More

Ami Turnbull

2022

Note to the Reader – Content Warning

More! briefly touches on sexual violence, this scene does not glamourise or romanticize in any way.

Acknowledgements

Firstly, I want to thank my mum and nan for getting me in to reading as a child, you both started my love of books and the escapism and pure joy a good book can bring. As a teenager, I found the books I love, romance is my niche and many a time I have found myself living in a book and never wanting it to end.

To my wonderful CCL crew: ten years, my first job and the support I had from everyone in the office whilst writing was very much appreciated. Sadly, we had no Ethan amongst us, but there are strands of so many of you in the book and the experience of call centre life and the friendships that are made at work. Thank you to all those who kept asking me about how writing was going, the excitement you showed at the prospect of reading it, both really helped to keep me on track. More! Is dedicated to our fun times together. Particular thanks to Steve for designing the cover for me.

To Ruth and Vicky, what can I say? I love the fact that whilst I was writing it, I read this book to you both over the phone in its entirety. I loved hearing your responses, your unwavering support and enthusiasm for my writing and the story. The hugest thanks go to Ruth for proofing and making my messy manuscript in to a tidy document, thank you so much!

Leila, it's been brilliant speaking to you about writing, a break from the day job of insurance, and I really appreciate the help with the self-publishing. Keep writing yourself, I want to see my name in your acknowledgements in the future.

Most of my friends don't read the trashy romances I love, but you all accept this about me and the encouragement you have all shown just confirms why I love you all so much. Thanks to my uni friends – Vicky and Ruth as above, with Cath, John, Mark and Phil, you all knew I was not going to write anything academic and this genre is right for me; to Matt for talking me through audio production; to Eran and Sara for always being there; to Sally, Rachel, Katie, Dan, Sam, Emily, Chrissi, Kirsten, Simon, Liz, and David for never tiring of me talking to you about Ethan and the book. Thank you all!

Chapter One

As I make the finishing touches to straightening my hair, I can hear him in the lounge moving things around and wonder why he is really here. He had sounded different on the phone when he'd called earlier, and when he'd arrived he had seemed anxious, awkward somehow. I shrug, switching off the straighteners. Whatever it is, it doesn't concern me any more. I reach for my favourite perfume, Insolence, and spritz generously.

I'm looking forward to this evening. It's my work's annual Summer party, a chance to drink from the free bar and to catch up with friends and colleagues. It's always been fun in previous years, and I can't help but think it will be more fun now I'm on my own. I pick up my new silver bag, grab my iPhone and head for the door.

"Have you found it yet?" I ask as I enter the room.

"No. Maybe it's not here after all," he replies and then turns to face me.

"Well, I'll let you know if I find it," I mumble, searching for the remote to turn off the TV.

He walks purposefully across the room towards me, and as I look up to meet his eyes I see something completely unexpected. It throws me, making me feel uncomfortable, so I look away and try to act casual.

"Is that all?" I ask.

"Why do I feel like I have made the biggest mistake of my life?" he responds quietly, sadly.

"Because you have."

What does he expect me to say, really? I force myself to look up at him again, and there it is, a look I haven't seen in a very, very long time. He wants me, desire is clear in his eyes.

"You look beautiful," he murmurs and before I know what is happening he pulls me close and kisses me hard, as if he has the right to.

As he kisses me, his tongue pushing into my mouth, his lips firm against mine, I realise with total clarity that I don't want him any more. For a moment I am furious: how dare he just show up like this and think I will fall back into his arms? But as I push him away, the anger evaporates and I don't feel anything but numb towards him. It's over, it's been over for a long time, and finally I don't feel heartbroken any more. Thank you, Tristan, thank you so much for making me realise that actually I'm OK now. There was no emotion in that kiss for me, just a familiarity, but no substance, no meaning. I'm over him, over us, we're done!

"No," I say, moving away from him. "What the fuck do you think you're doing?"

"I'm sorry, Rosie."

What for, I ask myself, for just kissing me? For cheating on me? For leaving me? I spy the control under a cushion on the sofa, grab it and turn the TV off. Whatever he is apologising for, I really don't care. I have a night out to enjoy and I am not going to let Tristan's apparent repentance get in the way of having a good time.

"I'm going out. Make sure you lock up when you leave," I say, and march out, leaving him standing dejectedly in the middle of the room.

Momentarily, I stand in the small hallway collecting my thoughts. I see his jacket hanging on the usual hook, which irritates me, and for some reason, I don't know why, I find myself twisting off my engagement ring and slipping it into his inside pocket. Without looking back, I open the door and step outside.

Unsteadily I start walking down the road, distractedly touching the slight indent to my ring finger. It feels odd, wrong somehow, but at the same time it feels ridiculously right, freeing, like something suffocating has been finally lifted. It is this latter feeling I am going with, I tell myself firmly, and pick up my pace.

***

It's a beautiful Summer's evening, perfect barbecue weather. A gentle breeze is now in the air, which is a relief from the earlier heat of the day. The late August sunshine is still shining brightly and birds are singing in the trees as I walk past the park. As the warm breeze brushes over my skin I realise I have forgotten my cardigan at home and hope that the temperature doesn't fall too much later this evening. There is no way I am turning back to go and get it. Just the thought of seeing Tristan again makes me shudder inwardly.

What was that all about, I wonder as I cross the road and start heading down the main street. I haven't seen him in about ten weeks and then, out of the blue, he rings to ask if he can come and look for a DVD he apparently forgot when he left me. I hadn't doubted him, but now I'm not so sure there was a film to find after all. I touch my ring finger again. I miss the delicate diamond ring that has been there for three years, but I don't miss him, not now.

I come to a halt, standing outside the door to Henry's, the bar in which I am meeting Libby and Will. I can hear the low murmur of voices through the open windows, a girl is laughing annoyingly shrilly and I find myself desperately wanting a drink. I take a deep breath and push the door open.

As I descend the small flight of stairs I spot Libby standing at the bar. She looks gorgeous in a white maxi dress. She sees me and we grin at each other, quickly embracing before we start to gush about how great each other looks.

"That colour really suits you," she enthuses, handing me a glass of white wine. "You're certainly going to turn a few heads tonight. Even Will might try his luck."

We both giggle and clink glasses. The wine is fruity, deliciously cool, and most definitely welcome. Our good friend Will is what can only be described as a womaniser, a loveable Northern scamp. He desperately wants to find 'the one', but all he manages to do is falter from dalliance to dalliance, sleeping with one pretty girl to the next, breaking hearts as he goes. He is an absolute nightmare with women but he is charming, kind and has been a constant friend to me since I started working for Mosen's Mortgages all those years ago.

"Thankfully, I don't think Will would ever try anything with either of us. He's like a brother."

"Cheers to Will not trying," laughs Libby and takes a big drink.

"Where is he?" I ask, surprised he isn't with her already.

"He's blown us out for Ethan," she replies.

"Ethan?" I ask.

"Ethan Harber. His new boss, our new Commercial Director."

Oh, Ethan. I remember someone mentioning we were getting a new Director starting last week. I had been miffed because I hadn't even known we were looking for a new Director and I had had no part to play in his selection. I've been on annual leave this week and had forgotten about him, not that his appointment will affect me in any meaningful way. I feel annoyed that not only was I not involved in his recruitment, but now he is stealing my friend away from me, even if only for a short while. I'm aware I am being irrational.

"He's very good-looking," Libby informs me. "Like absolutely drop-dead-gorgeous good-looking. I think he's a friend of Drew's."

"Glad to see nepotism is well and truly alive," I fume.

"Oh Rosie," she scolds. "He seems nice, at least from afar. I haven't had much to do with him yet, but Will seems to think he is OK." I shrug and suggest we go outside.

Henry's has a small garden out the back. Tables are scattered on the lawn, which looks over the waterfront. It's busier out here than inside, but there is a table free over near the water's edge and we settle down with our drinks.

"I'm thinking of moving," I tell her.

"I said you should move months ago," she replies. "I honestly think it is the right thing for you to do. It's a complete clean break, a chance for you to start all over again with no constant memories in your face all the time."

Libby Blake is one of those women who has conviction in everything she does. She's one of those very lucky people to have met her now-husband when she was eighteen;

he had taken a year out to travel around Australia, and had returned to England with a fiancée. Professionally, she has a reputation for being a bitch, but ultimately, she puts in the work and gets what she wants from life. She hadn't seen the point of university and had taken on junior office positions, paving out a successful career in Human Resources for herself. She is now part of the senior management team and I expect she'll move on to being a Director soon enough. Beneath all of the bravado she has a heart of gold and I feel lucky to be her friend.

We drink another glass of wine, chatting about my week off, and she fills me in with the goings-on at work. We are relaxed, at ease in each other's company, and I'd be happy to just spend the evening here putting the world to rights.

My phone chimes and I read a text from Ellie. She's outside, ready to give us a lift. We drain our glasses and head for the car.

"Hi," Ellie beams at us through the open car window. "You ladies look hot."

"You look great, Ellie," Libby says as she settles into the passenger seat. "Baby's certainly growing."

"I know, I struggled to find something to wear," she says and then looks apologetically at me.

I've become used to that look over the last four months since she announced her pregnancy. I hate the fact that she feels awkward around me, and it doesn't matter how much I enthuse about her upcoming arrival, she still seems wary of being too happy when I am around.

"Where's Will?" Ellie asks.

"He's ditched us for Ethan," I reply, relieved for the shift in conversation.

"Lucky Will," she swoons. "I'd ditch you two for him too. You haven't met him yet, have you Rosie? Oh my God, I thought I was going to go into premature labour when I met him. He is absolutely stunning." Oh no, not you as well, I think sourly and suggest we get going.

Chapter Two

Ed Mosen, my boss, grew up in Chelmsford and was the stereotypical cheeky Essex boy. He had an entrepreneurial flair and ventured successfully into the mortgage market in the late '80s. His big break, however, was a substantial lottery win. He decided to relocate across the border to Suffolk, where he built an impressive mansion for his family and moved his business to a new out-of-town development. He doesn't need to work, but still enjoys it and has continued to grow the company, diversifying products and recently joining the online platform. His baby, our call centre, continues to be the foundation of the business, tonight's party being his way of saying thank you to his staff.

I look out of the window at the passing farmland, seeing sheep in nearby fields and a horse looking over a fence. It's wonderful out here, so tranquil. It's so close to home, yet feels a million miles away. The car begins to jolt as we turn up a dirt track. Rounding the bend, we pass through electric gates and arrive in the splendour that is Greenacres, Ed Mosen's extravagant home. Ellie turns left into a field designated for parking. We can see a huge white marquee, and then to the right I see what looks like a fairground. I smile. He always has to lay on some kind of entertainment and tonight it appears he is treating us to a fair.

"I'm not sure letting drunk idiots ride on the waltzers all night was the best idea Ed has had," Libby comments disdainfully. She has a fair point, these parties usually get out of hand and adding some rides to the mix is obviously going to end one way – messy! But it'll be fun.

We get out of the car and begin to walk towards the marquee, saying hello to people as we go. Ellie says she will catch up with us later and goes on the prowl for the toilets, an annoying side effect of pregnancy, she complains.

The marquee is already busy as we enter. We both accept a glass of prosecco from a waitress at the entrance and join the throng. The men are looking smart in shirts and trousers, and the girls are wearing pretty Summer dresses. It's nice that everyone makes an effort, I think, and follow Libby past a group of the football team, saying hello to people as I go. She's walking purposefully over to a quiet corner, and then I catch sight of Will, who she is headed for.

His brown hair looks messy as always, he is wearing a crisp white shirt and grey trousers, and as he sees us he flashes his boyish smile that has left many a girl weak at the knees. He practically bounces the ten or so paces towards us and to my surprise swoops me off my feet and spins me around. It's a miracle I don't spill my drink everywhere.

I squeal, "What are you doing, you idiot?"

Over his shoulder, I glimpse the vision that undoubtedly is Ethan Harber. He's wearing a sapphire shirt with black expensive-looking suit trousers, a jacket casually draped over his arm. His hair is short, dark blond. I'd estimate him at being around six foot three or four, with a broad athletic physique. He is stunning, Libby and Ellie had not been kidding, he is beyond good-looking and even from a distance I feel intoxicated.

"You look hot," Will says into my ear and puts me down, his hands resting on my shoulders whilst he appraises me, utterly unashamedly.

I'm wearing a knee-length coral dress. It has a strap on my right shoulder, leaving the other bare. It falls low across my chest and back, clinging to all the right places to show off my newly acquired size ten figure. I'm wearing high-heeled silver sandals that match my bag. Teardrop earrings hang from my ears and on my wrist is a silver bracelet that has flower links with small coral jewels in their centres to match my dress. My long brown hair cascades down my back. I've had a French manicure and pedicure, applied some makeup and have to confess to have made an effort tonight.

I take a gulp of my prosecco, trying to slow my heart that has started thumping in my chest. I need to get a grip, I tell myself firmly, and take another drink to steady my nerves.

"Come on." Will takes me by the elbow, propelling me forward. "Ethan, let me introduce you to Rosie Fielding, our Recruitment Officer. She's responsible for hiring most of the deadbeats that are here this evening."

He stares down at me, his cool blue eyes meeting mine, pinning me to the spot.

"Hi," he says in a deep American accent, that seems to disarm me further.

"Hi," I manage, registering that Will has let my elbow go and has taken a few steps away and is now greeting Libby.

Ethan takes my hand in his. His palm feels cool against mine, his handshake powerful. For the briefest of moments we just seem to stand still holding hands, his dark blue eyes searching my face as I feel his gaze scrutinise me. My stomach somersaults and I find myself incapable of looking away. He lets go of my hand, his expression unreadable.

"So, you're responsible for hiring Will?" he asks.

I shake my head, composing myself as best I can. "No, I can't take the blame for that," I smile, a shy smile, and I can feel myself turning scarlet, feeling incredibly self-conscious. "We actually started on the same day. He's very good at his job, though."

"Is he indeed?"

There's the slightest challenge to his tone and I find myself wanting to defend and promote my friend. "Yes. Have you seen the portfolio of his partners?"

"I have," Ethan replies simply. "Well, it's good to put a face to the name, Rosie. I'll be needing your help soon."

"You're going to be recruiting?"

He nods. "For Will's role," he takes my now-empty glass from me. "Another," it's not a question, more a statement, and he walks away.

I can feel the colour drain from my face. He's going to be recruiting for Will's role, that's what he just said, he's getting rid of him and expects me to help find his replacement. No, I protest, he can't, I won't help him! But it's my job, it's what I do. Will obviously has no idea from his carefree attitude this evening, and Libby has told me Will likes Ethan. I feel awful, the expectations of a good time fluttering away on the non-existent breeze.

What do I do? Do I tell Will? No, the prospect of that conversation is not an appealing one. How dare Ethan have involved me in this! I'm outraged, mortified and completely in shock. I do the only thing I can under the circumstances, and head into the crowd, putting distance between myself and Will. The thought of telling him is horrific, but the thought that I am inadvertently keeping something from him is even worse. I take another glass of Prosecco from a different waitress and stop to survey my surroundings.

At the back of the marquee is the bar. There's a cluster of people standing around it, mostly call centre agents, clutching drinks and seemingly happy in animated conversation. Over to the right a dancefloor has been laid and a DJ is standing near his equipment, talking to Ed Mosen and his son, Drew. The left side of the marquee has tables running its length, leading to the exit.

I venture outside and join the smokers. Across the field I can see the small fairground, some bumper cars, waltzers, a big wheel and what looks like a ghost train. There's an ice cream van next to a candy floss stall. It's absolutely ridiculous, but so Ed Mosen. I join a group of call centre agents, all having just completed their induction. They look overwhelmed by it all.

"Hi guys," I say cheerily. "How's it going?"

A shrill screeching noise booms over the PA system, making us all jump.

"Get your arses inside!" our delightful MD commands unceremoniously.

The newbies look even more uncertain, so I go for a reassuring smile and herd them back inside. I always feel some kind of responsibility for everyone I recruit, I want them to be happy with us, I want them to succeed and to leave because the company has served its purpose. Obviously, that isn't always the case, quite a lot of the time it isn't the case in fact, but I still find myself being sentimental.

The marquee is full now, the chatter of two hundred colleagues suddenly seeming very loud, although I'm sure it will get louder the more alcohol is consumed. There is another screech from the PA system and Ed Mosen launches into his company address.

He thanks everyone for coming, for our hard work, and encourages us to let our hair down and to enjoy ourselves. He touches on some performance figures, which nobody seems to be listening to, and announces a 3% pay rise, with a new incentive scheme. Ed very much adopts the 'work hard and you will be rewarded' mentality and I think his staff respect him for that. He may be a millionaire, but underneath it all he is still the cheeky Essex boy, wanting to make a few quid where he can. Food, a hog roast, will be available from quarter to eight and the fair is now officially open. He toasts the company and wishes us all a fantastic evening.

And that is that. He has kept it to twenty minutes, which is unheard of, and now we are free to do as we please.

"Is the bar free all night?" one of the agents, Jack, if I remember rightly, asks.

"Yep, all night. You chose a good time to start working here, just in time for our Summer party. And wait until the Christmas one. It's always beautiful. Last year he had it all as a Winter Wonderland. It was spectacular."

The DJ bellows over the microphone, sounding hyper, and kicks things off with Taylor Swift. A few girls are straight on the dance floor and I admire their enthusiasm and the way they just dance so effortlessly, with what seems like a total disregard for everyone around them. They are young, in their early twenties, and at thirty-five I feel depressingly old. I need another drink and to be with people I actually like, so I bid my newbies farewell and head to the bar.

I order a glass of wine and find myself accosted by the Barrett twins. They are both already drunk, having been drinking for most of the afternoon, they inform me. They are absolutely adorable, ginger-haired, all freckles, tall and far too skinny. They aren't the most attractive of boys, but they are a delight to be around. They stand, one either side of me, and start appraising the girls.

"Look at Jade, the slag," Olly says, humour in his voice as he points to a blonde-haired girl dancing. "Her boobs will fall out of that dress in a minute."

"Like you'd complain," I say, noting her very short, very low dress, if you can call it that – a scrap of material would be more accurate.

"Already been there," he whispers conspiratorially. "She wasn't that good. All for show, nothing to back it up with."

"I don't want to know!"

"So have I," declares Jamie. "And I can confirm very disappointing."

I look from one brother to the other, trying to decide if they are winding me up or not. They both start laughing at the same time.

"You're shits, I never know when you're just taking the piss."

"You love us," they speak as one.

I melt. "I do, I just can't help myself." They look pleased with themselves and we spend another fifteen minutes together. They grill me about still being single, both asserting that they could help me move on. They are shameless – their high spirits are contagious, and my mood lifts.

“Boys,” we are suddenly interrupted by Drew Mosen, “I hope you don't mind if I steal Rosie away from you?” Neither Barrett protests, they wink at me and depart, no doubt to cause mischief. I turn to face Drew, smiling up into his kind face, genuinely pleased to see him.

“You look happier than I've seen you in a while,” he observes, uncharacteristically getting straight to the point.

“I feel a lot better. I guess you can't stay miserable forever, can you?”

“I'm glad,” he smiles and takes me by the arm. “Do you want to dance?”

I shake my head. “Not yet, but later, as always.”

“Are you seeing anyone?” he continues with his uncharacteristic line of questioning.

“No,” I reply, letting him lead me through the crowd. “What about you?”

“No,” he can't hide his disappointment at his answer.

“I’m not looking."

“They say that's when it happens.” He sounds dreamy.

We head to an unoccupied table and sit down. He seems like he has the weight of the world on his shoulders, and not for the first time I feel sorry for him. Ed Mosen is a hugely successful businessman and the pressure he heaps on his son is immense. Ed is shrewd, egotistical and arrogant, whereas Drew is kind, gentle and a daydreamer, and at times he just looks out of his depth. It is obvious that he doesn't want to follow in his father's footsteps, yet at nearly forty he hasn't had the heart to tell his father and Ed has failed to acknowledge there’s an issue. It's sad really.

We are joined by Libby and Will, and I know, without even having to turn around, that Ethan is standing directly behind me. I instantly feel on edge, bad that I’d let myself forget what he had told me, feeling like a shitty friend to Will.

“Drew,” the low American voice says, and Drew gets up quickly.

“Hi. Have you met Rosie, Ethan?”

“Yes, earlier.”

“Great. Look, I better go and check on Dad and that no one is trashing the place yet. We’ll catch up soon, we need to arrange dinner or something. I'll see you later for that dance,” he pats me lightly on the shoulder and departs.

“Where did you disappear to?” Will asks.

“I thought I'd do some mingling,” I reply, aware that Ethan is still standing behind me and purposefully not acknowledging his presence.

"Have you been on the fair yet?" Libby sits opposite me.

"No, not yet. You?"

She wrinkles her nose at me. "No thanks. I've been chaperoning Will, trying to save him from himself."

"And she's doing a good job, it has to be said. I even walked past Jade without being tempted."

"Oh, I wouldn't waste your time with her, the Barrett twins assure me she isn't worth it."

We laugh. 'Primadonna' by Marina and The Diamonds starts playing and Libby is up, dragging Will with her for a dance.

"Can I?" Ethan indicates the seat next to me.

I scowl at him, the alcohol making me brave, and don't reply. He sits down anyway. I do my utmost to ignore him, although I can't help a surreptitious glance out of the corner of my eye. He looks as if he is assessing me, which of course makes me feel ultra self-conscious. I reach for my drink at the same time he goes for his, our hands brush together ever so slightly. I shift away from him and take a very big gulp of my wine, whilst he just watches me, with no attempt to hide his scrutiny. It is unnerving.

"Are you OK?" Ethan finally breaks the silence.

I nod, unable to speak.

"You look," he pauses, thinking for a moment, "pissed off."

I shoot him what I hope is a venomous look, warning him to back off.

He raises an eyebrow. "Rosie?" Just the way he rolls the R on the tip of his tongue makes me feel giddy.

"What?" I snap, annoyed at myself for feeling so utterly overwhelmed in his presence.

He leans in closer. "Have I done something to offend you?"

"Are you serious?" I ask. He looks bemused.

"I don't think talking about work at a party is necessary or appropriate," I snap at him.

Ethan puts his chin in his hand, staring at me. "So, just to clarify," he drawls in his deep American tone, "you're pissed at me because I talked to you about work at a work's party?"

"No," I push back my chair, "because you're sacking Will and you thought it was OK to tell me about it before him. At the work's party of all places, and we've only just met. Couldn't it have waited?"

I practically leap out of my seat, turn on my heel and attempt to march away. I'm not the most co-ordinated of people at the best of times, and apparently the sudden movement, coupled with the alcohol and the fact I haven't eaten for a while don't go particularly well together and I feel myself tripping on an invisible crack in the floor. Shit! His arm encircles my waist and I feel a firm hand on my elbow. He is beside me in one fluid movement as he stops me from falling flat on my face.

"I'm not sacking Will," he murmurs, his thumb slowly moving up and down on my upper arm. "What gave you that idea?"

"You're not?" I breathe, confused.

"I'm not," he reiterates.

"You said you'd need my help recruiting for Will's role," I reply quietly.

The corner of his mouth turns up into the slightest of smiles. "I meant another Account Manager, Rosie. Someone else to do the same job as Will, that's all."

"Oh." I feel light-headed and need to sit down.

He sits next to me once more. "He's very good at his job, as you said earlier, but we need more resources. There's no point in us acquiring new business if we can't keep it. Will's overworked, he can't maintain effective relationships with partners, hence we're not monopolising on what we have. I need someone else. Is that OK?"

I feel stupid – how the hell had I jumped so spectacularly to the wrong conclusion? I want the ground to swallow me up. I look around at everything but him. I can't believe I got it so wrong and then, just to compound my humiliation, I nearly fell at his feet, literally.

"I'm sorry." Finally I turn to face him, composing myself and attempting professionalism. "I just thought... Well, you know what I thought. You'll need to talk to Libby about recruiting though, if that's what you want to do."

"Why? You're the Recruitment Officer, aren't you?"

"Yes, but there are procedures, it needs to be signed off by her before I get involved."

"Rosie, I'm on the Board, I have sign-off. I'll talk to you on Monday about it," he informs me, sounding so sure of himself. "Now," he indicates my empty glass, "another?" and this time it's a question.

"Please."

He stands and takes me by surprise by lightly placing his left hand on my shoulder whilst he leans over to take my glass. "Don't go anywhere this time," he commands.

I watch him stride away and feel utterly dazed. His touch has sent tingles through my body and my stomach feels jittery, all of a flutter. What the fuck? I am a mess, this is ridiculous, this is embarrassing! I need to snap out of it, quickly, before he returns. He's just a man, after all. Who am I trying to kid? There's something about him, self-confidence radiates from him, and for some inexplicable reason I was drawn to him immediately when I saw him over Will's shoulder.

I remember our handshake, his dark blue eyes locking with mine. I remember feeling transfixed and had felt a pang when he had let my hand go. I feel unsettled and I know I need to pull myself together before I lose all self-respect. I am at a work's party, getting to know a new colleague, there's nothing more to it than that.

As he returns and hands me a drink I find my resolve for cool professionalism, or so I hope.

"Thanks." I shoot him a coy smile as I take the glass.

Libby and Will reappear, all grins from their dance.

"One of your newbies is spewing in the ladies' toilets," Libby announces.

I shrug at the inevitable. "Is she OK? Is someone with her?"

"Yes, she's fine. I think someone has called her a taxi already."

I sit back, smile across at Will and feel content, glad to not be avoiding him now he isn't going to be losing his job. I listen to the three of them chat, occasionally commenting, but enjoying watching their easy interaction with each other.

I find my mind wandering into a daydream, where strong arms are encircling me and a deep American voice murmurs into my ear. I'm not sure if it is the alcohol or the daydream, but my head feels fuzzy and I am struggling to concentrate on what is going on around me.

"Oh my God," Libby says animatedly. "Rosie, you've taken your engagement ring off."

They are all looking at me and I realise I have been touching my ring finger again. I blush, aware that all attention is now on me, painfully aware that Ethan is watching me.

"It felt right," I mumble, taking a big swig of wine.

"About bloody time," Will remarks and toasts me. "To being single."

"To finding someone new," Libby grins.

They disappear again, apparently off to get shots to celebrate my lack of engagement ring.

"You were engaged?" Ethan turns to face me, fixing me with a cool stare.

"I was," I reply. "I'm not any more, obviously."

I wish I knew what he was thinking, but he just looks serious, his dark blue eyes watching my every movement. Once again I feel self-conscious in his presence and I reach for my glass.

"Rosie," he takes the glass from me.

"What?" I ask, surprised.

"Perhaps you should lay off the wine for a bit?" he replies, putting my glass down.

"Why?" I sound petulant and glare at him.

"Because," he moves closer to me and in a low voice says, "even the prettiest girl can look very unattractive when she is wasted."

I don't fully understand what he is saying, but I feel like he has physically slapped me right across the face. Deep down I know I am beginning to feel the effects of the wine and prosecco, and although taking it easy for a while is probably a very wise suggestion, I feel irritated that he has made it. Who the hell does he think he is?

"Ethan," I say his name for the first time, "you got me this drink, it would be rude of me not to finish it." I pick up the glass and down the remaining half under his frosty glare.

I slowly get to my feet, taking extra care to not trip over this time, thank him for the wine and walk away, not looking back. I head for the toilets, lock myself in a cubicle and sit and wait for my heart to stop pounding and for my head to stop spinning. I feel hideously drunk all of a sudden, verging on nauseous, but I swallow hard and tell myself that I am not going to join my newbie and become one of those girls who spews at the work's party. Getting to my feet I steady my breathing, run my fingers through my hair, straighten my dress and unlock the door. I check my appearance in the mirror and prepare myself to re-join proceedings.

Chapter Three

As I re-enter the marquee, 'Amazing' by Bruno Marrs begins and I find myself swept into a dance with Drew. I lean my cheek against his shoulder and close my eyes, naturally dancing in time with him. I'm not a great dancer, but Drew somehow makes it easy and when I dance with him I feel like a professional on *Strictly*.

"You OK?" he asks into my ear.

"I feel a bit drunk," I confess. "Your friend, Ethan, just told me to stop drinking, I think."

Drew's hold slightly tightens around me. "Did he?"

"Hmm."

"He can be a bit overbearing at times," he apologises. "Don't take it personally."

We dance in companionable silence, both lost in our own thoughts until the song finishes and is replaced with an upbeat dance track. Drew releases me: we never dance to anything but slow smoochy songs. I'm relieved to not see Will around, the last thing I need is for him to accost me for a lively dance, I don't think my head can take any more spinning! Drew promises to find me later for a repeat performance, kissing me on the cheek before he goes.

It's noisy, too noisy, and I am feeling stiflingly hot. I wander outside, past the smokers and away from the crowd, not really knowing where I am heading, but just wanting a moment to be quiet and alone.

It's dark outside now and pretty little lanterns provide gentle lighting as I continue, crunching across a gravel track which leads to the makeshift car park and the big house beyond. I stop by a tree, breathing in the country air and the smell of the hog roast on the breeze. It's a lot cooler now and I am grateful for the dip in temperature. I need to calm down and cool down.

I've never met anyone like him before. He has this aura about him, he seems so self-assured, confident, arrogant even, and I am uncontrollably drawn to him. I want to feel his dark blue eyes on me, they are intense, unfaltering and I don't want to ever look away. I remember his hold on me when I tripped, his thumb brushing against my bare skin, his hand lightly resting on my shoulder when he had reached across for my glass, and I remember the disappointment when he removed his touch.

Ellie and Libby had told me earlier that he was good-looking and stunning, but I had underestimated their appraisal of him and had found myself floundering when I saw him. I'm attracted to him, at least aesthetically, and I try to remember if I ever felt so nervy and on edge around Tristan.

The honest answer is no. I'd been attracted to him, of course, but it had been a slow process. We became friends, dated, fell in love and spent thirteen years together. But he hadn't wowed me at first sight. Tristan had been safe, reliable, he had gained my trust and I had loved him unconditionally. But I'd never felt intoxicated just being near him.

"Rosie, what are you doing out here all alone?"

It's Ellie, on her way to her car, having had enough and wanting her bed. She looks tired.

"I just needed a bit of fresh air," I reply.

She studies me, her hands unconsciously resting on her bump. "Are you OK?" She sounds concerned. "Libby said you have taken your ring off."

I nod. "Tristan came around this evening."

"Why?"

"I don't know," I say truthfully. "He said he had left a film, but he seemed strange. He kissed me."

Ellie's eyes widen. "Wow, what did you do?"

"I pulled away, I didn't want it, and I left."

"Do you think he's regretting leaving?"

"I have no idea, but it made me realise I don't want him. I left my engagement ring in his coat pocket before I left."

She asks me how I feel, and not wanting to discuss Tristan any more, I tell her I am feeling a bit drunk. She offers me a lift home, which I decline.

"I saw you and Drew dancing," she says brightly. "You dance wonderfully together. You'd make a lovely couple."

Poor Ellie, like most of the staff at work she has no idea that Drew is in fact gay. He is very private, and I don't think he will ever get up the courage to out himself at work. I find this strange, but guess it is his choice. Also, Ed isn't amazingly supportive, and I think to a certain extent Drew remains discreet for his father's sake.

"Drew's just a friend," I tell Ellie, dispelling any romantic notions she may be concocting. She breaks out into a huge smile, and then I see why. Ethan is walking towards us. Oh no, I don't need this, I came outside to get away from him, I realise.

"Hi Ethan," Ellie says in a girly, excitable voice. "How are you enjoying the party?"

"It's just about tolerable," he drawls.

"Well, I'm off now, I need a herbal tea and my bed, I'm afraid. Can I leave you to look after Rosie? She's feeling a little bit squiffy."

I am mortified, I can't believe she just said that!

“Of course, it will be my pleasure,” replies Ethan and then he says in a quiet voice, knowing perfectly well that I can still hear him, “but the thing is, I think she finds me irritating.”

“Oh no,” simpers Ellie, revelling in being so close to him. “It's not you she's irritated with, it's just that she didn't recruit you. She gets very protective about her work.”

I remember being angry a couple of weeks ago when Ethan's appointment had been announced. I had vented to Ellie then, but I had never imagined she would actually go and tell him of my annoyance. Ellie, oblivious to my embarrassment, hugs me hard and then bids us goodnight.

“I got you some water.” Ethan is the one to break our awkward silence. I glare at him. “Rosie.” His voice is menacingly low as he offers me a glass. I step backwards, once again affronted. Why is he bringing me water? Why is he out here at all?

“Why are you here, Ethan?”

“Because Ed told me my presence was required,” he replies, taking a step towards me.

I step away once more, but find I can go no further as my back collides with a tree trunk. “But why are you out here?”

“Because you are,” he responds simply. “I wanted to check you were OK,” again he offers me the glass. “I know I've pissed you off again, although I'm not sure how. I saw you come out here by yourself and I wanted to check you weren't going to fall over again and end up comatose in a field out here on your own.”

“I'm not that drunk,” I giggle, finding the thought absurd.

“I got you some water.” He holds out the glass.

I don't take it. “Ethan, I'm not that drunk," I repeat firmly. “I don't need you to tell me to slow down, and I don't need you to look out for me in case I pass out. I'm fine.” He puts the glass to my lips, not backing down, and in a bored voice says, “Just drink, Rosie. Indulge me, please?”

My lips part a little and he tilts the glass slightly, pouring water into my mouth. I swallow, aware of his proximity, consciously having to stop myself from reaching out to touch him. I blink up at him. His expression is deadly serious, his eyes dark.

“So, I'm wondering if you would have recruited me if it had been up to you?”

“I don't know,” I reply honestly, glad he has taken a step back. I move away from the tree. “I know nothing about you.”

“I'll send you my CV on Monday,” he says confidently.

“You really don't need to,” I stutter.

"I want to. I'm curious to see if I meet with your high standards. I don't think my CV will disappoint you."

"It's immaterial." I feel nervous again. "You are already here."

"Yes, I am," he flashes the most devastating smile, his eyes sparkle. "Now come back to the party."

He puts a hand on the small of my back, gently pushing me forward. His touch, again, sends tingles up my spine and I find myself co-operating, walking slowly back to the marquee with him.

"I'm sorry I offended you," Ethan stares down at me, suddenly stopping, removing his hand. "It wasn't my intention."

"It's OK," I concede, taking the glass from him and taking a long drink. "You were right, the wine was going to my head."

"Come out with me after this," again it feels like a statement, like he is telling me rather than asking and I have to admit, I quite like it.

"Everywhere will be closed," I reply despondently, knowing how late these parties go on.

"Not everywhere, trust me."

"We'll see," I respond noncommittally.

He trails his thumb firmly under my jaw, lifting my chin, forcing me to meet his gaze. It reminds me of how Tristan had looked at me earlier, although Ethan does smouldering to a completely different level I've never experienced before. I think he is going to kiss me, but regrettably he doesn't.

"Don't drink too much." His voice is low, harsh, and he releases me. The disappointment at not being kissed consumes me, distracting me from his arrogant perception that he has any right to tell me what to do. He brushes my hair away from my ear, taking my earlobe in between his finger and thumb and whispers, "I'll come and find you later."

"You do that," I attempt cool, knowing my shy smile betrays me. In silence we walk back to the marquee and join the party once more. A lot of people are outside now, screams and shouts coming from the fair.

I spot Libby sitting alone at a table and head for her, aware that Ethan is not following as he has turned into the marquee without bothering to say goodbye.

"Hi," I sit down, putting my glass of water on the table. "You OK?"

I'm surprised to see her on her own. People gravitate towards her and she loves being centre of attention, however much she denies it.

"I've just had to endure fifteen minutes of Ed leering over me," she sighs.

Oh dear, poor Libby. Ed can be hard work at times, and after a few drinks he can become unprofessional and inappropriate. Thankfully I have never had to deal with this, mainly because every time he speaks to me he is trying to set me up with Drew, pleading with me to end "his phase." Some people just shouldn't drink, and Ed Mosen is one of those people.

"You OK?" I ask.

She shrugs. "Yeah, yeah. You know me, I can handle Ed. Now where have you been?"

"I just needed a bit of fresh air. I saw Ellie. She's gone home."

"And Ethan. I saw you two just walking back together."

"Oh, I just bumped into him," I respond casually.

"You know he's been watching you ever since he met you?" Libby asks.

"No, he hasn't!"

"He has," Libby pushes a strand of her short blonde hair behind an ear. "I've been watching him, watching you. He can't take his eyes off you. I told you earlier, you look amazing, sweetie."

I nearly tell her about Ethan asking me out afterwards, but something stops me. The idea that he has been watching me is odd, because although I have been checking him out at every available opportunity I'd never thought he would be doing the same. Even though he has invited me out and so nearly kissed me, I am struggling to rationalise it all.

"Ellie completely dropped me in it and told him I was annoyed I hadn't recruited him," I say.

Libby grins. "Oh, you've got to love her, she has no sense of tact. What did Ethan say?"

I giggle. "He said he'd send me his CV."

"See, he's flirting with you!"

"Is he?" I ask uncertainly.

Libby nods enthusiastically. "Absolutely."

All of a sudden, I feel out of my depth. It was bearable chaos in my mind when it was just me being attracted to him, but if Libby is right and Ethan has been flirting, well that just may be too much to deal with. I feel like a teenager and like I don't know what I'm doing. I haven't had to do this for such a long time. I was never particularly good with boys back in the day, Tristan and I had stumbled into our relationship, but starting over is an alien prospect that I'm not sure how to do.

I think Libby senses my turmoil as she steers the conversation away from Ethan. "I lost Will to Jade. I left them dancing."

"Oh no," I groan. "When will he learn?"

"I thought he had higher standards." Libby makes no attempt to disguise her disgust.

Jade Williams is one of the very few people I really regret giving an interview to, let alone having to offer her a job. OK, to give her credit, she is great on the phone and is one of the company's top performers, but on a personal level she manipulates and uses people to her own advantage with no regard for anyone but herself.

Jade has a curvaceous figure, double-D breasts that she flaunts in the lowest tops possible, and long, toned legs that she shows off with no regard for the company's dress code. I've lost count of how many times HR have had to talk to her about appropriate work clothes, but she never listens, and nothing ever gets done. She has long platinum blonde hair, green eyes, and no one can deny she's a beautiful girl. She's an Essex girl, originally from Basildon, and calls everyone "babe" in her insincere, I've-smoked-far-too-much voice.

She's only twenty-two and is still very much enjoying being young and playing the field. She's the type of girl who walks into a bar and doesn't even contemplate buying herself a drink. Similarly to Will, Jade has slept her way through a staggering number in the call centre, so perhaps they would make a suitable match for each other, but I really hope not! I just don't like her. The thought of having to be polite to her for Will's sake is a depressing one.

We are joined by Peter and Sally from Finance. They have both been overindulging in the free bar and are in fine spirits. A group of agents joins us, the Barrett Twins among them, and we are regaled with a very detailed narrative of Kelly Harrison spewing on the bumper cars, which has apparently resulted in the fair beginning to shut down for the night.

I've finished my water and decide that the drunkenness has subsided adequately. I wander back to the bar and order another wine, deciding it is probably wise to stay with that and not mix my drinks. I catch sight of Will on the dance floor, but am pleased that Jade is nowhere to be seen. I wave to him and he makes his way over.

"Hey," he grins. "Having a nice time?"

I nod. "You? Libby said she left you dancing with Jade."

"She's not my type, don't worry." Will perches on a bar stool. "I think I might go home alone tonight."

"That would make a change," I say, pulling another stool out and sitting next to him.

"If we're still single when we're forty can we get married and get a dog?"

I laugh. "Sounds like a bloody perfect plan to me."

"Here's to us in five years then." Will clinks glasses with me.

"You're an idiot," I say lovingly.

"Ethan," Will calls suddenly. "Come and be the first to congratulate us. We're getting married in five years."

Ethan walks over, his eyes dark, his jaw set in a hard line. He glares at me and I feel myself wither.

"If we're still single in five years," I blurt out. "It's a joke."

"Oh." his expression softens.

I don't know if Will senses an atmosphere or whether he actually just needs the toilet, but he excuses himself and leaves us alone at the bar.

"What?" I ask him, and then realise he is looking at my glass of wine with a degree of annoyance. "I've only had this one. I'm being sensible."

"Good." His response is harsh.

How do I tell him that I need the alcohol to muster up the courage to go anywhere with him? I knew the whole 'moving on' thing was going to be hard, but I'd never expected to meet someone like Ethan who immediately attracted me in a way I seem to have no control over.

"Don't be moody with me," I say in a subdued voice.

"You and Will?" he asks seriously.

"What about us?" He doesn't answer, so I meet his gaze and read the question. "We're friends."

"Just friends?"

"God, yes, he's like an annoying brother to me."

"Is there a past? A future?"

"No," I assert. "There has been and never will be anything apart from a very good friendship." He surveys my face and then tells me to walk with him. He strides out of the marquee, past all the smokers and in the direction of the now-dark fair. I struggle to keep up with him, not being the most adept in heels, being mindful to not trip again.

"I can't go this fast in these sandals," I finally protest, slowing down. "Where are we going anyway?"

He holds his hand out to me. "We're going to the fair. Be rude not to as it's here."

"It's finished. Someone was sick on the bumper cars."

"The big wheel is still going," he says.

"It's all dark, I think it has all stopped."

"Humour me. Let's look, at least." I put my hand in his and he gives it a reassuring squeeze. He smiles, his face looking younger and less serious. It puts me at ease and I let him guide me further into the darkness.

All the other rides are now closed, as I had thought, but Ethan was right about the big wheel still being open. There is no one else around, except the ride operator, who seems pleased to see us.

"Hi," I say. "Are we too late? Everyone else seems to have gone."

"No, take a seat."

Ethan helps me into a cart, supporting me as I clumsily get in. "I'll be back," he says and goes over to the operator. I see them talking briefly and then he returns and joins me.

Slowly the wheel begins to move, shuddering as our cart gets going and begins to move forward and upwards. I look out at the darkness, seeing the pretty lanterns hanging from the trees and the light from the marquee. The music and noise from the party are distant, but also reassuringly close. We descend to ground level and then begin rising once more. As we reach the top I start to knot and unknot my fingers in my lap, struggling to muster up the courage to look at him.

I become aware that we have stopped moving and look down to see if we are being joined, but instead I see the ride's operator walking away.

"What's he doing?" I mutter and then loudly I call. "Hello, we're still up here, hello!"

He carries on walking, not even bothering to look back. I panic, I'm stuck up here, we're stuck up here, together. I think I must look worried as Ethan reaches and takes my hand once more, giving it a gentle squeeze.

"Where's he going?" I ask, concern evident in my voice and on my face.

"He'll be back," Ethan replies coolly.

I purposefully haven't looked at him since we have been on the wheel, but there's something about his voice, the certainty in his tone that makes me turn to face him.

"He'll be back," repeats Ethan, fixing me with a steadying gaze.

"Where's he gone, Ethan?" I ask, a tingle running up my spine.

"For a drink," he replies, a hint of a smile on his lips.

I'm perplexed by his answer, but distracted by his thumb which is slowly moving across the skin between my fingers and thumb. Back and forth, ever so slowly, back and forth. His touch is firm, rhythmical, and the gesture is intimate.

I blink up at him. "I don't understand."

"He'll be back in half an hour."

"We're stuck up here for half an hour?" I squeak.

"Is that a problem?" he asks.

"Why?" I ask quietly, confused.

"Because I wanted to be alone with you. And up here you can't walk away."

"Are you serious?" I can't hide the outrage from my voice.

Ethan nods, looking far too pleased with himself. "Rosie, is that a problem?"

Yes it's a fucking problem! I rage internally: if you want to talk to me you ask me, you don't get me on a big wheel and engineer it so that I can't get off. I want to be mad at him, this is just weird, nobody does this sort of thing. I do my best to look unimpressed.

Ethan shifts slightly, his knee now touching mine. "I thought you could interview me."

"What?" I'm appalled.

"I told you, I'll send you my CV on Monday, but I thought now was as good a time as any for the interview." I snatch my hand away, moving as far away from him as possible, which isn't very far on this bench seat.

"You've already got the job!" I say in exasperation.

"I want to know if you would have recruited me."

"It's irrelevant, you've already got the job," I reiterate. "My opinion doesn't matter, you've been appointed."

"Your opinion matters. It matters to me. I want you to interview me."

I put my head in my hands in frustration.

"Rosie," his voice is deep, slightly cracking on the R of my name. He sounds hot, sexy, irresistible. I mentally shake myself and vow to get a grip. I lift my head, aware that he has been watching me with some humour. He moves as if to take my hand once more and with every ounce of my being I shake him off.

Taking in a deep breath I say, "You are either really egotistical or have serious self-doubt issues. But if you really want me to interview you, then of course I will. If only to pass the time up here."

He smiles, a huge grin, exposing perfect white teeth from a toothpaste commercial. "Thank you."

As he reaches for my hand again I brush him away, sit up straight and square my shoulders. If we're going to do this then we're going to do it properly. I turn on the seat, my back flat against the side of the cart, and concentrate on a facade of professionalism.

He moves to his side of the cart, replicating my position, but casually he rests an arm across the back of the seat and if he wanted to, he could touch the side of my shoulder. Oh, how I wish he would. Enough, I reprimand myself sternly. He wants an interview, and I don't want to disappoint him.

Chapter Four

"Why did you apply for the job of Commercial Director?" I begin.

"I didn't," he replies.

"You didn't?" I'm momentarily flustered, but then recall what Libby had said earlier.

"I was headhunted." Ethan sounds far too pleased with himself.

"Your friend gave you a job, you mean?" I smirk.

"Trust me, sweetheart, I'm doing Drew a favour here, not the other way around."

"Really?" I go for bored disinterest.

"Really," Ethan says firmly.

He is so arrogant. "I'm sure Drew is very grateful."

"Next question." He is the one to sound bored now.

I don't know what to ask him, I have no point of reference to base any questions on.

"What were you doing before?" I venture.

"I was a Commercial Director for a multinational property development company. I worked in their legal department in London for around five years. Before that I worked in a bank's legal department in New York."

"From a multinational to a small independent mortgage company in Suffolk," I muse. "Quite a change. Why?"

"I wanted a break from the city," Ethan replies.

"So, this isn't a long-term thing for you?" I ask, resting my chin on my hand, my fingertips resting on my lower lip.

Ethan doesn't respond immediately. He looks momentarily undecided, an internal battle playing out across his face. I lock my eyes to his, his indecision a stark contrast to the arrogant confidence I have seen thus far. I dig my nails into my lip as I watch, enthralled.

"I don't have a five-year plan." The shutters come down and he is self-assured once more, his eyes burning into mine. "I've signed a contract for a year, which should be enough time for me to make some significant improvements to the business. We'll see after that."

My professional resolve evaporates and I find myself mute, unsure of what to ask next. I look down, feeling despondent that Ethan is not permanent. A year doesn't seem very long.

"I'm here because Drew asked me. Ed's being a bit," he pauses, choosing his words carefully, "erratic, unreliable. Drew's a geek, he doesn't know enough about business, so I'm here to ensure Ed doesn't fuck it all up and end up losing everyone their jobs."

"We've just been given a pay rise," I murmur, trying to digest this. "Doesn't that suggest the business is doing well? Ed's been doing this for over twenty-five years, he knows what he's doing, right?" I say, aware that there is no conviction to my voice, that I'm asking a question.

"Don't worry, Rosie, I won't let you lose your job. He's just having a minor blip, that's all," he slides towards me on the seat and pulls my hand away from my face. "Don't," he says gently, "I can't see you properly when you're hiding behind your hand like that."

I breathe in his fresh aftershave, bergamot and peppermint, a sensual masculine aroma enticing me. He trails a finger down my cheek, his touch light, but oh so powerful. I'm all sensation, touch tantalising my skin, fragrance invading my nostrils, and his eyes scorch with longing. I blink up at him. "I don't think this is appropriate interview etiquette."

"No," he agrees, looking down at me, his lips so close to mine. "Do you want me to back off? I can tell you about my transferable skills and other mundane hyperbole if you'd prefer?"

"You've already got the job," I whisper coquettishly.

He pushes my hair off my shoulder, slowly trailing his fingertips up my neck. The distant noise from the party, the squeals of laughter and drunken shouts, Jessie Ware's 'Say You Love Me' fade away and there is nothing except for me and him.

Deliberately slowly, he runs his thumb along my jaw, a finger moving across my lower lip, his eyes never leaving mine. Finally, he leans in, his lips touching mine. His kiss is gentler than I'd anticipated, lingering and sensual. I kiss him back, giving his tongue access to my mouth. My arms find their way around him, my fingers moving over muscular shoulders. His kiss intensifies, his tongue explorative. He tastes of mint and whisky and as we kiss on and on, desire pulsing between us, I know that in this moment I am lost to him.

Eventually we pull away from each other, breathing heavily. I've never been kissed like that before, never been so physically attracted to anyone as much as I am to him right now. It's disarming.

"I've wanted to do that all evening," Ethan declares, pulling me to him so I am in his arms, my body against his, my cheek resting on his chest. I can hear his heart beating steadily, unlike mine which I can feel hammering, about to explode. I close my eyes, savouring how it feels to be held by him, remembering his lips on mine, his tongue possessing me as he coerced me to respond. I feel dazed.

"You OK?" He asks, kissing the top of my head, inhaling the smell of my hair.

"Hmm," I respond, keeping my eyes shut. "What hyperbole were you going to try and tell me?"

"I don't know, some nonsense about working well in a team. Just the usual platitudes you are expected to say in an interview."

"And do you work well in a team?"

"Not particularly. I'm not a great team player," he admits. "What about you?"

"I don't think I'm a player at all," I reply, wondering if he will deduce that I'm talking about life in general and not just work. He raises my hand to his lips, planting brief kisses on each knuckle. When he gets to my ring finger his kiss is harder as he sucks my knuckle, his tongue touching the joint.

"When did you stop being engaged?" he asks, releasing my hand.

My eyes flutter open and I search his face, but he has a detached expression and I have a horrible feeling that our moment has passed. I wriggle out of his hold, sitting upright to face him.

"We broke up in April," I say, clasping my hands in my lap.

"You kept your ring on for a long time after," he comments.

"I liked the ring," I say simply. I can't explain why I hadn't taken the ring off as soon as we broke up, but I couldn't bear the thought of not wearing it, not until tonight that is, when something had finally clicked.

"Do you have kids?"

My eyes flicker away from him, staring into the lights of the wheel. "No."

I'm so tired of that question. It never gets easier to answer.

"Is this too soon for you?"

I shake my head vehemently. "No, no! It's fine, it's more than fine, I liked you kissing me," the words tumble out of my mouth, my brain not having the chance to censor them.

"Did you?" He cups my face, his thumbs pushing my chin up to meet his lips once more. "Good," he says, and deepens the kiss.

***

Hand-in-hand we begin to walk back towards the party. I feel like I'm walking on air, a goofy smile on my face. As we near the marquee, Ethan releases my hand and purposefully creates a distance between us. I falter, stopping. Why has he let go? Why has he moved away from me?

"I don't want people talking about us," Ethan says by way of explanation.

"Why?" I ask, not moving.

"Because my personal life is personal, and my professional life is professional."

This makes sense, of course it does, and to be honest the office gossiping about me isn't something I want either, but I seem unable to shift the feeling of rejection. I think Ethan must pick up on my mood because he suddenly pulls me back into the darkness, pushing me up against a tree, his body pressing deliciously close against mine.

"Ow, you're hurting me," I protest as rough bark digs into my back.

"I don't want to hurt you, Rosie," Ethan mutters into my hair, pulling my body tight against his. "This isn't about you, I just don't want people talking about me, OK? I've only been here a week."

"OK," I blink up at him.

"Come out with me after?" His eyes search mine.

"I don't know," I say, unsure of myself, the fear of the unknown engulfing me.

"We'll go for a drink," he says, as if reading my mind. "I want to know everything about you."

"I'm not that exciting, I'm afraid."

"Say yes," he urges.

"OK," I agree, unsure I can deny him anything he wants, even if I wanted to, which I don't.

"Good," he leans and kisses me briefly on the lips. "I'll come and find you later."

I nod, and we head back to the party together, but separately. I flash him a brief smile as I head inside and to the bar. If I am going to be going out with him I definitely need some more Dutch courage. The whole not-mixing-drinks plan goes out of the window and I order a gin and tonic.

Music is still playing, but it appears that people have begun to leave already. I lean against the bar, take out my phone and check my messages. There are five unread texts from Tristan, and two missed calls. I ignore them, briefly wondering if he has found the ring yet. I have a recent text from Libby, asking where I am and saying she and Will are getting the coach back. I quickly text her back and let her know I am staying a little longer and will see her on Monday. I know she will be intrigued as to why I'm not returning with them, but I'm not ready to share information about Ethan just yet.

Is staying the right thing to do, I muse. I want to be with Ethan, I do, but I don't know if I am brave enough to see this through. I think I had hoped that tonight would be the start of me moving on, I'd even thought that perhaps I would kiss someone, a meaningless snog on the dance floor or something, but I hadn't figured on meeting Ethan Harber and had never contemplated anything more than just a kiss. But Ethan's asking for more, isn't he? Or is he? Maybe we will just go for a drink. I'm so confused.

All I know is that I want to be with him, although I don't feel safe being around him. I feel like an awkward teen, frightened of the unknown, but now, unlike when I was sixteen, I know exactly what I want, even if it is just for one night.

I've never had a one-night stand before. I've never slept with someone on the same night I met them. I've never felt desire consume me so violently. I've never felt so powerless and vulnerable under a gaze and I wonder if he knows how he affects me. Tonight is the night to be reckless, I decide, and down my drink. I can do this because I want this badly enough.

"Where have you been?" Drew makes me jump, I hadn't noticed him coming up behind me. "I've been looking for you."

"I've just been outside," I reply. "Is everything OK? It looks like things are winding down."

"The first coach has just gone. I think another one leaves in half an hour."

"It's been a good night," I say as he leads me onto the dance floor.

We begin to dance to Ellie Goulding's 'How Long Will I Love You?' and I am lost to the music and to the dance, the inner turmoil forgotten. I close my eyes, falling in time with Drew perfectly. I wonder if Ethan is a good dancer. I fight the urge to bombard Drew with questions about his American friend.

"I'm sorry I haven't been around much this evening," Drew says as we find a table and I start on another gin and tonic. "Dad's being hard work. Thankfully, he has gone home now."

"Is he OK?" I ask, remembering Ethan's remark about Ed having some kind of a blip.

Drew looks troubled. "He's fine. He's just drinking a bit too much."

"Why have we got a new Director, Drew?" I try, hoping he will open up.

"Because I think eventually Dad will need a break from the business and I know I can rely on Ethan. Rumour has it you were quite perplexed to not be in on the action." I blush, mortified that this information has somehow got back to him. Drew pats my arm reassuringly. "We weren't so much looking for a Director, it just came up in conversation and one thing led to another and here Ethan is. He's an amazing businessman, my dad respects him, it just sort of happened. I'm sorry if you felt overlooked."

I shrug. "I was just surprised more than anything, that's all. It's fine. I was being oversensitive. He seems nice." Annoyingly Drew doesn't get the opportunity to reply as we are joined by Olly Barrett, who slumps onto the chair next to me, obviously having continued to drink since the last time I saw him.

"Rosie," he slurs, draping an arm clumsily around my shoulders, "you do look fit tonight, have I already told you that?"

"I'll leave you to deal with this," Drew says.

"Thanks," I reply, wishing that Olly hadn't interrupted my fact-find on Ethan Harber. "We must do lunch soon."

"Yes, I'll send you some dates." He kisses me on the cheek and leaves.

"Where's Jamie?" I turn my attention to Olly, vaguely aware that his hand is slowly moving lower down my chest.

"He's gone home," mumbles Olly. I feel my mobile vibrate in my bag on my lap and thinking it might be a reply from Libby, I pull it out. The number isn't in my contacts and I open the message:

"Get his hands off you now."

A shiver courses through my entire body and my eyes flitter around the marquee and settle on him standing at the bar, phone in hand. I'm conscious that Olly has his other hand on my thigh now, but I'm paralysed to do anything. Another text comes through:

"Before I come and do it myself."

It takes Ethan slowly sauntering in our direction before I find myself able to act. I shake Olly off, saying I need to deal with a phone call, and quickly start walking to the exit. I'm aware that Ethan is following me and am relieved he hasn't stopped to rebuke Olly. As I wander past the last of the groups outside I get another text, which I eagerly open:

"Right decision. A taxi is picking us up in five minutes from outside the house."

I read it again. Right decision, he is so arrogant! Do I even want to go out with him? Maybe the sensible thing to do would be to just go home and call it quits.

"I'm not sure I have made my decision yet," I text back with a smile to myself and wait.

"Is that so?" He makes me jump, coming up behind me, putting an arm around my waist. "Is there anything I can do to help you decide?" He nuzzles into my neck and I find myself leaning into him, feeling weak with desire, craving his touch. "Come back to my hotel with me," he murmurs, brushing my hair off my neck, kissing me seductively.

Hotel? He hadn't mentioned a hotel earlier and I had been imagining a bar somewhere, at least at first, perhaps his afterwards. Does it really matter if we just skip the drink and move to...?

"Are you cold?" he asks, and I realise I'm shivering. He drapes his jacket around my shoulders. "Come on."

"I don't know, Ethan," I stutter, not following him, unable to move.

He stares down at me, surprised, I think. I wonder whether he has ever been turned down before. I doubt it. I have drunk a lot tonight, but suddenly I feel depressingly sober. I pull his jacket tighter around me and stare down at the ground, willing myself to just take a chance.

He bends and kisses my forehead gently. "Come on," his voice is low, gentle and persuasive. "Let's just have a drink."

We both turn at the same time, having heard footsteps coming our way. Drew appears, heading back to the house. Ethan slips his arm around my waist and pulls me close. I feel awkward, remembering his earlier objection about being seen together, and wonder why the change of heart.

"We're just waiting for a taxi," Ethan says, his hold tightening on me.

"Oh, right." Drew looks embarrassed. I force a smile.

"Er," Drew seems flustered, "I'll see you both on Monday then. Er, have a good night."

"Goodnight Drew," Ethan replies coolly.

"That was awkward," I mumble, trying to relinquish myself from Ethan's vice-like hold. "I thought you didn't want to be seen together?"

"Drew doesn't count," Ethan responds, not letting go. "He can be discreet, I think we both know that. And how else do you think I got your number?"

"I hadn't even thought..." I trail off.

A silver Mercedes taxi drives through the electric gates and pulls up beside us. Ethan opens a door for me and it seems as if my decision has been made. I settle onto the back seat, breathing in a sickeningly sweet vanilla air freshener, and realise I am suddenly very tired. I suppress a yawn and wait for him to join me. The car begins to reverse and drives back through the gates. As we jolt down the dirt track, we pass a coach on the return journey for the last group of revellers.

"Don't look so worried, Rosie." Ethan pulls my hand away from my mouth.

The taxi driver engages Ethan in some mundane conversation and I find myself looking out of the window into the darkness, unable to concentrate on what is happening in the car. My mind wanders and I am back on the big wheel, very much back in the moment of our first kiss.

Chapter Five

"Hey." My eyes sleepily blink open as he unfastens my seatbelt. "We're here."

I rub my eyes, trying to orientate myself. Ethan gets out of the taxi and comes around to open my door. I get out, trying to shake off the tired fuzzy feeling, wondering where we are and how long I was asleep for. Ethan pays the driver and then turns to me, taking my hand in his.

"Where are we?" I ask as we crunch up a gravel path towards the hotel entrance, which has little lights illuminating the small flight of steps to the door.

"At the hotel," he replies.

"Where? Which one?" I ask, wishing that I hadn't fallen asleep enroute.

"We're at Tranquillity," he answers, placing his finger on a sensor, which opens the door.

Tranquillity, I know from the hype in the local paper, is a new upmarket hotel that only opened a couple of weeks ago. It's reportedly a very expensive haven for businessmen, elites and people with far more money than sense. Originally, the site had been set aside for an out-of-town shopping development, but a big American firm had apparently greased a few palms and at the last minute planning had been approved for a luxurious new hotel, boasting a golf course, tennis courts, a state-of-the-art gym and an Olympic-size swimming pool. Nobody can really understand why on earth the American company had chosen Suffolk to launch their first English hotel, but here it is, and here I am now walking inside.

The foyer is dimly lit, and I feel self-conscious as my heels clatter on the marble floor as we make our way to the large reception desk.

"Good evening Mr Harber," the upbeat American night porter behind the desk says far too brightly for this time of night.

"Aiden," acknowledges Ethan. "How's this evening been?"

"Pretty uneventful. The tennis team arrived at about eight."

"Any problems?"

Aiden shakes his head. "No. All good."

"Is the bar still open?"

"No, it's been pretty quiet tonight. You want me to open it?"

Ethan shakes his head, bids Aiden goodnight and leads me over to a lift, informing me he has a minibar in his suite. I'm too tired to argue with him and compliantly follow. We take the lift to the sixth floor and walk down a long corridor, passing through a couple of fire doors on our way. Ethan stops at a door which has Management written on it, he puts his finger to another sensor and again the door opens.

"Is that fingerprint recognition?" I ask as I follow him up a small flight of stairs and out onto a roof terrace.

"It is," Ethan replies, leading me through another fingerprint-activated door.

"That's odd," I comment. "I'm not sure I'd like a hotel having a copy of my fingerprint."

"It won't. It's not for guests."

"It said Management on the door back there," I recall as we wait for a second lift.

"It did."

"You work here too?" I ask, somewhat confused.

"Not exactly." Ethan pushes a button on the lift panel and turns to face me, an amused look on his face.

"What does that mean?" I ask forcefully.

"I own it," he says matter-of-factly.

I am dumbfounded, rendered speechless. This hotel has been described as 'high-end luxurious, extravagant, out of place, over the top, niche, amazing, paradise' in the media over recent weeks and here I am finding out that the man who has beguiled me all evening owns it. This revelation has certainly woken me up.

I remember his arrogance when he told me that he was the one doing Drew a favour here, and wow, talk about backing it up. I can't even begin to imagine how much Tranquillity would cost, but it's obvious that Mosen's Mortgages is mere child's play to Ethan. Again, he has overwhelmed me, and an unnerving feeling begins to uncurl itself in the pit of my stomach. Not only is Ethan Harber dreamily good-looking, but it appears that he is very successful and, most likely, hideously rich.

"You never disclosed 'hotel owner' in your interview earlier," I stutter.

"You're very sweet." He flashes me a brief smile and I can't help feeling he is patronising me.

As we exit the lift a deep, menacing barking begins and I jump backwards in alarm. Ethan catches me, enfolding me in strong arms.

"There's a dog up here," I breathe, collapsing against him, unable to even attempt cool, the noise being a surprise and not particularly a friendly-sounding one.

"Please tell me you like dogs?" He stares down at me, and seems positively relieved when I nod in response. "His bark is worse than his bite. Wait here." He releases me and goes over to the door where the noise is coming from. Ethan opens the door and out bolts a gigantic black-and-tan German Shepherd. I pin myself to the wall needlessly as the dog pays me zero attention and circles round and round his master.

Ethan clicks his fingers and the dog sits immediately, cocking his head to one side and staring up. Ethan rewards him with a stroke and a tickle behind the ears.

"This is Zeus," he says, his voice doting. "Zeus, go and say hello to our guest."

The dog slowly makes his way across the landing and sits in front of me, staring up at me with large doleful brown eyes. He raises a paw in greeting which I take and shake nervously.

"Relax, Rosie, he won't hurt you, he's a softie."

"Hi Zeus," I find myself gently stroking his head as I let go of his paw. He sighs contentedly, stands, wags his considerable tail at me and returns to Ethan.

"He likes you." Ethan sounds pleased.

Dispatching Zeus in the lift, Ethan explains that the dog is adept in pushing open fire doors and will use the stairs to find his way down to reception. Zeus is a very intelligent dog, I am told as I follow Ethan into his suite, which looks more like an apartment.

"Aiden," he says into a telephone, "I've sent Zeus down. Can you take him out and keep him with you tonight? Zach will pick him up at ten for his hydrotherapy. Great, see you tomorrow. Thanks."

I stoop down and take my sandals off, my feet sinking into soft cream carpet. I wander into the main living room, taking in the two leather sofas set either side of a coffee table. A huge TV is set up on the left wall, an immense desk near the window. To my immediate right is a door which I guess leads to the bedroom, and past that is a good-sized kitchen area. I wonder if Ethan is a good cook as I take off his jacket, fold it and place it on the back of the nearest sofa. Everything looks expensive, but it looks impersonal, like a showroom, and I feel hesitant to touch anything.

Ethan crosses the room confidently and takes my face in his hands, tilting my head back so our eyes meet. "What are you thinking?" His voice is soft.

"Honestly?"

"Always," his response is immediate and deadly serious.

"I'm thinking what the hell am I doing here, with you."

"Why?"

I step backwards, gesturing around the room. "All of this! You own a hotel!"

"So?" Ethan asks. I'm unable to articulate my feelings, but the question that keeps whirling around my head is, why me? He can have any woman he wants, why the hell did he ask me here?

"Does owning a hotel bother you that much?" he prompts.

"I don't know," I reply. "I wasn't expecting it, that's all. And how can you own a hotel and be a Commercial Director at the same time?" I run my fingers through my hair, unable to comprehend what the hell Ethan is doing working for Mosen's Mortgages. "It makes no sense."

"I'm not involved that much in the day-to-day running of the hotel. I told you, I worked in property. I'm good at helping to buy land or property for development. Tranquillity is my brother's baby really. I've just been able to help him financially, that's all. I'm like a silent partner, think of it like that. And I told you, I want a break, a change of gears for a bit."

He walks over to a sofa and sits down, beckoning me to join him. I shake my head and wander over to the window, pushing the heavy dark blue curtains apart, resting my elbows on the cool windowsill. I stare unseeingly out into the darkness, urging myself to pull it together. I'm not a gold digger, does it really matter if he is loaded? I'm here because I'm physically attracted to him, nothing more, nothing less, which means that actually his other credentials are meaningless, inconsequential.

I turn to face him and shoot him a shy smile. "I'm sorry, I'm not very good at all of this."

He gets to his feet and goes over to the kitchen. He clinks ice into a couple of glasses and pours two drinks, placing them on the coffee table before he comes and stands in front of me.

"Do you want to get back together with your ex?" he asks, looking down at me.

"No!" I shake my head, appalled and surprised by his question. "Definitely not."

"And am I right in thinking he was the one who ended it?" I nod. "And were you hurt very badly?" His voice is gentle, and I feel like I could tell him anything.

"Yes," I look up into his handsome face, aware he is utterly focused on me. "I don't know if I'll ever trust anyone ever again," I confide truthfully.

"You will," he pulls me into his arms, a hand stroking my hair, "I promise. I'm going to make you better."

For a moment I stiffen in his arms. What a ridiculously arrogant and peculiar thing to say! But as he continues to stroke my hair I find myself relaxing, wanting his bold statement to come true. I've been broken, damaged for a long time now, even before Tristan left me for a younger woman, and maybe it is time to put my pieces back together again. I glance up at him, tentatively raising my hand to stroke his cheek, feeling the beginnings of stubble on his skin.

"I really hope you're right," I whisper and raise my lips to kiss him, my arms going around his neck, my fingers curling into his short hair.

Ethan returns my kiss, his lips warm and firm against mine, our tongues slide against each other's as we lose ourselves to desire. His hands travel down my back, his fingers expertly massaging, making my body press up hard against his. My stomach lurches as I feel his hardness against me. His touch continues to work its way lower, his hands rubbing in downward circles. He lessens the kiss, his hands remaining fixed as he holds me to him. His lips press gently on mine, which is somehow equally as seductive as our passionate kiss.

"I wanted to fuck you the moment I saw you over Will's shoulder," he says boldly.

"Wow," I giggle with nervous embarrassment, "you're quite the smooth talker, aren't you?"

A part of me is thrown by his wanting-to-fuck-me line, but another part finds his straight-talking arousing. We're on the same page, it seems, physical attraction magnetising us together, a pull I find myself unable to resist.

He lets go of me and we sit together on the nearest sofa. He hands me a glass and I take a sip of an excellently made gin and tonic, of course he can mix a good drink, of course he can! Ethan picks his phone up from the table and a few seconds later Ed Sheeran is rather aptly singing something about how loving can hurt through the surround-sound.

"How do you know Drew?" I ask.

"We used to work together in New York."

"He's never mentioned working in America," I say, more to myself than anything.

"It was a long time ago. I think he had just finished at Cambridge and he wanted to travel. He spent about a year at the firm, working in our IT department. I was just starting out too. He's wasted at Mosen's, he's an incredibly intelligent guy."

Ethan's eyes soften as he talks about Drew, his expression kind, his fondness obvious. I listen, enraptured, as he goes on to tell me about how they have stayed in touch, how Ethan spent an entire summer staying with Drew and his family and had enjoyed England so much he had known he would return at some point to live. The Mosens appear to be his surrogate English family and I wonder if he feels obligated to Ed in a similar way Drew seems to. This would certainly explain him working for the company.

I lose myself to his sexy American drawl, his voice deep and incredibly hot. I could listen to him forever. As he puts a hand on my thigh and asks me whether I am listening I realise that I haven't been taking in a word he has been saying for the last minute or so, I have been preoccupied with the sexy way he says his Rs and how he elongates certain words in a delicious drawl and had lost focus on what he was saying.

He raises an eyebrow at me. "Am I boring you, Rosie?"

I blush. "No, I'm sorry."

"What was I saying?" he probes, his thumb ever so slightly edging underneath the hem of my dress, beginning to stroke my bare skin.

I blink up at him, my mouth turning dry. "I have no idea," I confess apologetically. "I was listening to your voice though," I blurt out, immediately cringing at my honesty and inability to think before I answered.

"My voice?" He sounds amused.

"Yeah, the whole American thing," I admit coyly. "It's very..."

"Yes?" he says, enjoying watching me squirm.

"It's very, erm, well it's very hot and kind of distracting."

"Kind of like you in this dress," his eyes glint devilishly at me.

His ring tone replaces the music over the surround sound and Ethan reaches for it, shooting me an apologetic smile as he greets somebody called Josh with annoyed irritation. I take the opportunity to find the bathroom, locking myself in.

The bathroom is exquisite, again in immaculate condition. I wonder if Ethan is a clean freak, perhaps even OCD, as I take in the spotless jacuzzi bath with its gleaming silver taps. There is a large shower cubicle, enclosed in frosted glass. The tiled floor is delightfully cool under my bare feet as I stand, flush the toilet and head to the sink to wash my hands with exotic-smelling soap. I stare at myself in the large mirror, my reflection lit in little spotlights above the counter. My face seems to have taken on a flushed complexion and my hazel eyes stare back at me in nervous anticipation.

Ethan Harber wants to fuck me, I think, remembering his candour as he had imparted his intent. I inwardly hug myself and stifle a giggle. Self-doubt begins to niggle at me, questioning whether sleeping with him on the first night is the right thing to do. Will he think less of me if I let him take me to bed on our first night? Should I be playing hard to get? I'm aware that all my concerns centre around what Ethan will think of me, not what I want or what I will think of myself. The only thing that seems to calm me, to stop me from overanalysing this, is Ethan's touch and that's all I really need and want right now.

***

When I return to the main room I find Ethan is off the phone and is pouring himself another drink. He turns to face me, a dark expression on his face. I'm startled and stop in my tracks.

"Are you OK?" I venture.

"Your phone rang," he replies, taking a drink.

"Oh, right," I say lightly, looking for my mobile on the table and no longer seeing it there.

"Someone called Tristan," Ethan's tone is unmistakably icy as he holds up my phone. "He seems very keen to speak to you, judging by the amount of texts and missed calls on here."

"It won't be important."

"Are you sure?" Ethan challenges.

"Yes," I reply.

"Who is he?"

"Nobody important," I say, stepping forward.

"You should lock your phone when you're not using it." Ethan drains his drink and hands me my mobile. "Whoever he is he seems pretty desperate to speak to you."

Momentarily I stare at him, registering what he is saying. I look down at my phone, open Tristan's messages, aware that they are no longer unread. There are over a dozen texts saying we need to talk, apologies, nothing of any consequence. I look at my call history, noting the missed calls from him. Glaring at Ethan, I tap Tristan on the call log and put the phone to my ear. He answers on the first ring.

"Rosie!" he exclaims.

"Tristan," my voice is calm, betraying no hint of emotion. "What do you want?"

"I need to talk to you," Tristan slurs. He's obviously been drinking too. "I shouldn't have kissed you. I'm sorry."

"It's fine, it doesn't matter," I say, my eyes not leaving Ethan. "Is everything OK? I'm kind of busy."

"Where are you?" Tristan asks.

"What do you want, Tristan?" I ask, sounding irritated.

"Can I see you tomorrow? I need to see you."

"Whatever," I agree. "Now leave me alone."

"I'll come around at lunch," he says quickly, desperately.

"Fine. Goodnight." I lower the phone. "Did you go through my mobile?" I ask, taking his silence as an admission. "You had absolutely no right to. Why?"

"Who is he?" Ethan repeats his question, his voice low. We both stand, glaring at each other. I refuse to back down here, I'm not the one in the wrong and I won't let him make me feel like I am.

"What exactly is your problem?" I demand, not bothering to disguise my annoyance.

"Is it so hard for you to tell me who he is?" Ethan responds, sounding equally annoyed. "I don't believe somebody unimportant wants to talk to you so badly as his messages suggest he does. It's two in the fucking morning!"

"Tristan is my ex," I respond angrily. "Are you happy now?"

"You said it was over," he says accusingly.

"It is over!"

"Then why is he calling you and leaving you messages apologising and saying he needs to see you? Doesn't sound over to me! I don't play games, Rosie."

I take in a deep breath. "Are you serious?"

"Deadly."

I flick through my contacts and make a call and order a taxi for as soon as possible. I turn away from him, owing him no explanation, and stomp across the room to retrieve my sandals. I sit on the floor, my hands shaking as I battle with the thin straps, willing myself to go with anger, to ignore the growing lump in my throat and the burning feeling behind my eyelids. I pick up my bag from the sofa, drain my drink and head to the door.

"I thought I had trust issues," I say.

Suddenly he is across the room, pushing the door shut, grabbing me by the shoulders and twisting me to face him. I have to stop myself from slapping him across the face.

"You can't go!" he says, desire and anger burning in his eyes.

"I can't stay," I respond, a knot of longing twisting deep down. Mad Ethan is incredibly hot, I am appalled at myself for thinking. "Why didn't you just ask me?" I blink up at him. "I'd have told you anything you wanted to know, you didn't have to go all weird and look at my phone."

His expression softens. "Then tell me now. Why was he calling you?"

"Honestly, I have no idea. We're certainly not getting back together. I wouldn't have come back here with you if there was any chance of that happening. I'm not like that, I wouldn't... I don't do this kind of thing..."

"I'm sorry."

"So you should be," my voice cracks slightly. "You've ruined everything."

"Don't say that." He rubs away an escaping tear with his thumb. "I'll make it better."

"You were supposed to be making me better, but I think you've made it worse," I bite down on my lip, unable to look at him.

"Stay," he urges, tucking a strand of hair behind my ear.

I shake my head sadly. "I really can't. I need to go home."

"OK," he releases me, accepting my decision. "How long did the taxi say they'd be?"

"Not long. I kind of have no idea how to get back down to reception, would you mind walking down with me?"

He nods slowly. "I screwed up, I'm sorry."

Ethan takes me by the hand, and I do nothing to stop him, and we leave his suite. In the lift he pulls me into his arms and holds me. I nuzzle into him, closing my eyes and wishing things had turned out differently, not having the energy to push him away, not wanting to.

"Not how I had hoped the evening would end," he murmurs into my hair.

"Me neither," I admit.

The lift doors open, and we walk across the roof terrace and back through the door that has Management written on it, down the long corridor and into the other lift.

As the doors slide shut Ethan corners me and his lips are on mine and we kiss passionately, urgently, trying to soothe each other. The moment may have been ruined but the spark is still there, flickering between us. He is the one to pull away and presses his forehead to mine, his eyes fixing me with a smouldering gaze.

"I will take you to bed, Rosie," he says matter-of-factly. "I promise you that."

"Promises, promises," I tease. "And maybe I'll let you when you're not being such an arse."

Ethan smiles, a gorgeous sexy grin spreading across his face, a gleam reaching his eyes. "Lock your phone."

"I will." I inwardly kick myself, I usually do.

The taxi is waiting for me outside as we pass through reception. We say a quick goodbye, Ethan telling me to text to say I have arrived home safely. I blow him a kiss as the car pulls away.

Thankfully the driver doesn't feel the need to engage in mundane conversation and leaves me to ponder the evening's events uninterrupted. Walking away from Ethan Harber is one of the hardest things I have ever had to do, but I comfort myself with the thought that I think leaving has only made him want me more. Maybe if I had slept with him tonight that would have been an end to it, but now I am certain he will seek me out again. I still can't understand why he had got all jealous and had looked at my phone, but maybe it wasn't the worst thing to happen. It had put a hold on things, temporarily slowing them down, but at the same time giving us a reason to continue.

My mind turns to Tristan, cross that he had chosen to come back into my life suddenly. I knew he had been weird earlier, and his texts and calls are in themselves worrying. I will deal with him tomorrow, but tonight, or should that be this morning, all I want to do is crawl into bed and dream of an arrogant, hot American.

I try to pay the driver, but he informs me it is on the hotel's account. Ethan must have arranged this quickly as I got into the car, I realise. I thank the driver and make my way inside, relieved to be home. I undress quickly, drink a glass of water and brush my teeth before falling into bed. I reach for my phone and text Ethan: "Home safely and tucked up in bed. Thanks for the taxi, you didn't need to. X" I smile as I hit send and wait, my fingers crossed for a response. My phone vibrates on the pillow next to me and a surge of excitement shoots through me as I open his message:

"Wishing I could have put you to bed. X"

"Me too. Goodnight, Ethan. X"

"Goodnight Rosie. See you Monday. X"

I roll onto my side, an excited and contented feeling consuming me, and before I know it my eyes have fluttered shut and sleep claims me.

Chapter Six

I wake abruptly, momentarily disorientated as I surface from a deep sleep. I'm tangled up in my duvet and feel far too hot. I push the cover off me, assessing what state last night's drinking has left me in. I register a dull headache, but my most pressing concern is an overwhelming feeling of nausea. I lay completely still, willing the stomach-churning to subside, whilst debating whether I even have the energy to make it to the toilet to be sick. I scrunch my eyes shut and urge sleep to rescue me from my delicate predicament.

Annoyingly, sleep evades me. Thirst becomes as much of a priority as concentrating on not vomiting. I have a craving for cold orange juice and try to muster the energy to get out of bed. Living alone has many benefits, but nobody being around to look after you when you feel rotten is not one of them, I muse indulgently. Tristan had always been amazing at looking after me when I was ill, even if I was suffering from a self-induced hangover like today, and for the briefest of moments I wish he was here now. It was one of the few perks of living with a GP. And then fragments of last night begin to take shape in my mind. I remember Tristan being here, him kissing me, me putting my ring in his pocket. And then all thoughts of Tristan are forgotten...

I open my eyes and reach for my mobile and read Ethan's texts. If I didn't have them as evidence I think I could quite easily believe the whole thing was a dream, an alcohol-induced hallucination. I reread the messages: nope, most definitely not a dream, it really did happen. He entered my life last night and has changed everything, changed me undoubtedly. Regardless what happens next, he has made me feel different, has made me experience attraction, desire, lust even, in a way I had never known to actually be possible. It had been like a scene from a film, Ethan Harber the male protagonist, captivating me with his sex appeal. Chemistry had magnetised us, not just me to him, but he had felt it too, I know he had. The wanting-to-fuck-me line replays in my mind, comforting me that it was definitely a mutual longing that had consumed us both. God, I regret leaving and wish I had woken up beside him this morning and not alone in my bed.

I look at my phone again, wanting to call him dreadfully, just to hear his voice. But what would I say? Hi? I groan in despair, knowing that of course I mustn't call him, it would be weird and far too desperate. No, last night I had been anything but desperate, I had walked away from him after all, and I have this gut feeling that he admired that, probably because it was a novelty to him. No, I must do nothing and let Ethan make the next move and all I can do is wait and hope that he does.

But what if he does nothing? What if he never even acknowledges me again? What if I have missed my only chance? And then I remember being in the lift with him and him saying he would take me to bed, and the panic lessens. He had been certain, it had been a statement of fact and I had believed him. I do hope Ethan Harber is a man of his word.

The nausea has subsided adequately enough that I feel able to slowly sit up and get out of bed. I put on my light pink Summer dressing gown and go into the kitchen and pour myself a glass of cold orange juice. I take a tentative sip, knowing that this will either revive or ruin me. I'm starving, but feel too weak to even make some toast, so settle for a packet of chocolate chip cookies and collapse onto the sofa.

I'm not sure how I am going to get through today and for the first time in my life I wish it was actually a work day, so our paths would at least cross. Then I would know whether he is still interested or whether it was just a one-off thing. Today has the potential for being incredibly long and I know I need to arrange something to occupy my time. I must not sit here procrastinating otherwise I'll be texting or calling him before I know it. No, I must keep busy.

I grab my phone as a text comes through, disappointed to see Tristan's name and remembering him wanting to come and visit. I reply saying yes, I am up and he can come around in an hour. At least his visit will be a distraction, I suppose. The cookies seem to have made me feel more human, and I feel well enough to shower and dress.

It's another gloriously warm Summer day and I regard my clothes hanging in the wardrobe, contemplating what to wear. I choose a white linen skirt and a V-neck pink and white striped top. I tie my hair back in a ponytail and return to the kitchen to make tea and toast.

I sit at the small kitchen table and check Facebook on my phone. I like a picture posted by Libby of Will asleep on the coach last night. My timeline is full of party pics and excitedly I scroll through them, hoping to get a glimpse of Ethan. But there is nothing, no sign of him anywhere. I type his name into the search, but he doesn't appear there either. Ethan Harber doesn't appear to be on Facebook.

I really want to text him and begin an internal argument about whether it really would be that bad if I just sent one message. What would be the worst thing to happen? He wouldn't reply, that would be the worst thing. Or perhaps he might reply and say last night was a mistake. He wouldn't, would he? I inwardly scream at myself for being so pathetic. The only way, besides contacting him that is, to deal with this excited energy is to talk to someone else about him.

And as if the universe is in synchronicity with me my phone starts ringing, and it is one of my closest and oldest friends calling to see if I want to meet in the park later this afternoon for a picnic.

"I was just about to call you," I say excitedly.

"Are you OK?" Chloe asks.

"I think so," I reply, a huge grin spreading across my face.

"Rosie?" Chloe sounds intrigued now. "Why were you going to call me then? Has something happened?"

"I think I might have met someone," I declare in a rush.

"Really? Who? I need details!" Chloe's voice is excited.

"I'll tell you later. I've got Tristan coming around in a few minutes, so will meet you in the park in about an hour. Is that OK?"

"Why's he coming around?" She sounds hostile now, venom trickling off her tongue.

"He wants to talk about something," I say dismissively. "I'm not really bothered, to be honest."

"You won't let him wheedle his way back, will you?" she checks.

"I definitely will not," I promise. "I can't wait to see you and to tell you everything. I'll text when leaving. Bye."

***

Tristan arrives at quarter past twelve. He looks tired and like he has aged suddenly, as if some burden is weighing him down. Momentarily I feel a pang of sorrow for him, but then I remember everything he has put me through and my heart freezes over once more.

"Hi," I greet him pleasantly enough and lead him into the kitchen. "Do you want a coffee? You look like you could do with one."

A slight smile creeps across his face as he sinks onto a kitchen chair. He looks forlorn, his eyes lifeless and dull, no sign of their usual warmth. He looks pale and in need of a shave. Did he look this bad yesterday? I try to remember as I wait for the kettle to boil. I'd noticed he had put on a bit of weight, and maybe he had looked a bit pitiful, but today he looks down and out. I make the drinks in an awkward silence, bringing the cups over to the table and putting one in front of him, and sit down opposite.

"So?" I ask, wanting to get this over with.

Tristan shuffles awkwardly on his chair and retrieves my ring from his pocket, dropping it onto the table with a clatter. "Nice touch," he says, with an unmistakable hint of annoyance to his tone. "I don't want your ring back, Rosie."

"It's not my ring," I respond calmly. "You bought it, I think it's only right you have it back. Do whatever you want with it, but I don't want it."

"You kept it long enough," he observes.

"I kept it too long. Look, Tristan, I don't want to argue with you about this. If you don't take it then I'll just throw it in the bin."

"Oh, for fuck's sake Rosie!" He grabs the ring again and shoves it back into his pocket, glaring at me.

I glare back at him, surprised by his outburst. "Sell it," I suggest.

"I thought you would just keep it," he says. "I mean, after all this time. I'd like you to keep it."

"I can't. I need to move on."

"You don't have to wear it, obviously. You could just put it somewhere safe."

"Why would I want to do that? I'd know it was there, reminding me of what I thought we had and what you did... No, I honestly don't want it."

Tristan looks sad and troubled and reaches across the table, trying to take my hand. I flinch away from him, not wanting him to touch me, not wanting to give off any mixed signals, definitely not wanting him to try to kiss me again. He looks uneasy and shifts once more on his chair, his eyes darting around the kitchen before he finally plucks up the courage to make eye contact with me.

"Carla wants to start a family," he mutters and stares down into his coffee.

I am flabbergasted at his lack of consideration for my feelings. Like I really want to get into discussing his future plans with the younger woman he left me for. I can't believe he could be so insensitive. I'm stunned into silence.

"We had a bit of a scare," he continues. "Thankfully it was just a false alarm and she wasn't pregnant. God, Rosie, it was awful... I thought it was going to start all over again. And then she did the test and it was negative and I was so relieved, and she was so disappointed. I couldn't deal with it, with her, and I wanted you. That's why I came around last night. I know it's probably wrong, but I thought you would understand."

"Are you serious?" I ask in horror.

"Well, yes," he replies, apparently not finding this inappropriate at all. "I haven't told her about what happened with us." I grip the side of the kitchen table, the familiar hurt awakening and bubbling just beneath the surface. "I guess I just panicked," Tristan ploughs on, oblivious. "I mean, she's never even hinted at wanting a baby before. Perhaps if she had then I would have mentioned it."

"Mentioned it?" I whisper. "What, like over a cup of coffee? I can't believe that you think this is OK, to come here and talk to me about you and her and the possibility of babies..."

"So, do you think I should tell her about everything?"

"I think you should go," I say, getting up.

"Don't be like that," Tristan says placatingly. "I mean, you'll meet someone eventually, what will you do?" I think of Ethan. I feel unsettled, knowing that I don't want to have that conversation with him. Everything is perfect, untainted, that conversation would inevitably change everything one way or another.

“I don't know,” I reply, unnerved. “If it's serious then I guess it has to come up. I don't want to do this,” I say, backing out of the room. “I really want you to go now, please?”

“I don't want to upset you...” Tristan gets up slowly.

“Well you have,” I say sadly.

“Look, about the kiss,” he mumbles, following me to the door. “You won't say anything, will you?” I look up at him, his face anxious, and I realise that ensuring I keep my mouth shut is really why he is here. His baby predicament is just a lame excuse, a smokescreen to hide the fact that he is worried I might blab and his indiscretion might find its way back to his new girlfriend.

“Fuck off, Tristan.” I open the door. “And don't bother coming back. I'm so over you.”

I slam the door and march back into my bedroom and fall onto my bed, burying my face in my pillows as the first tears start to fall. I'm not sure why I am crying really. Is it the fact that he potentially could have the baby with someone else that we never could? Or is it the fact that at some point I will have to explain everything that has happened to someone if I am ever going to have a meaningful relationship in the future? All I know is that the sadness for what I can never have has resurfaced and I am powerless to fight it. The feeling of life just being so unfair takes hold and I am lost in my own grief-stricken world, where nobody can make it better or take the pain away.

The sobs, as always, lessen and I lay quietly on my stomach, waiting for the calm to return, to give me the strength to wipe my eyes and get up and face reality once more. I look at my watch and sit up, closing the shutters on the hurt again, and concentrate on getting ready to go out.

***

On the way to the park I stop off at Waitrose to buy picnic provisions. I dump Pringles and hummus in my basket, joined by some sausage rolls and mini cheese and onion pasties - I'm in need of some stodgy food after last night's drinking. I throw some wine gums and Minstrels into the mix, select a chilled bottle of Pinot and pay a depressed-looking man at the checkout.

“Doing anything nice this afternoon?” he asks in a bored voice.

“Just meeting a friend,” I reply, equally not in the mood for polite conversation.

“These are on special offer, buy one get one free,” he indicates the Pringles.

“Oh.”

"Just grab another on your way out."

I thank him and take another tube as I leave.

The park is packed with people out to enjoy the sun. Picnickers sit on blankets, kids run around noisily playing together. Dogs are wandering around listlessly, too tired to run in the heat, but content enough to search out any leftover food from lunch or to snooze in the shade. The sun really does seem to make everyone happier, I observe, and walk up the hill, away from the duck pond.

I find Chloe soaking up the sun on a red-and-white picnic blanket, her attention on completing the Guardian crossword. She is lying on her stomach, propped up on her elbows, her long, slender, tanned legs stretched out behind her.

"Hi," I drop my shopping and settle down beside her. "What a lovely day."

"I know," she sighs, smiling at me and folding the paper. "I intend to spend the whole of next week in my garden, I've got to make the most of the school holidays while they last."

"I wish I had another week off, although..." I trail off. No, that's not true, another week off without seeing Ethan again would be hell. I mean, a day is bad enough!

"Although?" she prompts, missing nothing.

I blush. "I don't know where to start."

"OK," Chloe sits up expectantly. "Let's get food, drink, and you can tell me everything. Bloody hell Rosie, you look, I don't know... Happy?"

"I look over Tristan, finally," I say, indicating my ringless finger.

Chloe unpacks her John Lewis picnic hamper, pours wine into two plastic wine glasses and hands me a slice of her infamous homemade quiche.

"And you've met someone. Who is he? When? Where? I want to know everything."

And so I tell her everything, in minute detail. The way he looks, the way he made me feel, what he said and how much I am attracted to him. As I babble on and on her smile broadens and I know she is happy that I am finally happy. Admittedly I do notice her raise an eyebrow when I tell her about Ethan checking my messages, but she doesn't pass comment.

"I don't know if it will lead to anything," I say, opening the Pringles and dipping one in the hummus, "but I've never felt like this before."

"Reckless Rosie," Chloe says, encouragement in her voice. "This is fantastic. I've never seen you so excitable over a man before. It's brilliant! He really must be something special to make you go all doe-eyed."

"He is," I breathe, the butterflies returning as I speak about him.

I tell her about Tranquillity and before I know it she is Googling him, intent on finding him, assuring me he won't have avoided an online presence. It doesn't take her long before she is whistling in appreciation and shows me her phone.

“Is that him?” she asks, impressed.

“Yep,” I reply, inwardly hugging myself as my eyes absorb every inch of the picture.

The photo is from his banking job, the caption informs me, relating to some significant story about a settlement. My eyes fail to take in the text in any meaningful way. I wonder when the picture was taken, he looks exactly the same, cool, controlled and completely unreadable.

“And you walked out on that? Are you mad? I mean, he's not my type, but even I can recognise that you won't meet a man like that every day.”

“I know,” I groan, taking my first sip of the wine, wondering if I should have bought lemonade instead. “I don't intend to make that mistake again, if I get a second chance.”

“Good,” Chloe sounds serious all of a sudden. “If anyone can fuck Tristan out of your system I reckon it could be this man here.”

I find myself blushing again and mumble something about Tristan already being out of my system. This prompts me to tell her everything about what had happened with him last night and earlier this afternoon. She is outraged on my behalf, utter hatred pouring from her for everything he put me through. Chloe's determined, unwavering contempt for Tristan has been invaluable over recent months, particularly when I had started to blame myself for our demise. She has stayed over many a night, let me cry on her countless times, and has pulled me through to the other side, where I can see a future without him and where the sadness and pain have dwindled.

The conversation turns to Chloe and her growing disillusionment and dissatisfaction with teaching. It's sad to think that ten years ago she was so enthusiastic and committed, but now she appears tired and frustrated. Bureaucracy seems to have extinguished her love for the profession, management reducing morale to a depressingly low level. And then she talks about the kids she teaches, and her eyes light up with the old passion, the same resolute determination to make a difference and to encourage her students to achieve their potential.

“We've got a meeting at the beginning of September with the new Head,” she tells me. “Apparently another restructure is on the cards. My Head of English is off with stress, so I imagine we'll all be expected to cover his workload. I feel drained just thinking about it.”

“Maybe another school would be different?” I suggest.

She shakes her head miserably. “I don't think so. Now, let's go back to Ethan,” she grins, “what's your plan of attack for tomorrow? Are you going to barge into his office and say 'take me right here, right now'...?" I giggle and wonder what his reaction would be, suspecting that he might just oblige. That is a distracting thought, one I might revisit later when I inevitably won't be able to sleep with the anticipation of tomorrow's meeting.

"Do you think I need a plan?"

"Of course you do. Like what are you going to wear? It needs to be professional, yet sexy."

"I don't do sexy," I shrug, and open the Minstrels.

"No, you didn't do sexy with Tristan," corrects Chloe, popping a Minstrel into her mouth. "But now you do. I saw your photos on Facebook last night, that was a hot dress."

"I do like that dress," I murmur.

"Rosie, just be yourself and allow yourself to have some fun. It doesn't matter if it's just one night or for the rest of your life, this Ethan of yours has finally dragged you kicking and screaming into the world post-Tristan and I want to meet this man, if only to congratulate him for making you smile again. Go to work tomorrow in a come-hither dress and allure him. He's obviously into you, I mean the whole big wheel thing shows that, doesn't it? He wants you like you want him, so turn your phone off for no interruptions and go and get him."

She makes it sound so simple and the more she goes on and on, the more I begin to believe her. I lay back, staring up at the perfect blue sky, relishing the sensation of the sun beating down on me. Tomorrow, anything is possible. I just need to go and get it.

Chapter Seven

Monday morning has never felt so good, I think as I breeze into the office and walk over to my desk, which is situated in the corner next to the kitchen door. I sit down, switch on my PC and log in. I check my email, which has a staggering number of unread messages, and decide I definitely need a strong coffee before I can begin working my way through them. I'm just about to stand up when the kitchen door opens and out comes Will and Ethan in mid-conversation. And so it begins, I smile, as I push back my chair and get to my feet.

"Morning," I say to them both.

"Morning, Rosie," Will responds brightly. "Where did you disappear to on Saturday night? I thought you were getting the coach back with us."

As I redden at Will's question I am disappointed to see Ethan stalk past me without even an acknowledgement. My eyes follow him, watching him stride purposefully to the door and then out into the corridor, presumably towards his own office. So much for the come-hither dress – he hadn't even noticed I existed, let alone anything else. He had completely blanked me, and the disappointment stings. I focus on Will and mumble some lame story about being with Drew, which he thankfully accepts without any further questions.

"Well, I'm off to Manchester shortly, so I'll see you tomorrow sometime," he informs me.

I make coffee and return dejectedly to my desk and sink onto my chair. I scroll down my emails, seeing the familiar names of work colleagues and recruitment contacts. Nothing jumps out at me as demanding my urgent attention, but just as I am about to look away a new email appears and it's from Ethan. I open the message immediately, my hand trembling slightly on the mouse as I read:

"Good morning Rosie,

Please find my CV attached as discussed.

Check your calendar. I've scheduled in a meeting for this morning to go over the Account Manager role.

Kind regards,

Ethan Harber

Commercial Director."

How horribly formal, I think as I open the attachment and skim-read it quickly. First class law degree at Harvard, of course, as if it could have been anywhere else! Junior positions in a couple of banks, proceeded by an impressive set of promotions, with his last position being Director of the British division of a property company. I know none of the companies he has worked for, but his history of promotions suggests he is successful and that he isn't one of those people who just settles.

Dispassionately I reread the document, approving of its structure, admiring the content, and I know that if this had just fallen onto my desk one day that I would have wanted to know more about this person. I consider whether to ping him a quick reply, but decide against it. He hadn't even had the good manners to say hello this morning, his reply can wait. I obligingly check my calendar though and see he has scheduled a meeting for us at ten to discuss recruitment. I accept without leaving a comment.

The office begins to fill with people, a buzz of conversation about the party spreading across the floor. Although people are discussing horrendous hangovers and drinking too much, they all seem incredibly upbeat for a Monday morning, delighting in the opportunity to regale each other with their blurry memories. Sanji, one of the IT Developers, apparently fell down the coach steps and ended up in A&E with a suspected broken ankle. His arrival, limping with a crutch but no plaster, prompts much mocking. He looks slightly embarrassed at the attention and I doubt he has ever felt so popular in his dull life before. Ordinarily I would join in the office gossip, but my mood is suddenly gloomy and I just sit at my desk, vaguely listening, but not really concentrating.

Libby arrives, dropping her bag on the desk opposite me.

"Nice to have you back," she says, sitting down and switching on her computer. "I've got a few meetings this morning, but thought we could have a catch up later, give you a chance to go through your emails beforehand."

"Sure," I reply. "I've got a meeting with Ethan at ten to discuss an Account Manager, but apart from that I'm free all day."

"Have you?" Libby sounds surprised.

"Yes, has he not invited you?" I pretend to look at the meeting request, knowing full well he hasn't.

"Oh, whatever," shrugs Libby. "You can deal with him. I'll most likely still be in a senior manager meeting anyway."

"I can reschedule," I offer.

"No, don't be silly. Do you want a coffee?"

"I've got one, thanks."

She goes into the kitchen and I relax. She didn't seem bothered about the meeting and didn't quiz me about Saturday, so that's good. I turn my attention to work and begin the task of going through my emails, prioritising as I go. I have rejections to send out to candidates who have been unsuccessful after interview. I need to talk to call centre management about the current bunch of newbies to see how they are getting on and to check nobody has left as yet. I have quite a few notifications from our recruitment section on our website and make a note to check in later on to have a look at new applications. I also need to update the 'Current Vacancies' section on our website. I look down glumly at my list and sigh despondently. I add the meeting with Ethan and decide that I should prepare for that first.

I bring up Will's job spec and print it off; this is as good a place to start as any. I've never recruited for Business Development before, so need to look at which agencies will best suit us. I also make a note to discuss internal advertising.

Libby returns with her drink and smiles over at me. Oh no, she has that look in her eye, that inquisitive look. "So?" she asks pointedly.

"What?" I reply, hiding behind my computer screen.

"Ethan," she replies.

"There's nothing to tell. Nothing happened. I would have come back with you and Will, but I ended up getting talking to Drew."

"How boring!" grumbles Libby and turns her attention to tidying up her chaotic desk.

I breathe a sigh of relief and pretend to concentrate on my work. It's killing me not telling her the truth, but Ethan had made it clear he wants to keep professional and personal lives totally separate and I feel I must respect that. And anyway, it doesn't look like there will be much to tell if this morning is anything to go by.

I'm unable to concentrate, so decide to go and check on my newbies. I tell Libby I am off to the first floor and make my way downstairs. As always the noise in the call centre is overwhelming with agents taking calls, but it doesn't take me long to absorb the noise and be able to focus. It's always full of energy down here, some days verging on a crazy hysteria, while on others a horrendous depression engulfs the entire floor. Thankfully today is a positive one, people feeling motivated by Saturday's party.

"Rosie," Olly Barrett, looking sheepish, calls me over as I walk past.

"Hi," I say, stopping at his desk. "You OK?"

"Yeah. Look, did I say or do anything dickish on Saturday? I vaguely remember talking to you..."

"You were fine, Olly," I reassure him.

"So I didn't try and kiss you or anything?"

I shake my head and smile. "No, you didn't."

"Jamie must have been winding me up, the bastard."

A call comes through and Olly immediately switches into agent mode, his greeting to the customer sounding genuine. I leave him to sweet-talk a Mrs Khan and head over to a quieter corner where the Operation Managers sit. Two of them are carrying out

Return to Works, but Tom is free and seems happy enough for me to distract him from updating call monitoring guidelines.

"One of your newbies has phoned in sick," he says accusingly in his strong Glaswegian accent. "Where do you get these people from? And one of them is late! She called in ten minutes ago to say she's started her period and has gone to buy some tampons! Like I want to know that! I mean, why couldn't she just have lied and said the alarm didn't go off?"

"Because if she told you her alarm didn't go off you would have balled her out, whereas the period excuse, I imagine, made you all embarrassed and lenient. In all probability she did oversleep. What did you say to her?"

"I told her not to worry and to take her time." Tom looks pissed off. "I hate women, you're all lying bitches. And I hate this fucking job. I need to get out of here." Oh no, I wish I hadn't said anything now as Tom launches into a rant about being better and worth more than this. I attempt to change the subject back to my newbies, but after informing me they are all still here he continues his diatribe against the company, and in particular its agents.

Tom Warren has been here even longer than me. He originally started out as an agent and had been good on the phone, unintentionally staying, working his way up from Agent to Supervisor and now to Operations Manager. Nobody expects the Call Centre Manager to leave anytime soon, so realistically there is nowhere else for him to progress to and it is this knowledge that seems to be frustrating him. But however much he vents and complains, which he does frequently, you only have to watch him stroll around the call centre, interacting with the agents, to know that actually he does enjoy his job and is in fact very good at it.

I glance down at my watch and am shocked to see it is ten past ten. I'm late! I rudely interrupt Tom and leap to my feet, telling him I need to be somewhere. I speed upstairs and hurry to my desk to grab my notepad and pen before I quickly make my way to Ethan's office. I stand outside for a moment to catch my breath and then knock.

"You're late," he says as I open the door, and returns his attention to his computer monitor.

I falter, my hand clinging to the handle. "Sorry, I was in the call centre."

"I don't want to hear excuses. You're late, it's not good enough. I don't have time to be waiting around for you. If you were going to be busy at ten you shouldn't have accepted the meeting."

"I just lost track of time," I admit, my heart sinking. "It's only ten minutes." I move from the door and make my way to the chair opposite him.

"It's ten minutes that I can't overrun, Rosie." Ethan's voice is harsh. "I don't tolerate lateness."

"Of course you don't," I mutter miserably to myself. "I don't need that long," I say hopefully.

"Well, I do," he replies. "I don't like to be rushed. We'll reschedule," he checks his computer. "I'll see you at four. You can go now."

Feeling well and truly dismissed, I turn around and go to the door. "Don't be late next time," he warns me as I open the door. I leave his office, not looking back, fighting the urge to turn around and tell him to get over himself. Shit happens, sometimes people are late, it doesn't have to be a big deal. We could quite easily have done the meeting if he had wanted to, but oh no, he wanted to exert his authority over me.

By the time I reach my desk I have gone from feeling apologetic to bloody fuming at his rudeness. He hadn't even shown me the professionalism of looking at me, well not properly, and what with him blanking me earlier I feel bloody annoyed and incredibly disappointed. This wasn't how I had imagined seeing him again would be and I'm pissed off, pissed off with him for just being him and pissed off at myself for hoping that something good could come out of Saturday.

I open up his CV email and hit reply. Fuck you, I think as I angrily type my reply, my fingers loudly crashing on the keyboard.

"Your CV is impressive, however, I would have to question whether you would fit into the culture here. I'm not sure you would, or do ..." I hit send and wait. After five minutes with no reply I begin to regret emailing him, wishing I knew if he has read my email and is just ignoring me or whether it is just sat in his inbox, unread.

Libby returns and looks surprised to see me. "I thought you would still be with Ethan," she says.

"He rescheduled," I reply flatly. "I was a little bit late and he wasn't very impressed with me."

"How late?"

"Just over ten minutes. I was downstairs, checking up on the newbies, I just lost track of time. Anyway, Ethan doesn't tolerate lateness and well and truly dismissed me."

"Oh dear," she sighs. "It's unlike you to be late."

"I know," I shrug.

Just as I'm about to get up from my desk to make a drink I get accosted by Ellie, carrying a bouquet of red roses. She hands them to me excitedly, a huge grin spreading across her face.

"These have just been dropped off downstairs for you," she tells me.

I stare down at the dozen red roses, a flutter awakening in my chest. With shaking hands I open the card and read: 'Roses for Rosie'. That's it, no signature. I can feel the office's attention turn on me and begin to flush the same colour as the flowers.

"Who are they from?" Libby asks.

"It doesn't say," I hand her the card.

"Could it be Tristan?" Ellie whispers.

"No," I shake my head. "He never bought me flowers, ever. Definitely not him."

"I think there's a vase in the kitchen," Libby says. "They're lovely. Somebody obviously wants to impress you or thank you for something."

I take the bouquet into the kitchen and find a vase at the back of the cupboard underneath the sink. I rinse it and settle the roses into it, feeling dazed. They must be from Ethan, I think, nobody ever sends me flowers, ever. So perhaps all is not lost after all.

I need to thank him, I decide as I return to my desk and put the vase down. I tell Libby I am off to the toilet, but instead of turning left when I leave our open plan office I turn right and as if walking on air I glide down the narrow corridor to the office at the end. I nervously knock on the door, a jittery excitement consuming me. He's not rejecting me after all, we're still on the same page.

Hearing permission to come in being shouted through the door I enter, finding Ethan standing next to the window, his mobile clamped to his ear. He looks surprised to see me, but indicates a chair and then turns back to the window.

"Mom, just tell Josh to let me know when he has booked the flight. I'll meet him at the airport. OK, speak later," he ends the call and faces me. "And now you're hours early. Time management doesn't seem to be your thing." His voice is cold.

"I got the flowers," I say happily. "They're beautiful."

"What flowers?" he asks dispassionately.

"The roses." I hand him the card.

He looks down at it, then looks at me. "How original," he says mockingly. "Roses for Rosie, Jesus Christ," and hands me back the card.

Oh shit, I realise in horror, they're not from him after all. Feeling flustered I stand and mumble an inarticulate apology on my way to the door, feeling humiliated and embarrassed. As I pull the door open Ethan casually crosses the room, pushing it quietly shut.

I spin around, intent on pushing him away, but as my hands encounter firm biceps I find my fingers curling to hold onto him. I feel his muscles initially tense, solid beneath his crisp white shirt, but as I make no attempt to repel him and continue to cling to him, he relaxes. It feels good to touch him and I ache for him to touch me too.

"I've got a conference call in ten minutes," he says, making no attempt to touch me.

"Oh," reluctantly I let go.

"I read your email," he says, placing a hand either side of me, his palms resting flat against the door, imprisoning me. "I'm here to improve things. I'm not going to apologise for that, even if that means I don't fit in, right?"

"Well, then don't expect to be liked," I say.

"Sweetheart, I'm not here to make friends."

"Fine," I snap.

"Fine," he responds coolly.

"Don't let me hold you up," I say, feeling trapped by his arms either side of me. "I wouldn't want you to be late for your call."

"How considerate," he drawls. "If only you were as diligent about your own time management."

"Ethan, I did apologise at the time, I'm not going to keep on apologising, so get over it and move on," I say boldly.

He laughs. "Rosie, I like you. You've got spirit." Do you? I want to ask, desperate for his confirming approval. But I can't even bring myself to meet his eyes, and as he steps away I find myself leaving his office in a rush.

I return to my desk gloomily, glaring accusingly at the roses as I sit down. Briefly I wonder who sent them, nobody ever sends me flowers, so it had made sense that they were from Ethan. But they definitely weren't from him and I find myself resenting that. But he had said he liked me, even if he had sounded condescending, and I am comforted by this.

I sit staring vacantly at my computer, feeling dejected, rejected and super uncool. Deciding to harness this negativity, I send the rejection emails to unsuccessful candidates. I usually feel slightly apologetic for our rather brief and impersonal rejection email, but today I find myself unashamedly glad to be sending out bad news, finding the thought of others having a shitty day mildly pleasing. As I work my way systematically through the list of names I find my professional focus and take refuge in the world of familiar work, refusing to let any thoughts of that horrible American distract me.

***

The thing I love about my job is that I get to meet new people all the time and am in the position where it is OK to judge them. There's no defined formula for recruiting, it's primarily based on instinct, on my ability to be able to assess people's qualities and deficiencies and to be able to successfully match individuals to suitable job roles. First impressions are crucial in recruitment and I've always been good at reading people, being able to see through the fakes, adept at reading between the lines, finding sometimes the things people don't say equally as poignant as the things they do.

Call centre recruitment isn't glamorous by any means, but what I really love is finding someone who on paper isn't that special, and then being able to bring them out of their shell in interview to find out that in fact they are worth taking a gamble on. Angelo Lopez immediately springs to mind, one of my most cherished appointments.

Angelo had originally applied for a call centre agent position a year ago. His CV had been passable, nothing spectacular, but enough to gain him a telephone interview. His previous call centre experience, working in PPI, had served him well. His soft, polite telephone manner had captivated me and I had had this niggling feeling that there was so much more to find out about him. He was incredibly nervous at interview, his confidence over the phone not initially translating to a face-to-face meeting. He was surprisingly shy, clumsily stumbling over his answers in a strong Brazilian accent. I had been beginning to doubt myself, wondering if I had been mistaken, but then we moved onto his studies and Angelo came to life, passion emanating from him. It was contagious. His call centre experience was from a part-time job to support him through his Graphic Design degree, which he enthused about. His eyes lit up, his whole demeanour exuded confidence and commitment, his enthusiasm for graphic design was undeniable and as if it was meant to be, I knew that we were soon to be advertising for a junior graphics position within our IT department.

When I had called him a few days later to say I didn't think the call centre was right for him he had been impeccably polite, although I registered that he sounded demoralised and defeated. I wanted to hug him down the telephone, to reassure him that everything would be OK. My gut instinct was screaming to not let him go, so I mentioned that we were soon to be advertising for a junior Graphic Designer and would he be interested in applying. Excited gratitude had poured down the line, leaving me feeling all warm inside.

Drew and I interviewed him a couple of weeks later and my initial hunch about him was right, he was special. Angelo won Drew over with his recommendations for the new website and had shown us an impressive portfolio to illustrate his work so far. He is young, keen to learn and has an eye for amazingly good design. I had been thrilled to offer him the job, delighting in his disbelieving surprise and then his euphoric acceptance.

Angelo is charming to be around. He's an artist really, with a useful technological knowledge that enables him to carry out his job. His gentle, laidback personality is soothing to be around and he has brought a sense of calm to an otherwise stressed-out IT department. The only concern I have about him is how we are going to keep him, knowing deep down that soon enough he will be off to work on something more impressive than dull design for a mortgage company.

I find myself absorbed, working through lunch, reviewing applications received directly through our website. Most of them are unsuitable, but I arrange a couple of telephone interviews for later this week. I then have a meeting with Libby, where she tells me that our Personnel Assistant has handed in her notice and would I be able to help cover some of her workload whilst we look for a replacement.

“There's not much I need you to do,” Libby says. “I just need help with minuting meetings I can't attend. The Ops Managers are going to take on quite a bit of the work and we'll just see how we get on for a bit. Ed isn't in a hurry to get a replacement really. It's really FOF that I want you to help with as we need someone who isn't from the call centre in the meetings.”

FOF is shorthand for what is affectionately known by Head Office as Fuck Off Friday, as it’s the day where disciplinary meetings are held and where staff find themselves dismissed. I already minute for staff forums and occasional management reviews, so it isn't surprising they are drafting me in. FOF is not something I relish being involved in but I agree, not really having a legitimate reason to say no.

“I know it's not ideal,” concedes Libby, “but things will most likely be rather quiet over the next few months. I don't envisage us needing another induction after October until the new year, and with the exception of the Account Manager I don't think we are looking for any other roles. It'll be good for you to branch out a bit.”

I wrinkle my nose at her in protest. My first ever job was as a Personnel Assistant and it really hadn't been for me. I don't want to branch out; I like what I do.

“And now,” Libby smiles and pushes a piece of paper towards me. “Here's some good news.”

“What is it?” I ask, picking up the sheet of paper and beginning to read.

“It's our nomination for you for the National Recruitment Awards.” I'm incredibly touched as I read the submission, which acknowledges and celebrates my impact on the business. If you are to believe this then I am bloody amazing at what I do!

“It's lovely. Thank you...” I trail off, lost for words.

“You deserve it. You work hard, it's about time it got recognised properly.”

This puts me in a good mood for the rest of the afternoon and I start work on updating the ‘Working For Us’ section on the website. I realise, gleefully, that Ethan's profile will need to be added and go to get the camera so I can take his photo later. I consider writing some copy for his bio – after all, I do have his CV – but decide he can jolly-well write it himself. I'm sure he will relish the opportunity to say how amazingly great he is.

The minutes begin to start to crawl by and I find myself occupied by thinking about who sent me the flowers. I literally have no idea and am annoyed that there is no signature or clue as to whom they are from. Their presence on my desk is annoying:

somehow they seem to be mocking me, delighting in my utter humiliation with Ethan. Why hadn't I done some digging first before just wading in and thanking him? He must think I'm a real idiot. Why the hell would he buy me flowers anyway? He wouldn't, he didn't.

At ten to four I find myself in the ladies, quickly running a brush through my hair and touching up my makeup. Slowly I make my way to his office, clutching my notes and the camera, focusing intently on professionalism. At exactly four o'clock I lightly knock on the door.

"Hi," I say.

"Hi." Ethan leans back in his chair and for the first time today he looks at me, really looks at me. Pretending not to notice, I stride confidently over to his desk, depositing my belongings before I sit down.

"So," I begin, taking control, not wanting a silence, "I've printed off Will's job spec as a starting point." I push a copy towards him. "I thought you could have a look and let me know what you need changing. I mean, are they going to be doing the same thing, or is Will going to focus on new business and the new manager on dealing with the ongoing relationship? That kind of thing. I've got a call with Hartley's on Wednesday to see if they can be of any help. They're the local agency who help us with call centre staff, and to be honest I'm not sure they will be ideal, but it's a starting point and they'll recommend someone else if it's more appropriate. And there's a couple of online job boards we can use. And of course we can put the advert up on the 'Recruitment' section of our website and internally advertise as well. I'll need to know salary and benefit details."

"I use an agency in London. I've arranged a meeting with them for Friday."

"OK," I falter, choosing my next words carefully. "A London agency may not necessarily be the best option for us."

"Why not?" he challenges abruptly.

"Because we're not in London," I reply simply.

"I am aware of that," he replies.

"What's the agency called?" I ask.

"Bianca. I've worked with her for years. She's very good."

"I actually meant the name of the agency, not the agent. I can at least have a look at them."

"You don't need to. I'll deal with her myself."

"OK," I say slowly, resting an elbow on his desk, leaning slightly towards him as I rest my chin on my hand. "What exactly do you want me to do then? It sounds like Bianca will have everything covered."

"I'm just showing you some professional courtesy," he says, mimicking my pose and resting his chin on his hand.

"Are you?" I question, an edge to my voice. "How, exactly?"

"Well, I'm consulting with you."

"No you're not!" I explode angrily. "You don't want my help, you've got Bianca all lined up. You go to London, knock yourself out. I'm sure you'll find loads of people willing to commute to Woodbridge."

"Travel is part of the job. They won't even have to be here that much."

"Well Will is in the office quite a bit," I counter.

"They might want to relocate," Ethan says. "I mean, I did."

"Whatever. In my opinion you'd be better looking, at least to start with, for people who already live locally. We've got a good reputation and that goes a long way. But you do what you want to do."

We both sit, glaring at each other, neither of us backing down. I can feel myself beginning to get uncomfortably hot, not helped by the sun that is beaming down on me through the window. In contrast Ethan looks cool and I can smell his aftershave. It triggers a memory from Saturday night and I drop my gaze.

There's a knock and Libby pops her head around the door. "Sorry to interrupt, Will's on the phone and I can't seem to transfer him through to you, Ethan." He gets up and follows her out, saying that IT are supposed to be fixing the issue. As the door closes I stand and go to the window, grateful for the gentle breeze that blows in at me.

The minutes crawl by and I begin to get restless. I decide to write him a note, gather up my belongings and head for the door. But just as I am about to reach for the handle I find myself stepping backwards as Ethan fills the doorway. He stares down at me, taking in the fact I was about to leave.

"I left you a note. I wasn't sure how long you were going to be and to be honest it doesn't look like you need me anyway."

"Will's had a car accident." Ethan closes the door. "He's OK," his voice softens as I pale. "The car is probably a write-off, but he's absolutely fine. He's getting the train back tomorrow after his meeting."

For a moment I'm in a trance, the words 'car accident' catapulting me back in time. I hardly register Ethan taking the camera and my paperwork from me. I drag my mind back to the present and pull myself together.

"But he's definitely OK?" I check.

"Yes. Now, shall we carry on where we left off?"

"Was there much more to discuss?" I ask, my anger now dissipated.

"Libby just told me about your nomination for a recruitment award. She told me I was in very capable hands with you." He takes my hands in his. "Shall we start over? Pretend that the rest of the day hasn't happened?" I look up at him in surprise, his expression now reassuring, his eyes inviting, their previous hostility nowhere to be seen. All day he has been so detached or dismissive, I find myself completely thrown and unable to speak.

"How about I talk to your agency with you and you speak to mine with me? Then we can have lunch together and decide on a strategy? Does that sound reasonable?"

"Yep," I manage.

"Good."

I stare down at our joined hands, remembering our handshake at the party, feeling the same spark in his firm, domineering hold. His palms are warm but not clammy, and as he lazily runs a thumb down the side of my index finger, applying a gentle pressure, I'm unable to fight the feeling of desire.

Ethan slowly releases me, a slight smile touching his lips as he steps past me and over to his desk. I turn to see him pick up the camera and he shoots me a questioning glance.

"I'm updating the 'Working For Us' section on the website," I explain, taking a few steps towards him and taking the camera. "All the directors have profiles on there, so I thought you'd need one and I wanted a photo to put up with it. Can I?"

"If you must."

I go to the window and pull the blind down slightly to reduce the sunlight, indicating where I want him to stand. I stare through the lens at him, his expression serious, high-powered success emanating from his blue eyes. With trembling fingers I begin to take some snaps.

"You are allowed to smile," I encourage. "Try sitting at your desk," and as a hint of a smile flickers on his lips I know I have the shot I need. I lower the camera. "Perfect. Do you want to see?"

Ethan comes around the desk and looks over my shoulder and nods. "It'll do."

"Great. Well, if you can just send me a quick bio, like a paragraph about yourself, I can get it uploaded ASAP. And if you can send me salary and benefit details I can at least make a start on the internal advert."

"Do we have to advertise internally?" Ethan asks.

"Why wouldn't we?" I gather up my papers.

"Is it likely there'll be anyone suitable?"

"Possibly. There's a couple of people who I think might apply. They may not necessarily have the experience you are looking for, but they do have the company knowledge and product background. I can tell you're not convinced, but you can at least try, you never know."

For a moment I think he is going to argue with me, but I can see him checking himself and instead he tells me to email him the time of the call with the agency on Wednesday so he can make sure he is available. He sits back down and I take the cue to leave.

“Thanks, Rosie. Until next time.”

As I close the door on him a huge grin spreads across my face. That had been a difficult meeting, he is infuriating, but I know I am going to love working with him, going to relish proving to him that he really doesn't need a high-powered recruitment agent in London. I need him to respect me professionally, to value my opinion, to trust my judgment. At the moment he doesn't and I'm determined to change his mind, and am going to enjoy doing so.

Chapter Eight

At five to five, just as people are beginning to finish their work for the day and are preparing to leave, I make the rather foolish decision to answer my desk phone to an unknown number. As people begin to head out, I find myself politely entertaining a marketing executive from a national mortgage publication who is intent on trying to sell me some advertising space. The excitable young man, ignoring my objections, continues his pitch, offering a specially discounted rate which I'd be mad to miss, apparently.

Initially I am quite polite, but as he continues with the hard-sell I begin to get irritated with his inability to listen and to accept what I am telling him. The office is completely empty when finally, I assert myself and tell him for the last time we are not looking to advertise with him and hang up on his persistent sales chatter.

I go into the kitchen to wash up my cup and as I stand at the sink a flash of lightning seems to act as a catalyst to start one hell of a downpour. Rain begins to fall ferociously and water begins to come through the open window. I lean across the work surface, struggling to reach for the handle to pull the window shut. I stand on tiptoes, my outstretched arm getting battered by raindrops as I fail to reach the handle. Why the hell do people have to push it out so far, I wonder as a roll of thunder cracks through the air.

"Allow me." Unheard, Ethan appears behind me, resting a hand quite unnecessarily on my lower back as he easily closes the window.

As I straighten his hand travels across my back, until his arm is around my waist, his palm now gently resting on the side of my stomach. I shift slightly, grabbing some paper towels from the dispenser on the wall so I can dry off my damp arm. Another flash of lightning illuminates the sky as he takes the towels from me and throws them in the nearby bin.

"I hope it lets up soon, I left my umbrella at home."

"You'll just have to stay here with me until it stops," he replies into my hair as he pulls me closer. "We've got unfinished business, if I remember rightly."

I lean into him, taking comfort in the feel of his solid physique. "I thought you had changed your mind," I mumble, my eyes darting to the door, painfully aware we could be interrupted at any moment.

"Seriously?" He trails a finger down my cheek, running it under my jaw and applying pressure so I am forced to look up at him. "Why would you think that?"

"I don't know, maybe because you blanked me, dismissed me..."

"You were late," he interrupts. "And I never blanked you," he gently places a finger on my lips to quiet my protest. "You, on the other hand, have been disparaging about my CV, kept me waiting, and come to mention it you still haven't sent me a time for Wednesday, so I think perhaps you may be the one who has changed your mind."

I remove his finger from my lips, my fingers entwining with his, locking together as our eyes meet. There's something about his eyes that captivate me completely. They can be the coldest blue, harsh and threatening, which alarmingly I find incredibly attractive, or they can radiate a softer blue that smoulders with an enticing intensity that leaves me longing for him. It's like they have this ability to transcend from the iciest look to a scorching ferocity I have never seen before. A click and a sudden loud humming noise from the fridge jolt me back to reality.

"I think I said your CV was impressive," I smirk, "but it was you I have concerns about."

We spring apart as we hear footsteps heading our way and seconds later the kitchen door is flung open and in strolls Tom. Not wanting to endure any awkwardness, I acknowledge Tom as I slip past him and out of the room. My phone is ringing as I head to my desk and I pick up the receiver, relieved for the distraction.

"Hello, Mosen's, how can I help you?" I collapse onto my chair.

"Rosie?" A muffled male voice crackles down the line.

"Yes," I reply.

"Did you get the flowers?" he asks, his voice eerily quiet.

"Who is this?" I stutter, taken aback.

"I thought roses would suit you," he continues. "Roses for Rosie, I thought the moment I met you."

"Sorry, this is a really bad line. Who is this?"

"Beautiful flowers for a beautiful lady," he purrs, a slight Birmingham accent to his voice. "I like the pretty dress you are wearing today, very summery. Blue suits you."

I shiver. "Who are you?"

"You made a bad decision today," he continues, breathing heavily down the line. "I sent you the flowers because I thought I could rely on you, but you've let me down."

I'm vaguely aware of Tom walking past me and leaving the office as I begin to start pushing buttons on my phone to try and find out the caller ID.

"Rosie," the voice leers, "I'm not an unreasonable man, so I've decided to give you another chance, a chance for you to change your mind and make things right."

"I don't know who you are," I manage, struggling to keep my voice calm. "Who are you? What are you talking about?"

Ethan makes me jump as he rests a hand on my shoulder. I roughly shrug him off, the heavy breathing down the line making me feel sick. There's something vaguely familiar about the voice, the slurry, stoned sounding Brummie accent, but my mind seems unable to place it.

"I'll give you some time to think," he continues. "I am sure you will see sense. I'll be in touch... Oh, and Rosie, do be careful when you leave the building, it's very slippery outside with all this rain, I would hate to think of any harm coming to you," and he hangs up, leaving me in a state of panic. I fumble to put the receiver down, my fingers clumsily hitting the buttons as I continue to try to find the caller ID. Withheld number appears on the display and a feeling of uneasiness engulfs me. His warning about it being slippery and not wanting for me to come to any harm had sounded threatening, and throughout the entirety of the call his tone had been sleazy. I am unnerved.

"Are you OK?" Ethan asks in concern.

"No, not really." I get up and push past him. "I need to speak to Drew."

Hurriedly I make my way out of the office and to Drew's room, which is next to Ethan's. I knock on the door, but it is locked. He isn't there and my anxiety heightens.

"He's in London," Ethan says, having followed me. "What is it? You look terrible."

"I just had a really weird phone call," I say. "He said he sent me the flowers."

"So, who was it?" he asks.

"I don't know," I reply, beginning to feel lightheaded, worry consuming me.

Ethan puts a steadying arm around my waist and guides me into his office, pushing the door shut behind us. "You're shaking," he observes and pulls me close, enfolding me in strong arms.

"I don't know who he is," I babble. "And it was a withheld number."

"What did he say exactly?" Ethan asks calmly.

"That I had made a bad decision about something, I don't know. He said he liked the dress I'm wearing."

Ethan's hold on me tightens. "It is a nice dress," he concedes. "You look gorgeous in it."

The compliment, the one that I have been hoping for all day, is completely lost on me. All I can focus on is the memory of the heavy breathing, the threatening warning and the fact that some unknown person has declared they sent me flowers.

"He knows what I'm wearing, which means he's been watching me." Alarm pitches in my voice at this prospect.

"Sweetheart, calm down," he soothes, a hand gently rubbing my back. "Let's pull up the call and listen to it together. You'll probably recognise who it is because you'll be able to focus properly. It'll be fine."

He pushes me gently down onto a chair and goes behind his desk to his computer. He seems relaxed and I find myself wondering if I have overreacted. Maybe he is right, maybe if I hear the voice again I won't be so thrown and it will be recognisable. I mean, he said we'd met, so I must know him, right? But as the call begins to play through the computer speakers I feel my skin begin to crawl and I'm on edge once more, only compounded by Ethan looking grimmer and grimmer as the call plays out.

"What an asshole," he says harshly.

"He sounds unhinged, doesn't he?" I ask, my voice low and trembling.

"The CLI is unknown on the call recording as well."

"I didn't know if Drew would be able to find out the number."

Ethan reaches for his mobile and within seconds he is speaking to Drew, explaining what has happened. He starts clicking the mouse and relaying information, but I can see the frustration on his face and hear the irritation in his voice. He gets up and goes to the door, telling me not to move, and leaves me on my own.

I sit in silence, desperately trying to get my mind to remember who the voice belongs to. There is something slightly familiar about it, but it's such a distant, insignificant memory that I'm unable to recall fully. It could be anyone, I realise, just someone I've spoken to once in a shop or at a pub. All I know for sure is that I don't know him, we have no friendship, no relationship on which to base it being acceptable for him to send me flowers. And what really bothers me is this feeling that he has been watching me without me even knowing he exists. Has he just seen me by chance today and therefore been in the position to pop my dress into conversation, or is he purposefully looking out for me? Fear of it being the latter whirls uncontrollably around in my head, and I feel vulnerable.

A beam of sunlight begins to slowly creep its way across Ethan's desk, and I realise the rain has stopped and the sun is out again. I glance down at my watch, it's just gone five thirty and I decide I want to go home, to have a bath and to fall into bed. I'm tired and emotionally drained and need a good night's sleep. When Ethan returns I feel calmer and back in control of my emotions. I shoot him a shy smile and stand up.

"Drew's driving at the moment, but when he gets home he'll remote in and have a look at your call log, see if there is anything he can find out, although he isn't that hopeful. He said we can deal with it in the morning, and in the meantime you can stay at Tranquillity."

"What? Why?" I ask in surprise.

"We – I – want to know that you're safe."

"I'll be fine at home."

"I'm sure you probably will be," Ethan replies, "but I'm not willing to take the risk. He sounds like a nut job, and the fact that he knows what you are wearing today means he has seen you today. He could be watching you. I don't want you on your own until we know who he is."

I pale at the fact he has verbalised my own fear. "I can stay with a friend," I suggest.

"No." His tone is harsh and the severity with which he disagrees makes me meet his gaze, a churning feeling starting up in my stomach.

"I'll be fine," I try unconvincingly.

"Please don't fight me on this, Rosie," he says coolly.

"I can't afford Tranquillity!" I protest.

"Think of it as a new company benefit then," he responds lightly. "Drew agreed. He obviously knows where you work, we don't know if he knows where you live, and as your employer we feel a responsibility to keep you safe. He intruded into your work life, that implicates the company. It's just for tonight."

"You think I should be worried?" I ask nervously.

"Not if you're with me, I don't. Come here," he commands enticingly, his voice soft.

I find myself incapable of moving, my feet rooted to the spot, unable to walk the short distance across the office to him. I feel my pulse quicken and am unsure if it is the anxiety from the telephone call or the thought of Tranquillity and Ethan that is responsible for the acceleration. I stare down at my hands, my fingers knotting and unknotting. I feel on edge, wanting to quarrel with Ethan for being so vile for most of the day, whilst another part of me wants to fall into his arms and close my eyes and let him keep me safe. This isn't how I had imagined today would be. I thought it would be lingering looks, provocative comments, but not this...

"Rosie, I don't want you to worry." Ethan's voice is gentle, caressing even, and I feel myself melt. When he says, "come here," for a second time I am unable to resist and practically fall into his waiting arms. He runs a hand slowly down my back, his finger trailing my spine, whilst his other hand glides through my long brown hair. Reaching my bum, he pulls me closer, his body firm against mine. His lips meet mine, his kiss hard, his tongue possessing me completely. Gently he pushes me backwards and effortlessly lifts me onto the edge of his desk. My arms instinctively make their way around his neck as I cling to him, desperate to touch him, to be as close to him as possible. I've yearned for this all day and am lost in the moment.

Ethan is the one to break away, his teeth gently grazing over my lower lip as he sucks it seductively. He takes a step away from me, forcing me to release him, my hands settling in my lap as I try to catch my breath.

"How the hell can you think I haven't noticed you?" he asks. "I haven't stopped noticing you since the moment I first laid eyes on you. I noticed you first thing this morning when you came into the office practically skipping, all smiles, I had to close the kitchen door so I could concentrate on what Will was saying."

"You saw me come in? Why didn't you say hello?"

"Because I find small talk tedious." He pulls me to my feet. "We need to go before I end up screwing you over my desk."

I inhale sharply, initially shocked and then excited, remembering my conversation with Chloe yesterday. The come-hither dress I had agonised over seems to have finally paid off. I'd selected a short-sleeved light blue dress, with a scooped neckline to reveal a suggestion of cleavage, but not too much, subtlety being what I had been aiming for. The knee-length dress moulds itself perfectly to my figure, complimenting my narrow waist and broader hips. Inwardly I applaud myself for my choice.

"How did you get to work today?" Ethan asks, sounding business-like once more.

"I walked."

"Excellent, I can drive us to the hotel then."

"I need to go home first," I say. "I'll need to collect some things."

"We can stop off on the way."

Ethan gathers up his belongings, locks his office and follows me as I go to collect my bag. I falter when I see the flowers. Ethan follows my gaze.

"Bin?" he checks as he picks up the vase.

I nod gratefully as he wanders into the kitchen. I hear him deposit the flowers in the bin and then turn on the tap to rinse the vase. I'm relieved they are gone.

He returns. "Where's the card?"

"I threw it away when I..." I trail off and look away.

"When you realised they weren't from me," he completes my sentence. "Where is it?"

"I ripped it up. It's in the bin. It was just a plain card, nothing to identify where the flowers were bought."

"OK. Let's go." We travel in the lift in silence. I follow him out into the underground car park assigned to our building, wondering if anyone will see us leaving together, but it's completely empty. Head Office left at five o'clock and the Call Centre works until nine, so really there isn't any reason anyone should be down here.

"Nice car," I observe as he opens the passenger door of the Maserati Turismo Sport.

I give him directions to my flat, lean back against the cream leather seat and admire his driving. There is something so masterful about the way he handles the car, it's distracting, it's hot. I wonder if he will handle me so expertly, with such control and precision.

My mind races. I'm going back to Tranquillity again, but uncertainty as to what to expect begins to make me feel on edge. Am I going back to finish off what we started on Saturday? He had kissed me with the same undeniable longing, which would suggest he wants to pick up where we left things. But there is a niggling thought that maybe he has only invited me because of the phone call. After all, he did mention the company being obligated. I need to know, one way or the other.

"Where am I going to sleep?" I ask him hesitantly.

"It's a hotel." He fails to disguise the laughter in his voice as he pulls up outside my flat. "I'm sure we'll find you a bed somewhere."

"Don't laugh at me," I say quietly.

"I'm sorry," he says, his voice soft and genuine. He turns off the engine and drums his fingertips on the steering wheel whilst he considers my question. "With me, hopefully." I can't bring myself to make eye contact with him and have no clever reply to come back with. I feel flustered, awkward, and clumsily fumble with the door handle and get out of the car. I'm aware of Ethan following me and with a shaking hand I manage to put the key in the lock and open the door to my ground floor flat.

"I'll just get a bag ready," I tell him and indicate the lounge. "Make yourself at home. Do you want a drink?"

"Rosie, stop." I comply automatically, his tone authoritative. "Look at me," his voice softens and gently he turns me to face him, his hands resting lightly on my shoulders.

I have no idea why I suddenly feel like I do, but the need to know what he wants, what he expects from me, is overwhelming. On Saturday Ethan had been totally unexpected, and although I had been nervous in his presence I had been happy to go along with it, happy to just see what happened. Maybe the alcohol had relaxed me, made me lose my mind, but honestly I don't think it was that. All day I have wanted him and wanted him to want me in return, to really bloody well want me. And if he had hitched up my dress in his office and had tried to screw me over his desk, as he so eloquently put it, I think I would have let him.

The rational part of my brain knows that he does want me, he said he had noticed me, he had kissed me hungrily, with unrestrained longing. But the irrational me is questioning everything, desperate for answers, to feel like I have some kind of control, or even a say in what happens next. I don't want him to take me back to Tranquillity as some protective company gesture, I want him to take me back with him because he wants to. Self-doubt hits me like a thunder bolt, reminiscent of the earlier storm, rumbling through my head. I feel stripped, as if I'm hurtling towards the edge of an abyss, unable to stop myself from plummeting over. All of my insecurities, some I didn't even know I still had, lurch to the forefront of my mind, pushing and pulling me off balance.

"What's wrong?" he asks quietly, his hands slowly travelling down my arms and then up again to my shoulders.

"Nothing." I try to shake him off. "I'll pack."

Ethan doesn't release me, instead he slips an arm around my waist and guides me into my lounge and across the room to the sofa. He sits down and pulls me onto his lap. Surprisingly I don't try and fight him and I find myself nuzzling against him, resting my cheek against his firm chest, taking refuge as his arms encircle me and he inhales my hair. I close my eyes, soaking in the feeling of being held by him, his strong muscular arms reassuring me, making me feel safe. My heart flutters and my brain is forced to react, to rebuff the sentimentality as just pure naive madness.

"I'm sorry," I whisper, moving slightly and resting my head against his shoulder.

"Ssh," he soothes, placing a kiss on the top of my head.

My hand automatically raises to my face, my fingers resting on my lower lip, a childish defence mechanism I have never kicked. I dig my nails in, hard, fighting the lump in my throat and the pricking feeling behind my eyes. I must not cry, I tell myself, my nails sinking in so deeply to my skin that I register a dull pain, which distracts me, giving me the space to push down the impending tears.

"I'm sorry," I say again. "It's just been a crappy day."

"I don't believe you," he replies quietly.

I catch my breath and feel my body tense. His response is to hold me tighter and he plants a kiss on my forehead. As I sit all huddled up on his lap, snuggling into his broad toned body, I feel like Thumbelina, small and delicate, but completely safe. I've never craved someone to protect me, not really, but here I am sitting on a practical stranger's lap on my sofa, feeling the safest I have felt in a very, very long time.

I wonder when the last time was I felt like this, and for a fleeting moment a memory of my dad flickers, a distant childhood memory of him scooping me up in his arms after I had fallen off my bike. I had been crying, but he had said something, I don't remember what exactly, but it had made me laugh. The memory recedes.

I've never been one of those girls, those irritating Princess types, and certainly Tristan had never tried to look after me in a massively protective way. I've always been independent, for as long as I can remember, and that's been fine, completely fine. I haven't desperately craved, yearned for some macho man to come and be my superhero, but right now, I can't help but feel that I've been missing something, something so integral that I don't know how I've survived without it. It just feels good, unbelievably good. And right, it feels incredibly right. Ethan sits quietly with me and lets me rest against him. Slowly he begins to brush the hair away from my face and takes my hand, removing my fingers from my lip. He shifts slightly and gently moves me onto the sofa.

“There's absolutely no pressure,” he finally breaks the silence. “You can have your own room. I don't want you worrying, thinking that I expect you to sleep with me tonight, because I don't. You're not a sure thing. Let's just have dinner together, talk,” he looks sheepish when he says ‘talk’ and it makes me smile.

“Thank you,” I lean up and kiss him briefly on the mouth, before standing and heading towards my bedroom. “I won't be long.”

Quickly I select some clothes, not having the time to agonise about what outfits will impress. I pack my iPad, and stuff my makeup, hairbrush, deodorant and perfume into the side pockets of my rucksack. I dash to the bathroom to collect my toothbrush and toothpaste and within minutes I am back in the lounge, ready to leave. The distance away from him has been restorative and I feel normal, in control and far away from the emotional cliff-edge I had just been precariously perched on.

“Can I drive your car?” I ask brightly.

“Sure,” he stands and throws me the keys.

I catch them in delighted surprise. “Really?”

He strides towards me and takes me in his arms, bends me backwards and kisses me. “No,” he reclaims his keys. “Don't be ridiculous. Like I would let you drive my car.” He takes my bag and we head for the front door together. The atmosphere has shifted and we both seem at ease, happy to be in each other's company.

As I get back into the car I realise that I wouldn't mind if Ethan thinks I am a sure thing, I am definitely hoping he is. I shoot him a smile, which he returns, our eyes meet and are full of promise. The chemistry, the spark is most definitely back. I'm sure we both feel it and I know that it is only a matter of time until it detonates, engulfing us in the explosion.

Chapter Nine

I unclip my seatbelt and am about to open the door, but I stop and look at Ethan who has remained seated. A muscle twitches in his jaw, he looks tense. I sit back and turn to face him and wait.

"I lied to you back at the office," he finally says.

"About what?" I ask.

"Drew has no idea you are here. You coming back to Tranquillity was my idea, I didn't run it past him, even though I told you I did. I know you get on really well with him and figured that if I said he thought you coming here was sensible then it would make it easier to convince you."

I process what he is telling me, aware that I should be mad at him – after all, he has manipulated a horrible situation for his own advantage. I can see that Ethan expects me to be annoyed with him and is preparing himself for my outburst. But the truth is that his confession is peculiarly reassuring. His admission had been self-motivated, I hadn't had to drag it out of him, he hadn't waited until tomorrow morning to 'fess up when there was a possibility I might find out the truth.

"Thanks for telling me," I say and get out of the car. The honest truth is that I don't really care if Drew does or doesn't know I'm here. Of course, Ethan shouldn't have said that he was all for Tranquillity to be my safe haven when he wasn't, but the fact is I am glad I am here, relieved I am not on my own and ecstatic to be with Ethan.

"I thought you would be pissed at me," he says, meeting me at the back of the car.

I shrug. "I probably should be. Just don't do it again." Ethan physically relaxes as he realises he has been let off the hook. He grabs my black and pink rucksack from the back of the car and puts an arm around my waist, dropping a light kiss on my head.

"Let's go and get you a room," he says, back in control.

"Ethan." He stops. "What if I don't want my own room?"

He drops my bag on the concrete floor, a huge smile spreading to the corners of his mouth. He stares down at me and takes my face in his hands. He bends down to kiss me, his lips soft and warm on mine, his tongue entering my mouth, exploring, conquering, claiming me in the middle of an underground car park. And I let him.

"No pressure," he murmurs.

"I know," I whisper back, snuggling into him.

We pull apart and he swings my rucksack onto his shoulder and strolls to the lift, his arm firmly around me, holding me close. The lift brings us straight outside his suite, no need to go via reception and the hotel like we did on Saturday.

"Where's Zeus?" I ask, expecting barking. Ethan unlocks the door and I follow him in. He drops my rucksack on the nearest sofa.

"He's with Zach, his owner," he replies.

"Oh, I thought he was yours."

He shakes his head. "I look after him a fair bit, walk him most days. Zach can't get out too much now. And Zeus is a great dog. I like spending time with him. You remembered his name?"

"Of course," I smile and walk across to the large window, now able to appreciate the view. To the right, through the trees, I can see a lake, the sun reflecting off the water. To the left are tennis courts and beyond is a golf course. There's no sign of anyone, it's peaceful, tranquil as the hotel's name suggests. I smirk at my own observation.

"It must be lovely to live here," I say.

"I actually miss somewhere I can just call home, somewhere that is just mine. I'm house-hunting at the moment. I don't plan to stay here for too long, particularly as my younger brother is about to show up."

"You don't get on?" I ask.

"We get on great. Josh likes to socialise a lot in an attempt to find himself Miss Right, but he only seems to find a lot of Miss Right Nows. He insists on trying to do the same for me."

"And what does he find you?" I ask, focusing my attention on a blackbird in a nearby tree.

"Annoyingly unsuitable women." Ethan comes up behind me, brushes the hair away from my neck and kisses me, but goes on to ruin the moment by continuing. "I'm monogamous in my promiscuity, unlike Josh who is a bit more relaxed about crossovers."

"Sounds delightful," I bristle.

"And you sound disapproving," Ethan responds.

"Can I get a shower?" I opt to change the subject, feeling I could do with cooling off.

"Sure." There's a definite smile to his voice.

"On my own," I clarify.

"Jeez, Rosie," Ethan says in exasperation.

"What?" I follow him across the room as he grabs my rucksack and strolls over to what I presume is the bedroom door. But it leads to a corridor with two doors to the right and a windowed door straight ahead, leading outside. Ethan pushes open the second door and enters his bedroom, dropping my bag on the four-poster bed. He retrieves a white towel from a nearby wardrobe and hands it to me.

"Thanks," I say.

"There's shampoo and stuff in the bathroom," he indicates a door to my left. "Help yourself to whatever. And there's a lock, make sure you use it, just to prevent any confusion."

And with that he turns away and moodily stalks out. I thought he had been annoyed at my supposed disapproval regarding the Harber brothers' dalliances with women, but I now realise the whole showering-on-my-own clarification has really pissed him off. I feel like I've insulted him somehow, but can't understand why.

I perch on the edge of the bed and survey the room. It is cream-carpeted the same as the rest of the suite. The bed is in the centre, made up with white bedding with pale blue swirls that match the blue drapes hanging, pulled back, from the four posts. Sliding mirrored wardrobe doors take up the wall to the end of the bed; a dark oak bedside table to the right matches the chest of drawers to the left. A large window is directly opposite the door, letting in plenty of the evening sunlight. The door to the ensuite is across from the head of the bed and beyond that, in the corner, is a light blue armchair next to a brass floor lamp and a small oak bookcase. A hint of new wood is in the air, mixed with a masculine aroma of aftershave.

I quickly undress and head for the shower, locking the door behind me. Bottles are lined up on the counter next to the sink, most of them unopened. I select shampoo, conditioner and body wash, all scented in zesty grapefruit, promising to revitalise and renourish. I pull the glass door closed behind me and luxuriate in the powerful, warm torrent of the shower, cleansing away the trials of the day.

I meticulously rub in the body wash everywhere, allowing my mind to imagine Ethan's hands running over my body, massaging the soapy foam into my skin with a tantalising sensuality that makes me regret the solitary shower clarification. Just thinking of his touch on my bare skin is exciting, erotic, too much! I hurriedly wash off the body wash, step out of the shower and quickly dry myself. I smile at my flushed reflection in the mirror as I open the door.

I return to the bedroom, wrapped in the large, luxuriously soft bath towel. I pull out the clothes from my rucksack, disappointed with my selection, wishing I had taken more time to consider what to wear. The storm has helped to shift the clinging humidity, the temperature having dropped slightly, so I opt for a black capped-sleeve dress which has white and pink flowers dotted on it to add a summery feel. It's casual, but pretty. Chloe would no doubt wrinkle her nose up at my choice, I can hear her admonishing me for not choosing something with a lower neckline. But it's a dress I'm comfortable in, and as I stare at my reflection in the mirror I feel like I have made the right choice by sticking to something safe. I don't need the added pressure of feeling paranoid about my wardrobe decisions. No, I'm out of my depth as it is!

I towel-dry my hair as I try to comprehend the cause for Ethan's irritation. I am convinced it was my comment about showering on my own, his quip about me locking the door compounding my theory, but I can't understand why it had exasperated him. Was it so wrong to be clear, to set some boundaries? Maybe, the thought pops into my head, just maybe he thinks my comment was egotistical, that I think he needs boundaries set because he is struggling to control himself around me. He wouldn't think that, would he? Because it's so untrue it's farcical. It had just been a throwaway comment, I hadn't meant anything by it, it had meant to be a diversion from talking about his promiscuous, albeit self-proclaimed monogamous past.

The idea of Ethan with countless scores of women before me isn't one I want to entertain. He's unmarried, gorgeous, successful, overt male sexuality exudes from him, it's not a surprise he has a history, but the thought of being one in a long line of many before me, and even worse, many after me, is unsettling. And there it is, I realise with complete clarity: the thought of Ethan moving on is painfully distressing. I pull the hairbrush roughly through my hair, irritated by this revelation. I'm falling for him, plummeting at an alarming speed, and I realise that even if I could stick my hands out to break my fall I don't think I would.

This is ridiculous. I wince as I brush out a knot. I am not, I must not fall for him. This can't be about raw emotion, because if it is then in all probability I am choosing to get hurt. No, I reason with myself, this is about me wanting him, being physically attracted to him, and that's all it must be about. I'm sure he isn't considering my feelings right now. No, I expect he's considering the best and quickest way to bed me before he moves on. But as I stand and straighten my dress, preparing to go and find him, I catch sight of my reflection in the mirror and am aware that it's too late, I'm actively choosing to freefall. Emotions are already involved for me, I admit, because the thought of Ethan moving on twists painfully low in my gut.

My history is not a promiscuous one. I have slept with three men and was in relationships with all of them. And for the last thirteen years there's only been Tristan and I'd never imagined there would need to be anyone else because I had trusted we would be forever. But here I am, very much imagining Mr Promiscuous in there, in the knowledge that I am not his girlfriend and that this is most likely just a fling. I must think about short-term gain and ignore the prospect of long-term pain.

***

I find Ethan in the kitchen, busy chopping vegetables. His hair is damp – presumably he has used the bathroom I saw on Saturday – and he has changed into a black shirt and blue jeans that show off his muscular thighs and toned behind. Wow, smart casual is hot on him.

“Hi,” I say quietly, desire uncurling in my stomach at the mere sight of him.

“You eat steak?” he asks, efficiently chopping a pepper.

"Yes. Can I do anything to help?"

"No. I'm fine," he replies coolly. "I would offer you a drink, but I wouldn't want you to think I was trying to get you drunk so I can take advantage."

I take a step backwards: wow, he's still pissed off at me and I have no clue what to say or do. I look around for inspiration and catch a glimpse of the view from the window. Bingo, I need some fresh air.

"Can I go outside?" I ask his back as he continues chopping.

"Of course you can, you're not a prisoner. You can escape from the door near the bedroom."

"You're being horrible," I say and march out of the room.

The windowed door leads out onto a private roof terrace. There is a sheltered area with a table and chairs and an open paved area which has potted plants dotted around. I lean my elbows on the brick wall that runs around the perimeter and look down onto the lake through a gap in the trees. I breathe in the smell of wet concrete mixed with damp foliage. It's so quiet, the only noise being from the birds, their chirping and flapping wings as they call and fly to each other occasionally breaking the silence. It feels like Ethan and I are the only people here, it's so desolate, and I wonder where the hotel guests are.

I hear the door behind me open and slowly I turn to face him. We stare at each other for a long time, both trying to assess the situation, to read each other. Defensively I cross my arms and try to wait it out. He leans against the doorframe, his eyes roving over my body with such intensity it feels like he is physically touching me. I shiver, my heart pounding uncontrollably. How can he affect me so dramatically by just looking at me? I can't bear it any longer and turn away, staring back down into the clear water below. I hear him move towards me, sense his body close behind mine. I stiffen as his hands rest on my shoulders, his fingers beginning to expertly massage my knotted muscles.

"You're very tense," he says in a low voice, applying pressure.

"Are you surprised?" I ask, an edge to my voice.

"No," he replies gently, "I'm not. I'm sorry for being horrible. I wouldn't have walked in on you in the shower uninvited, you know?"

I turn into him, leaning my cheek against his chest. His arms close in around me, a hand beginning to stroke my hair away from my face. He smells gorgeous, all freshly showered and of the familiar scent of his aftershave. I tentatively raise my hand to his, our fingers entwining and locking together. He shifts me slightly, so I'm in the crook of his other arm, his palm flat, fingers splayed over my stomach.

"I'm really crap at this," I say apologetically.

"Oh Rosie," he sighs, raising my hand to his lips. "But you want this, whatever this is, right?"

"Yes," I respond unequivocally.

"Good." He lets go of my hand, his fingers trailing down my cheek, my neck, over my collarbone. "Because I really want this." His hand reaches my breast, his thumb deliberately brushing over my nipple through the thin fabric of my dress. "I really want you." I turn to face him, my breast now resting in his hand as he begins to explore, my nipple hardening under his touch. His other arm slides from my waist as he pushes me back against the wall, giving him access to my other breast. My hands travel over his broad muscular chest up to his face, my fingers encountering the beginnings of stubble. I stare up at him, our eyes locked.

"How hungry are you?" he asks, blue eyes burning into my soul, locating desire within me I never knew existed.

"Not very," I whisper, my eyes widening.

He lowers his lips to mine, his kiss firm, his tongue entering my mouth possessively, leaving me in no doubt that this is it, he really does want me. And I respond equally as fervently, my hands travelling over taut shoulder muscles, gliding down over his back.

Ethan pulls away and takes me by the hand, unceremoniously pulling me inside and into his bedroom. He tells me to wait whilst he turns the cooker off, leaving me alone. I cross to the window to draw the curtains, trying to regulate my breathing and to still my now quivering body. I can't believe I am about to do this with the most gorgeous man I have ever seen in my entire life. I've never been so exhilarated and nervous at the same time.

Ethan returns, closing the door behind him and switching on the dimmer lights, mood lighting now illuminating the bed. I'm sure I must look like Bambi caught in the headlights and I watch his expression soften as he crosses the room confidently towards me.

"You OK?" he asks softly. I swallow, my eyes darting around the room, aware that I am turning red with embarrassment, unable to answer him. I bite on my lip, a sudden urge to burst into tears overwhelming me and it takes all of my strength to not fall into his arms right now in floods.

Slap! It hits me hard across the face: I'm absolutely terrified of sleeping with someone that isn't Tristan. Thirteen years with the same man, knowing him so intimately, him knowing everything I did and didn't like. And yet here I am about to have sex with, let's be honest, a complete stranger, who knows nothing of any importance about me. Ethan's earlier self-proclaimed promiscuity, coupled with his overt male sexuality, make me feel lacking, inadequate. God, it's like losing my virginity all over again, although this time it's a million times worse as at least when I was fifteen it was

OK to be nervous and the boy in question had no expectations for me to live up to. I'm thirty-five, a sexually liberated woman, I shouldn't be feeling so intimidated, so completely out of my depth.

"Do you want a drink?" he asks.

"I'm good," I reply.

"Are you sure?"

I nod and smile weakly. Taking his outstretched hand, I let him guide me over to the bed and perch on the edge as indicated. He kneels down in front of me, his eyes searching my face as he removes my sandals, his hands running over my feet, caressing my insteps with his thumbs. It's alarmingly arousing, desire shooting upwards as his hands trail lightly up my legs, his eyes never leaving mine. I feel bewitched, my skin super-sensitive under his gentle touch, arousal beginning to throb through my body, physical desire quietening the inner turmoil in my head. Any self-doubt dissipates as he pulls me to my feet, hard against him.

"No pressure," he murmurs sincerely. "If you want to stop this then we just stop, OK? Any time, Rosie, we'll just stop." He looks earnestly down at me and I have the strongest of feelings that he can read my mind. It's both unnerving and reassuring.

"You might change your mind," I suggest bleakly.

"Don't be ridiculous," he responds vehemently. "You have no idea how restrained I am being."

I stand on tiptoes, bringing my lips close to his and in a low voice murmur, "You don't need to be."

Our lips meet with a seductive tenderness that builds with every lingering kiss, our tongues dancing a passionate tango together, making me feel deliriously lightheaded. With shaking fingers I start unbuttoning his shirt, clumsily struggling as if the buttons are too big for their holes. His skin is warm under my touch, his muscles rippling, his stomach flat and rock solid. He is toned, well-defined muscles tensing under my fingertips. His hands slowly caress their way up my back, his fingers entwining in my hair, which is still damp from the shower. On and on we kiss, revelling in each other's touch, passion pulsing between us.

Ethan lets me go and shrugs off his shirt to expose a lightly tanned and svelte torso.

"Turn around," he instructs, his hands now resting lightly on my shoulders as he turns me away from him.

He brushes my hair off my neck and slowly begins to kiss my ear, his teeth nipping the lobe, before he traces soft kisses down my neck. His hands find their way to the zip at the back of my dress and slowly he begins to inch it down, before he lowers the sleeves off my shoulders, down my arms and then before I know what I am doing I am stepping out of my dress, my hand shooting out to cling onto his arm to stop myself tripping.

I right myself, suddenly aware I am practically naked, with the exception of my skimpy lingerie, and feel horribly self-conscious. Instinctively my arms fold across my chest. Although the room is warm and I am not at all cold I can feel the beginnings of goosebumps prickling under the surface of my skin, in stark contrast to my blood, which is boiling its way through my entire body. My heart is hammering as my eyes flitter around the room, resting on my feet, spotting a chip in my nail polish. Ethan moves to my right, turns around and sits on the bed and pats the space beside him.

"Don't overthink this," he says as he snakes an arm around my waist and pulls me closer, "because if you do I think you'll bottle this and that would be a real shame. For both of us," he adds as an afterthought. He's right, I'm so on the edge of bottling out, of putting my dress back on and making a lame excuse neither of us would believe.

"Trust me," he urges enticingly, a hand stroking slowly down my arm, prising it away from my chest. I want to pull away and remind him that I never intend to trust anyone again, but his hand finds my breast, his finger and thumb begin to stimulate my nipple through my bra and any rational thoughts are lost to physical desire.

Ethan begins to kiss the hollow of my neck, the hand around my waist moves upwards, unclasping my bra with effortless efficiency and drops it to the floor. He pulls me up the bed and his lips find mine as he pushes me down onto the pillows and begins to kiss me deeply. His hands skim over my skin, my breasts, my nipples hardening under his touch. And then he is kissing my neck, my collarbone, his tongue languidly trailing over my skin until he takes my right nipple hungrily into his mouth, his tongue circling and flicking, whilst a hand caresses my left breast. His other hand glides over my stomach and he pushes my legs apart, his hand brushing over my underwear and then travelling down my right inner thigh. My skin feels on fire as he strokes, kisses, sucks me. He kisses his way to my left breast as a hand makes its way up my left thigh, rubbing me through the black lacy fabric of my underwear. He pulls the material to the side and begins to fondle me, his thumb finding my clitoris, lightly caressing my hardening bud, circling and teasing. I let out a moan of pleasure as he bites down lightly on my nipple, a finger entering me, sliding in and out.

"Ethan," I murmur into his mouth as his kiss claims me. My hands explore broad shoulders, defined back muscles, a gorgeously toned bottom. With some trepidation I feel his erection through his jeans and with shaking hands I manage to unfasten the button and zip, sliding my hand clumsily into boxer shorts, encountering his hard cock. My fingers curl around him, my thumb stroking the smooth tip as I slowly work my hand up and down.

"Do not move," Ethan commands, gently placing a final kiss on my lips before he pulls away.

I lie quietly, trying to catch my breath as I watch him quickly undress, my eyes widening as his hard cock springs free. Either the three men from my past were lacking or Ethan Harber is very well-endowed. Holy shit. I turn my head to the left, unable to look any more. I jump in surprise as I feel Ethan lifting me slightly off the bed as he yanks off my knickers. He crawls up my body, his skin hot as it glides over mine. He looks down at me, tucking a strand of hair behind my ear, and kisses my cheek.

"Sweetheart, look at me," he drawls in his deliciously seductive American accent as his hand grazes purposefully down my body. "Rosie," I blink up at him, his expression the softest I've ever seen, his eyes gentle, inviting, and my heart melts. "You OK?"

"Yes," I reply quietly, because actually I am, I'm more than OK, I feel amazing.

He kisses me lightly on the forehead, on the tip of my nose, dropping kisses on my cheek, working his way lower as he gently nips and sucks. Slowly he moves a finger in and out of me, circling my clitoris once more, waves of pleasure crash over me. I reach out for his cock, but he gently pushes my hands away. He shifts position so that he is in between my legs, his tongue licking its way up my thigh and then changing sides. I squirm under him as his hands reach up to my breasts and begin to circle my nipples once more. I let out a low moan as his tongue dips into me, sliding in and out, before he kisses his way to my clitoris and I shudder under him.

As he kisses, licks, gently bites and slides in and out of me I know I have never felt so aroused in my life. I feel like I'm on a precipice of pleasure and Ethan Harber is bringing me to the edge, preparing to push me over. As he flicks at my clitoris and with deliberate slowness runs his warm, wet tongue up and down I can feel my muscles tighten and as he plunges his fingers deep inside me I give way and fall over the edge, the orgasm violently wracking through my entire body, tremors rippling again and again as I lose myself.

I'm vaguely aware of Ethan reaching into the top drawer beside the bed and pulling out a condom, unwrapping it quickly and rolling it on.

"I need to fuck you right now," he declares, rubbing his cock against my entrance. "I need to be inside you." I'm powerless to speak, but to show him I want that too I tilt my pelvis up invitingly.

I gasp as he drives fully into me, my body accepting his unfamiliar presence. He stills, staring down at me, his expression now of lust. I move slightly and curl my legs up around him and slowly, with utter control, he begins to move. As he picks up pace I find myself meeting every thrust, yearning for him. A finger finds my swollen bud again and as he plunges into me, harder, faster, deeper, he circles, bringing me to the brink again. I feel my muscles tighten around him, my back arching in ecstasy as my second orgasm claims me, aftershocks of pleasure rippling on and on. Ethan locks his eyes with mine as he moves forcefully in and out of me, reaching his own powerful climax, collapsing on top of me as he buries his cock deep inside for the last time.

We lie quietly together, all tangled limbs, our bodies fused together in a postcoital heap. Ethan rolls onto his side, taking me with him and I find myself lying in his arms, my cheek resting against his solid chest, his spattering of fair chest hair tickling my skin. Wow, I reflect, just wow. Ethan had been gentle, but forceful, controlled, instinctively knowing my body intimately, playing me like a musical instrument, quiet fortissimo, building to a powerful crescendo of pure pleasure.

"I hate condoms," complains Ethan as he pulls out of me, kissing me on my shoulder before he goes into the bathroom to deposit it.

I stretch out, adrenalin tingling through me. This isn't how I had expected it to be with Ethan, I'd imagined glasses of wine beforehand to manage my nerves, to take the edge off the anxiety, but in reality I hadn't needed the alcohol because it had just felt right as soon as he had touched me and kissed me. I close my eyes, listening to the running tap in the bathroom. I hear the door open and feel the bed dip as Ethan joins me.

"This was not how I imagined my Monday evening would turn out." He remains seated, resting a hand on the side of my arm.

"Me neither," I blink up at him.

"You OK?" he asks gently.

Excellent question, and one I don't have the answer for, not really anyway. I've spent the last two days fixated on what it would be like to sleep with him, insecurities plaguing my thoughts, but I'd never considered how I would feel afterwards. On Saturday it hadn't been about anything more than a one-night stand: however crude it sounds it had just been about physical attraction, sex. But now, a strand of consciousness is meandering its way determinedly to the front of my mind and it's undeniably telling me I don't want this to be over. If I'm honest I think I had known that this morning, when he had ignored me in the office, because it had hurt. But now, after the most amazing sex, I am sure that I want more, whatever that means.

I sit up and shoot him a bashful smile, shuffling to the edge of the bed beside him.

"I'm good," I manage, unwilling to articulate my true feelings.

"You are," he replies, insinuation in his response. "Very good."

I blush at his innuendo, unable to speak.

"You hungry?"

"A little bit."

"Then let's eat." Ethan stands, taking my hand and pulling me to my feet. In silence we retrieve our scattered clothes from the floor and dress.

"I just need a minute," I say, fumbling with my zip.

"Sure." He pushes my hands away and completes the task of doing up my dress. Lingeringly he kisses my neck. "Do you want wine with dinner?"

"Please."

"Don't be long."

When he has left the room and the door has shut I collapse in a giddy heap onto the bed. I did it, I had sex with a virtual stranger for the first time in my life and it had been absolutely fucking amazing. I'm completely lost to him, the first hit of addiction overwhelms me and just like a junkie I want more, I need more!

Chapter Ten

"No Josh, that is not happening. Go back to Jackson today and tell him he either wants the reservation or he doesn't. And tell him we need to know by the close of day. We're running a business here, not a charity."

I stand awkwardly at the entrance to the main room and let my eyes travel appreciatively over his body from behind. There's something so masculine about him, toned shoulders, long muscular legs. He obviously looks after himself and I wonder what exercise he does to look so fit. I blush as he catches me checking him out and take a step back to leave. Maybe he doesn't want me overhearing his telephone conversation with his brother, maybe I should make myself scarce. But as I go to take another step out of the room Ethan approaches me quickly, gesturing me to wait.

"Look, I've got to go. Say hi to Chelsea for me. OK, bye," he lowers his mobile. "Sorry about that. My brother is trying to close a potentially lucrative deal for the hotel, but he's awful at negotiating."

"I didn't mean to interrupt," I say, suddenly concerned I might be invading his privacy. What if he has plans for tonight? What if I'm in the way and he's just too polite to tell me? "If you've got things to do..."

Ethan quietens me, his hand stroking down my left cheek. The usual fire that burns through my body when he touches me lights up deep within me. Just the slightest touch, even a mere glance in my direction and I'm lost under his spell. And I know the more time I spend with him the further I will lose myself to him, and I don't care. I want to be lost, I somehow need it, need him like a drug addict needs their next fix. His right hand copies the left and he cups my chin and tilts my head back to meet his gaze. He stares at me for a long time, trying to read me, I think.

"No, Rosie," he replies, "I have nothing to do. Do you? Did you have any plans for this evening?"

"No. I was going to go for a run, that's all."

"You run?" He sounds impressed.

"A bit."

Running is in fact a recent activity to my life, a by-product of the broken heart. Somehow pounding the pavements had helped, I had found it therapeutic. Running gives me a freedom, a detachment from reality, a mechanism to rid myself of my anger. I enjoy it now, it comforts me, calms me. And physically I'm now in the best shape I have ever been.

"Maybe we could go for a run together at some point," he suggests, leading me over to a sofa. We sit down and I accept the glass he offers and take a long drink. I realise he's waiting for an answer and I don't know what to say. I'm not a particularly great runner, it's just something I like to do, whereas I have this instinctive feeling that Ethan is particularly good.

"Maybe," I say noncommittally.

There's interest in his voice as he asks, "Why do you run?" I hold his gaze, struck by the oddness of his question. Nobody has asked me that question before, but I just sense he knows the truth.

"Because it helps me forget," I reply quietly, my eyes dropping.

"I get that," he says. "It's good, isn't it?" I nod, a shyness overwhelming me. We're only talking about running, yet it somehow feels like we are sharing this mutual, intimate secret. Briefly I wonder what he is trying to forget. I put my glass down on the table and turn to look up at him, my mouth going dry, unable to speak.

Ethan brushes my hair off my shoulder, his fingers trailing down the side of my neck and then they move, tangling in my hair, pulling my head back as he lowers his lips to mine and kisses me hungrily. He pushes me back onto the sofa, my head resting on the arm as he continues to kiss me, his lips demanding, his tongue licking away a drop of wine from my lower lip as he enters my mouth, tasting me with a passionate intensity. A low knot of desire begins to uncurl deep down in my stomach, and I know that the amazing sex we have just experienced together isn't enough, that we both want more.

Ethan pulls away, staring down at me, releasing my hair from his hold. "We'll go running together at some point," he says quietly.

"Why?" I breathe, feeling trapped by his solid body looming over me.

"Because I want to." His eyes darken and his voice changes, deepening, sounding resolute. A tingle travels up my spine. It's unnerving as the atmosphere shifts from intimate to something darker. I think he picks up on this as his expression softens and he kisses me lightly on the mouth, each skilled kiss relaxing me, ridding me of the sudden bout of anxiety. I'm not sure if he is trying to manipulate me with his sensuality or whether he is trying to gain my trust but whatever it is, my body responds, my arms finding their way around his neck, pulling him closer as I open my mouth to him and let him deepen the kiss.

Once again Ethan is the one to pull away, saying he needs to check on the food. I sit up, trying to regain a sense of equilibrium, and wait for my breathing and heartbeat to normalise before I offer my assistance. He declines, of course, saying he has everything under control, and as I watch him move around with organised precision it's utterly apparent that he is more than capable in the kitchen.

I pick up my iPhone and check my texts. I have one from Will in response to a message I sent him earlier upon hearing about his car accident. He assures me all is well and that he is off out for a meal this evening with a prospective client. I also have one from my nan, asking how my first day back at work was. I quickly reply to her, saying it was fine and I will try to get to visit her this weekend.

"It looks like it's going to rain again," Ethan says.

"Typical English Summer weather," I reply, wandering over to where he is cooking. "Are you sure there's nothing I can do to help?"

Ethan shakes his head. "Sit," he indicates the nearby table. "It won't be long."

I sit down and notice a mortgage publication on the table. I pick it up and flick uninterestedly through the pages.

"You read this?" I ask scornfully.

"I intended to," he replies, sliding steaks onto two plates. "As you know the mortgage industry is quite new to me, I thought I might find something useful in there."

"Doubtful," I scoff. "I got a call from their advertising department today."

"Oh good." Ethan sets the plates down on the table and sits opposite me. "A call came through to me earlier, I gave them your number. Maybe we could advertise for my Account Manager in there. I believe it gets a decent readership."

"No," I reply vehemently. "The rates are ridiculous, and the sales guy was a complete sleaze."

"You know best," Ethan replies, a hint of mockery to his tone.

"I do!" I shoot him a smile even though I know his comment was flippant.

"Sleazy how?" There's an edge to his voice. I don't answer straight away, becoming preoccupied with his mouth as he pops in a chunk of steak and begins to chew. There's something so alluring about that mouth, his lips... I look down at my plate, coming out of my trance.

"Rosie," Ethan prompts.

I shrug. "You know, just punctuated every sentence with darling or love."

"Oh, that old trick! Does come in handy sometimes, I've used it myself." I cut into the steak and tentatively take a small mouthful. The meat is rarer than I would usually eat, but I don't feel as if I can make a comment now. The steak is in fact deliciously tender and well-seasoned, probably the best I have ever eaten.

"This is lovely," I say appreciatively. Ethan smiles, obviously pleased. "Do you cook a lot?" I ask, cutting into a new potato cooked in parsley butter.

"A fair bit," Ethan responds. "I'm not particularly into fancy food, but I like good food."

"And this is most definitely good," I groan as I sample the homemade salad dressing, which is just to die for.

“What about you?” Ethan leans back in his chair, taking a swig from his bottle of beer. He looks like arrogance personified, so self-assured and in control. “Do you cook?”

I nod and take a sip of wine. “A bit.”

“And what's your signature dish?”

I consider this for a while, chewing on another piece of succulent steak as I do so. “I don't know. I like simple things as well. What I really like to do is bake.”

“Excellent. What do you bake?”

“Anything. I make a good lemon drizzle cake. I sometimes make cakes for the office, so if you keep on the right side of me, you never know.”

“Hmm,” he spikes potato onto his fork and slowly brings it to his mouth. “I'll keep that in mind.”

We eat in companionable silence; every now and then our eyes meet before I look away, unable to bear the intense scrutiny he fixes me with. Instead I concentrate on the delicious food, and before I know it I have cleared my plate and drained my glass.

“Do you want dessert?” Ethan asks, taking my plate and putting it into the slimline dishwasher.

“No thank you, I’m full.”

“More wine?” He takes my glass, continuing, “I think you might need it.”

“Why?” I ask, instantly feeling unsettled.

“Because there's a few things we need to talk about.”

“Like what?”

Ethan pours me another glass and gets himself another beer before he strolls back to the sofa and places them on the nearby coffee table.

“Well,” he remains standing, “we need to talk about the phone call for a start.”

Oh, that. I had temporarily forgotten about the creepy call from earlier, had banished it to the back of my mind, allowing Ethan to monopolise my recent thoughts. And now, as time has elapsed, I don't feel as worried as I had done before in the office. The stress has evaporated away and I'm able to think more clearly.

“There's not really much to say,” I reply. “It was probably just a one-off thing and I'll most likely never know who it was or hear from them again.”

Ethan sits down. “You were worried earlier,” he observes.

“Because it was unexpected,” I say, going to join him on the sofa.

"Are you sure you haven't got on the wrong side of anyone lately?" Ethan asks sternly. "You need to think, Rosie. I don't know, perhaps a neighbour you have had an argument about parking with, or a guy who you have managed to piss off?"

A giggle escapes me. "My neighbours don't have a car."

"And?" he prompts harshly.

I blush, sitting forward to perch on the edge of the sofa. My fingers curl around the stem of the wine glass but I don't attempt to lift it, not actually wanting a drink. For the first time since I have arrived here this evening I am aware there is no background noise, no music or television, and the silence is suddenly suffocating me in its nothingness. I can feel myself tense, my skin beginning to prickle self-consciously.

"There hasn't been anyone," I finally give in, needing to break the silence.

"Are you sure? Think: a drunken mistake perhaps?"

"No! I don't do drunken mistakes. I never... I don't usually do this."

"Define 'this'," Ethan encourages, sitting forward and putting his arms around me from behind, resting his chin on my shoulder and kissing the side of my neck.

"I, erm..." I can feel myself getting flustered, my body rigid against him.

"You don't usually fuck strange men you meet at parties?" His warm breath caresses my skin.

"No," I shake my head.

His hand covers my clenched fist, purposefully releasing my fingers from the glass. "Thank you for making me the exception," he drawls. "Are you regretting it already?"

"No. Are you?" I ask uncertainly.

"No, of course I'm not." I feel my body becoming pliant in his arms as he twists me, my ear crashing against his chest as he sits back, taking me with him. "So, you've been single since your breakup? No dalliances?"

"No. I wasn't ready."

"Rosie," there's something sharp in his tone that makes me look up at him. "You do know I can't make you any promises, don't you?"

"Of course I do," I respond, an undercurrent of defensiveness to my voice. "This is nothing, I know that."

"That's not what I said." His hold on me tightens as he prevents me from wriggling away. "Don't block me out because you think that's what I want you to do. It isn't."

"Then what do you want me to do?" I ask in confusion.

"Tell me what you're feeling."

"You don't want to talk about feelings," I contradict harshly. "I may not have done this before, but I do know you don't talk about that. I don't need you to pretend like you care."

And this time when I try to escape his hold he doesn't try and stop me. As I get up I briefly catch a glimpse of a troubled expression on his face. I head into the bathroom and lean my back against the closed door.

Fucking, screwing, sleeping with Ethan, whatever the correct terminology is, had been beyond anything I could have imagined. I had let go, let him take control and oddly it had felt exhilarating. But now all I can think about is the empty void he will leave behind when he goes.

When I eventually come out of the bathroom I find him in the kitchen standing next to the open window, his elbows resting on the high sill as he watches the second storm of the day unfold.

"Ethan." I quickly go to him, nervously placing a hand on his lower back as I join him to watch a sheet of lightning illuminate the now dark sky. "I'm sorry," I say in a shaky voice.

"You don't need to apologise," he slips an arm around my waist. "You don't trust me, I get that. If you don't want to talk, then that's OK. But if you change your mind, I will listen, because I want to understand you and because I think it will help."

"You think?" I ask.

"I do," his voice is gentle, but encouraging.

I consider what he has said and bizarrely I reach a decision easily. On Saturday night he had told me he didn't play games – well, neither do I. I take a deep breath and opt for the truth. I want him to like me so badly that it hurts, but I won't pretend to be something I'm not.

"I didn't think I'd have to start over again," I begin. "Tristan and I were together for so long, I'd gone way past thoughts of it not working. I guess that was naive of me. Maybe that's why he cheated on me," I trail off, mulling this thought over.

I remember the first couple of years with Tristan, remember the times I had thought we may break up. But the longer we were together, the less I considered that. And when he had proposed to me I had believed that that would be it, we would be together forever. I'd had no doubts, I'd been comfortable in our relationship.

"He cheated on you?"

I nod. "Thirteen years down the drain, just like that. I don't want him," my hand falls to my side, "but it just feels odd, the thought of being with someone else, even if it's just for a one-night stand."

Ethan twists me to face him, his hands roughly pressing on my shoulders as he fixes me with a cold gaze, his eyes like shards of ice. “And that's what you think this is, do you?” he asks fiercely. “A one-night stand?”

My eyes widen as I stare at him. We're back to moody Ethan, pissed off Ethan, I realise. I knew talking was a bad idea, I knew it wasn't the done thing. So why had he encouraged me to open up? Why had he made me want to tell him everything? I try to step backwards, but his fingers sink into my flesh as he stops me from moving away. I blink at him, inhaling sharply.

“Well, isn't it?” I stumble over my words.

“No.” His reply is so quiet I hardly hear it.

“No?” I breathe.

“No.” This time his voice is low, but firm, definite.

He lessens his pressure on my shoulders, his hands stroking down my arms before he pulls me against him. I take solace in his masculinity, his physical strength encircling me. I feel suddenly weak in his hold, a heady mixture of desire and relief flooding through me. This isn't a one-night fling, and although I have no idea what that realistically means for us, I can't stop myself from feeling like he has just offered me a reprieve. I'm not foolish enough to kid myself that this is a relationship, but it's not just one night either and for some inexplicable reason that both thrills and terrifies me.

“You look tired,” he murmurs, trailing a finger down my cheek.

“I didn't sleep well last night,” I admit, leaning shamelessly into his touch.

“Really?” he asks. “Why was that?” His eyes have softened now, the muscles in his jaw less tense, and I sense he knows he was the cause of my sleeplessness.

“I had things on my mind,” I reply neutrally.

“Let's go to bed,” Ethan says decisively, taking my hand and leading me out of the kitchen to his bedroom. As soon as we enter he pulls me back into his strong embrace, his lips capturing mine in a passionate kiss.

“Get ready for bed,” he tells me, letting me go as he heads into the bathroom, closing the door behind him. When he returns I am in the process of putting my nightie on. He makes me jump as he comes up behind me and removes the material from my hands and slips it back over my head. I twist to face him and watch him inspect my choice of nightwear.

“Nice,” he says as he folds the skimpy black material and hands it back to me, “but completely unnecessary.”

Ethan undresses quickly. His movements are confident, and it is obvious he isn't at all bothered about being naked around me. In contrast I feel awkward around him, shy of my nudity, so I dart into the bathroom to brush my teeth.

I don't know why I'm freaking out so much. He had seen me naked earlier, but then he'd undressed me and it had felt natural, whereas now the thought of just opening the door and strolling across the bedroom, with everything on show, seems a daunting prospect.

"Rosie?" I'm not sure how long I have been in the bathroom before Ethan is knocking on the door. "Are you OK?"

"I'm fine," I say, coming out and side stepping agilely past him, quickly covering the distance to the bed, hurriedly sliding between the sheets, pulling the lightweight duvet up around my shoulders.

I turn onto my side, facing away from him, and let my head sink into the soft pillows.

"Sweetheart," he gets in beside me, planting a kiss on my bare shoulder. "What's wrong?"

"Nothing," I reply, aware of the warmth of his body behind mine.

He props himself up on an elbow and studies me, his right hand resting on the side of my arm. He leans down and starts to kiss the side of my neck, his tongue trailing sensuously over my skin. I melt into him and become aware of his arousal as I feel his erection hard against my lower back. His hand leaves my arm and slips into the covers as he pulls my body hard against his, his hand now cupping my breast as his finger and thumb toy with my hardening nipple.

"I want you," he declares, his American accent seducing me further.

I roll over, the urge to touch and be touched by him overwhelming me. "I want you too," I reciprocate, my hand stroking down his firm chest, grazing over his stomach until my hand finds the shaft of his cock. He twitches against me as I slowly run my hand over him, feeling him grow harder under my touch. A quiet noise escapes my throat as he clamps down on my nipple, stretching it.

Our lips meet in a passionate union as our tongues duel in erotic battle, physical desire consuming us both. We kiss on as his hand pushes my legs apart, his fingers exploring me, teasing my clitoris as they brush it lightly and then move away. He slides a finger inside me, stroking my inner walls as his thumb pushes down hard over my throbbing bud. As he moves in and out of me with his fingers, my hand matches the rhythm on his cock. I feel my orgasm rush up on me suddenly, taking me by surprise as it crashes over me. His mouth catches my cry of pleasure and I feel myself quiver against him as the orgasm rolls on.

Ethan grabs a condom from the bedside drawer, swiftly unwraps it and puts it on. I'm still in a post-climatic trance as he takes control of my body, arranging me on my knees in the centre of the bed, my fingers entwined in the sheet. As he positions himself behind me, he kisses me, surprisingly gently, up my left shoulder blade, and another burst of desire begins to swell within me. This time when he enters me it is rougher than before, more primal. As he grabs my hips and begins to move I realise he needs this, is as lost to the moment as I am, and I find myself even more aroused by him. He seems to be able to enter me deeper this way, stretching me as he pounds me forcefully. I soak in the feeling of being completely taken by him and bury my face in the pillows to muffle my moans of ecstasy as he finds my clitoris once more. The building sensation grows with every thrust and I can feel myself begin to sweat beneath him. His breathing is hard behind me, his breath tickling my ear as he kisses the hollow of my neck. His kiss, the feeling of his tongue reaching a sensitive spot is enough to send me flying over the edge as I let go. I'm aware of him driving into me for the last time, his cock pulsing deep within me as he finds his own release. I collapse underneath him, unable to stay upright any longer, feeling well and truly fucked.

Ethan slowly withdraws and lifts his body off mine. I stay lying on my stomach, my eyes closed as I let my body slowly recover. I'm conscious of him removing the condom before he sprawls out on his side next to me.

He tentatively strokes my arm and asks, “Did I hurt you?”

I roll onto my side to face him and open my eyes, blearily staring at him. “No.” I feel a bit sore, well used, but not hurt.

“Are you going to tell me what was wrong before?”

“It doesn't matter,” I say dismissively.

He presses his lips gently to mine and says, “Tell me. I want to know.”

“It sounds ridiculous,” I falter.

He kisses me again, gently, by way of encouragement I think. What is it about this man that makes me want to tell him everything? It's as if he instinctively knows what to say or do to crack me, to make me want to share my inner thoughts with him. Rationally it just feels odd, over-the-top somehow, but there's another part of me that doesn't want to analyse his bizarre desire for knowledge, and it's that part of me that I find myself wanting to listen to now. He's ultimately asking me to be honest with him, that's all, and honesty is something I crave now, Tristan's betrayal only intensifying this basic need.

I train my gaze on an imaginary crack in the wall over his shoulder and open my mouth to speak. “I felt shy about being undressed around you.”

“Why?” He sounds genuinely surprised. “You've got an amazing body.”

“It's just how I felt.”

“Because I'm someone new,” realisation flickers across his face. “You just need time, right?”

I smile at him as he puts an arm around me and pulls me against him. I snuggle into him, feeling like I belong. A wave of contentment envelops me, and I find myself fighting to keep my eyes open.

“It's OK.” He strokes my cheek, sensing my fatigue. “Go to sleep, sweetheart.”

“I’m sorry,” I subdue a yawn.

“Ssh.”

“Goodnight,” I manage drowsily, before my eyes flicker shut and I give into sleep. As I drift off in Ethan's arms I'm aware of a physical contentment and a feeling of happiness, and I struggle to remember the last time I had felt either.

Chapter Eleven

As I rush through the doors my stomach sinks as the delayed London train on platform 2 begins to pull slowly out of the station, not quite as late as me, it would appear. Bollocks, I inwardly curse, and go to purchase a ticket from an exceptionally upbeat man.

"You've just missed the 10.08," he informs me jovially, making me want to reach over the counter to strangle him with his tie. I saw the fucking train pull out, I don't need him to rub it in further. "There's signalling problems near Stowmarket. The next train to London will probably be here at around eleven, it's just left Norwich."

I buy myself a coffee and sit at a table, preparing myself to call Ethan to tell him I have missed my train and am going to be late for our twelve thirty meeting near Moorgate.

We haven't seen each other since Tuesday lunchtime, when he had apologetically emailed me to say something had come up and he wouldn't be in the office for the next couple of days. I had tried to hide my disappointment, being practical and arranging for him to be able to call into the conference with James White, my recruitment contact, on Wednesday. James had started the call by mentioning we needed to do dinner soon and that it had been far too long since he had seen me, which had instantly annoyed Ethan, and I had spent the entirety of the call trying to manage testosterone-induced egos. I'd wanted to call Ethan afterwards to explain mine and James's relationship, but something had stopped me, and now instead of looking forward to him meeting me off the train I find myself nervous, certain of his irritation regarding my lateness.

Waking up in his arms on Tuesday morning had felt amazing, and although we hadn't talked much, being in a rush to get to work on time, the atmosphere had been charged with desire. His lingering kiss before we left served to demonstrate no regrets, signifying the promise of more. He had dropped me off in a quiet side street near work so I could arrive independently, arousing no suspicions.

When, later that morning, PC Kelly had turned up to take my statement regarding the phone call Ethan had sat next to me, his hand resting unseen on my thigh under the table. The young policeman had asked me a few questions, similar to Ethan's from the night before, had listened to the recording and spoken to Drew about our IT system. As he was leaving he had handed me his card and told me to get in touch if I thought of anything. He hadn't seemed worried and had left me feeling like I had wasted police time. And that had been the last time we had been together.

Taking a steadying breath, I scroll down to Ethan's name on my mobile and hit call.

"Hey, you," his voice caresses me down the line. "Are you on the train?"

"I got stuck in traffic," I mumble.

"You missed it?" His tone becomes clipped.

"Sorry," I say contritely.

He sighs. "What is it with you being late for meetings with me? I can't wait for you. We're supposed to be meeting Bianca at half twelve."

"I know. The next train is due at eleven, so I can get into Liverpool Street by about quarter past twelve and it's only one stop on the tube. Do you still want me to come?"

"Yes. I'll text you the address and you can join us at the restaurant."

"OK."

I stare out of the window onto the platform. A couple of people are milling around under umbrellas, the rain falling hard and from the look of the dull grey sky it's here for the day, all signs of Summer becoming nothing more than a cherished memory.

My phone vibrates on the table and I read the text. It's just the restaurant address, he hasn't said anything else, no greeting, no looking forward to seeing me, no kiss, just an address. I know I've screwed up and inwardly I berate myself for ruining everything. It's not only the fact that I have inevitably pissed Ethan off, but turning up late just looks unprofessional and this really bothers me. When he had mentioned his London contact it had riled me and I had been intent on proving to him that he doesn't need her. I bet Bianca will be there on time, the woman he rates, the woman whose judgment he appears to respect. I let the frustrated anger wash over me, because if I don't focus everything on that I'm going to be crying with despair into my coffee.

***

At five minutes to one I find myself outside the brasserie, ready to see Ethan again and to annihilate Bianca. The train trip has given me the time to put things into perspective. It hadn't been my fault that there had been an accident in the one-way system that had delayed me, and it wasn't my fault that trains were late either, it was just bad luck. I've apologised to him, I'll apologise to her and then we'll move on and get down to work. I push open the door and enter, shaking the raindrops off my umbrella as I struggle to wrap it up.

The restaurant is small, tables squashed in tightly to accommodate as many diners as possible. It's busy, full of smartly dressed businessmen, giving it an aura of being the venue for business lunches. It's noisy, the clatter of cutlery on plates, a cork popping over to my right, loud voices all clamouring to be heard, and oh God, there's the insincere chortle of a middle-aged man, making my skin crawl with the pretentious city fakery of it all. I scan the room, searching for Ethan, but don't see him.

"Madam," a waiter looks me up and down with noticeable disdain, "do you 'ave a reservation?" I slip off my jacket and hand it to him along with my umbrella. "I'm meeting a colleague," I plaster on a smile, aware that my whole outfit, pink blouse and black trousers, probably costs less than the ties in here.

"Name?" the waiter prompts coldly.

"Rosie Fielding."

Without looking at the book he smirks at me, trying to hand me back my belongings as he goes to open the door. "We 'ave nobody of that name."

"Ethan." I don't move, the smile slipping from my face and replaced with a look of pure contempt, similar to the one he had greeted me with. "I'm meeting Ethan Harber."

It's his turn to alter his expression, his eyes widening in surprise before he defrosts and beams at me. "Ah, you are Mr Harber's guest," he hands my jacket to a hovering cloakroom attendant and beckons for me to follow him across the restaurant and to a private room at the back. He opens the door and ushers me in. The room is intimate, only having six tables, although now only the one by the window is set. The room is empty, except for Ethan, who gets up as soon as I enter.

"Give us five minutes," he orders chillingly.

"Of course, Mr 'Arber," the waiter fades into the background, closing the door behind him, leaving the two of us alone.

Ethan slowly walks towards me, his eyes dark, his jaw set in a hard line.

"Hi," I swallow.

"You're wearing trousers," he observes, stopping in front of me. It's an odd remark, probably inappropriate, one which I am unable to respond to, so instead I ask, "Where's Bianca?"

"She just had to pop out, her mobile reception is terrible in here, some urgent work thing. And as you weren't here."

"I'm sorry!" I interrupt.

"Are you?" He reaches for me, his fingers curling inside the top of my silk blouse as he pulls me closer.

"Yes," I reply shakily, feeling the heat from his body.

"Have you missed me?" he asks, his long fingers unfastening a button on my blouse.

I inhale sharply, looking down at his large hands, his fingertips skimming over the small section of newly exposed skin. I lift my gaze and swallow, his proximity and brazenness catching me off guard. "I thought about you," I admit.

"Good." Happy with my response he leads me to the table and pulls out a chair for me and then settles beside me. He runs a hand slowly down the side of my arm and asks, "You haven't had any more flowers or calls?"

"No, not exactly."

"What does that mean?"

"I had a couple of silent calls at work yesterday. I'm sure they were probably just sales calls that didn't connect," but deep down I'm anything but sure.

"Why didn't you call me?"

"And say what?"

"Anything."

The door opens and Ethan moves away as Bianca enters with a flourish. I watch her confidently approach, her perfume overpowering as she nears. She's as I expected, dressed in a perfectly fitted grey pinstriped skirt and cream satin blouse. Her red wavy hair tumbles around her shoulders, framing her narrow face. I meet her eyes as Ethan introduces us and a chill runs through me as I stare into the cold grey eyes of a woman who undoubtedly has used her stiletto heels to trample her way up the ladder of success. Instinctively I recognise her for the super-bitch that she is and prepare to battle.

"Sorry about that, Ethan," she says in a low husky voice, her attention fixed on him. "Incompetence, we struggle to escape it, don't we?" I pick up a menu in an attempt to ignore her, certain she is insinuating I am one of the incompetents.

"Let's order some drinks," Ethan says and beckons the waiter standing at the door. "Wine?"

"They do a good Shiraz here," Bianca says, browsing quickly through the wine list. "That one?" She points, checking with Ethan.

"Sure," he nods.

The vague headache that started on the train is probably a good enough reason to order a mineral water, but as I spot Bianca's scarlet acrylic fingernails unnecessarily graze the side of Ethan's hand, and observe him not even flinch as she takes a menu, I know I need alcohol to endure her.

I watch their easy interaction, observing the way she flutters her long lashes at him, and an unfamiliar flicker of jealousy slowly ignites. I watch their leisurely chatter, their relaxed familiarity. Unlike me, Bianca isn't fazed by him, and equally he appears at ease with her. I can't imagine him telling Bianca to modify her drinking, and I certainly can't imagine her taking it. I wonder how much is professional courtesy on his part, but as she moves onto mentioning a birthday party they both seem to be attending on Sunday I begin to suspect they have a personal relationship also.

I zone them out, my participation in polite conversation seemingly not required, and concentrate on deciphering the appallingly ostentatious dishes.

"Rosie," I jump as I feel his hand gently touch my arm, dropping the menu to see three sets of eyes staring expectantly at me. "Do you know what you want to order?"

"The calamari is amazing," Bianca suggests.

"Erm," I rake my eyes quickly over the menu again and order the wild mushroom risotto, it being one of the few recognisable meals on the wordy menu. I feel the headache ramp up a notch as I catch sight of the waiter and Bianca sharing a look, certain they are judging me. I take a tentative sip of the red wine and decide it is time to move onto business.

"So," I lean back in my chair and do my best to not glare at Bianca, "shall we make a start?"

"If you want," Ethan says, a hint of amusement to his voice, his thigh pressing against mine underneath the table.

I move away, not wanting to be distracted by him. We're here for a business meeting, he was the one that instigated it and I want to get it over with as quickly as possible. He shoots me a sideways glare, presumably unhappy with my need to distance myself from his touch, but I ignore him.

"You lead," I say in a quiet voice. "This is your meeting."

With a bemused expression on her face Bianca reaches down to pick up her briefcase and retrieves a slim file, which she slides over the table to Ethan. "It's really rather simple, Rose," she drones patronisingly, "you're looking to recruit a Bus Dev Exec and I have loads of them on our books."

"It's Rosie," I say coolly, picking up the flimsy folder. "And it's only simple if you have the right kind of people."

"I have excellent people," she replies haughtily. "The best."

"It's about suitability," I counter and then in a more conciliatory voice I say, "thanks for these."

There are five CVs in the folder, all for men, all of whom are working at corporate companies in the city. This is exactly what I had feared. I'm aware that Ethan and Bianca are talking again about things I have no involvement or interest in, so I pull a pen and a notepad out of my bag and concentrate on the file.

I skim over the documents, noting down current positions and companies. Connecting to the restaurant's WiFi, I go onto Google and start researching the companies and individuals, checking company websites, LinkedIn and Facebook. My hunch was right: unless they want a considerable decrease in salary, along with relocation or a lot of travel, there is no way they will entertain Mosen's as their next career move. I finish scribbling as the food arrives and put my pen down.

"I can give you feedback on these," I say as the waiter retreats.

"Can it wait until after lunch?" Ethan asks harshly.

"Sure," I reply, feeling reprimanded.

"Have you ever thought about working in London?" Bianca asks.

"I did work in London for a couple of years."

"Really?" She sounds surprised. "Where?"

"I worked at Black & White in Farringdon."

Black & White is a highly successful recruitment consultancy, so I'm not surprised that recognition flickers across her face. She pushes her hair off her shoulder, and I can see she is reassessing me.

"Who did you work with there?"

I swallow a mouthful of the risotto and answer. "I worked with James White predominantly. He mentored me."

"The guy we spoke with on Wednesday?" Ethan looks up from his lamb. I nod. "You never mentioned it," he says accusingly.

"He has a terrible reputation for being a womaniser," Bianca says, holding out her glass for Ethan to refill.

"Well not with me he wasn't," I respond coolly and excuse myself.

I sit on the toilet with my head in my hands, willing the now throbbing headache to let up. I've only eaten a couple of mouthfuls of my lunch, but I have no appetite and am beginning to feel a little queasy. I want to wrap this up and go home to bed. I flush the toilet and take a steadying breath as I unlock the door.

For a moment I don't register his presence as I walk to the sink to wash my hands, but then something out of the corner of my eye catches my attention.

"What are you doing in here?" I hiss, warming my hands under the powerful dryer. "Someone might come in."

"They won't." Ethan stalks towards me.

"What do you want?" I ask.

"I want you to be nice," he drawls, running his fingertips slowly down my cheek. "What else could I want? Stop being so standoffish."

"This is a complete waste of my time."

"It's called networking," he says as if speaking to a child. "Bianca works for a good company, you never know what opportunities she could offer you."

"Are you serious?" I ask in disbelief. "I don't need or want any help with my career. I'm happy with what I'm doing and I'm sorry if that's not good enough for you."

"Rosie," he looks startled.

"Get lost, Ethan." I push at his chest, ducking under the arm that he reaches out to grab me with and marching out. My head is pounding now, transitioning into a migraine. Bianca looks startled as I stride back to the table and start tidying my belongings back into my bag.

"I'm really sorry," I say calmly. "I'm not sure what Ethan has told you we are looking for, but it certainly isn't this." I drop the folder next to her, aware of Ethan standing at the door.

"They're great guys," Bianca says defensively.

"I'm sure they are, but they're corporate, international travel, they're on salaries that we cannot even begin to meet. And you might want to update your records because according to Facebook Tony Pearce has emigrated." Her mouth drops open. "I'm sorry if Ethan has wasted your time. Nice meeting you and all that."

"Are you not going to finish your lunch?" she splutters. I shake my head and walk to the door, past Ethan and back through the restaurant to collect my jacket and umbrella from the cloakroom attendant.

The streets are quieter now, people having returned to work for the afternoon. The rain has abated but the sky is still grey, pending rain hanging in the air. I walk quickly, head down, my focus on reaching the underground station, getting to Liverpool Street, and catching the train home. I want my bed, need darkness, silence, and sleep.

"You alright love?" An upbeat cockney voice asks as I join a crowded platform.

I blink rapidly at the long-haired man who posed the question. He's staring at me with considerable concern.

"I'm fine," I reply in surprise. "It's just been one of those days."

He shoots me a bashful smile as he repositions the guitar case he is carrying. He's probably early twenties, tall, exceptionally thin, his long, unwashed mousey brown hair falling to his shoulders. He's wearing a loose grey t-shirt and ripped jeans. I catch the unmistakable smell of cannabis clinging to him. He looks messy, the type of man I would usually rush past in the street, but there's something about his awkwardness that draws me closer. I stare into large hazel eyes, their kindness chasing my anger for Ethan away.

"Thanks for asking," I say.

He shrugs as if it was nothing. "Where are you heading for?"

"Liverpool Street," I reply.

"You sure you are going to be OK?" he asks, studying me. "You look very pale, if you don't mind me saying so?"

"Migraine," I explain, "not helped by a horrible business lunch."

“The food or the company?”

“Both,” I smile. The train arrives at the platform and we board together. We don't speak until we pull into the next station.

“I hope you feel better soon,” he says as I stand and move to the door.

“Thanks. Goodbye,” and with that the doors are sliding open and I am stepping down onto the platform. I don't look back but I have the oddest feeling he is watching me. I hurry up the stairs to the mainline concourse and scan the boards for an Ipswich-bound train. I've just missed one by a matter of minutes and the next one isn't due for half an hour. Disheartened, I find an empty bench and sit down, preparing to wait.

Ten minutes later I feel my phone vibrate and without really paying attention, I hit answer.

“Where are you?” His voice is razor-blade sharp down the line.

“I'm waiting for a train,” I respond automatically.

“At Liverpool Street?”

“Yes.”

“Don't move,” he commands. “I see you.”

I look up and there he is, coming down the escalator, and before I know it he has me by the arm and is pulling me sharply to my feet.

“You complete bitch,” he snarls. “You were totally out of line back there.”

“I'm surprised you even noticed I'd gone,” I flare back at him.

As I go to push him away I'm aware of my vision fading fuzzily, and a sudden wooziness swamps me.

“Fuck, Rosie!” he exclaims as he catches me, preventing my fall.

“Is everything alright?” I'm vaguely cognisant of a stranger asking.

And as the blackness pulls me under I hear the lilt of an American voice say, "She's OK. She's mine." And then the darkness wraps around me.

Chapter Twelve

It's noise that returns first, the hustle and bustle of the station, heels tapping on the floor as people move hurriedly in all directions, the gentle whoosh of suitcase wheels sliding across the smooth floor, a booming voice coming over the Tannoy. It's followed quickly by touch, my bum on a cold surface, being held against someone. A man, my nose tells me from the masculine smell of aftershave that fills my nostrils. It's a familiar smell. Cautiously I open an eye, followed by the other, blinking rapidly as I take it all in, the memories returning in a jumbled chaos. And finally there's pain, a searing ache that threatens to split open my skull.

"What happened?" I ask, putting a hand over my eyes to shield them from the light that is intensifying the throbbing in my head.

"You fainted," Ethan replies calmly. "How are you feeling?"

"My head's pounding." I relax against him and close my eyes. "I think it's a migraine."

"Have you drunk enough, eaten enough?"

I consider: I'd drunk half of the coffee at the station and a glass of red wine, but the couple of spoons of risotto is the only food I've eaten today. "I could have done better," I admit. "I just need to go home to bed and sleep it off."

"Are you OK to walk?" Slowly he gets up, pulling me with him, a supportive arm around my waist. I nod.

We begin to walk, but I realise he is heading for the escalator that leads to the exit.

"You're going the wrong way. We need platform 10."

Ethan slows and for the first time since I have come round, our eyes meet and hold. "You're coming back to my apartment," he states uncompromisingly.

"Ethan, I just want to go to bed," I protest weakly.

"And you can," he replies. "At mine. You can sleep, eat, and when you're feeling better I'll drive you home." Feeling dazed, embarrassed and in pain, I can't muster up the energy to fight him on this, so I let him guide me through the crowd and into a black cab.

"You should have said you weren't feeling well at the restaurant," he says after giving the driver an address, his arm sliding behind me on the back seat, his fingers stroking the side of my neck. I rest my ear on his shoulder and reach for his other hand, our fingers fusing.

"I didn't know I was going to faint," I reply. "I've never before. And I haven't had a migraine since uni. Where's your apartment?"

"Knightsbridge."

“Nice,” I sigh. “Are you still mad at me?” I ask, the memory of him calling me a complete bitch pricking sharply into my consciousness.

“Yes,” he responds darkly.

“You left Bianca,” I realise. “Why?”

“Because I wanted you,” he replies quietly.

I raise his hand to my lips, placing a kiss on his knuckles.

“Do you want to see a doctor?” Ethan swerves away from our intimacy. “Are there any tablets you need?”

“No. I've taken some painkillers already, I just need to sleep.”

“Then bed it is. Now, no more questions,” his hand moves from my neck, his fingers combing through my hair. “Close your eyes, relax against me, I’ve got you.”

I comply, my body dissolving against him. Occasionally I squint out of the window as we make our way slowly through the traffic. I recognise Sloan Street as we pass, shortly followed by Harrods. We are in the heart of the exclusive metropolis that is Knightsbridge. It's familiar, I've been here before and seen it plenty of times in films and on television.

The taxi pulls to the kerb outside an apartment building and we get out.

“You live here?” He nods, taking my hand and leading me through the door that has just been opened by a concierge.

“You OK with heights?” Ethan asks as we enter a glass lift, his finger hovering over the button.

I nod and the lift moves quickly upwards, the view of London sprawling out below us.

“It's impressive, isn't it?” He smiles, following my gaze. “I love London.” The lift doors slide open and Ethan bustles me to a door, which he unlocks and leads me through into a hall and then into a large lounge. My eyes are immediately drawn to the full glass wall that leads out onto a balcony overlooking the city. I remember the impressive view from Tranquillity, but this is stunning in a completely different way. Ethan definitely has the eye for picking great landscapes to appreciate out of his windows.

“This is what is going to happen,” he says, taking my jacket and bag from me and depositing them on a sofa. His arms find their way around my waist and pull me so my back crashes against his chest. “We're going to go upstairs,” his voice is close to my ear. “You're going to let me undress you,” his hands trail up my stomach, slowly across my breasts. “And then,” he begins to kiss the side of my neck, working his way to my jaw and up to the corner of my mouth. “I'm going to lay you down in my bed and let you go to sleep,” he smiles, the sparkle of triumph glittering in his eyes as he witnesses my longing and my frustration.

I spin around, my lips pressing to his, my tongue sneaking its way in between his lips, exploring his mouth, urging him to respond and claim me. A throbbing low down in my core temporarily distracts from the agony in my head, liquid lust pooling through my body as a craving for him consumes me.

“Hey,” his hands capture mine as I loosen his tie.

Rejection dampens the fiery desire immediately and I step backwards, ashamed of my neediness, embarrassment spreading across my face. What am I doing? I put a hand to my forehead, the migraine shooting me a sharp pain to register its protest.

“You need to feel better before you kiss me like that,” he says, his eyes glued to my face. “When you are feeling better we can continue that, but for now you need rest.” I nod my agreement and follow him through the high-ceilinged, oak-floored apartment, upstairs to his bedroom.

There's a real masculine presence to his home, making it feel lived in, like this space represents him. Downstairs a huge TV hangs on the wall, with an Xbox and shelf of games residing below. A glass cabinet hosting CDs and DVDs had caught my attention as I left the room and if it hadn’t been for the pounding in my head I would have loved to have a browse, intrigued to discover his tastes. Paintings of city landscapes brighten up the walls and I am drawn to a city skyline painting on the wall near his bed as I enter his large bedroom.

“That's amazing,” I say, walking towards the painting of New York at night. “It feels like I'm there, looking out of a window. You like art?”

Ethan closes the black curtains and switches on a light. “I like paintings that remind me of places and people I know. You look wiped out,” he drops a tender kiss on my temple before he starts to unbutton my blouse. Two minutes later Ethan carries my naked body to his bed and lays me down on crisp white sheets, pulling a summer duvet up around my shoulders.

“Can I have the light off?” I ask, turning onto my side to face him.

“Sure,” he obliges. “I'm going to go and get you a drink. Do you want something to eat?”

I shake my head, relaxing into the pillows. He returns moments later with ice cold water which he insists I drink. I follow his instruction, the water sliding welcome down my throat, its chilliness making me shudder inwardly. I hand him back the glass and stretch out a hand to him, not wanting him to go.

“I've never stormed out of a meeting before,” I say, a mixture of apology and pride to my tone.

Ethan removes his shoes and lies down on his side on top of the duvet facing me. “And I've never gone after a woman in a rage before.” His voice is husky, a quaver of vulnerability reverberating low in his voice that makes something deep inside me ache. “And I have no intention of repeating it,” the familiar control returns. “What was wrong with you anyway?”

“I felt like I didn't need to be there,” I reply hesitantly. “Like it was a catch-up between two friends. I felt like a third wheel. And also,” the toilet conversation flashes in front of me, re-igniting a surge of anger, “I felt like you were both looking down on me.”

“Paranoia,” he responds dismissively.

“Really?” I challenge. “Because if I remember rightly, you suggested that Bianca could help me with my career, like I should be grateful or something. You may thrive working in London, but it's not for me and it's not what I want.”

“OK,” he leans forward and kisses the tip of my nose in a conciliatory gesture. “I'll back off.”

“Not completely?” I edge closer, needing his physical contact.

Ethan drapes an arm across me and pulls me against him. “No, not completely,” he confirms.

I snuggle into his chest. “I'm glad you came after me.”

A hint of a smile twists at the corner of his mouth as slowly he brings his lips to mine and kisses me. His lips are gentle, his tongue slow and measured as he entices me to respond. He sucks my lower lip into his mouth and lightly bites down, a shot of desire spiralling down my body.

“Hold that thought,” he says, his voice a sexy low purr. "Now turn onto your other side, I want to try something."

I stare at him wide-eyed for a moment and then roll over. He pulls me against him, and then he places his hands on my temple, his fingers applying gentle pressure in a circular motion.

“Close your eyes,” he whispers as he continues to massage, his thumbs trailing from the bridge of my nose up my forehead. It feels comforting and my body relaxes, tension oozing away. The pain is still there, but it feels like it is shifting slightly, as if the poker-sharp agony is dulling, becoming less immediate.

“That's good,” I sigh. “Where did you learn that?”

“My sister used to get really bad headaches. Massage helped her, so I learnt. You don't need to do it for long, but it can help to loosen the tension.”

He continues for a while longer in silence, whilst I begin to drift. When he has finished and I have drunk some more water as instructed he spoons me from behind, his hand slowly stroking from my shoulder down my arm and back up again.

“Can you stay the night?” he asks.

“I guess,” I reply.

"Good," he kisses my cheek tenderly. "Are you doing anything Sunday?"

"No," I yawn.

"Come to Zach's birthday party with me. We're having it at the hotel. I want you there."

"OK." I roll over, nuzzling into his chest, taking refuge in his strong muscular arms. Emotionally zapped, I melt against him, inhaling his scent, relishing the touch of his fingers sliding through my long hair. Sleep is beckoning me but I try to fight it, not wanting this moment to end.

Today had not been what I hoped; it had been a wash-out, a disaster. I hadn't fallen off the train into his arms, I hadn't wowed him in front of Bianca, nothing had gone as I had planned or imagined it would, but yet here we are together in our own little bubble and it feels incredible, as if it were meant to be.

My eyelids begin to feel heavy, fatigue weighing them down, and finally I succumb to a deep sleep.

Chapter Thirteen

I wake suddenly, unsure of where I am until the memories begin to return hazily. I sit up and look around the dimly lit room, a light coming from the bedside lamp. I run a hand across my forehead, relieved that the pain has gone. I feel a conflicted mixture of well-rested and emotionally drained. Glancing down at my watch, I'm surprised to see it's ten to seven in the evening. He must have just let me sleep, and then I wonder where he is, what he's doing. I get out of bed and look for my clothes, but they are nowhere to be seen. Not wanting to leave the room naked I open a drawer, pull out a black t-shirt and put it on.

I use the ensuite. My mouth feels dry, the taste of red wine lingering on my tongue and teeth. I search the bathroom cabinet for a spare toothbrush but not finding one, I settle for his. I splash water over my face, removing my makeup with a flannel. I pick up a comb and detangle my long hair as best I can. I look pale in the mirror, swamped in his baggy t-shirt. I shrug, knowing there's nothing I can do to improve my appearance.

Self-consciously I go downstairs in search of him. The place is quiet, the lounge and kitchen empty. I return to the hall and stand nervously outside a closed door.

"Ethan," I tap and push the door ajar, peeking through.

He looks up at me from behind a huge desk, littered in paper and folders. His eyes travel down my body, a grin inching deliciously across his lips as they crawl upwards once more, settling on my face. "You're awake," he says, dropping the pen he had been holding onto the desk with a thud and leaning back in his black leather chair. "How are you feeling?"

"Much better, thank you. I couldn't find my clothes."

"They're in the laundry," he replies. "That t-shirt looks better on you than it does on me." My heart skips a beat. "Come here."

I'm unable to move, my breath caught, my hand clinging to the door handle. The atmosphere is charged, I sense his longing from the other side of the room and shyness overpowers me. All I'm wearing is his t-shirt, no underwear, and I feel exposed. I stare at him and his eyes soften, beckoning me to come closer.

He looks gorgeous sat behind his desk, an aura of high-powered professionalism emanating from him. He looks comfortable, as if he belongs there, completely in control. He's changed into a grey t-shirt and jeans, a casual look that clashes with the professional demeanour of the room, but somehow it just makes him appear even hotter. I swallow and relinquish my hold on the door and begin to walk towards him, stopping just short of his desk.

"Closer." He indicates for me to walk to his side. I edge around the corner and Ethan moves on his chair, his hands reaching for me, clamping tightly on my hips as he draws me near.

"Hi," he says, looking up at me.

"Hi," I reply.

"You moved away from me earlier at the restaurant," he says quietly, accusingly. "Why did you do that?"

"What?" I struggle to concentrate as his eyes begin to travel lower again, certain he can see the hardness of my nipples prodding through the thin material. It's too much, he's too much, and I try to step away, but his fingers sink into my skin as he holds me in place. I force myself to meet his gaze. "Because I didn't want you to distract me," I say.

He nods, apparently satisfied with this answer, and suddenly pulls me onto his lap. I lean against him, inhaling his scent mixed with the smell of freshly laundered clothes.

"It didn't matter anyway," I continue, "I still managed to mess it up."

"Did you?" He cups my chin in his hand and tilts my head backwards so our eyes meet. His thumb begins to stroke back and forth on my jaw, whilst he stares questioningly at me. "What makes you think that?"

I shrug. "I left. I wasn't even professional enough to finish lunch. I wanted..." I trail off.

"What did you want?" he asks.

I shake my head. "It doesn't matter."

"It matters," he replies determinedly. "Tell me, Rosie, what did you want?"

"I wanted to impress you," I answer.

"And what makes you think you haven't?"

My eyes widen as he fixes me with a smouldering look, his hands now trailing up either side of my neck to my cheeks and then he shifts, sitting upright, and his lips find mine. His kiss is gentle, lingering, his tongue tangling with mine. "You have no idea," he whispers against my lips. "You're adorable," he begins to kiss my earlobe and then starts kissing down my neck. "You were everything I needed you to be today. You were hot, you said what you thought needed to be said and you didn't take any crap."

His words, the feel of his breath tickling the side of my neck, send tingles through my body. His desire for me is clear, his erection hardening beneath me. As a hand slides under the hem of the t-shirt, his fingers beginning to stroke up my thigh, an urgent feeling of needing to slow things down overwhelms me. I want him, I'm pleased that he obviously wants me too, but I don't want to be screwed over his desk, which is where this is undoubtedly leading. I know that if I don't push 'pause' and instead give way to the physical yearning that is permeating my entire being, I'll end up feeling cheap.

"Ethan." I pull on his wrist, removing his wandering hand.

"What's wrong?" He looks pissed off. "Don't you want this?"

"No," I slide off his lap. "Not like this."

"Like what?" he asks in exasperation.

"Like a cheap fuck over your desk," I blurt out, leaping to my feet and marching out.

"Rosie," his tone is firm as he pursues me. "Don't be stupid."

But I'm unable to stop and my pace quickens as I head into the lounge. But there's nowhere for me to run to and Ethan corners me in the kitchen, grabbing my arm and sharply turning me to face him, backing me up against the fridge. Adrenalin pulses through my body as my hands shoot up and I push hard against his chest. He captures my wrists easily in one of his hands, glaring down at me.

"You're wearing my t-shirt!" he says as if that explains everything, as if that means I'm a sure thing just waiting for him to take me.

"You've taken my clothes," I say, a strand of fear beginning to unwind its way through my veins.

I think he sees the fear on my face and his expression softens, his grip on my wrists lessening, but not releasing. He leans down, his forehead resting against mine, and closes his eyes for a moment, trying to compose himself.

"Oh, Rosie," he breathes, opening his eyes and staring down at me. He lets go of my wrists and walks away, leaving me alone.

I slide down the fridge and sit on the floor, pulling my knees up to my chest and hugging myself tightly. I let out a slow breath, aware that I'm shaking. What the hell just happened? I had just needed things to slow down, that's all, but he'd acted like I'd just offended him. I'd been afraid of him, not because I thought he was going to hurt me, because actually I don't think it had been that, but when he had chased me across his apartment and caught me I had felt trapped by him. I want my own clothes, want to know that I can leave whenever I want, but I'm stuck here in his t-shirt! Why had he taken my clothes? Why would he do that? Does he want me to feel trapped? I can feel my throat tighten, a lump building painfully. I rest my head on my arms and squeeze my eyes shut in an attempt to stop the burning behind my eyelids.

I hear him return a couple of minutes later, sense him sitting down on the floor next to me.

"I left you a note." He begins to rub my shoulder. "I should have realised you didn't see it when you mentioned not having your clothes, but I was so distracted by how gorgeous you looked standing there in the doorway to my office. I thought you wanted to have your wicked way with me." He slides his hand down my arm to my hand and gently squeezes. "I'm sorry, Rosie, I misread the situation. Please come and read the note?"

I let him pull me to my feet and guide me back upstairs to his bedroom. I bite down on my lower lip, unable to speak, scared that the lump in my throat will burst, that the unshed tears will begin to fall.

He points to a scrap of paper on the pillow. I pick it up and sit down and read:

"You look beautiful when you sleep! I stupidly scooped up your clothes with mine and sent them to the laundry. I'm off out to buy us some food, so I'll pick you up something to wear whilst I'm out. Call me when you wake. X p.s. Your new clothes are in the bag in front of the wardrobe. Looking forward to seeing you model them. If you ever wake up that is."

"Do you want to see what I got?" he asks, picking up a shopping bag.

I manage to nod and he pulls out a coral cotton summer dress, near enough the same colour I wore at the party. It's plain, short-sleeved, a respectable V-neck that doesn't look too low. It looks like something I myself would have chosen. It's understated, but pretty at the same time. I bring my hand to my mouth, the lump detonating in my throat.

"I'm so sorry," I whisper shakily. "I'm such an idiot." A tear escapes, streaking down my cheek, followed by another and then another. I blink, desperate to stop myself from falling to pieces, the humiliation bad enough already, but I can't stop the tears from spilling over.

"Please don't cry," Ethan drops the dress on the bed and swiftly moves to me, sitting down beside me and gathering me into his arms. "Baby, don't cry," his voice is pained as he kisses the top of my head and slowly begins to stroke a hand up and down my back in reassuring little circles, his hold tight, protective even, as he consoles me. I turn into him and rest my head on his shoulder, no longer trying to fight the tears.

Turning up late, being jealous of Bianca, storming out of the restaurant, fainting, the migraine, missing his note and then making a complete fool of myself in his t-shirt... It's been a horrible, horrible day and I'm incapable of pulling myself together. And he's being sweet, kind, which seems to make me cry even more.

"You're not an idiot," he murmurs into my ear. "Look at me," he moves me from his shoulder and holds my face in his hands, his fingertips brushing away the tears. "I looked at the CVs from Bianca whilst you were sleeping. You were right, completely unsuitable. Do you often use social media to check prospective employees out?"

"Sometimes." I wipe my eyes with my hands, control returning.

A knowing smile creeps across his lips, a sparkle glinting in his eyes as he asks, "Have you looked for me?"

I blush. "Possibly."

"What were you looking for?"

"Background information."

"Like what? Give me an example."

"Erm," I straighten up. "Your age."

"Well as I imagine you worked out, I'm not on Facebook, Twitter, LinkedIn. Any questions you have about me you're going to have to ask. Now," he takes my hands in his, his expression serious, "are we going to talk about what just happened in my office?"

I shake my head. "Do we need to?"

"I think we should." He begins to run a thumb across my knuckles. "There's nothing cheap about fucking you, OK? I don't think of you like that, I don't want you to think I do. The simple fact is that I'm sexually attracted to you, very sexually attracted to you, and if you're honest I think you feel the same too. But," he focuses me with an intense stare, "I know this isn't easy for you, so if you felt like I was rushing things back then, rushing you, then I'm sorry. I would never do something you weren't OK with. Just don't think too much about this."

He leans down and kisses me gently and then gets up and strolls into the ensuite bathroom. I hear him start running the water and a few seconds later he sits back down and pulls me into his arms.

"I'm running you a bath. I've got a little bit of work I need to finish, so you can relax. Then I'll cook for us. You need to eat, you hardly touched your lunch. I don't want you passing out on me again."

"Thank you." I nuzzle against him.

"You will of course have to repay me with your body," he says, a mischievous glint in his eyes.

"Oh, really?" I challenge.

"Really," he replies huskily, sending a shiver down my spine.

I playfully push him away. He smiles before he moves quickly and pins me down on the bed. I squeal in surprise and laugh up at him as he brushes the hair away from my face, making it fan messily over the white pillows.

"Never change," he whispers and leans down to kiss me tenderly on the mouth.

He goes back into the bathroom to check on the bath, leaving me swooning after him. He warned me to not overthink, but I can't help it, can't stop the thoughts and questions from whirling frantically around my mind. This man, this gorgeous man has triggered something inside me, something so overpowering I feel like I have no control. I know that Tristan has fucked me up, left me with vulnerabilities and insecurities that I didn't have before, but I'm horribly conscious that Ethan has the ability to screw me up infinitely more. I'd known it on Saturday, bizarrely I think I'd known it the moment I clapped eyes on him over Will's shoulder. Ruin me or repair me, I don't know which he'll do, but I do know I can't stop this.

"Bath's ready," he says.

"Thank you," I reply, standing up.

"What do you want for dinner?"

I shrug. "Something simple. I'd be happy with toast, to be honest."

"Toast?" he scoffs.

"Just something plain. I still feel a bit..."

"OK, I can do that."

"I can always cook," I suggest. "Or we could cook together?"

"Enjoy the bath," he kisses my cheek and then moves and murmurs in my ear secretively. "I'm 39, 40 in December. Any questions you have about me you're going to have to ask. And ask me, Rosie, not Drew, not anyone else, just me."

He kisses me quickly on the lips. It's a hard kiss, a fleeting but controlling touch of the lips to back up what he has just said. And then he walks out of the bedroom and closes the door behind him.

Chapter Fourteen

Having luxuriated in a decadent-smelling bubble bath, I return to the bedroom to dress. I find underwear in the shopping bag, a cute white lacy set. They're demure, not slutty, and they fit perfectly. I try on the dress and stare at my reflection in the full-sized mirror. He has chosen well. I dig in the bag in search of the receipt, suspecting a high price tag, but find nothing. He'd also taken the labels off, so I guess that's a conversation to broach with him.

I find him in the kitchen, setting two places at the breakfast bar. He stops when he sees me and just stares for a moment.

"It fits, then," he says proudly, stalking towards me.

I nod. "Thank you. You have very good taste. How much do I owe you?"

He shrugs. "You don't."

"I don't want you buying me clothes," I say.

"The only reason you needed something to wear was because I'm a dumbass and chucked your stuff in the wash. Therefore, it's just a gift to say sorry for not thinking." He puts a finger to my lips to hush my objection. "I'm not trying to buy you or anything seedy. I don't want to argue with you about this. And if you feel that strongly about it you can leave it here tomorrow, like you're just borrowing it for the night, although I would prefer it if you didn't do that. Don't overthink this," he warns, and leans into kiss me. "Come and help me cook."

"You're letting me help?" I ask in surprised excitement.

"Yeah," he flashes me a quick smile.

"What are we cooking?" I ask.

Ethan goes to the fridge and takes a carton of juice from the door. "You need to drink." He pours some orange juice and hands me a glass. "Could you manage an omelette?"

"Sounds perfect."

"Well, get grating then," he says, pushing a block of cheese towards me on the counter.

I get started, watching him chop onions and mushrooms efficiently, the blade on the knife flickering through the vegetables at an alarming, yet controlled, speed. We don't talk, the Goo Goo Dolls play quietly in the background and we share the occasional smile.

"Did you get your work done?" I ask as he takes the grated cheese from me.

He nods and indicates me to sit at the breakfast bar on one of the high stools. “I had to check over a contract for Josh. He arrives tomorrow evening. I wanted all the loose ends tidied up so I can hand over to him.”

“And what are we going to do about recruitment?”

Coming up behind me, he wraps his arms around me and kisses the top of my head. “Let's deal with work on Monday, shall we?” Then he moves away and focuses his attention on cooking.

I sit on the high stool, my legs swinging as I watch him. This is what I imagined today would be like, us together, just being... A feeling of belonging here, with him, envelops me like it's the most normal thing in the world. I finish my drink, slide off the stool and go to wash the glass.

“How long have you lived here?” I ask, staring out of the window, spotting a London red bus pulling away from a nearby stop.

“Nearly five years.”

“It's very bachelor,” I observe.

“That's me.”

“But you've had girlfriends, right?” I ask.

“Not meaningful relationships, no,” he replies, his tone casual. “Not in England, anyway.”

“Why?” I ask, finding it apparently easy to ask him personal questions if I don't look at him, don't see his face, don't have to stare into those mesmerising clear blue eyes.

“I haven't met anyone that I wanted more from,” he replies. “The flings I’ve had have been just that, flings.”

“Did you have a fling with Bianca?” I ask hesitantly.

“Not exactly.” There's a subtle but unmistakable edge to his voice.

“What does that mean?” I find myself asking, ignoring the warning sign to change the subject.

“It means we're not having this conversation,” he replies harshly.

“Did you want to...?” I know I should back down but I can't stop myself, I need to know.

“No.” his response is fierce.

“Did she?”

“For fuck's sake,” he bangs down a plate on the work surface, making me jump. Spinning me around, he glowers down at me. “I said we're not having this conversation.”

"Is it so wrong that I want to know something about you, Ethan?" I hold his gaze.

He runs his fingers through his short blond hair in exasperation. "Let's just eat."

He walks away, back to the cooker. I return to the breakfast bar as my phone begins to ring. It's my nan. I answer, relieved for the distraction. I confirm that I will visit tomorrow afternoon and then hang up.

The atmosphere is tense, neither of us speaking. He is radiating some kind of anger, and I'm pretty sure I'm giving off a pissed off vibe as well. I don't know if it's some bizarre jealousy or mistrust on my part, but "not exactly" as a response seems to have been a catalyst for rationality, sanity, to leave my brain. Not exactly implies something... I put my elbow on the breakfast bar and lean my chin on my hand and glare into space.

"You know moody doesn't suit you?" Ethan says from the cooker as he removes the Le Creuset pan from the heat. I look away, wanting to preserve my irritation, not wanting the glimmer of a smile he just gave me to affect me. I need to stay annoyed with him, because I know it's the only way I'll ever find out what "not exactly" meant.

"Do you want a drink?" he asks stiffly, opening a bottle of beer and taking a long drink. "Gin, vodka, wine, beer?" I gesture towards the bottle of Tanqueray and he pours me a strong gin and tonic. He places it in front of me and holds me from behind, resting his chin on my shoulder.

"I came after you," he says quietly into my ear. "I chose you."

"You sound like I should be grateful."

"Maybe you should," Ethan sighs and walks away to plate up our food.

We eat in silence. The omelette is great, all fluffy, with just the right amount of strong cheddar, crispy bacon, onion and mushroom. Omelette is one of my favourite foods, it reminds me of my mum...

"I need to leave pretty early tomorrow." I crack first. "I need to go to Felixstowe and visit my nan."

"OK."

"I'll probably get the train there, so I can just leave from London."

"I'll drive you, I said I would. And it's not much further."

Ethan fixes me with an intense look. I'd been aware of him discreetly watching me as I ate, but now he's making no effort to disguise his interest, and unless I am mistaken it is desire flickering intensely in his eyes. It's distracting and threatens to undermine my annoyance. The corner of his mouth twists into a delicious smile as he leans forward and takes my hand.

"You're pretty cute when you're pissed," he says. "Your nose does this whole crinkle thing."

Bingo, his words refuel my irritation. I don't want him to find me cute, I want him to take me seriously, I want him to say something real, to tell me something honest, true, just like I have him. I snatch my hand away and glare at him as I get down from the table and go to put my empty plate in the dishwasher.

"Cute, but quite easily could become boring," he says, coming up behind me to put his plate and cutlery in. "Don't become boring," he whispers into my ear, an arm snaking its way around my waist as he pulls me backwards and closes the dishwasher. He kisses the side of my neck, his lips pressing against the hollow near my collar bone. "You need to cool down," he says, a hint of excitement to his voice. "Come on, I want to show you something."

He pulls me back into the hall and opens the door opposite his study, which leads into a dark, narrow passageway. He turns on a light and quickens his pace, turning a corner and opening a door to a self-contained gym, weights to the left, a treadmill and rowing machine to the right. And then I see it through the window straight ahead: a swimming pool.

"Is this yours?" I breathe as he opens the adjoining door from the gym to the pool and flicks a switch, spotlights reflecting down onto the crystal blue water.

"All mine," he says, squeezing my hand as we walk to the poolside.

"Wow! It's amazing!" The dim lights shining on the water, along with the view of London at night from the glass walls around three sides of the pool, manage to create some kind of magic that captivates me completely. It's beautiful, stunning, and there's only the two of us here to enjoy it together.

"Are you coming in?" Ethan asks, hauling his t-shirt over his head and throwing it on a nearby chair.

"I haven't got anything to wear," I blush.

"Neither do I." He leans down and kisses me, his fingers trailing slowly down my cheek.

"Is this what you usually do with your flings?" I ask, staring up at him.

He inhales, frustration flickering across his face.

"I'm sorry." I step back, appalled. What am I doing? I'm jealous, clingy, desperate for his reassurance. This isn't me and I hate feeling so out of my depth, so lost.

"No," he replies softly and steps closer, taking my hands and drawing me to him. "You want honesty, right?" I swallow and nod, a shiver travelling up my spine. "Most of the women I've fucked haven't come back to my apartment. A couple have, but no, I haven't brought them in here. I thought you might like it, that it would be fun to just mess around, that's all. And whilst I'm being honest and upfront, nothing major happened with Bianca. We got drunk at a recent party and she made a pass at me. I told you I don't usually screw people I work with. Apart from you, you're the exception to that rule. Bianca was embarrassed, it's been a bit awkward, which is why I like to keep business and personal separate," he runs a thumb across my bottom lip, pulling gently at the corner that I have been distractedly chewing. The tip of my tongue touches his skin. His eyes meet mine with a look of unrestrained intensity.

I reach up and caress the side of his arm. "I don't want to feel like this."

"Then don't," he says huskily as his hand moves away from my mouth and cups my chin.

We stare at each other in silence for a long time. Desire emanates from him, a muscle twitches in his jaw as he restrains himself. Goosebumps prickle on my skin as I feel a low ache begin to intensify, burning away the anger and self-doubt so that there is only desire for him flickering through me.

"You were right," I say, "I think I do need to cool down."

His restraint dissolves as he spins me around, pushing my back hard against the now-closed door, his lips finding mine. His kiss is forceful and just what I need to forget everything apart from him. My fingernails scrape across his shoulder muscles as I cling to him, needing the warmth of his body hard against mine. I kiss him back, our tongues swirling and tangling together, our lips desperate for each other's. My hands make their way lower down his back, my fingers massaging his rigid muscles, and then I'm clumsily fiddling with his belt and unfastening his jeans. Everything up until now has been about me, he has been amazingly attentive, playing my body like a well-versed musician, and now I want him to unravel at my touch, just the way I do for him. I push his jeans and boxers down his legs, freeing his erection.

"Wait," I breathe as his hand moves to the side zip on my dress. I run my tongue along my lower lip, my eyes lowering to his cock and then returning to his face, my intention obvious. A lazy smile touches his lips as he steps out of his clothes, completely naked before me. I kiss him briefly on the mouth and then start kissing my way down his body, my tongue flicking across his skin as my lips press against his jaw, the side of his neck, down his muscular chest, across a nipple and down to his stomach, his abs rippling under my touch.

My hands slide their way up muscular thighs, kneading the tight muscles, before I cup his balls in one hand, a finger trailing across his skin. His cock twitches at the contact. I inhale his skin: he smells clean, a masculine aroma of shower gel, which arouses me further. I lower myself to my knees, my other hand skimming over his cock as I blink up at him through my long lashes. My tongue sneaks shyly out, slowly and lightly licking his tip, my eyes trained on his. I trail my tongue down his length, taking time to kiss his balls.

His eyes begin to glaze over as I slowly lick upwards, and in this moment I know I have him. I take him into my mouth slowly, inch by inch, his hardness reaching the back of my throat. A low groan escapes him as I apply suction, my mouth exploring his hard shaft. Slowly I begin to set a rhythm, my tongue teasing him as I begin to quicken the tempo. He responds, his pelvis crashing against me. His balls lift upwards in my hand, my other hand reaches up to his stomach, needing something solid to cling to. It's hard and it's fast now and I can feel him reaching the edge, willing him to crash over down my throat. But just as I think he is about to he grabs my hand, squeezing it painfully tight, and fists his other hand in my hair, yanking my head back. I open my mouth in surprised pain and he withdraws.

He pulls me to my feet and claims my mouth with his tongue, reasserting control. I feel lightheaded, unsure why he had stopped and disappointed that I hadn't taken him over the edge.

"You're a siren," he murmurs against my lips, his kiss becoming gentle, his eyes blazing.

I lean against him, my heart pounding, my body high on the sensation of his kiss, his touch, as his fingers pull down my zip and slide into my dress to my breast. My nipple hardens under his touch. I let him undress me as if in a trance, his hands warm, powerful on my skin as he slowly removes my clothes, his lips seducing me further with skilled kisses. I squeal as he suddenly scoops me off the ground, an arm firmly around my shoulders, the other holding me behind my knees.

"Hold onto me," he instructs, stepping forward.

My eyes widen, but I comply, clinging to him as he carries me to the poolside.

"Don't throw me in," I say, my hold on him tightening.

"I won't," he smiles down at me. "I promise."

The word had sounded casual enough, but as our eyes meet I instinctively know he is testing me to see if I believe him. I freeze in his arms, aware he is playing me, and even more conscious that somehow he is unwittingly winning because I do believe him. I loosen my hold and rest my cheek on his shoulder, nuzzling into his neck. I feel weightless in his arms, floating away in an intoxicating haze as he lowers his lips and kisses the hollow of my neck, shooting tingles of desire low down in my body. I close my eyes, giving way to sensation.

The water hits me hard, splashing me in the face, my arms shooting out as I squirm out of his hold and right myself in the cool water. He had kept his promise, he hadn't thrown me in – instead, he jumped in with me in his arms, submerging us both. I swim a few strokes until I can touch the floor and stand.

"I kept my promise," Ethan says, holding me from behind, resting his chin on my shoulder.

"You did," I agree and smile up at him, turning and wrapping my arms around his waist. "Thank you for coming after me today."

"You're welcome."

"It's amazing." I indicate the Knightsbridge backdrop, the lights of cars twinkling through the one-way glass as they slowly make their way through traffic.

"Yeah," he nods, "it's pretty awesome. I'm kinda attached to the place."

We sink into the water so that our shoulders are under the surface. I feel overwhelmed in this amazing setting, skinny-dipping in a private pool at night, the spotlights hitting the water and romanticising the setting. And then there's Ethan, the man who has turned my world upside down in a matter of days. The man I want more than I think I have ever wanted anything or anyone in my entire life. He reaches for my hands and our fingers entwine.

"Are we OK?" he asks, his voice jolting me back to the here and now.

I nod and shoot him a playful smile as I pull my hands away and swim to his left, calling over my shoulder as I begin a fast front crawl, "Race you, there and back." I turn ahead of him, getting a solid clearance off the wall as I head at full throttle for the shallow end. I can feel the stitch growing in my side, but I kick, strong hard kicks as my arms propel me forward with controlled precise strokes. For a split-second I believe I can beat him, but just as I am about to touch the wall he beats me to it with a firm slap. I'm heaving and in considerable pain, whilst Ethan doesn't even seem to have lost his breath, a triumphant smile spreading across his face.

"Rosie?" His smile fades as I double over, clutching my right side.

"Stitch," I gasp, scrunching my eyes closed as the pain spikes.

"That's what happens when you race straight after food," he says.

"This was your idea," I accuse through gritted teeth.

"The pool was my idea, sure," he murmurs into my ear. "Not the racing, that was all you." He puts an arm around my waist and pulls me close. "Breathe through it," he instructs, his hand stroking my shoulder in reassuring circles. "You haven't had a great day, have you?"

"I don't know," I reply, straightening and shooting him a shy smile. "It's not all been bad."

"Is that so?" he asks.

I blush and try to step away, but he clasps me tighter and slowly leans down to kiss me lingeringly. It's a sensual kiss, seductive, leisurely and demanding all at the same time. I begin to feel dazed, my arms somehow finding their way around his neck as I lean up against him, our wet bodies colliding, skin on skin. It's hot, it's erotic... And the stitch is no more.

His hands travel up my back and slowly around to my chest as he cups my breasts in his large powerful palms. His thumbs graze across my nipples, which harden like pebbles under his touch. Arousal throbs between my legs, his cock jabbing hard into my stomach as desire consumes us both.

"I haven't been able to stop thinking about you," he says huskily, lowering himself in the water as he sucks my right nipple roughly into his mouth.

"Me too," I breathe as his hand slides between my legs, he finds my clitoris and slides a finger slowly inside, his tongue flicking over my nipple. I rest my hands on his shoulders, my body going into sensory overload. He wraps his free arm around my waist as he kisses his way to my left breast, slipping a second finger inside as he circles my clit. He brings me to the edge quickly, his fingers skilfully fucking me, hitting a sensitive spot inside that makes me moan his name in pleasure. My muscles tighten, his touch becoming somehow too much as his lips begin to kiss their way sensuously up my chest to my throat. His fingers move quicker now, harder, his thumb teasing my clitoris as he draws me closer to the brink. No one has ever made me feel like this, so close to sheer abandon. His eyes meet mine confidently, he knows he is undoing me from the inside out and it seems to please him.

"You're beautiful," he whispers, slowing the pace as his lips find mine.

I know he's playing me, holding me on the edge because he can, and there's a bit of me that wants to wriggle away and for him to stop, but as he rubs once more and plunges into me hard, I know that I need this from him.

"Ethan," his name escapes my lips again as my body responds. The orgasm washes over me, making my legs feel like jelly. His touch becomes gentle, sensual strokes making the pleasure ripple on. We drift deeper into the water, Ethan holding me tightly against his chest. The intimacy makes my body feel like it's merging into his, like I'm being consumed by him.

"I want you," he says in a low voice.

"I want you too," I whisper shakily, my heart hammering as he tilts my head back, so I meet his unwavering gaze.

"Wrap your legs around my waist," he orders. I comply, immediately aware of his cock, jutting hard against me. My eyes widen as he looks at me expectantly.

"Are you sure?" Ethan asks, holding me against his body, his cock twitching against my skin.

"Yes," I reply, adapting my position slightly, pressing down invitingly on his tip.

We continue to stare at each other. The sensible voice in my head is clamouring about a condom, but the much louder voice of lust is shouting to just go for it. I've got the implant, so no risk of unwanted pregnancy. Ethan kisses me suddenly, his tongue dipping into my mouth as his lips press against mine possessively and the merits of protection are forgotten. He enters me, easing his full length slowly into me, stretching me inch by inch. I don't know if it's the position, the fact that we are submerged in the pool or that he isn't wearing a condom, but he feels bigger somehow, his shaft warm and strong inside me. It's intense as he stills, now fully inside, filling me in a way that verges on pain, but not quite. As I lose myself to his kiss, his tongue exploring my mouth expertly, his lips firm and demanding on mine, I feel myself relax around him and welcome the feeling of fullness.

His hands settle on my hips and he begins to move me, slowly at first, then faster as he begins to drive into me hard, hitting the sensitive spot he touched earlier. It's hard, fast and I gyrate against him, lost in the moment. The water splashes in ripples around us, the lights dancing on the surface. "Ethan," I gasp, pulling away from his kiss in an attempt to catch my breath.

He stills and holds me close as he nuzzles against my neck. "We need to take this out of the pool," he whispers, slowly pulling out of me and resting my feet on the ground.

I nod, unable to speak, and let him guide me to the edge and help me out. He holds my hand and leads me towards a lounger. He bends down to recline it and then motions for me to lie on my back. He hovers above me, his eyes burning molten pools of lust, and then thrusts powerfully into me, filling me. I hook my legs around his waist, drawing him deeper. "I want everything you've got," I whisper.

He kisses the side of my neck, his teeth grazing over my skin. His hand slides between our bodies as he begins to move, his thumb circling. I cry out into his shoulder, my nails digging into his skin as I feel my climax building. He withdraws and glides his erection over my throbbing bundle of nerves. He pushes into me forcefully, making me gasp. He bends over me, his breath tickling my skin as over and over again he drives hard into me. I moan as he pinches my clitoris and then softly rubs across the top. I'm vaguely aware that I scream out as my muscles clench against him and then I detonate violently around him.

"Fuck," he rasps as he slides into me for the final time, he comes deep inside and then he collapses onto me.

I close my eyes, my heart pounding in my ears, his weight pinning me down onto the lounger, and try to regain a sense of equilibrium. But it's no use: emotionally and physically, I'm overwhelmed.

"You OK?" he asks, kissing my shoulder softly.

"Yeah," I manage quietly.

He slides slowly out of me, sits and then gathers me up into his arms and holds me, a steadying hand stroking my back. I'm trembling against him, endorphins whizzing wildly through my veins.

Finally, he breaks the silence and suggests we shower together.

"You look shattered," he observes as he scoops me up into his arms.

"Put me down," I protest, but he ignores me and carries me back through his apartment and upstairs to his ensuite.

We shower together, unable to keep our hands off each other, washing each other in a refreshing citrus-smelling body wash. He shampoos my hair, his fingers massaging my scalp like he's a pro. I'm in a daze when he turns off the water and wraps me in a fluffy white bath towel.

Back in the bedroom we sit on the edge of the bed and he towel-dries my hair.

“I could get used to this,” I sigh contentedly.

“You do that,” he murmurs against my ear.

I twist to face him, my towel slipping from my breasts as I move. We stare at each other for a moment before our lips meet and we lose ourselves to each other again.

Chapter Fifteen

I stare at myself in the mirror, straightening the strap of the emerald-green cocktail dress that I purchased a couple of hours ago for tonight's party. It's a long, clinging dress that emphasises my curves and narrow waistline. The plunging V-neck shows ample cleavage and I've accessorised with a silver pendant that nestles between my breasts.

"Oh, Rosie," my nan opens the door and stares at me, her eyes glistening with unshed tears. "I wish your parents could see you now. They'd be so proud."

I cross the room quickly and gather her to me, holding her slight frame tightly as we momentarily indulge ourselves in wistful memories.

"They'd approve of your handsome American chap as well."

Ethan and Nan had met each other yesterday when he had dropped me off. I hadn't counted on her being out in the garden when we pulled up, and before I knew it she was beside the car and insisting that my "friend" must come in for a cup of tea. Ethan had grinned at her and switched the engine off. For the next thirty minutes I had witnessed them charm each other, with the icing on the cake being when Milly, Nan's grouchy, man-hating Jack Russell, joined proceedings and somehow ended up on Ethan's lap, nuzzled in the crook of his arm, snoring. No man has ever won that dog over, until Ethan, the Dog Whisperer.

"He's not my chap," I say, sitting on the bed to fasten the straps on my nude sandals.

I'm looking forward to seeing Ethan again, but anxious about tonight's party. We haven't discussed it in any detail and I'm unclear as to what I am going as: his date? A work colleague...? I'd wanted to ask him last night when we had spoken on the phone, but when he had called he had his brother in the car with him and the conversation had been stilted.

I drive Nan to the train station, thanking her for coming shopping with me, and despatch her back to Felixstowe. Then I set the satnav and head for Tranquillity. I park and call Ethan, but it goes straight to voicemail. I try twice more and get no luck, so head towards reception, the nerves jumbling around in my stomach. The door shoots open and it is only my quick reaction of jumping to the left that saves me from getting smashed in the face. I glare at the culprit as he comes outside.

"Sorry," he says. I know that face, I've seen it on Google, and the distinct American accent is familiar, although the voice is a notch higher.

"Are you here for the party?" he asks. I nod. "Great. I'm Josh." He extends a hand.

"Rosie," I respond.

"Ethan's Rosie?" A flash of realisation crosses his face and he beams at me.

"Ethan's brother?" I clarify.

The family resemblance is unmistakable, although Josh is a softer version of his older brother. His blond hair is the same colour, but slightly longer; his eyes are the same startling blue, but warmer – they're pretty eyes, but not captivating. He's a couple of inches shorter and not quite as broad, but still fit, aesthetically and physically. He has a look of the boy next door, friendly, and his huge smile makes me feel at ease.

"Sorry," Josh digs in his pocket and pulls out his ringing mobile, listening a moment before he says, "Chill out Ethan, it's under control. I've just spoken with the caterers, it's fine. Come downstairs, I'm about to have a drink with Rosie," and he hangs up and turns to me. "He'll be with us in a moment." He winks at me and opens the door. "I need a drink, I know nobody at this party, it sounds hellish, some old guy's birthday."

"I know nobody either," I reply, my heels clattering on the marble floor as I try to keep up with him across the foyer. "Apart from Ethan."

And there he is, stepping out of the lift to intercept us. He glowers at Josh for a second before he sees me, his expression softening as he walks towards me and kisses me briefly on the mouth, sliding an arm possessively around my waist.

"Hey you," he murmurs into my ear.

"Hi," I reply, the butterflies surfacing giddily.

"We'll join you in a bit," Ethan tells Josh, and ushers me towards the lift doors.

"Nice meeting you," I look over my shoulder and shoot Josh a quick smile. Josh turns and walks back to the door, presumably heading for wherever he was going when he met me. Ah, I see him pull out a packet of cigarettes as he opens the door and walks outside.

"Are you OK?" I ask as the doors slide shut. He seems pissed off, a muscle twitching in his jaw. "Ethan?" He doesn't reply, just pulls me close and holds me, inhaling my hair. His body is taut, his muscles rigid, angry stress exuding from him.

"It's not you," he eventually speaks. "Just hotel stuff." His arm remains tightly around my waist as we walk down the corridor to the second lift. It's as if he doesn't want to let me go and it feels good, any physical contact with him suits me just fine. Outside his door he stops and turns me to face him, a finger caressing my cheek. "Zach's here," he says in a hushed voice. "So, before we go in I need to kiss you."

His lips claim mine, his tongue invading my mouth as if it belongs to him. It's possessive, like he's letting me know I'm his, completely his. I run my hand over his jaw, feeling the tension under my fingertips as he halts the kiss. I stroke up his cheek, his skin feeling moisturised and freshly shaved. I pull him closer, inhaling the masculine scent, which is different tonight, but equally as alluring. It's classically male, a hint of bergamot, a fresh tang of lemon and an undercurrent of ginger. They talk about people being able to look you into bed, but right now this man could seduce me with his aftershave alone. It's hypnotic.

"Nice dress," he says. "You look beautiful. Although," he kisses the shell of my ear, "I do prefer shorter."

"I'll try and remember that," I say lightly, and straighten the navy tie that matches his tailored navy suit. "I like this," I trail a finger across the thin grey stripes of the tie. "You wear a suit well." He looks surprised by the compliment and kisses me quickly once more before his arm returns to my waist and he opens the door.

Zach is sat on the sofa reading a newspaper when we enter and stands when he spots us over the top of the sports column. He smiles, a kind smile that reaches his brown eyes, and heads straight for me.

"My dear girl," he booms in an Etonian voice and kisses my cheek. "How jolly lovely to meet you."

"You too," I stammer and shoot Ethan a what-the-fuck glance.

"Dear boy, the Japs have just tried to call you on Zoom. I'm afraid I disconnected the call, you know me and technology. I suggest you call them back and iron over Josh's blunder. I'll entertain this young lady of yours whilst you do," he pulls me to the sofa. "Let's have some Pimm's, shall we?" And off he goes to pour me a drink.

"Sorry, sweetheart, I really need to deal with this. Would you mind?" Ethan takes my bag. "I won't be long, this can't wait."

"OK." I nod and sit down.

"Don't scare her off, Zach," Ethan calls as he heads towards the bedroom.

Zach returns with two glasses and for the next fifteen minutes entertains me, regaling me with anecdotes from his retirement. He fondly speaks of Ethan, about how they met at work and of their successful deals together. I listen attentively. Zach is an amazing orator and he has me enthralled.

"You know something?" He puts his empty glass down and leans conspiratorially towards me. "I've known Ethan for a good few years now and I don't think I've ever known him to turn up to a function with a lady before. Leaves with plenty, but never arrives with one."

"Really?" The enormity of what he is saying is not lost on me. "I like him," I find myself admitting.

"I can tell," Zach says kindly. "He can be difficult at times, bloody annoyingly so, but keep with him. He needs somebody like you in his life, someone sweet, grounded and totally smitten with him." He puts a hand up to hush my objection. "I saw it as soon as you walked in the room together, and when I talk about him your eyes have this far-off lovestruck look."

"That's ridiculous," I interrupt. "We hardly know each other."

"So? Something's there, a spark between you. Tell me I'm wrong."

"You think?"

He pats my knee. "Knowing Ethan as I do, he won't make it easy for you, but hang in there, old thing: he's worth it, even if he doesn't think so. Now, drink up."

"Happy birthday," I say, and take a drink of the very strong Pimm's.

I wonder how old Zach actually is. His hair is peppered grey, his movements awkward, caused by arthritic pain, I suspect. His eyes are warm, genuine, but below the surface tiredness lurks. When he talks he is full of life, animated and sparky, but physically there's an obvious frailty.

Zach excuses himself when Ethan returns and leaves us alone in the suite.

"Is everything OK?" I ask tentatively, following Ethan to the kitchen where he pours himself a whisky and knocks it back, banging the empty glass on the counter.

"Come here." He beckons me closer and nervously I cross the kitchen to stand in front of him, my eyes locked to his. He rests his hands lightly on my shoulders, his thumbs absentmindedly trailing over my collarbone. His jaw is set in a hard line, his eyes resonating a harshness I haven't seen before, and a vein pulses in his neck. I swallow and reach a hand up to slowly touch his cheek. Something happens when my fingertips touch his skin, I see it, I feel it even, it's as if the stress ebbs away.

"What's wrong?" I encourage, my lips gently pressing to his, my eyes glued to his face. His right hand strokes down my chest and he picks up my pendant, the side of his hand brushing my cleavage. He scrutinises the silver heart before gently returning it between my breasts.

"God, I want to bury myself in you," he says hoarsely, his voice laced with fire-filled lust that makes my knees go weak. I feel the redness scorching my cheeks as my eyes dart away from his. It feels good to be wanted, albeit his directness is a little crude, but ultimately he is under the spell of desire like I am and it feels good that I'm not alone. I wrap my arms around his neck and kiss him sweetly on the lips. "Later," I whisper as muscles low down clench at the prospect.

He stares directly at me, as if he is looking straight through a window into my consciousness. Whatever it is he sees, it calms him, the tension draining from his face, and the suggestion of a smile teeters on his lips. His arms encircle me as he pulls me even closer, his hold firm as he brushes the hair off my left shoulder and bends down to breathe in the perfume at the side of my neck. I relax into his hold.

"Are you going to tell me why you're so stressed?" I murmur into his chest.

For a moment he tenses, but to my surprise he answers. "Josh promised something for a Tokyo client and hasn't delivered within the agreed timescale. The guy wanted to pull out, he nearly did."

"But you sorted it?"

"I managed to negotiate a deal to keep him onside. In the long-term it won't be a big deal. Josh needs more help than he would care to admit, so I guess I need to step up."

"What does that mean?" I ask, terrified that he will bail from Mosen's to help his younger brother.

"Just be around for him a bit more, I guess."

"Will you go back to America?" I ask quietly.

"No," he replies reassuringly and presses a kiss to the top of my head. "He's here for a while and after that we'll just talk more online. Now, are you doing anything tomorrow?"

"No," it's the August bank holiday, "nothing set in stone."

"Let's spend it together."

"Yes," I smile up at him, "let's do that. Why don't you come to mine, I can cook, you can stay over if you want?"

"I want," he replies, a sexy undercurrent to his drawl. I twist in his embrace and wrap my arms around him, hiding my smile over his shoulder. Zach was right, I am a hundred percent smitten.

Chapter Sixteen

Ethan reaches for my hand as we exit the lift, offering a gentle reassuring squeeze. We walk past a group of suited men, Zach's contemporaries, I guess from their appearance and age. I recognise the man sat behind the reception desk as Aiden from last Saturday night and smile shyly at him as we pass. As we enter the bar my attention is drawn to the grand piano, a Mozart concerto being played beautifully, setting the sophisticated tone for the evening ahead. The bar area is all leather sofas and low oak tables, a couple of intimate alcoves are to the left and a gleaming bar takes up most of the right wall, curving to a door which I can see leads through to the dining room. Directly in front of us, glass doors are open and lead out onto covered decking and then down onto a lawned area. People have started to arrive, some already sitting comfortably at tables, a few milling outside and another group chatting at the bar.

Ethan tells me to go and find a table outside whilst he gets the drinks. I leave him and cross the bar, heading outside, but I stop, getting the oddest sensation someone is staring at me. I survey the room and my eyes meet warm hazel eyes from behind the piano. The music stops abruptly as the musician scrapes back the stool, stands and grins at me.

"In all the bars," he says, approaching.

"Wow!" I beam up at him in surprise. "Hello again." It's the man from Moorgate, albeit a considerably smarter version. His hair has been washed and scraped back into a ponytail, his scruffy clothes now replaced by a smart dinner suit.

"You look better than last time I saw you," he says, his eyes fixed to my face.

"Thank you for checking I was OK," I reply. "What are you doing here?"

"It's my uncle's party. He asked me to play for a bit."

Of course, the kind eyes are an obvious family resemblance, but different shades.

"What about you?"

"Charlie," Zach appears at my right shoulder. "You've met Rosie, I see. She's Ethan's date, you know the American I told you about, so no chatting her up, please. Now," he places a gentle hand on his nephew's shoulder, "there's a Bach piece I really would love you to play."

"Catch you later," Charlie winks over his shoulder as he is returned by Zach to the piano stool. I nod and make my way outside, off the decking and across the lawn. I crunch down a gravel path to the left, inhaling the sweet scent of the flowers. Roses, gardenias and lilies perfume the gentle breeze, their reds, pinks and whites splashing colour to the peaceful garden. I extend a hand and slowly skim my fingers across the cool delicate petals of a pale pink rose. A nearby sound of running water catches my attention and I continue down the sloping path, rounding the corner to a clearing, where a fountain gurgles in the centre, surrounded by beech trees. Lamps are dotted around the fountain's stone wall and I imagine it being incredibly romantic out here at night.

"Hey," Ethan's voice makes me jump and swing around. "I was calling you."

"Were you?" I brush a strand of hair off my face. "This garden is so beautiful."

Ethan settles the glasses on the ground and wraps his arms around my waist. "I'm glad you like it."

"It's so unspoilt," I sigh. "Thanks for inviting me tonight."

"You might not feel like that shortly," he replies, releasing me and picking up the drinks.

"Why?"

"My sister's here."

"Oh. Well I met your brother and that went OK."

"Chelsea's quite prickly."

"I could avoid her?" I suggest and take my drink.

"She already knows you're here," Ethan replies, sitting on a bench to the right of the fountain, patting the space beside him.

"What have you told her?" I sit.

"Not much." He looks away, brooding, shutting me out.

I sigh and rub the side of his arm. "It'll be fine."

"Maybe I shouldn't have invited you to something my brother and sister were going to be at," he muses. He's anxious, I realise, although I'm not sure if he is bothered about what they will think or what I will. I hadn't wanted him to meet Nan yesterday, it had felt like it was happening too soon, and I'd been worried it would burst our bubble. Maybe he feels the same...?

"Ethan." He meets my gaze. "Do you want me to go? I can go."

"No." His response is immediate, definite. "I want you here, I want you full stop."

I smile. "I want you too," I say and get up. "Come on, let's do this."

***

"OMG." Instinctively I know the disdainful female drawl that floats across the lawn is the prickly sister. "You're not Ethan's usual type."

"Chelsea," Ethan warns, and slides an arm around my waist, drawing me closer. I melt against him, grateful for his warmth, as I stare into the ice-cold eyes of Chelsea Harber. She's sitting in a wheelchair, a slender arm resting on the table. She looks like a doll: porcelain skin, shoulder-length blonde hair, layers cut to frame her long narrow face. There's no meat on her and momentarily I wonder if she is anorexic. She looks like a delicate little princess sitting there in a pretty white short summer dress, but then my attention returns to the shards of ice she has trained on me. She pouts at Ethan and my first impression formulates: she's a rich, spoilt, American brat who is used to getting things her own way.

"Chelsea, this is Rosie," Ethan introduces us awkwardly. "Play nice."

"Hi." I plaster on a fake smile.

"Hello again." A low, husky voice prompts me to look to my left. How had I not seen her as we crossed the grass? Sitting next to Chelsea, smoking a cigarette, is Bianca. I shoot Ethan a sideways you-could-have-fucking-warned-me glare, and somehow manage to maintain the fake smile and join it with a similarly insincere greeting.

"You really should have said something on Friday," Bianca scolds Ethan as she takes in the situation.

"Why?" Ethan asks frostily. "I wasn't aware my personal life was any of your business."

Bianca's face momentarily crumples, and I feel sorry for her. She puts out her cigarette and gets up. "Quite," she says silkily, "absolutely none of my business."

"B." Chelsea's chair whooshes into action as she follows the red-headed woman inside. "Wait up."

"That was shitty," Josh says. "I don't know who's worse, you or Chelsea."

"Shut up Josh," Ethan snaps and sits down.

"This is going to be a fun evening," I mumble, and take a gulp of wine.

Josh looks at me before laughing. His amusement alters the atmosphere and we spend the next twenty minutes chatting. Josh is funny, a comedian with a cheeky grin. He's easy to be around, holds nothing back, what you see is what you get. He's an open book, and I like him. Chelsea returns but doesn't join in with the chatter – instead, she eyeballs me across the table with what seems like contempt. I rest my hand possessively over Ethan's on the table and fix her with a fuck-you-bitch glare. I don't know if the men just don't pick up on the animosity, or whether they choose to ignore it, but they seem more than happy enough to leave the two of us alone whilst they go for more drinks.

As soon as they leave Chelsea lounges back in her chair and asks, "I take it you haven't known my brother long?"

"No," I reply, twirling a strand of hair around my finger.

"Figures." She sits forward, placing her elbows on the table. "Don't expect to. He'll fuck you and chuck you," a malicious smile crosses her lips. "You're so not his type, it's unbelievable."

"What happened to you," I ask, staring directly at her, "to make you such a bitch?"

She blinks rapidly, her long fake lashes fanning her lower lids. "Don't try and fuck with me," she hisses.

I stand up. "I'm fucking your brother," I reply coolly. "I have zero interest in fucking you."

I watch her mouth drop open in surprise and then I spin on my heel and march back inside. Heart pounding, I head through the bar and to the ladies' toilet, walking slap into Bianca on the way out.

"Sorry," I apologise as she steps backwards, holding the door for me.

She looks down at me as I pass and quietly murmurs, "He'll hurt you," and with a flick of her red hair, she saunters out.

When I return to the bar five minutes later, Ethan is waiting for me.

"Hey." He walks towards me and cups my face in his hands, his eyes searching mine. Neither woman has told me anything I don't know but somehow, someone else verbalising my worries has unsettled me and right now all I want to do is hide away. Hide from him, hide from them, just shut it all out. And then I remember what Zach said about Ethan not taking women to parties and a flicker of hope ignites: that means something, I know it does.

"I'm sorry about Chelsea. I'll tell her to back off."

"No," I say dismissively.

To my surprise he leans down and kisses me. For a moment, as his arms encircle my waist and he pulls me hard against his body, everything around us ceases to exist. His tongue slides into my mouth, lazily tasting me, his lips teasing mine, their touch gentle, making me crave more, much more.

"You OK?" he whispers. I nod, conscious that most of the bar are watching us. My cheeks begin to burn. Ethan looks like he doesn't give a shit about the onlookers as he tucks a tendril of hair behind my ear and kisses my forehead. "Come on." He takes my hand and leads me through the bar into the dining room. Thankfully, we sit nowhere near Bianca or Chelsea and we spend the next hour and a half enjoying good food and company. Zach had insisted I sit next to him and had conspiratorially given me the lowdown about pretty much everyone in the room, as we enjoy smoked salmon followed by roast beef and all the trimmings.

"I saw you had a run-in with Bianca," he murmurs as Ethan excuses himself for a few minutes. "Don't let it ruin your evening." He pours more wine into my glass. "And certainly don't worry about Barbie in the wheelchair over there."

I giggle. “She hates me.”

“So what if she does?” Zach pats my arm encouragingly. “Ethan doesn't.”

Ethan returns and Zach turns his attention to the man on his right and starts discussing the cricket.

“You OK?” Ethan asks, his hand running up my thigh under the table. I nod, placing my hand on his, stopping his wandering fingers. He shoots me a deliciously sexy smile, which promises so much. He starts a conversation with an elderly couple sitting opposite about an investment in some new property development in Boston. I zone out, his palm now resting on the back of my hand, his thumb slowly trailing circles across my skin. He commands the table, conversations stopping as attention drifts to him. I have no idea what he is on about as he rattles through projections for year one, two and three, but I'm magnetised to him as he confidently talks, answering questions easily, exuding competence and control.

The business chat continues over dessert. I push my plate to one side, my appetite no more. My stomach flutters with desire, my attraction spirals to dizzying heights as I watch him, see him for the first time in the role of successful businessman. He's self-assured, ironing over objections from the balding man sitting opposite, who obviously doesn't like Ethan. It's compelling viewing, it's hot, he's hot! As coffee is served, a saxophonist begins playing an Ella Fitzgerald song and people start leaving their tables, small clusters of people beginning to form, drifting slowly back into the bar. Most of our table leave and we are joined by Chelsea, Josh and Charlie. The men sit to my right, whilst Chelsea slides her wheelchair next to Ethan.

“So Rosie,” she says loudly, all eyes on her, “Charlie told us over dinner how you two met.”

Ethan's hand tightens over mine as he searches my face and asks quietly, “You know each other?”

“We met on Friday,” I mumble.

“We met at Moorgate at the Tube,” Charlie says, completely at ease. “She was looking unwell, I asked if she was OK, that's all.”

“I've just read a book about a couple meeting on a train,” muses Chelsea. “They got together in the end, all very sweet.” You bitch, I think as I see a muscle tighten in Ethan's jaw. She's riling her brother on purpose, while sitting there as if butter wouldn't melt.

“Well, she wasn't OK,” Ethan says accusingly to Charlie.

“Oh?” Concern flickers in Charlie's eyes.

“Ethan,” I say in a low voice, my eyes imploring.

Josh clears his throat. “Shall we go to the bar?”

Ethan nods and pulls me up with him, possessively holding me to his side as he scowls at Charlie and leads me away through the bar and back outside to a quiet corner of the garden.

"What the hell is your problem?" I ask, shaking him off.

"That useless asshole of a nephew of Zach's has been checking you out all evening."

Has he? I wonder, because I certainly hadn't noticed. In fact, Charlie hadn't even entered my head since our random meeting. My attention, my thoughts had been for this brooding, pissed-off man who is now glowering down at me.

I shrug. "Get a grip! He's nice. He took the time to ask if I was OK, he noticed something was wrong, which is bloody more than you did."

As soon as my outburst finishes, I regret it. Ethan looms over me, a muscle throbbing in his jaw as I see him battling with... With what? Anger? Jealousy?

"You fainted," Ethan finally says in a low voice.

"So?" I ask, exasperated.

"He noticed you were ill and did nothing about it. What if I hadn't been there?"

I sigh. "But you were."

"I don't like him looking at you with those lovesick puppy-dog eyes."

My mouth falls open as I hold his unwavering gaze. "Are you jealous?"

He rests his hands on my shoulders, his fingers pressing down hard. "Don't fuck me around, Rosie," he says chillingly. "You're with me, only me."

"What, so I can't even talk to him?" I clarify. His lack of a response serves as his answer and a slither of rage begins to slide its way through my veins. "You're being a complete bastard!"

"I know," he replies unapologetically, a smile curving at the corner of his mouth. "Just keep away from him."

"No," I say firmly. "I've known you for a week, you haven't earnt the right to tell me what to do and who I can and can't talk to. No man will ever do that."

"Is that so?"

"Ethan," a screeching Chelsea's voice reaches us.

"Yes," I reply determinedly. "I think you should go and see what your sister wants, don't you?"

He turns and stalks away and I stand alone, my heart thudding in my chest. Minutes ago I had been transfixed by him, fantasising about what would happen between us later, but now I'm angry, fucking fuming. How dare he tell me what to do, how fucking dare he! I stomp back towards the bar, but spotting Josh and Charlie standing on the decking I head for them, making the decision to deliberately ignore Ethan.

"You OK?" Josh asks, a knowing look on his face. His brother behaving like a nob mustn't be a surprise.

"Fine."

Charlie reaches into his jacket pocket and as he pulls out a lighter, a small plastic bag falls to the floor. Quickly I bend down and pick it up and at the same time Ethan comes out of the door. For a moment we stare at each other and then everything happens really quickly. He marches towards me and grabs me by the shoulders, glaring down at me with unbridled rage, his attention on the small bag I'm holding.

"Drugs!" His voice is deadly low and I'm aware the surrounding noise fades as if someone has hit pause, all attention is directed on our little group as I shrug him off, my heart pounding at being touched like that, the rage evident in his eyes.

"It's mine," Charlie says, taking the bag. "It's only a bit of weed, chill out."

Ethan looms over Charlie, grabbing him by the tie. A few people come outside, aware something is happening and either wanting to help or spectate, I'm not sure as the only one who moves is Josh, grabbing his brother ineffectively by the arm. "Get the fuck out of my hotel," he orders, releasing Charlie who staggers backwards, losing his balance and ending up on the grass.

"Ethan," I say, shocked, but he ignores me and strides away.

"Leave him," Josh says calmly to me, gently holding me back.

Charlie tentatively stands up, brushing himself down, and people start to move once more, aware the show is over and beginning to dissect the upset, guesses of what it was about on the tips of tongues.

"I'm sorry," Josh says sincerely. "He's got some issues. Drugs are a definite 'no' for him."

Once I've reassured myself that Charlie seems to be OK, albeit shaken, I walk away in a daze, unsure of where I am going. I end up in reception, asking Aiden if he can get me into Ethan's suite, feigning a headache and pretending I can't find him. Aiden hands me a key-card.

"Use this," he smiles. "Do you know where you are going?"

I nod and head upstairs on autopilot. When I open the door I am surprised to see Ethan sitting on the sofa, a glass of whisky in his hand. My eyes dart around the room, landing on my handbag. I remember he took my other bag into the bedroom, so I go and collect it off the bed. I return and drop the key-card on the coffee table in front of him before I give him a reproachful look and head to the door.

"Where are you going?" he asks, draining the whisky and finally getting up.

"Away from you," I respond. "I don't want to be anywhere near you."

Ethan glares at me. "I won't apologise," he says adamantly.

"I doubt you ever apologise for anything you do," I say, fury coursing through my entire body. "You overreacted. It was a bit of weed, Ethan, not some heroin he was shooting up with on the lawn. And he dropped it, I don't think he intended to light up and smoke a spliff down there."

"Drugs are non-negotiable," he says fiercely, taking a step towards me, his eyes burning hot rage into my soul.

I take in a deep breath. "Whatever this is between you and me, I don't want it, I don't need it." I walk confidently out and back to the lift.

"Rosie!" His bellow hits my eardrums as the lift doors slide shut and I begin the descent to the car park. I won't apologise, his words spin around my head, joined by mine, I don't want it, I don't want it, I don't want it...

Chapter Seventeen

"Rosie!" His angry voice carries across the eerily quiet and dimly-lit car park. He's some way behind, having come down the stairs to find me. Chirp: my car alarm bleeps as I push the button to unlock it, running the final distance, his footsteps nearing every second. Adrenaline rockets through me, a heady mixture with the alcohol I've already drunk. I clumsily grapple with the door handle and scramble inside, slamming the door behind me as he rounds the corner.

"Get out of the car!" he shouts, banging his fist down on the roof above my head, making me flinch.

"Go away!" I yell back.

"Don't be a stupid bitch. You've been drinking, you can't drive."

His words smother the anger, the adrenaline, everything. For a moment it feels like everything just stands still in time, a horrible stillness that freezes me, making it difficult to breathe. I detach the key from my keyring and push open the door, only vaguely aware of Ethan's surprise as he is forced to step back.

"I had no intention of driving." My voice sounds strained and far-off as I get out of the car. I launch the key into the darkness, hear it clatter and scrape on the concrete. "I just don't want to be near you." I see the anger drain out of his face by the light he is standing under, and watch as it is replaced with something I can't register.

He inhales and asks, "What's wrong?" I shake my head, unable to find the words as the walls of the past begin to rise up. I get back into the car and rest my elbows on the steering wheel, my head on my arms, my eyes scrunched shut. The notion that he could think I would drive whilst drunk and upset whizzes round and round my head, making me feel dizzy. I hear him open the passenger door, feel him sit down, his hand reaching to lay flat on my shoulder.

"I want you to go," I whisper into the darkness. "Please go."

"No." His reply is firm, but gentle. "Come back upstairs. We can talk."

"I don't want to talk to you," I murmur.

"OK, we won't," he sighs. "We'll just go to bed."

"I don't want to go to bed with you!" It's not much, but there's a suggestion of fight to my tone, and I cling to that sliver of the present, forcing it to expand, to push the past back.

"Separately," Ethan says. "We can deal with everything else in the morning."

"Separately," I agree, having no better plan myself, unless you count sleeping in my car.

Ethan watches me closely as I get out of the car and we head back to his suite. He looks confused, concerned, and somewhere I glimpse a hint of apology to his expression. I turn to stare at my reflection in the lift mirror and look into huge, haunted eyes, my complexion pale. The sensation of not being quite with it is painted clearly on my face and I'm not surprised Ethan's anger has faded.

I concentrate on holding it together but suddenly I'm scared, terrified that Ethan unwittingly has catapulted me back fourteen years ago, back into pain, back into grief. There hadn't been a trigger, no hint of a warning so that I could either distance myself or at least prepare myself. Ethan had thought I was going to drive, and logically I can't blame him for jumping to that conclusion. I had been angry, but the fact is that I do blame him: I hate that he could think that of me and I hate the memories, the feelings that he has evoked.

"I want you to leave me alone," I say flatly as I head towards his bedroom.

"Can I get you anything?" he asks, holding back.

"No. just leave me alone, Ethan."

It's not until I am in Ethan's bed, snuggled tightly in his duvet, inhaling his masculine scent on the pillow, that I realise I should have gone in the spare room. I can't bring myself to move, though, and I sink into his pillow, oddly comforted that I'm in his bed, even though I've pushed him away. I suck in the side of my cheek and chew gently, refusing to let myself cry, battling the tiredness, determined not to sleep. I have no idea how long I lay awake for, but in the end sleep captures me, dragging me back into the familiar nightmare.

***

My graduation ceremony had fallen on a sunny July day. The ceremony had been tedious, lots of clapping and dull speeches, but my friends and our families had felt buoyant, felt so upbeat and enthusiastic about life and our futures. We'd gone to a local Italian restaurant afterwards to celebrate, everyone happy, smiling.

My parents had been among the first to leave, wanting to get back to Nan, who was unwell. I remember hugging them goodbye, shrugging them off as they told me how proud they were, dismissing them so casually so I could return to my friends. Eventually we had left the restaurant, parentless, and headed off for a beach party. I'd felt free, completely clueless about what I was going to do next, but not caring.

I'd been lying on my back, staring vacantly up at the stars just after midnight, the smoke of the nearby campfire filling my nostrils, someone playing 'Fade Out' by Radiohead on an acoustic guitar, a few people drunkenly singing along. And the next minute I'm staring up at a young, quite good-looking policeman. I'd sat up, smiled up at him and then boldly reached for his hand and stood shakily.

“Hi, Officer,” I hiccupped, and giggled, losing my balance. He'd caught me awkwardly. “You've got nice eyes,” I'd slurred, but he hadn't smiled, he'd looked serious, and I'd stopped giggling.

***

It's always the noise of the lorry horn first, followed closely by my mum's scream, a flash as I see my dad's face, his expression one of dread, but acceptance. The screech of tyres, the smashing as metal collides and crumples, glass shattering. A smell of petrol, a whoosh of flames, followed by the deafening rumble of an explosion. And heat, so much heat!

“Rosie, wake up!” I push away the hands that are gently shaking me. “Rosie,” the voice becomes louder, the hands firmer as they pull me from the nightmare. “Sweetheart, it's just a dream, it's just a bad dream. You're OK, I've got you.”

I'm aware of screaming and as my eyes flutter open, I realise it's me that's making the noise. I'm trying to push Ethan away but he manages to clamp my arms by my side, his eyes finding mine in the lamplight. “Rosie, look at me.” His voice is commanding, sharp, just what I need to snap me back to reality. My body goes limp as I stare up at him, my chest heaving with panicky, shallow breaths. He pulls me into a sitting position and holds me tightly against his chest, a hand gliding up and down my trembling back. “It was just a bad dream,” he whispers soothingly. I'm comforted by his warmth, his tenderness, his patience as he continues to rub my back, his words reassuring. Fragments of the evening begin to return and I remember I'm supposed to be mad at him, that he had acted like a complete arsehole, yet in this instant, in the void between my nightmare and real life, he saved me.

“I’m sorry.” Embarrassment floods my body. With one hand Ethan stretches to plump up the pillows, before he positions me against the headboard.

“Do you want to talk about it?” he asks quietly as he arranges the duvet around me.

I shake my head and lower my gaze. He moves on the bed, so he is sitting beside me. “I'm sorry,” he murmurs, sliding an arm around my shoulders. I swallow the lump that is trying to lodge itself in my throat and give in to his touch, leaning my cheek against his chest, grateful as his other arm closes around me. I'm not sure what he is apologising for, but it's enough to make it feel OK for him to be in bed with me in just a pair of boxers.

“Do you have bad dreams often?”

“No. Not any more.” His warmth merges into me, a knot of desire unravelling surprisingly quickly. I turn and brush a kiss to his skin, his muscles tightening under my touch, and stare up at him.

“Don't.” He pulls away. “You don't want this. Lie down, I'll stay with you in case you have another bad dream.” I want to argue with him, want to tell him that right now I do want him, that I don't want this to end, but the rejection is sharp and renders me speechless. He relinquishes his hold on me and I turn away, dejected, and lie on my side. He reaches over and switches off the lamp before lying down and turning away from me.

I don't know why I feel surprised, I'd known this would end the very first time he kissed me, but right now I'm left feeling that I've somehow caused this. Had I overreacted? Would it have been such a big deal if I had simply avoided Charlie? And then I remember Ethan's deadly look when he had seen me with the weed, the way he had put his hands on me, the way he had looked at me, the way he had turned on poor Charlie. No, I'd been right to walk away, and Ethan was right just now to make sure I go through with it.

I must have drifted off at some point, because when I wake again I have my head on Ethan's chest and he has an arm draped across my body. I suck in a deep breath. Why does this feel so right? His breathing is steady, he's fast asleep. I try to move, feeling hot against him, but his arm tightens around me. I relax, comforted by the notion that in sleep he wants me, he's not pushing me away. I sigh and begin to log the feeling of his touch to memory, saddened that this is all I will have of him tomorrow.

When I wake again I'm alone. I stretch out, my thoughts foggy, disjointed. I sit up and rub my eyes. The bedroom door opens and Ethan leans against the frame and stares at me. He looks detached, unreachable.

“I'll drive you home,” he says abruptly. “I can't see your key anywhere in the car park. Get dressed, let's not make this more difficult than it needs to be.”

I nod, the fight draining from me. He is cold, chillingly so, and it's clear his mind is made up. Whatever this was, it's finished, and I need to get out of here, away from him, as soon as possible for my own sanity and dignity.

Chapter Eighteen

I shower and dress. Ethan offers me breakfast, which I decline, suggesting I call for a taxi, which he says won't be necessary and that he will drive. Not wanting to be on my own, I ask him to take me to my nan's and tell him I will deal with my car later.

The drive is quiet, neither of us in the mood for insincere chatter. I'm a volatile mixture of anger and sadness, desperate to contain both emotions as I stare unseeingly out of the window. Ethan is calm, controlled, resolute. He hasn't touched me all morning, he's hardly looked in my direction; being so close to him but not having the physical contact is hellish.

"Thanks for the lift," I say dully as he pulls up outside. I get out and collect my bag.

"See you at work," he says casually. I don't respond, don't look back. I focus on one foot in front of the other as I walk up the garden path and push the doorbell.

"Rosie," Nan looks surprised to see me, her gaze travelling over my shoulder.

"Can I stay?" My face crumples.

"Of course," she pulls me inside. "Go and get settled."

I end up in the spare room where I usually stay. Tears pour down my cheeks as I collapse onto the bed and bury my face in the pillow, not even trying to stop the sobs that wrack my entire body. A thought, a realisation, battles its way to the surface. I never had that nightmare when I was with Tristan. When we had started going out I had been terrified that I would, I made so many excuses as to why I couldn't spend the night with him because I'd been worried I'd wake up screaming. And when I had started sleeping over Tristan had known everything, but the nightmare hadn't returned. My counsellor had warned me that at any time, particularly in times of stress or grief, the dream could resurface, and when I had had my miscarriages I had expected it, but there had been nothing, not even a hint... Why do I feel like the fact I had that dream in front of Ethan signifies something so much more than the fact that I never did with Tristan? It's crazy, irrational, but somehow I feel like my subconscious trusts Ethan more than it ever did Tristan. I can taste the salt of my tears as they trail down my cheeks. My head begins to pound with the intense emotion. I cry quietly, a hand to my mouth, my nails sinking into my lower lip.

I hear the door open slowly, but I don't move. Nan's seen me cry like this before, she'll no doubt put a cup of strong sugary tea on the bedside table and leave me be until I am ready to talk. After a while I'm aware the door hasn't closed, that I haven't heard her move across the room to put the cup down, and I lift my head slightly to see Ethan, watching me. My breath catches as I stare through the tears.

"What are you doing here?" I whisper.

"Your grandmother didn't give me much of a choice," he replies softly.

“What do you mean?” I ask.

Ethan smiles and slowly crosses the room. “She marched outside like a woman on a mission, told me in no uncertain terms to make things right and practically hauled me out of my car.” He crouches next to the bed and tentatively brushes the hair off my face. “I hate seeing you cry.”

“I'm fine.” I pull back, wiping my eyes. “Honestly, you can go.”

“Actually, I can't. She’s taken my car and told me she'll be back in a few hours.”

“She’s what?” I sit up and move to the edge of the bed, my feet touching the ground.

“She seemed quite determined.” Ethan sits next to me. “She screeched off like a boy racer. I hope my car's going to be OK. I've never let anyone else drive it before.” A glimmer of a smile teeters on my lips as I imagine my formidable nan speeding away in Ethan's Maserati. I reach for the box of tissues, blow my nose and wipe my puffy eyes.

“I'm going to ask you one question and I need you to be honest, no holding back, I just want the truth.” I nod. “Forget last night, forget what happened with Charlie, Chelsea being Chelsea, forget it all. This thing between you and me, whatever it is. Do you want it to end? Because although I think I probably should let you go, the truth is I don't want to, and I'm not sure I can.”

My eyes widen in surprise, warmth pouring through my body, melting away the anxiety. I inhale shakily and meet his gaze.

“Truthfully, I don't want this to be over, to end like this. But last night was not OK, you were not OK, you were horrible and angry and I can't just forget it.” I stand and move away from him, knowing that I need to say this, that I can't just fall back into his arms like nothing happened. He needs calling out on his actions and I know that I’m gambling, that he certainly has it in him to close down and walk away, but I can't ignore it. I cross my arms and face him.

“I need you to tell me why, to make me understand.” He had been jealous of Charlie, that much was obvious, and bizarrely I don't mind the misguided jealousy, not really. But it was the cannabis that had pushed him over the edge, and I need to know why. “I know it had something to do with the drugs.”

“I can't be around them.” He stands up and runs a hand through his short hair in exasperation. “I've seen how they fuck people up, ruin lives, people I care about have been hurt. Do you take drugs?” Concern flashes across his face, as if this is the first time he has considered the possibility.

“I've experimented,” I reply cautiously. “Mainly at uni, a bit when I worked in London.”

“With what?” His voice is laced with anguish.

“Ecstasy. I haven't taken it for years, and I’m OK to never take a pill again.”

"When I saw you holding the weed I saw red. And you're right, I overreacted, but I hate being around drugs, any drugs. I know it's ridiculous, that there's nothing sinister about a bit of recreational weed, but I just don't want to see it. Chelsea ended up in a wheelchair because she got off her face with," he pauses and looks away, "a friend. They ended up having a car accident whilst fucked on coke. Addiction screws people up. She broke her back. She had her whole life ahead of her, and because she was fucking reckless she ruined it."

"I'm sorry."

It sounds lame, but I don't know what else to say. I want to run the short distance across the room and pull him close, to tell him that it's OK, that I want him, want him so badly. But I find myself rooted to the spot, awkward, unable to look anywhere but at him. The silence is unbearable, the seconds feel like minutes. Anxiety builds once more, my stomach twisting itself painfully into knots. "I know I fucked up last night," Ethan says finally. "I should never have grabbed you like that. I would never hurt you. I hate that I upset you."

He's apologising without saying sorry, and it's enough. We meet in the middle of the room and I relish the way he pulls me into his arms, the feel of his strength as he squeezes me so tight it nearly hurts. He strokes my hair, his hand skimming from the top of my head down my back in an assured motion. I snuggle against him.

"Has Nan really taken your car?"

"She has," he murmurs.

"Sorry."

"I'm not," he murmurs, a hand cupping my chin and tilting my head so our eyes meet. "I want you to tell me about your dream," he says matter-of-factly, a thumb caressing my jaw.

"It doesn't matter," I say defensively.

"You're thirty-five and having nightmares," he says. "I'd say it matters, wouldn't you? I'm not judging you, but you were upset last night, even before you went to bed you were upset, and I think I might have caused it. One minute you're mad at me, the next you looked so sad. All I wanted to do is hold you."

"Why didn't you?"

"What?" He looks confused.

"Hold me? You know I wanted you last night, but you pushed me away."

"You were upset, I didn't want to take advantage of you. I'm not a complete asshole."

"You overwhelm me," I whisper. "You're asking me to tell you stuff that most people, good friends, don't know about. A few minutes ago you wanted to leave this, to drive away."

"That's not true," he says vehemently. "I've never wanted to leave this, not from the very first fucking moment I saw you. There's something about you," his tone softens. "I want all of you," he caresses my cheek. "All of you, Rosie."

I blink up at him, my insides melting. I take a deep breath, deciding to go for it. "My parents were killed in a car accident. The other driver was drunk. I had no intention of driving last night, I just needed some space, but when you thought that I was going to drive, it brought back memories – the worst memories."

"I'm sorry." He brushes his lips lightly to mine. "The dream?"

"I wasn't in the car, but I heard enough from the police to get a really vivid picture of what happened. That's what I dream about, it's like I'm watching it in slow motion. I haven't had the nightmare in a very long time. After the accident I pretty much had it every night for around six months."

Ethan leads me back to the bed and we lie down on our sides, facing each other. He props himself up on his elbow, his other arm resting across my side, his hand placed against my lower back.

"Can I stay at yours tonight, like we agreed?"

I hesitate. "I don't know."

"Let me make this right."

"It's not that. We're OK."

"Then what?"

"I think I should sleep alone tonight."

"Why?" he persists.

I try to sit up, wanting to break the intimacy, but Ethan's arm clamps me to the bed.

"Talk to me," he snaps. "Give me something to work with."

"I'm scared." The words come out shakily.

"Scared of what?"

"That I could have the dream again. That it's back," I eventually say.

"And?"

"And I don't want you seeing me like that."

"What?" He sounds genuinely incredulous. "Why?"

"I dealt with it on my own before. I'll be fine on my own now."

"Like hell you will." His eyes darken. "You're not going to go through this by yourself. I'm staying. I told you before, I want all of you, and if that includes bad dreams then so be it."

"Ethan!" I protest. "We only started this a week ago. Dealing with bad dreams shouldn't be on the table yet. It's too much!"

"It's not enough, I want more, I want everything you've got. And be honest, Rosie – with yourself, if not with me – you wouldn't be happy if I fucked you and then left. You want me to hold you whilst you drift to sleep, to feel my lips on your skin as I wake you in the morning."

I sigh at the thought. He's right, of course I want the cuddles, the waking up together, of course I do!

"And surprisingly, I want that too," he says huskily. He lowers his lips to mine, his touch confident, his tongue dipping into my mouth. Pushing me onto my back the kiss intensifies as he rolls on top of me, his body crushing me into the mattress. I wrap my arms around him, my fingers trailing up his back, revelling in the sensation of firm muscles beneath his shirt. It's intense, my lips feel bruised against his. It's all-consuming, the type of kiss that literally leaves you breathless. Gradually the kiss lessens into something gentle, its softness tantalisingly seductive in contrast to the unrestrained passion.

"Call your nan and get her to bring my car back," Ethan says, returning to his side and pulling me into the crook of his arm. "Then let's go to yours, where we won't be disturbed. I want you, but the thought of your scary grandmother bursting in on us is not doing it for me."

I giggle. "Me neither. I'll call her in a minute, but can we just stay like this a little longer? It's nice."

He places a gentle kiss to my temple, his lips lingering unhurriedly on my skin as he trails a finger lazily down my cheek. "Let's never go to bed like we did last night," Ethan murmurs. "If we need to argue all night, then let's do that, let's not ignore each other and go to sleep with things unresolved."

I sigh and close my eyes, feeling contentment float over me.

"Hey, don't you go to sleep on me," he orders. "Go and make that call. The sooner I get my car back, the sooner I can get you to yours." He lowers his voice, his lips brushing across my earlobe. "The sooner we can have the best make-up sex you could ever imagine."

Chapter Nineteen

"Tea, coffee?" I ask, stooping down to pick up an envelope off the mat, discarding it on the coffee table as I cross the lounge and enter the kitchen. I pick up the kettle and go to fill it at the sink.

"No." Ethan stalks close behind me and takes the kettle, placing it back in its stand, unfilled. He spins me to face him, backing me up against a work surface. My breath catches as I stare up into smouldering pools of desire, his eyes sparkling with unbridled need. He lifts me effortlessly onto the counter and fixes me with a lingering gaze that pings desire through my entire body.

"Saturday morning seems a very long time away," he says pointedly.

Colour heats my cheeks as I remember how he had woken me up on Saturday.

"Yes," I swallow, "it does."

His hands capture mine in my lap, his hold firm, his thumbs skimming lightly over my knuckles. With frustrating slowness, he lowers his lips to mine, heat pouring through my body as his kiss disarms me. His lips are firm, his tongue plunging into my mouth, and I find myself responding equally as fervently, needing to taste him, my lips crashing against his. I shuffle precariously close to the counter's edge, craving his firm body against mine. Ethan's arms find their way around my waist, his hands sneaking under my top, his fingers stroking up my back. Adeptly he unclasps my bra, his hands sliding under the thin satin material to cup my breasts. His touch is gentle, his fingers barely touching me. His kiss, in contrast, intensifies as he sucks my lower lip roughly, his teeth grazing over my skin. My arms tighten around him as I lose myself to the intoxicating mixture of gentle and dominant. I slide off the work surface, my body rubbing against his as I dismount, and still kissing passionately we clumsily make our way back through the lounge to my bedroom.

Unceremoniously he pulls my top over my head and pulls my bra straps down my arms, discarding them both carelessly on the floor as his lips find mine once more. Ethan moves to my bed and perches on the edge, his hands holding me upright as his lips trail kisses down to my breast. His tongue flickers across a hard nipple before he takes it into his mouth, his tongue sliding over the erect peak, eliciting a low moan from me. His fingers skim over my stomach and to the zip at the side of my skirt, making easy work of undressing me further. His knee nudges my legs apart and his fingers move slowly over the fabric of my knickers, a finger sneaking its way inside my underwear. A low appreciative noise vibrates deep in his throat, his warm breath tickling my skin, as his finger enters me, feeling my slick desire. I'm aroused, already on the edge, just his lustful gaze in the kitchen had been enough to make my body quiver in anticipation for him.

"Look at me," he instructs, his eyes finding mine, their sparkle registering how close I am as his finger slides to hover over my clitoris. "Step out," he says, pushing my underwear down my legs. I comply shakily and his arm pins me back into position, his thighs clamping around me. His hands travel down my skin, goosebumps prickling under his fingertips, his controlled gentleness tantalising. A hand cups me between the legs, the warmth of his palm coursing through my sensitised skin. Two fingers rest at my entrance, his thumb dipping inside, trailing up to my clitoris, where he begins to circle, the nodule of throbbing nerves responding under his touch. His lips begin to trail kisses to my other breast, his tongue brushing over my skin, before his mouth takes hold of my nipple. His fingers enter me sharply as he sucks my nipple roughly into his mouth. His tongue and thumb mirror a circling, flicking motion, whilst his fingers move in and out, slowly and gently to begin with, but as my body responds the pace increases. Ethan's free arm holds me as my orgasm beckons, my legs trembling and my knees threatening to buckle.

“Go with it,” he says, his voice hoarse.

Pleasure peaks suddenly, his thumb slows as the first spasm begins and then he begins to move again, drawing the orgasm on to a plateau, which feels amazing, but at the same time as if it's too much. I try to push his hand away, but he grasps my wrist. The second wave of pleasure explodes violently through my body, and then I find myself on Ethan's lap, cradled in his arms as a sharp, warm tingling sensation overwhelms my entire being. I close my eyes, trying to process the intensity of the physical feeling that has overwhelmed me.

Ethan places his lips to my temple and asks, “Feel better?”

My eyes flutter open and I stare up at him blearily, a shy smile twitching at the corner of my mouth. I sigh contentedly. Yes, I feel better, like a weight has been lifted. “Hmm.”

“Good.” He kisses the tip of my nose and moves me to the bed so that he can stand and undress. I watch the carefree way in which he removes his clothes, self-confidence oozing from each fluid movement. I inhale sharply, his naked form a vision of masculine perfection.

“Come to the edge of the bed,” he says, his hand stroking up his cock. “Lie on your back.” He positions me so I'm right at the bed's edge and holds my legs straight up in the air.

He enters me, inching his length slowly in until his cock is fully buried, our bodies united as one in the most intimate of ways. His hands tighten around me as he begins to move. Make-up sex with Ethan is hard and fast, his thrusts driving deep. I allow my eyes to close, soaking in the feeling of his possession, the sound of his thighs slamming against my bare skin, our breathing coming in short, ragged pants. He folds my knees so they rest on my chest, inching me higher off the bed so I am resting more on my shoulder-blades. The position change is subtle, but it allows him to power deeper. I stare up at him, our eyes locking, the connection intangible, but so powerful it undoes me, my body jolting as his touch radiates pleasure through my veins.

His release shoots, spilling deep inside. Ethan thrusts a couple more times, his release crashing over us both in waves. He stills slowly, a look of contentment on his face, a satisfied smile that reaches his eyes. That look, I realise, that look of satisfaction, I had something to do with that. I roll onto my side, feeling a sticky trail forming on the inside of my thigh. I reach for the box of tissues and dab at the mess, tossing the tissue into the bin.

“Better?” I ask as Ethan flops beside me, pulling me against him.

“Much,” he replies, pushing the hair off my shoulder and pressing his lips to my skin.

“Good,” I whisper, reaching for his hand. We lie quietly for a long time, our breathing returning to normal, the satiated feeling like a cover over both of us. There's a calmness, a blissful content that we are both sharing.

This morning I had woken feeling miserable as sin, but only hours later I’m cradled in his arms and I know I've fallen in love with him. It's ridiculous, and it's not something I'm ready to share with him, with anyone, but I know it's there, beating in my heart. Maybe it's madness, desperation, I don't know, but right now it just feels right, so right that it just needs accepting for what it is. I'm in love with him, and acknowledging it is somehow a relief. It's like I have no control over it: it just is, and I need to accept it rather than fight it.

“What are you thinking about?” Ethan asks.

“You. This.”

He nods. “I thought so.” He kisses me tenderly. “Good thoughts, I hope?”

“Good thoughts.”

***

I must have dozed because when I wake, Ethan is not with me. Rubbing my eyes, I get up and slip into my dressing gown. I find him in the kitchen, dressed, sitting at the table, his attention on his phone. He looks up as I enter.

“You should have woken me.” I stifle a yawn.

“You looked so peaceful, I didn't have the heart.” I perch on his lap, one of his hands sliding inside the dressing gown to cup a breast, his lips pressing against the hollow of my neck. I lean my cheek on his shoulder, inhaling his masculine scent. “Good sleep?”

“Hmm.”

“Josh called, your key has been found. Stay at Tranquillity tonight and drive to work from there in the morning.”

"I wanted you to stay here," I grumble. "I'm supposed to be cooking."

"I'll stay tomorrow."

The doorbell makes me jump and I stand, refastening the dressing gown belt.

"I'm not expecting any visitors," I say apologetically and head to the front door.

"Hi," Chloe says brightly. "I've been calling you," she enters like a whirlwind and breezes into the lounge. I turn to see her mouth fall open as she catches sight of Ethan in the kitchen. She recovers quickly, shrugs her shoulders and marches to introduce herself, whilst I am left floundering, nearly forgetting to close the front door. I watch them, fascinated, as he stands and they both size each other up.

"No wonder you didn't answer your phone." Chloe winks at me. "Sorry to interrupt your bonk holiday Monday. I was bored and popped in on the off-chance you might want a movie marathon. But I can see you're busy." I redden, feeling like a teenager that has been caught in the act. Ethan, however, doesn't look at all affected.

"I was just about to make tea," he says, turning away to pick up the kettle.

"Well," Chloe slips off her jacket, hangs it on the back of a chair and sits down, "that works for me," and she shoots me a mischievous smile.

"Erm, Ethan, this is Chloe," I say nervously. "We went to school together."

"We are friends," Chloe clarifies. "In fact, some might say best friends."

"Understood," Ethan replies calmly as he crosses the kitchen to me, tucking a strand of hair behind my ear. "Don't look so worried," he murmurs. "Go and get dressed."

I hesitate, not wanting to leave them together, anxious what Chloe might say in my absence. She's wary of him, I can tell, and I'm pretty sure that Ethan can tell too, although he doesn't seem fazed. "Go!" He kisses my forehead, before moving away to ask Chloe how she takes her tea.

I dress quickly, unsure if I'm comforted or unnerved by the murmurs of their voices from the kitchen. I scrape my hair into a low ponytail before returning to them, spotting and picking up the envelope from the coffee table as I pass through the lounge.

"Rosie's done it," Chloe says as I pull out a chair and sit. "The boys loved her."

"I bet they did," drawls Ethan.

"Done what?" I ask, opening the envelope.

"Come to the careers workshops I co-ordinate at school. I'm trying to persuade this super-successful businessman to come and be a speaker, perhaps even help with some work experience placements."

"What is it?" Ethan interjects sharply as the colour drains from my face. I stare down at the note, which simply states in bold writing: "To my flower girl, roses can be broken just like that, snap!!!" Unable to speak, my mouth going dry, I push the sheet of paper in Ethan's direction and watch his expression darken.

"Oh my god!" Chloe says as she casts her eye over the note. "Do you think this is from the guy who sent you the flowers at work?"

"Of course it is!" Ethan responds harshly.

Chloe, pissed off by his tone, squares her shoulders and glowers at him. "Well, she never had any flowers or notes before you came on the scene."

Ethan looks outraged. "What are you suggesting, exactly?"

"Well," Chloe considers, "if you're a crazy psycho then getting Rosie scared and then offering her comfort works pretty well for you. You were there the first time, after the phone call, and look how that night ended. It's just a theory," she concludes sweetly.

"It's ridiculous!" Ethan scrapes his chair back and stands, beginning to pace the kitchen.

"Oh, chill out," Chloe also gets to her feet. "It was just a possibility, a whim. I need to be sure that Rosie isn't being played by another loser."

"I guess I get that," he says grudgingly. "And if you're in any doubt..."

"I'm not," I interrupt. "I don't know who this is, but I know it's not you."

"Great," Chloe says casually, "so glad we've got that cleared up." She drains her cup, depositing it in the sink and picking up her jacket from the chair. "I guess you'd better let the police know."

"Yes," I agree. "I've got a card with contact details from Tuesday."

"Do you want me to stay?" she asks.

"No, I'll be fine. You go."

"You look after her," Chloe instructs Ethan as she hugs me. "If you want to stay at mine, just turn up."

"She'll stay with me," Ethan says firmly.

"I thought you might say that," she responds.

I see Chloe out and return to the kitchen. Ethan pulls me into an embrace and I crumple against him, soaking in his warmth and strength.

"Chloe was sensible to question whether this is me," he says, his hold tightening.

I blink up at him. "But it isn't?" A shiver courses down my spine.

"No. I want you with me because you want to be, not because you're scared."

"I do want to be with you, Ethan."

"I don't want you to have any doubts about this, no niggles. Look at me. I need you to trust me, implicitly."

"I do, completely. I'm sorry about Chloe, who knows where she got the idea from? She's a bit dramatic."

"I like her," he says. "She warned me to look after you without actually saying it, I approve of that. She's a good friend, I can see that."

"She is." I wrap my arms around his neck. "I'm not going to be frightened by whoever this is."

"Good. But if you feel unsettled then talk to me, OK? Let's call the police, then pack some things and go to mine."

Chapter Twenty

The November sun is surprisingly warm on my back as I sit at a table outside the pub opposite work and wait for Charlie to return from ordering our lunch. I chose here on purpose, hoping that Ethan might materialise from the door across the road, that his eyes might travel across the street and rest on Charlie and I eating together. I imagine his irritation and find the prospect pleasing. Right now I want to piss him off, like he has pissed me off the entire morning. Sometimes he can be an absolute jerk, and I don't even like him.

"He's not there," Charlie says, placing a glass of wine in front of me and taking a seat opposite.

"I have no idea what you are on about," I protest grumpily.

Charlie smiles, a knowing smile. "What's he done?"

"Is it that obvious?" I pout. "You don't want to know."

"You're right," he sighs, "I don't, but you want to tell me, you need to tell me, because he still insists on keeping you and him a secret at work. Come on," he leans back, "I'm listening."

And for the next ten minutes Charlie is true to his word and listens, just letting me vent about my shitty morning. We'd started with the interviews for the Business Development Relationship Manager, which I should have known would be a nightmare. I mean, we'd fought over the shortlisting process, so why the hell would the interviews be any better? Libby was meant to be interviewing with us, but she'd called in sick this morning and Ethan was adamant that we would do it on our own. We'd been OK interviewing two external candidates, both mediocre, nothing to write home about. But then Jamie Barrett, whom I had pretty much begged Ethan to give a chance, had interviewed and things had spiralled out of control. Ethan had been condescending, rude, and Jamie left looking humiliated. I'd bollocked Ethan before the next candidate, telling him to not be such an arrogant nob.

"I'll try and be nicer," he had murmured as the door opened and in walked Jade.

Where Jamie had got arrogant, egocentric Ethan, Jade got the complete opposite. He was kind, encouraging, and fuck him, he flirted with her, and she flirted back.

"What?" he had laughed as the door shut and we were left alone. "You told me to be nice."

"You're an idiot," I had fumed, scooping up my things.

"And you're hormonal," he had drawled, coming up behind me.

"Fuck you," I'd hissed, pushing his hand off my back. "I'm going to lunch."

"We need to debrief."

"Debrief yourself," I'd snapped and marched out, not looking back, not wanting to see his smile, the amusement gleaming in his eyes.

"Your plan's about to work," Charlie interjects my rant.

"What plan?"

"He's just walked out of the office, and yes, he's seen you with me."

"How does he look?" I whisper.

"I can't tell. And there was me thinking you just wanted lunch with me, no strings attached."

"I did, I do! We arranged this last week, remember? I couldn't have known Ethan was going to be such a shit, could I?"

"I don't know, I'd say the possibility was quite high," Charlie grins. "Do you want me to snog you or something to really piss him off?"

I giggle. "I couldn't possibly use you in such a way." I take a sideways glance and see Ethan striding down the street, his mobile to his ear.

"So, I went to Chloe's school this morning," Charlie says as our food arrives.

"How did you get on?" I ask.

"Pretty good, I think. They've offered me some supply hours because the music teacher is on the verge of a nervous breakdown and they don't know when he'll be back. I start next week."

"That's brilliant. Well done you."

We clink glasses, and a satisfied smile creeps across my face. I've met Charlie a few times over the last couple of months. He's kind, gentle-natured, and for some inexplicable reason I find him soothing to be around. He gets mine and Ethan's relationship, and although I know he doesn't approve, he indulges me, and actually is the only person I can be completely honest about it with. Charlie suspects I'm in deep, too deep, but doesn't judge me. Chloe, who has met Charlie a couple of times now, thinks he is falling for me. I'd dismissed the idea as ridiculous, but honestly, sometimes I catch him looking at me, like he is right now, and wonder if she might be right. Charlie is lovely, but even if Ethan wasn't in the equation, he isn't my type.

"Chloe invited me to join you at the fireworks display," he says, dipping a chip into ketchup before popping it into his mouth.

"Excellent," I say, pushing away my plate, my chicken salad hardly touched. "A few people from work are coming too."

"Chloe said I could ask whoever."

I nod.

"I thought I might ask Josh and Chelsea."

"If you want," I say unenthusiastically.

I've seen the Harber siblings a couple of times since Zach's birthday party. Josh continues to be charming, friendly and funny. We get on really well, maybe too well, because Ethan seems wary when we are together. Chelsea hasn't warmed to me, still insistent on making digs whenever she can. Ethan adores her and panders to her every whim. I've tried to talk to him about his relationship with them both, but he shuts down, and I haven't pushed it.

"Be nice, they don't know anyone here. Are you asking Ethan?"

"Probably not. I don't think he'd come. Although maybe he would if I can get Will to ask him."

Charlie sighs, failing to hide his irritation. I'm not sure if he is annoyed by the fact I want Ethan there, or whether it's because of the secrecy. I have a feeling it's the latter; he keeps subtly suggesting that Ethan needs to get over himself and just be honest about our relationship at work. But he's not ready, I know he's not, and I'm reluctant to rush him.

"You look tired," Charlie observes.

"Ethan's been in London the last couple of nights. I decided to stay at mine last night, and I didn't sleep very well. I guess I'm more on edge than I like to admit. I kept hearing noises, and half-expected a bunch of crumpled roses to be posted through the door, or for the window to be smashed."

"What are the police doing?"

"Logging instances. Trying to trace phone calls and emails. They don't seem that concerned. I mean, he hasn't done anything, just sent a few creepy letters, some flowers, some dead flowers, called me a few times to comment on my attire."

"I thought you were staying at Tranquillity?"

"I was supposed to be," I answer, finishing my drink. "But I just wanted some normality. I need to take some control back." Charlie nods, seeming to understand. We pay for lunch and then he walks me back across the road to work.

"Rosie." I turn to face him at the door. "I get you wanting to take back control, but consider whether actually it is this weird flower-sending man that's making you feel like you aren't in control. I think you deserve better than you are getting at the moment. That's all I'm going to say. See you Friday."

I return to my desk, feeling gloomy, Charlie's words ringing true. I hate this, hate being secretive to people who are my friends. I want to tell Libby and Will, I want to vent to them when Ethan is annoying; I want to bore them with how amazing he can make me feel. I want it to feel real, meaningful.

“Hey, gorgeous,” Will says, stopping at my desk.

“Hi.” I look up.

“How's interviewing? Ethan doesn't seem to think you have found the one yet. I saw Jamie at lunch, he said Ethan was a right cunt.”

I giggle. “He was. If Ethan doesn't think we have found the one, then we probably haven't. I'm not sure my opinion really counts.”

“Have you heard the news?” Will pulls out the chair next to me and sits down.

“What news?” I ask, seeing an email from Ethan pop up on my screen. I don't open it and turn to Will for gossip instead.

“Apparently, Ed is taking a sabbatical, and has asked Ethan to act as MD for a few months. Rumour has it that Ed is off to the south of France to chill out for a bit. Has Drew said anything?”

I shake my head. Neither has Ethan, which compounds my misery.

“I think it will be a good thing,” Will continues. “Ethan has ideas, good ideas, I think he could make some positive changes around here.”

“You think?”

Will stretches and stands. “I like him.”

“You like everyone,” I point out.

“You want a drink?” he offers.

“I'm fine, thanks.”

Will heads into the kitchen and I take a deep breath before turning my attention to my computer screen. His email subject ‘Debrief’ holds my attention as my hand hovers over the mouse. I find I want to ignore it, to open a memo about overtime, or any of the other emails that are unread in my inbox, and that is exactly what I do. For the next fifteen minutes I respond to emails, my eyes resting on Debrief, before I ignore it again and open the next email below. It's childish, I know, but it makes me feel better. My desk phone rings, making me jump.

“Hello, Mosen's.”

“So, you're ignoring my email?”

“What email?” I stammer, turning scarlet.

“Open it now,” he instructs.

I comply, and read:

“Boardroom.”

"Sorry, am I supposed to know what that means?" I say. "Your emails need to be a little more specific." I smile, amused at myself, and then the smile disappears as I catch sight of him striding across the office towards me. I put down the telephone receiver.

"You're late for our meeting," Ethan says loudly, so that most of the office can hear.

"We don't have a meeting," I flounder.

"Yes we do," he leans over my shoulder, clicks my mouse and brings up my calendar. "2pm, in the boardroom. Get your notes," he lowers his voice, "and your arse downstairs now." He straightens and walks away, saying loudly as he goes, "Whenever you're ready."

I stare at my calendar, certain I hadn't seen the entry before. I sigh and get to my feet, catching Will's eye as I pick up my folder.

"Run along," he mouths from the kitchen door, making little sweeping gestures with his fingers. I scowl at him and march across the office and down the stairs to the boardroom on the first floor.

Chapter Twenty-One

The boardroom exudes an atmosphere of no-nonsense formality with just the right undercurrent of foreboding. It's painted in a very pale sage green, its walls bare, with the exception of the large projector screen. The wall opposite the door hosts large windows, with Venetian blinds which are now closed, shutting out the glorious sunshine, which would, if given half the chance, help to warm the room up. I hit a button on the heating panel just inside the door and hope it doesn't take too long to kick in, goosebumps pricking up on my arms.

The large dark mahogany table takes up the majority of the room, surrounded by sixteen black leather chairs. To the right, midway down the wall, is a door which leads to a small kitchen that houses a fridge, kettle and microwave. My heels sink into the soft, dark grey carpet as I cross to the table, plonking my folder opposite Ethan.

“Don't,” he says, as I'm about to take a seat. I stop, my hand resting on the back of the chair. Ethan stands and slowly stalks around the head of the table. “Did you miss me when I was away?”

I swallow, my eyes finding his automatically. “I did.”

“Where did you sleep last night?” he asks quietly.

“Does it matter?” I ask, wondering how he knows I didn't stay at Tranquillity like we had agreed I would.

“Yes, it matters.” His tone is low, harsh.

“I went home.”

“You never said,” accusation reverberates through his voice, his eyes, his entire being. “When you spoke to me last night, you never said you were at home.”

“How do you know?” I ask. “Are you keeping tabs on me or something?”

“Or something,” he replies.

“What does that mean?”

“It means it came into conversation, by chance, with Aiden over the phone. Don't you look so outraged, you're the one in the wrong here, not me.”

“How am I in the wrong?” I say indignantly, raising my chin.

“Because you lied.”

“I did not lie,” I protest fiercely.

“OK, you omitted full disclosure about where you were last night,” he drawls, his tone condescending, as if he is speaking to a child. “And you know why you did that?” I stare up at him challengingly. “Because you knew I'd be fucking mad.”

"I hate being at Tranquillity when you're not there," I complain. "I wanted my own bed. Is that so wrong?"

"Yes!" he explodes. "We agreed you wouldn't stay on your own, not until Roseman has been identified."

"I'm sorry," I put a hand out and caress the side of his arm. "I had a crap day yesterday, you weren't here, I just wanted my own things, my own space. Please, Ethan," I look up at him imploringly and take a step closer. "It was OK, you don't need to be annoyed."

Lightly he brushes my hand away and steps back, retracing his steps to his chair, where he sits.

"I can't deal with you now," he says detachedly.

"Deal with me?"

"Yes, deal with you. Sit down Rosie, let's debrief."

"No," I object.

"Sit." His voice is low, his expression dark, sending a chill through my veins. I sigh and sink into the chair, feeling like I've been well and truly reprimanded.

"I don't know why we're bothering," I say dully. "You've already told Will you haven't found the one."

"Do you disagree?" Ethan rests an elbow on the table and puts his chin in his hand. "Let me look." He reaches for my folder and slides it across the table and begins to flick through my notes. "You're very detailed, aren't you?"

"Can I look at your notes?"

"I didn't make any."

"Yes, you did! You were writing in the interviews."

"You're so kind to these people," he says, closing the folder and pushing it back in my direction. "Candidate 1 had a lisp, it was distracting, I couldn't concentrate on what he was saying, which means our partners won't concentrate, which means he isn't the man for the job. Candidate 2: completely dull, no charisma, absolutely no personality, and that means he won't sell, he won't clinch the deals for us. Candidate 3: the lovestruck puppy who wanted to pull you at the work party..."

"That was his twin brother, actually," I correct.

"He has no experience."

"He could learn. He is due to finish his Business degree in the Summer."

"Fuck the Business degree," scoffs Ethan. "He doesn't have the business experience. Haven't you read the job spec? I want an experienced business development manager, someone who has a history of getting results. What I don't want is some kid just out of university. Now, Candidate 4: promising, I thought," he leans back and smiles.

He's winding me up, I know it, he knows it... He wants me to react, and the clever thing to do would be to completely ignore him, but I can't restrain myself. This man brings out the extremes in me, and right now I'm pissed.

"Really? Maybe you're right. I mean, you'd know more about it than me, wouldn't you?" He looks questioningly at me. "Young, pretty girl, probably quite happy to sleep with whoever for a deal. I guess that still works."

"That's bitchy," he says.

"Accurate, though."

The boardroom telephone rings, and Ethan stands to answer the call.

"Sure, of course, I'm sure Rosie will be delighted. Come straight in." He replaces the receiver and comes to my side, kissing the top of my head. "Smile," he whispers into my ear, before he opens the door and in bustles Ellie with her new-born and a multitude of baby paraphernalia.

"Sorry to interrupt, but I didn't want to leave without seeing Rosie."

"Absolutely no problem," Ethan smiles. "Congratulations."

"Thank you," Ellie beams, motherhood suiting her.

"You look great," I say, getting up and staring down at the most perfect baby girl, all wrapped up in a pink blanket. "She looks adorable. Congratulations."

"Do you want to hold her?"

I nod and carefully accept the bundle of sleeping baby. "Hello Tessa," I coo. She wriggles slightly, her eyes momentarily opening, before her little fingers clamp around my thumb and she returns to sleep with a sigh.

"You're a natural," Ethan murmurs.

I look away, unable to meet either his or Ellie's eyes. He's right, of course, I am a natural. I've always been good with babies, just not good enough to carry one of my own. My heart squeezes for what I won't have. I swallow the lump and compose myself.

"Libby's sick, she would have loved to see you."

"Yes, Will said. Never mind. I can't stay long, anyway. I just wanted to come in and say thanks for the beautiful flowers and baby clothes. You'll have to pop round for tea soon."

"I will," I reply as I carefully hand Ellie her daughter back.

"Well, we'd better be off," Ellie says, kissing her baby's head tenderly. I hug her, promising to be in touch. Ethan holds the door open and Ellie leaves. I sink back into my chair.

"Did you and Tristan not want kids?" Ethan surprises me by asking as he pulls the chair to my left out and sits down.

"We did," I reply, looking away.

"I can imagine you with babies," he murmurs, a hand stroking the side of my arm.

I flinch away. I hadn't envisaged having to have this conversation with him, because 'the talk' about babies would mean this was serious, and serious was certainly not something I had imagined. Passionate, all-consuming, but not serious, not for him, anyway... But here we are, and for some reason I feel like I need to be honest.

"We tried," I say quietly. "I had miscarriages, then an ectopic pregnancy. I had to have a tube removed. We went through three rounds of IVF after that..."

"I'm sorry. Did you consider adoption?"

"Tristan didn't want to adopt."

"Did you?"

"Maybe," I say quietly. "I don't know. It didn't matter, he didn't. I gave up on the idea, I had to."

"I'm sorry."

I push his hand off my arm and stand, irritated by his consolation. I don't need it, and right now I most certainly don't want it.

"Are we done?" I ask. "I've got things to do."

"Rosie," Ethan gets to his feet and tries to pull me into an embrace, but I push him away.

"No!" I protest. "I hate the way you get me to tell you things when you tell me absolutely nothing. I don't want your sympathy, I don't want you telling me where I can sleep at night. You tell me absolutely nothing."

"What do you want to know?" he asks in exasperation.

"Anything, something!"

He takes a step closer and leans down, his lips inches from mine. "All morning I've been thinking about what it would be like to fuck you on this table."

"That's all I am to you, isn't it?" I step backwards, the desire to slap his gorgeous face overwhelming. "Will mentioned that you were going to be taking over for a bit, that Ed is taking a break, and that you are going to be in charge. And you know what I thought? Why don't I know that when Will does? I've spent the last couple of months going to bed with you every night, but I know nothing about you. You fuck me, but that's it."

Ethan sighs. "What exactly are you asking here? Just so I understand what is it that you want from me?"

"I want more," I surprise myself by saying. I don't think I had consciously realised that I actually wanted more until now. I'd been OK at accepting the fact that I'm in love with him, and I thought it was OK that he wouldn't feel the same, but right now I want to feel like there is at least something between us apart from the physical. "You told Will about taking over, do you have any idea how shit that was having to hear that from him and not you? You say you want all of me, but you give me nothing."

"Nothing's a bit harsh," he interrupts, an amused glint in his eye, a suggestion of a smile turning up at the corner of his mouth. "I'm sorry I told Will and didn't tell you first. Is that better?"

"Don't mock me." I pick up my folder, preparing to march out. "I'm staying at mine tonight. On my own."

"Not on your own, you're not." He grabs me by the arm and spins me forcefully to face him. "I get it, you're hormonal, on your period, whatever, and if it makes you feel better you can hate me for a few days, but let's not completely overreact here, shall we?"

I'm outraged: how does he even know that I'm on my period? Embarrassment scorches my face as I step back, dumbfounded by his sheer lack of discretion, the total insensitivity, how inappropriate his comment is. His crass remark about fucking me over the table I can deal with, but the current state of my cycle, for some ludicrous reason, seems to overstep a mythical boundary of what is acceptable. His phone chimes, and I watch him read a message.

"Look, I've got to go," he says, full of composure as he stalks towards me. "God, your tits look amazing in that top." He reaches out and places his palm on my stomach comfortingly. There's something so tender about his hand resting there that it takes every inch of self-control to not fall into his arms sobbing in a hormone-induced breakdown. I hardly ever get periods these days, not since I had the implant fitted, so this morning's unexpected arrival caught me by surprise and in all honesty I feel on the edge. I inhale, meet his gaze, and try to muster up a disapproving scowl.

"I'll send out the rejections," I say.

"Jade?"

"What about her?"

"I'll give her feedback, and Jamie too. I'll try and be constructive. Leave it with me." He places a swift kiss on my forehead. "Cheer up. I'll see you later. And Rosie," he says as his hand reaches for the door handle, "I'm staying over tonight."

Chapter Twenty-Two

I spend the next hour at my desk, with every minute crawling by. I'm miserable, I feel like a horse has kicked me in the stomach, and I feel drained. I'd returned to my desk to receive an email from Roseman, Ethan's nickname for my unwanted admirer, although today's email isn't particularly admiring. Usually his emails, or leering telephone calls, focus on what I am wearing, making it obvious that he has seen me that day. But occasionally, he references me disappointing him, that I need to fix something. The one-line email today simply says: "I can't believe you've done it again! You snobby bitch!" And then in line with the rest of his emails and letters there is a picture of roses, today's picture showing withered flowers that are about to die.

It's odd, I think as I screenshot the email and send it on to the police, that I don't feel scared any more. At the beginning I had tried to pretend I wasn't frightened, but deep down I certainly was unsettled. But now I just want it to stop, or to know who he is and why he's doing this. The feeling that I have met him is now something I am sure of, but I'm still unable to place the voice. This inability infuriates me, but however much I try to wrack my brain for a memory, nothing of any use materialises.

"Are you coming?" Will stops at my desk. I stare up at him questioningly. "Ethan's taking everyone off the phones. Haven't you read the memo?" I shake my head and click open the internal memo link on the intranet. "All Staff announcement: 3pm on the first floor. Attendance required."

Wearily I stand and follow Will and the others downstairs. Agents are already unavailable, the wallboard red with calls waiting. There's an odd atmosphere, uncertainty on most people's faces. Ed never takes people off the phones, so their concern is not misplaced. I join the Ops Managers, slinking into the corner behind Tom.

"Do you know what this is about?" he asks.

"Haven't a clue," I say.

"OK everyone," Ethan's voice carries masterfully across the call centre floor, the murmurs of worried staff ceasing immediately. "I'm here with good news." There's a sigh of collective relief. "As of now, I am taking over from Ed. He's taking a sabbatical, and the Board has asked me to look after the business whilst he is away. This is a strategic decision and won't affect your jobs. I'm not looking to make redundancies or anything like that, and I don't want people leaving here worried. I am going to be reviewing all functions of the business. What we are doing as a company is good, but I think we can do better."

Ethan gives a motivational speech for the next ten minutes. I watch the expressions of my colleagues, watch their concern transform into excitement. Ethan is proposing a new chapter, encouraging staff to join him on a journey of success, and by the looks on the faces of people around me he is easily converting the staff. By the time he finishes there seems to be a positive buzz to the call centre.

I return to my desk and close down my PC. My stomach is now agony, and I'm beginning to feel unwell. I need a hot water bottle and to go to bed. I knock on Drew's office door and tell him I am leaving early.

"You look wiped out," he says.

"I feel it," I admit. "Maybe I'm getting what Libby has." I leave Drew's office, momentarily tempted to knock on Ethan's door, but decide against it. He doesn't need to know.

I drive home, take some painkillers, and snuggle up under a blanket on the sofa with a hot water bottle. I put the TV on but am so tired that I don't really take any notice of what is on. I close my eyes, hoping that the shivery sensation that started during Ethan's company address stops soon. My mobile, still on silent, vibrates, the low buzzing sound registering with me, but I can't muster up the energy to get up and retrieve it. I turn onto my left side and begin to doze.

***

I jolt awake, disoriented, before I remember I am at home. The doorbell chimes and I think it must have rung before and pulled me out of my slumber. I rub at my eyes, blearily making my way to the door and opening it to find Ethan brooding on my doorstep. I shouldn't be surprised to see him, yet I am.

"Let me in," he commands, and gingerly I open the door fully so he can enter. "You didn't tell me you were leaving work early," he says, dropping his bags on the floor and removing my hand from the door handle so he can close it behind him.

"I told you I was coming home tonight," I reply, retreating back into the lounge and sinking onto the sofa. "I really don't want company. I feel crappy, I just want to sleep." Ignoring me, he takes off his coat and wanders into the kitchen with a carrier bag. I sigh and pull the blanket up around me and sink back into the comfort of the plump cushions. Ethan isn't listening, and I haven't got the energy to argue. Let him do what he wants, I decide, and begin skipping channels to find something to watch. Emmerdale is on – I glance at my watch to see it is already 7.20pm, I must have slept for a couple of hours, but I still feel utterly wiped out.

Ethan returns, scooping me up so he can sit on the sofa, nestling me against him, my head resting in the crook of his arm. He's cold, the November wind making his touch chilly, a subtle smell of bonfire smoke clinging to his shirt.

"Do you often bunk off work early?" He eventually breaks the silence.

"I didn't bunk off," I respond. "I told Drew. I'll make up the time, don't worry."

"I'm not. I have no concerns about your work." He trails a finger slowly down my cheek.

"That's something, I suppose," I say huffily.

"Are you in a lot of pain?" His hand delves beneath my blanket and rests on my stomach.

"Yes. Look," I try to sit up and to disentangle myself from him, "Ethan, I'm really not in the mood."

"Ssh." His arms clamp around me, drawing me against his chest. "I know," he kisses the top of my head lightly. "I thought we could order a takeaway, watch a movie. I've missed you."

Moving position slightly, I stare up at him. Sometimes his eyes captivate me with lust but conversely, now, they are the most gentle pools of brilliant blue, it's not about sex but belonging and I want to lose myself to this look right now. He is turning me to mush. Sighing, I snuggle into him further, accepting he is here to stay the night.

"You know we can't? I mean, I don't..." I murmur, embarrassed.

He returns his hand to my stomach, rubbing gently. "I know, it's fine. But I can stay?"

"If you must." I feign resignation.

"But do you want me to?" he asks, and for a moment I am sure I see uncertainty flicker across his face, a crack in his voice that needs reassurance.

I nod and move so I can wrap my arms around his neck. I brush my lips against his, before resting my cheek on his shoulder, closing my eyes. "I missed you too," I whisper. "Being at Tranquillity, with you not there, it was horrible. I thought coming back here would make me feel better."

"And did it?" he asks, his fingers tangling in my hair as he shifts so he can look down into my face.

"No," I admit. "I couldn't sleep. I was on edge, every noise making me jump. I half expected a bunch of flowers to smash through the window. I was nervous, and I know it's mad but I wanted him to show himself. I just want it to be over, one way or another. I know you are worried about me, and really, it's sweet, but I can't let this make me lose control. I don't want to be scared, I'm tired of feeling anxious, wondering if he is there, behind a bush, sitting opposite me at a coffee shop. It's driving me mad, and the only way I can deal with it is to try and be normal." I go on to tell Ethan about today's email, and he just listens, a brooding look on his face. "I'm glad you're here," I finish.

"Then why did you object earlier?" he asks, cupping my chin and staring down at me.

"Because I don't want to become reliant on you," I answer. "Because I'm on my period; because you've been a shit most of the day; because I feel rubbish, which is why I left work early."

"You do look pale," he says, moving me so he can stand. He bends down and picks me up and carries me into my bedroom, where he undresses me.

"Ouch!" I complain as his hands squeeze my breasts. "Ethan," I try to push him away. "I'm sore, I'm bleeding, I don't want to..." I trail off in embarrassment. Periods, sex, they don't do it for me, but I wonder if he is one of those men that really don't care.

"I know," he sighs, sitting on the bed and pulling me onto his lap, his arms embracing me tightly. "Access denied, I get it," he rests his chin on the top of my head. "But when it's finished, you let me know immediately. I've missed you. I want you. Sleeping with you and not fucking you is going to be an unwanted novelty."

"You don't have to stay," I whisper, swallowing a lump that has begun to form in my throat.

He cups my face in his hands and stares at me. "You really think the only thing I want from you is to fuck you, don't you?" he asks, his voice low.

"Maybe," I reply, and try to look away.

"Why would you think that?" he asks, his eyes trained on mine.

"I don't know," I shrug. "Because everything ends up with sex! Because we've been seeing each other for just over two months and hardly anyone knows."

"People know!" he interjects.

"Nobody at work does!" I counter. "I feel like I'm lying to people, people who are supposed to be my friends. I hate it!"

"I'm not going to out us at work, Rosie." His tone is firm, his expression set. "I said that from the start."

"You did," I agree despondently, and slide off his lap to busy myself with putting on pyjamas. I'm aware of his eyes on me, watching my every movement.

"Look," I eventually say, crossing my arms and meeting his gaze, "I'm tired, I'm overemotional."

"And you're trying to push me away," he interrupts, standing and pulling me into his arms. "It's not going to work," he whispers into my ear. "I'm not going anywhere. I like spending time with you," he brushes his lips gently against mine, his hold around my waist tightening.

"I won't be any fun," I blink up at him. "I feel rotten."

Placing a hand to my forehead, Ethan's expression softens. “You're burning up,” he says, concern etched on his face. “I thought you felt bad because you were on your period, not because you're getting sick.”

I snuggle against him, relaxing in his arms, comforted by the masculine strength that always seems to engulf me when he pulls me into an embrace. I inhale his scent and close my eyes.

“I think I might be getting what Libby is off with,” I finally say. “I don't want to give it to you.”

"Ssh," he puts a finger to my lips. “I'm going to look after you. No arguments. Are you hungry?” I shake my head. “Tired?” I nod. “Paracetamol and bed it is, then.”

“What will you do?” I ask.

“Work.”

“You always work,” I respond as I get into bed and lie down.

“You can take the day off tomorrow,” he says, perching on the side of the bed and taking my hand in his.

“I'll probably feel fine after a good sleep.”

“I'm your boss now, and I'm telling you that you are having the day off.”

“Shit!” I exclaim. “I'm sleeping with the boss.”

“Yep,” he grins.

“I never thought I would be that person, the type to sleep with the boss,” I yawn.

Ethan chuckles. “And I never thought I'd be the boss sleeping with one of my staff.”

“Will it always be like this, a secret?”

“I don't know,” he replies, kissing my hand. “You're beautiful, and I know you deserve more than this, but I can't let you go.”

“Then don't,” I say quietly.

Our eyes meet, and for the very first time I believe that this could be more for him too. We've always had the physical attraction, from the very first time I saw him over Will's shoulder, but right now, in this moment, there's a flash of an emotional connection. Dare I dream that this could be more for him as well...?

Chapter Twenty-Three

I become aware of voices, male voices, their tones hostile. I recognise them, but for a while I struggle to connect them to their respective person. My head is pounding, pain throbbing behind my eyeballs, a general achiness seeping down the back of my neck, my joints stiff as I sit. I'm hot but can't stop shivering as I stand and make my way unsteadily to the door. They are standing in the entrance to the lounge, squaring up to each other, Ethan's tall, broad frame making Tristan's shorter, slighter body seem smaller than it really is.

"Tristan," I say, surprising them both and temporarily distracting them from their masculine preoccupation of sizing each other up.

"I didn't know you'd have company," Tristan says, slightly apologetically. He looks particularly uncomfortable in contrast to Ethan, who seems his usual confident self as he crosses the room and puts an arm around my waist, scowling across at the other man. Wow, this is awkward, I think, looking from one to the other, unsure of what the correct etiquette is for this situation.

"Tristan, this is Ethan." I opt for polite introductions. "We work together."

"And sleep with each other," Ethan adds, glaring, his jaw set in a hard line.

Tristan shrugs. "I didn't know you were seeing anyone."

"Well, she is," Ethan draws me closer, "and now you know. Rosie's not feeling well, so I think you should go."

"Are you OK?" Tristan steps closer, his eyes scrutinising my face. "Do you want me to take a look at you?"

"I just need to sleep," I say awkwardly, feeling my body leaning into Ethan, unsure if it is because I'm feeling weak, or because I want to make a point.

"Hey," Ethan's other arm circles my waist, as if he is holding me up.

"Take her to bed." Tristan's voice is clipped. "I'll get my bag from the car."

"He's a doctor," I explain. This is surreal, I think, as Tristan returns with his doctor's bag and starts checking me over, Ethan watching, leaning in the doorway.

"How long have you been feeling unwell for?" Tristan asks, looking down at the thermometer reading.

"Just this afternoon," I reply.

"Hmm." He turns and orders Ethan to go and get me a glass of water and then tells him where to find the paracetamol in the bathroom cabinet. "You didn't tell me you were seeing someone else," he says when we are left alone.

"Neither did you," I respond, amused by my quip.

Tristan frowns. "Why didn't you tell me the flat was on the market?"

"Because it's not really any of your business any more, is it?"

"We need to talk." He leans closer, his eyes searching mine.

"We really don't," I reply, shuffling away from him. "Why are you here, Tristan?"

"Because I want you back," he whispers.

Any remaining colour drains from my face, and for an instant I think I'm going to pass out. I regain composure as Ethan returns with a glass of water and painkillers.

"What's the verdict?" he asks.

Tristan stands. "She's got a bit of a temperature, nothing major, but worth keeping an eye on. I'll come back tomorrow to see how you are feeling," he says to me.

"That won't be necessary," Ethan says harshly, glowering down at Tristan.

"See you tomorrow, Rosie," Tristan calls over his shoulder, and leaves.

Ethan begins to pace moodily up and down my bedroom until we hear the front door click shut. Then he turns and glares down at me.

"What?" I ask, slumping back against the pillows.

"What?" he explodes. "Why the hell is your ex coming around at eleven at night?"

"I don't know. The last time I saw him was the day after the work party in August. Don't look at me like that because I haven't done anything wrong! Oh, and thanks for outing us to him, really classy."

"I'll sleep on the sofa," he says quietly, too quietly.

"No!" I say crossly, pushing back the cover, preparing to fight, and trying to ignore the achiness that is consuming my body. Physical pain I can cope with, but not emotional, not now. "If Tristan turning up has made you feel like you need to sleep on the sofa, that you need space from me, then you can go. I don't need you here, in the next room, pissed off at me for no reason. I haven't done anything wrong, and I won't have you make me feel like I have! You've done it all day, I've had enough, Ethan. I don't like you when you're like this. Stay with me or get the fuck out."

Ethan stares down at me, a muscle twitching in his jaw, his expression unreadable. He sighs and heads for the door. I cling to the side of the bed to stop myself from running after him and begging him to stay. I want him to stay so badly that it's like another pain, only worsening my malady. I lie down again, scrunching my eyes shut, fighting back unshed tears. I hear the sound of the shower and realise Ethan hasn't left.

My mind wanders to Tristan and his declaration. What the hell? Shamelessly, when he had left me, I had begged him to come back, to give us a second chance. He had become my constant after my parents' death and I'd wanted to cling to him, needing that security I felt with him. Looking back at it now, I shudder at my weakness. When my parents had died I'd felt this overwhelming, all-consuming loneliness that was bone-deep. Tristan had understood that, he'd made me feel something other than grief, and his infidelity had threatened to push me back into the void of hopeless solitude. I'd wanted to fight for us, for him, for me; I'd wanted to cling so tightly and never let go. Somewhere along the way of his betrayal I'd lost my self-respect, and bizarrely Ethan had helped me find it again. I'd ended up needing Tristan in a destructive, obscure fashion, but not now. The spell has been broken, the neediness has fizzled away.

It's different with Ethan: I want him, but I don't need him. I'm magnetised to him, desire for him consumes me every moment I am in his company, but there's always the niggling feeling that this won't be forever. I dread the inevitable, the conclusion of us, but being alone again doesn't scare me, not like it did with Tristan. I'll be sad, devastatingly heartbroken even, but I don't think I'll feel so intimidated being on my own. Ethan wants me the most when I am fighting him, it's been like that since the first moment we met, the bickering keeping alight our fire. I must never lose myself to him, because as soon as I do I will lose him, of that I am sure. I don't know what is going on in Ethan's mind right now, why he is annoyed with me, but what I do know is that I don't deserve it and I mustn't let him walk all over me.

Ethan doesn't speak when he returns, he simply pulls back the duvet and slides in beside me, his arm circling my waist as he pulls me back against him. He trails kisses up my shoulder to the hollow of my neck.

“I'm sorry,” he murmurs.

“What for?” I whisper into the darkness.

“For whatever you need me to be sorry for.”

“That's not good enough.” Sighing, I turn to face him and slide my arm around him. “But right now, all I want is to fall asleep with you. We can continue this in the morning.”

Ethan strokes my cheek, brushing a tendril of hair away from my face. He kisses me lightly on the mouth. “OK,” he agrees. “You're so hot. Do you want me to let you go?”

“No.” My hold on him tightens. “Please don't.”

He nestles me closer, so my head rests against his chest. I inhale his scent, his skin smelling freshly showered, the masculine aroma of shower gel lingering seductively. I fall asleep feeling far too hot, but oddly at rest with his arm draped across me, his fingers splayed out on my lower back.

I don't sleep well, waking to kick off the duvet, waking shivering to pull it back on. I seem to drift into episodes of really deep sleep, but wake suddenly and feel even more tired. My inability to settle disturbs Ethan, but he doesn't complain; occasionally he kisses my neck or squeezes my bum, but he doesn't speak.

"Good morning, beautiful." He bends down to kiss my cheek as he reaches across me to turn off the alarm. "How are you feeling?"

I yawn, rubbing my eyes. "Tired, achy. I'm sorry I kept you awake."

"Luckily, I've never needed a lot of sleep." He smiles down at me. "I'll get you some more pills, I think you still have a temperature. Are you hungry? Let me bring you breakfast in bed."

"I am hungry. I'll get up."

"Don't you dare." He puts a hand on my arm to hold me down. "You need to rest. What do you want? Let me look after you."

"Just some toast would be great, thank you."

"Peanut butter?"

"Yes please," I nod.

"Tea?"

I nod again. "I just want to have a quick shower first. I feel minging."

"You look gorgeous," he replies smoothly.

Ethan relents and lets me get out of bed, but insists I am too weak to shower alone. Afterwards, I am permitted to snuggle up under a blanket on my sofa to watch TV whilst he makes us breakfast. He brings my toast to me just as I send a text to Libby, letting her know I am not coming into work today.

"Who are you texting?" Ethan asks, sitting down next to me.

"Libby."

"I've got a meeting in London this afternoon. I can work from here until around eleven. I'd feel better if I dropped you off at Tranquillity before I get the train."

I shake my head. "I'm staying here."

"Because you want to stay so your asshole ex can visit?"

I shrug. "No. I want to stay here because it's my home. We had this discussion yesterday. Don't try and bully me."

"I'm not bullying you!" he objects. "I'm trying to keep you safe."

I put my plate on the coffee table and move onto his lap. "You're sweet," I murmur, kissing his cheek. "What time will you be back from London? Can you stay over again?"

"Early evening." Ethan brushes a strand of hair off my face. "I'm not happy about leaving you on your own," he frowns down at me for a moment before acceptance registers. "But I don't want to argue, and I have a feeling I'd be onto a losing battle."

My arms find their way around his neck as I nuzzle against him, my cheek resting on his shoulder, my lips twitching into a smile against the side of his neck.

"You're very attractive when you're being reasonable," I murmur. "You should try it more often."

"Eat your breakfast." He squeezes me quickly, before sliding me from his lap. "What about Tristan?"

"What about him?" I scrunch up my face.

"Will he come round?"

"I don't know," I sigh. "Are you jealous?"

"Completely." His tone is serious, and the amused smile leaves my face. A stupid thing to say, I realise as soon as the words have left my mouth.

"You shouldn't be," I say, reaching for his hand. "Tristan is nothing to me. You know that. I told you that the very first night, remember? Ethan, I want you." I bring his hand to my mouth and kiss it. He doesn't look fully convinced but doesn't push it. I decide not to tell him about Tristan telling me he wants me back. What would be the point? It's not going to happen. Ethan doesn't need to know.

He spends the next couple of hours on his laptop, studiously working, whilst I doze in and out of consciousness. I'm no longer shivery, and don't think I have a temperature any more, but I feel totally zapped, my energy levels worryingly low. Thankfully, my period seems to have stopped, just being a one-day blip, which has happened before with my implant.

"Sweetheart," Ethan bends over me and gently kisses my cheek. "I've got to go."

"Hmm." I blink up at him, admiring his navy-blue suit, the way the jacket emphasises his broad shoulders, the trousers moulded to show his muscular thighs and long legs. "You look nice," I say, smiling up under my long lashes.

"Why, thank you," he grins and softly kisses me. "Get better soon. I really want you."

I sigh contentedly. "Have a good meeting."

He grimaces. "Doubtful. Rest up. I'll text you when I'm on the train back."

"Missing you already," I murmur, repositioning myself on the sofa.

"I hate leaving you."

"Just go," I giggle, play-pushing him away. "I'll be waiting."

"Good." He kisses me again, a fleeting but firm touch of his lips to mine. "I'll see you later." He picks up his coat and bag and heads out. I sink into the sofa, pulling the blanket around me. God, I need to get better quickly because even when I'm poorly I still really, really want him.

Chapter Twenty-Four

I spend most of the morning snuggled on my sofa, drifting in and out of sleep. By lunchtime I feel considerably better, more like I am suffering from fatigue rather than feeling ill. My spirits are lifted further when my smarmy, fake-tanned estate agent calls to tell me he has a very keen man who wants to view my flat on Friday afternoon. We arrange a time, and I hang up feeling hopeful. I get up to make myself a sandwich and cup of tea.

“I'm missing you.” I quickly type out the text to Ethan, wishing he were here to talk to about the possibility of somebody being interested in the flat. He surprises me by calling me back, E flashing up on the screen.

“Hello.”

“Hey you. Are you OK?” he asks.

“I didn't mean to interrupt.”

“It's fine,” he soothes. “I can talk. How are you feeling?”

“Lonely,” I grumble, collapsing back onto the sofa. He doesn't respond. “How is the meeting?” I ask, feeling deflated. Does he miss me when I'm not with him? Or does he just carry on as if I don't exist? He misses fucking me, he'd said that, but does he actually miss me?

“Rosie?” His voice has an edge to it, and I realise I hadn't been listening to his reply.

“Sorry.”

“What's wrong, sweetheart?” His voice is low, husky, and it sends shivers through me. God I love his voice, his super-sexy New York drawl. I love the way he says my name, the way he calls me ‘sweetheart’. I love the way he lowers his voice, like now, a huskiness to his tone. It does things to my body, my stomach twisting itself into a knot of desire.

“I'm fine,” I sigh.

“Are you sure?” he asks gently. “Do you need me to come back?”

“No,” I reply weakly, wondering if he would if I said yes. “I'm sorry. I'm just feeling a bit,” I pause, searching for the right word to describe my mood, “emotional. I'm sorry. Honestly, I’m fine. Ignore me.”

“Are you sure?”

“Yes.” I force myself to sound bright. “I'll be fine. See you this evening.”

“OK. I'll pick up a takeaway on the way home. We never did the whole movie and food thing last night.”

After saying goodbye, I start browsing the property pages online. To date I haven't found anywhere I want to buy, I'm not really sure I even know what I am looking for. The plan, if you can call it that, is simply not to live here any more. I can move in with Nan for as long as I want and put the rest of my stuff in storage. I don't need to rush into anything.

I'm bored with looking at properties, having traipsed around enough the last couple of months to help Ethan in his own search. He had put an offer in on a converted barn and at the last minute, at the end of October, the seller had pulled out. He had been pissed off at the time, and the whole affair seems to have put me off wanting to bother looking for myself. The property market is quiet at the moment, Ethan has assured me, and I'm tempted to leave looking until the New Year, like he has decided to do.

The doorbell rings and I find Tristan standing in the rain. Fuck, I'd forgotten he had said he would come to check on me. I had meant to text him this morning to put him off. He gently pushes past me, hanging his wet coat on the hook and taking off his shoes.

"Make yourself at home," I say sarcastically, closing the door.

"Let me look at you," he says, his hands resting on my shoulders as he turns me to face him, his eyes travelling down my body and then back up again to rest on my face. "How are you feeling? You look better," he rests his hand lightly on my forehead. "Your temperature is down."

"Get off." I shrug him off. "Cut the crap, Tristan. Why are you here? What do you want?"

"I told you yesterday," he replies, his eyes gentle as he stares down at me. "I want you back."

"I said you would." The words tumble out of my mouth before I have chance to stop them.

"You were right," he trails a finger down my cheek. "I was stupid, I was wrong. Forgive me."

When Tristan had broken the news of his affair and had told me he was leaving me, I had been so shocked, so unbelievably hurt. Tristan wasn't an arsehole, so his betrayal had stung even more. It was so out of character for him. He was kind, loyal (or so I thought), he was decent, a hardworking GP at the local surgery. Even though he had ripped my reality to pieces and stomped his size eleven feet all over our life together, I had known Carla, the cliche nurse, was just a phase and not for keeps. I'd known that he was going through some ridiculous midlife crisis, where a younger woman acted to massage his ego. And I'd told him, begged him not to be so foolish. And here he is now, telling me what I had always known: he had made the worst mistake of his life.

"Tristan." I back away, not wanting him to touch me.

"We were good together," he says, taking a step towards me.

"'Were' being the operative word," I respond, putting up a hand to stop him. "I'm with Ethan."

"The American guy from last night?" I nod. "With the flashy car? God, Rosie, he's not you."

"And you are?"

"Yes."

A blanket of sadness smothers me because Tristan's too late. I sink onto the sofa and put my head in my hands. Uncertainty uncurls itself in my brain. Would I be sending Tristan away if it weren't for Ethan?

"Rosie," Tristan takes a seat beside me, a hand gently rubbing my shoulder. "Please!" He sounds like he is begging, and as I peek sideways to look at him, I see desperation. "I love you," he whispers. "I don't think I ever stopped loving you."

I swallow, looking down, not wanting to see the sincerity in his eyes. It hurts because I believe him, because I know he is speaking the truth. "I'm sorry," I say quietly, "but I don't love you."

"And you do love the American?" There's something condescending about his question; it irritates me.

"Yes," I reply, sitting upright, shaking his hand off my shoulder. "But I stopped loving you before Ethan came on the scene. When you kissed me in the Summer, I stopped then, or I knew I'd stopped then. Whatever we had, Tristan, it's gone."

"But we can get it back," he implores.

I shake my head. "I don't want to."

"Fuck." He runs his hands through his damp hair, tousled from the rain.

"I stopped believing there could be an 'us' the night I gave you the engagement ring back." The realisation calms me. I'd stopped loving him before I'd even met Ethan, and somehow that clarity helps rationalise my decision now. Ethan is not the reason for me saying no, Tristan is, time is...

"Are you going to move in with him? Is that why you're selling? Is it serious?"

"No." I see the glimmer of hope this information brings and know I must crush it immediately. "I love him, though." The flicker fades, replaced with resignation.

"I can't make this better, can I?" he asks.

"No." I shake my head.

"What if I said I wanted us to try another round of IVF?" I'm shocked by his question, and my silence spurs him on. "I know I thought we should stop, but maybe I was wrong. We'd make great parents, you'd be an amazing mother."

"You bastard," I whisper, fury pulsing through my veins. "You think if you dangle the possibility of a baby it will get me back?"

"I think we've been through too much to give up."

"I will never forgive you for cheating on me." I glare at him.

"But you wanted me back not so long ago," he says in confusion.

"I was scared of being on my own, of starting again. I'm not scared any more."

"And you've got Ethan now," Tristan mutters bitterly.

"Kind of," I nod.

"He's not the man for you. He'll break your heart."

I shrug. "Maybe. Probably. But I don't care."

"Are you sure?" Tristan shuffles closer and stares into my eyes, trying to will me to waver. I stare back, unblinking, relieved to feel no old feelings stir.

"What we had," I say, "it's gone, Tristan. I think it went a long time ago. We were so fixated on babies that we just didn't notice. We are one of the many couples who lose each other through the depressing, uncompromising, unrewarding cycles of unsuccessful IVF."

"Tell me you don't love me any more," he insists. I oblige, my words soft, acceptance grudgingly registering on his face. There's an odd finality to this moment, we both sense it, the acknowledgement that this really is it for us. Bizarrely, I think I'd always known he'd come back; maybe he'd known it as well, but here, in the present, this is the end, no second chances, no clinging on to false hopes of babies, just our conclusion.

Chapter Twenty-Five

Tristan's visit has left me on edge, my desire for Ethan increasing by the hour. It's an ache for him at the pit of my stomach, a need to feel him, his skin against mine, to inhale his scent, to taste him, to be seduced by his voice, to be magnetised by his eyes.

I run myself a bath, soaking my weary limbs in the hot water, my mind calming. I slip into a pale pink pair of silk pyjamas and take residence back under my blanket on the sofa. Fatigue crashes over me again, a concoction of physical tiredness caused by feeling under the weather, mixed with emotional exhaustion. I'm too weak to fight sleep, my mind going vacant as my eyelids close.

I wake to the sound of the doorbell. Springing upright, I rub at my eyes and get to my feet, hurtling out of the lounge.

"Hey." Sounding surprised, Ethan drops the carrier bag he had been holding on the floor and catches me, pulling me into his arms. "Are you OK?" I don't answer, shivering against him, the November coldness clinging to his clothes and hands. I wrap my arms around his waist, snuggling against him, my body pressed hard against his. He tilts my chin up and stares questioningly down into my face, searching for answers that I'm unable to give him. He bends, his lips gently pressing against mine, his tongue searching, his lips cool, his mouth warm in contrast, tasting of peppermint, something I now associate with him. I slide my hands up his chest and around his neck, and he squeezes me so tight it borders on painful, a delicious pain that morphs into intense pleasure. I kiss him like we haven't seen each other for years, my tongue greedily exploring his mouth, my kisses hungry, like I can't get enough of him. He walks me backwards, pushing me up against the wall, kicking the front door shut, his hands slipping under my silk pyjama top, stroking up my back, his fingers kneading my tight muscles.

"Feeling better?" he asks, breaking our kiss, leaning his forehead against mine and staring intensely down at me.

I nod, unable to speak, my heart hammering in my chest. "Sorry," I finally say, embarrassed by my passionate outburst.

"Don't be," he replies hoarsely as he takes off his jacket and hangs it on the peg, before he pulls me away from the wall and back into his arms. "I like this kind of a welcome back."

I smile up at him, his eyes the warmest blue, his lips twitching into an amazing grin. There's something so devastatingly sincere about the way he is looking at me, it makes my heart squeeze tight for him.

"You look so much better," he says, stroking down my cheek and placing a kiss to my forehead.

"I feel better. I've slept for most of the day. It seems to have helped."

"Did that asshole ex of yours show up?" I'm about to answer but his mobile interrupts, taking his attention away from me. He reaches for his phone, checking the caller ID before he answers. "Hi Mom."

I slip out of his arms and pick up the carrier bag he has dropped, smelling Chinese food. I head into the kitchen and begin to dish up. I pour him a whisky and a glass of lemonade for myself. I smile contentedly as I scoop lemon chicken onto chow mein noodles, touched that Ethan has remembered my favourite dish. I serve his, a Chinese curry with boiled rice, and sit at the table, snacking on the prawn crackers whilst I wait for him to finish his phone call.

Five minutes later he saunters into the kitchen and sits opposite me, taking a drink.

"God, I needed that," he sighs.

"Difficult day?" I ask, popping a chunk of chicken into my mouth.

He nods, slowly chewing on a mouthful before he responds. "Difficult people, made harder by the fact they are assholes."

I listen to him vent about his day, his frustration with the partner he had been visiting, their apparent lack of vision and willingness to think outside the box, and their open hostility when they learnt Ed was no longer in charge. He goes on to grumble about how behind the times Mosen's is, particularly bearing in mind they have Drew's computer expertise. Things are going to change, he declares, a tingle traversing up my spine with the ferocity in his voice. Success drives him, being good isn't enough for him, being the best you can be is his motivator. Staying still is not an option, and apparently Mosen's has been stationary for far too long.

"Ed and the Old Boys' network have been holding the company back; some of the dead wood we have at a senior management and Board level is tantamount to business suicide."

"What are you going to do?" I ask, sipping at my lemonade, smiling as he forks a bit of my lemon chicken and pops it into his mouth. Sharing food is something we just naturally did right from the beginning. He'd want me to try things, or he'd just reach across and help himself. There is something intimate about it, a familiarity that I like.

"I'm going to review resources," he replies, leaning back in his chair.

"Redundancies?" I say despondently.

Ethan gets up and pours himself another whisky. He leans against a work surface and stares across at me. "You'll be OK, I told you that right at the beginning. Don't look at me like that," he chides, unremorsefully.

"Like what?"

"Like you're disappointed in me."

I consider his response for a moment, trying to process my feelings. “People are going to lose their jobs and you don't even seem sorry about it.”

“I'm not,” he says immediately. “People will lose their jobs if they are not up to fulfilling them properly. I'm a businessman, not a philanthropist. The vast majority of people will be fine, and in a year's time they will most likely be better off because profits will be up. We can do proper pay reviews, bonuses will go up.”

Deep down I know he is right – we certainly have some fossils at work – but it makes me feel uneasy that Ethan is going to be the one to bring about the change. He pulls me to my feet and holds me, his face softening.

“This is why I don't fuck people I work with,” he murmurs. “It complicates things.”

“Maybe I should look for another job?” I suggest.

He shakes his head. “It complicates things, but I like working with you. I like watching you, knowing that you're close.”

“Will you make anyone redundant that I'm friends with?” I say quietly.

“I don't know,” he replies, his eyes transfixed to mine. “I can't promise you that I won't.”

“Is my job safe because I'm sleeping with you?”

“No.” He shakes his head vehemently and cups my chin in his hands. “You are good at your job. You get people, you know exactly what to ask to get the best out of them.”

“Then why do you fight me on pretty much every decision I make?”

“Just because we disagree, it doesn't mean I don't respect you professionally.”

He looks and sounds like he means it, and I relax into his hold.

“Can I ask you about one person?” I ask, hiding my face against his chest. “Will?”

“Will will be fine,” he whispers into my ear.

I want to ask about Libby, but don't, scared of what his answer will be. Their relationship is tempestuous to say the least. She may have found him attractive at the start, but she now finds him arrogant and overbearing, whilst he finds her cold and obstructive. She may be good at her job, but I know Ethan would relish her departure.

***

We spend the rest of the evening snuggled on the sofa, watching TV and sharing a tub of salted caramel ice cream. Ordinarily, we'd end up in bed, but Ethan doesn't know my period has finished, and for some reason I don't tell him. All I want tonight is this, the tender kisses, the caresses. Usually our closeness is defined through sex, but tonight there's something more.

"My parents have decided to visit England for Thanksgiving," Ethan says, switching off the news. "They're staying with some friends in Kensington and Mom wants Chelsea, Josh and I to come over for lunch. I'd like you to come."

"Oh," I say in surprise, twisting so I can see his face. There's something uncertain in his expression, and I realise he is nervous.

"Thanksgiving is on Thursday 26th. I thought we could take a couple of days off work, stay at mine in London."

"OK," I murmur against his lips.

"Good," he murmurs back, our lips touching in fleeting, delicate kisses. He moves so he is lying on his back on the sofa and pulls me on top of him. Our kiss intensifies, our tongues tangling. I can feel the twitching of his cock against me, and it fuels my own arousal. His fingers reach for the buttons of my pyjamas, making quick work of them, so that he can push the top off my shoulders, exposing my breasts. His hands cup them, squeezing, his finger and thumb rubbing and pulling at my hardening nipples. I slide a hand between our bodies, rubbing at the bulge in his suit trousers. I pull my lips away from his, breathless, gently kissing his cheek.

"I want you," I whisper in his ear. "Take me to bed."

He pulls my face back to his, his eyes burning. "I thought sex was off-limits."

"My period has finished," I say.

"Fuck." His tone is laced with pure need and he pulls me back into a rough kiss. His hand slides down my body, slipping into the waistband of my pyjamas. He slips a finger inside me, his thumb homing in on my clitoris, his kiss so intense it makes me feel lightheaded. His lips leave mine and I collapse against his shoulder. He wriggles beneath me, manoeuvring us slightly. His lips find the hollow of my neck and he sucks on the sensitive spot, his tongue teasing my skin.

"Ethan," I moan, as he pushes in a second finger, his thumb relentless against my throbbing clit. "Oh my God!" I close my eyes, the pleasure consuming my body.

"Open your eyes," he whispers, kissing my ear. "Look at me. I want to see you." My lids blink open as his fingers increase the pressure, their hard thrusts sending me over. His mouth captures my moan as I let the orgasm crash over me.

I'm vaguely aware of him rolling us precariously over on the sofa, and then he moves away, quickly undressing and pulling my pyjama bottoms off. He pulls me up by the hand, positioning me so my arms are resting on the back of the sofa, his hands sliding down to my hips, pulling me slowly onto his cock, filling me inch by hard inch. He pulls out and sinks back into me, repeating the motion, each thrust getting quicker and harder. His fingers dig into my skin as he sets up a pounding rhythm, our skin slapping together. I feel the warm tingling sensation in my lower stomach begin to build once more, loud noises spilling uncontrollably from my mouth as he fucks me to oblivion. Sensing how close I am, he moves a hand and circles my clitoris, slowly, precisely. We come together, my muscles tightening around him as he spurts deep inside, our moans of ecstasy unite, and we lose our minds to everything but each other.

Chapter Twenty-Six

"Sorry I took so long," I say, finding Ethan in the kitchen.

"Are you ready?" he asks tersely, his tone making me stop to stare across at him. "Rosie?" he snaps.

His mood had been fine before I'd left him to shower but there's a definite shift, and I can't place it. I go to him, slipping my arms around his waist, nuzzling into him. His arms grudgingly pull me closer, but there's something mechanical and cold about his touch, his arms feeling heavy around me, as if his action is automatic and lacks emotion. I blink up at him, his expression blank and unreadable.

"Are you OK?" I ask.

He cups my face in his hands and stares down at me, his eyes serious, penetrating to my very core. "Let's go to work," he replies, his lips touching mine quickly before he lets go and strolls towards the front door.

The journey to work is awkward, an odd atmosphere engulfing the car. The easy conversation we usually have on these journeys is absent, and there is a lack of the familiar touches: his hand doesn't rest on my leg, he doesn't reach across to stroke my arm as we wait at a red traffic light. Everything is off. His hands clutch the steering wheel, his eyes on the road, his jaw set in a hard line. I put a hand on his thigh and squeeze, shooting him a nervous smile. His muscle tenses under my touch, as if he is recoiling from me. Feeling slighted, I remove my hand and stare unseeingly out of the passenger window.

As has become customary, he drops me off on a quiet side street five minutes' walk away from work. He doesn't lean over to kiss me, and barely manages to say goodbye.

"You're coming to the fireworks tonight, right?" I ask, having subtly managed to get Will to ask Ethan, making Will think it had been his idea and not mine.

"I'm not sure."

"But Will said..." Disappointment flickers through me.

He sighs. "Go to work, Rosie."

I stare at him, desperately trying to understand his iciness towards me, but he gives nothing away, and as soon as I'm out of the car he accelerates, the Maserati disappearing around the corner. I straighten my dress, take in a deep breath, and make uncertain steps to the office.

"Morning," Libby greets me with a concerned smile. "You OK? You look a bit pale, are you sure you are well enough to be here?"

I shrug. "I'm fine. How are you?"

"Better. Sit down, I'll get you a cuppa."

"Thank you," I reply gratefully.

Will saunters over and perches on my desk. "So, I'm working a half-day today. Thought we could meet up before the fireworks?"

"Great, me too. Why don't you come to mine this afternoon. I have a flat viewing at 4pm, so come around some time after that. The Barretts are coming over later as well."

"I hope Jamie doesn't feel too awkward around Ethan," Will muses.

"I hadn't thought about that," I say, feeling shitty for Jamie.

"Ethan debriefed him," Will continues. "I think he was nicer than in the interview. Jamie seemed happier, anyway. How are you feeling?"

"Much better."

Libby returns with our drinks and we spend some time catching up, talking about how wiped out we had both felt with the horrible bug that is sweeping through most of Head Office. She grimaces as she glances at her monitor and curses something under her breath.

"What?" I whisper, catching her eye.

"Email from Ethan, demanding I arrange a Senior Manager meeting for 10am. I think he thinks I'm his PA now he's in charge."

I look away, the familiar awkward feeling snaking its way through my body. Libby detests Ethan, finding him egocentric and rude, and boy, she loves to bitch about him. I always try to deflect the conversation elsewhere, feeling like my silence is a betrayal of both of them.

My phone rings, giving me an out from Libby's burgeoning rant. The line crackles, and instinctively I know it is Roseman.

"You're going to pay, you stuck-up bitch," is all he purrs before he hangs up.

"Another call?" Libby asks, eyeing me with some concern.

I nod, replacing the receiver. "I need to call PC Kelly," I say, picking up my mobile and scrolling through my contacts. I update him, adding to the contact log. So far the emails, notes and calls have been untraceable, and it all feels so futile. I was surprised when Kelly answered on the second ring, used to getting his voicemail. He listens dutifully, sympathetically, and attempts to reassure me. I thank him and hang up, feeling a tingle of tension bunching inside my stomach. The leers, the rants, I can deal with those; but the calls where he threatens, asserts I am going to pay, these calls leave me feeling on edge. The fact that the police haven't been able to identify him in the last few months doesn't help matters. Their lack of concern is irritating, they don't even seem bothered. PC Kelly is nice enough, he says the right things, but my faith in him has dwindled as I listen to the platitudes that have heeded no results. I'm fed up with it all.

Ordinarily, after such calls, I'd find Ethan and would be comforted in his arms, his touch, his words reassuring me. But today I just stay at my desk, brooding about everything and nothing all at once. I go through the motions, beginning to collate recruitment data for analysis, pulling up exit interview sheets to ascertain trends for departing employees. I'm geeky, I usually love this type of work, but this morning my heart isn't in it.

At half past eleven I find myself outside Ethan's office, knocking tentatively. The need to see him has grown until I couldn't bear it any longer. He stares up at me as I enter, a look of surprise on his face. His eyes darken as they travel down my body, a lust-filled gaze taking hold as he eyes my curves in my figure-hugging navy jersey dress.

"Close the door and lock it." His voice is low but forceful. With shaking hands, I comply. He moves over to the window and closes the blind. He turns and stalks back to his desk and sits back down, pushing his chair out.

"Come here," he beckons, and with uncertainty I make my way to him. His hands reach for my hips and he pulls me so I collide with his knees. Again his eyes travel down my body, making me tremble under their intensity. There's something off about him, a detachment combined with something darker, a volatility I haven't seen in him before. Standing, he turns me, a hand gently pushing at the centre of my back, pushing me down across his desk. My eyes widen as he pulls up my dress, bunching it around my hips, sliding my tights and underwear down my legs.

"Ethan," I gasp in shocked protest.

"I need this," he replies hoarsely, and I hear the zip of his trousers. There's something about him that stops me arguing, doesn't try to stop him from plunging hard, deep into me. We've never fucked in the office before, I'd never been comfortable with it, needing to keep a semblance of professionalism. We've kissed in this office, long, seductive snogging sessions, but it was as if there was an unspoken line that he had known not to cross.

He thrusts hard, long harsh strokes, his fingers digging into my hips as he powers again and again into me. There's nothing tender about this, and I know for the first time with him I'm not going to come, I'm not going to be pushed over into the world of pleasure that he always takes me to. No, this is just sex, uncompromising, an angry, punishing fuck. I consider stopping him, but as he pushes into me over and over, relentlessly, I find myself unable to move, unable to think straight. Even though this doesn't feel right, doesn't feel like us, it doesn't feel wrong enough to stop it. His body crashes against mine, and I hold my breath as I feel his release deep inside me. A single teardrop escapes, splashing onto the desk, and I'm consumed by an overwhelming feeling of cheapness. I scrunch my eyes closed as he pulls out of me. I hear his zip, but still, I'm frozen to the spot. I tense as he uses a tissue to wipe me. A switch flicks, and finally I find the strength to move, to push him away and to pull up my underwear and tights, straightening my dress.

“You will never do that to me again,” I say, my voice shaky. On unsteady legs I cross the room, unlock the door and leave, not looking back, scared of what I will see.

I sit on the toilet seat, trying to gain some composure. I'm angry and devastated all at the same time. How could he? Why did I let him? Why didn't I tell him to stop? The questions carousel around my head, on and on, spiralling without any answers. I sink my fingernails into my lower lip, a trickle of blood at the corner of my mouth jolting me back to reality. I blink rapidly, my breathing slowly calming.

When this had started back in the Summer, I had been panicked about feeling cheap, worried that fucking him would make me feel worthless. He had known that, he had made assurances, and unconsciously I had pushed away my fears, I'd trusted him. I'd stopped preoccupying myself with the troublesome thoughts as time had gone on, and I had believed him. Today, just now, he'd shattered it all. I'd felt like a hollow vessel as his cock had pounded into me, disconnected from him. I want to go back upstairs to have it out with him, to find out what his problem is, but I don't. Instead I return to my desk, feeling jolted, and pretend to work.

My mobile buzzes and I pick it up to read the text from Tristan: ‘I found my wallet.’

I text back, ‘What?’

He replies immediately. ‘My wallet, I found it.’

Confused, I hit call and wander into the empty kitchen.

“Hi.” He answers on the first ring.

“I didn't know you'd lost your wallet,” I say, smiling at Will as he comes in to make a cup of coffee.

“Oh, did your new boyfriend not tell you?” There's a sneer to Tristan's tone.

“What? When?” I ask.

“This morning. I came round this morning. Didn't he tell you? You were in the shower. I thought it might have fallen out of my pocket yesterday, and as I was passing...”

“Right,” I reply, the pieces clicking into place. “Just call me next time. In fact, you know what, make sure there isn't a next time.” I end the call, dropping my mobile onto the side with a clatter, a hand going to my forehead in realisation and exasperation. I hadn't told Ethan about Tristan's visit: he had asked, and I hadn't told him. Tristan showing up this morning, making it obvious he had visited yesterday, would definitely rile Ethan, and explains the moodiness. Shit, fuck, why hadn't I just told him?

“What's wrong?” asks Will.

“Nothing.” I shrug. “Just give me a hug.”

“Any time.” He squeezes me into a bearhug, something I love about him. Will is one of those friends who give amazing, wonderful hugs that just make things seem so much better than they actually are.

“Am I interrupting?” a far-too-familiar drawl asks. Will doesn't let go, and I leave my face buried against his chest, not wanting to see the man at the door.

“No,” replies Will unabashedly, and I love him for that.

“Something’s come up in London,” Ethan tells Will.

“OK. I'm off soon anyway, I’ve got a half-day. See you this evening, though.”

“Great.” I hear him turn, and sneak a glance at his departing back. “As you were,” he says over his shoulder, an unmistakable tinge of condemnation to his voice that I know is completely lost on Will and totally aimed at me.

I wriggle out of Will's arms, quickly saying goodbye and that I will see him at my flat later. Then I stride purposefully across the office, out into the corridor and to the door at the end. I don't even bother knocking, just fling the door open and march in. Surprise flickers across Ethan’s face momentarily, before he irons out his expression to something more neutral.

“Did you forget to tell me that Tristan came by this morning?” I shoot at him abruptly.

“Did you forget to mention he came by yesterday?” he retorts harshly, his large frame crowding me against the closed door. “I told you right from the start, no games.”

“And I told you I didn't want to be screwed over your desk like a cheap fuck,” I fire back.

I watch him step back, I see his expression falter, a troubled look flashing across his face.

“Oh, was it not good for you?” he asks harshly. “Did you feel cheated I didn't make you come?” he growls, his eyes darkening.

“You think I'm playing games,” I accuse, glaring up at him.

“You lied!”

“No,” I interrupt forcefully. “You asked me a question, did Tristan come round, and I would have told you, but your phone rang and then I forgot. I didn't make an active choice to not tell you, it just wasn't important enough for me to remember. What you've done is so much worse!”

“Don't get hysterical,” he patronises. “I wanted you, and you weren't exactly complaining, so don't act so prim and proper.”

“You're a bastard, Ethan.”

“I've been called worse.”

“You're not even sorry?” I stumble over my words.

“You deceived me,” he says in a deadly low voice.

“So what, you fucked me hard over your desk like some cheap bitch because what, you wanted to punish me? To teach me a lesson?”

“I told you, I don't think of you as cheap,” he says.

“Well, I felt cheap.”

“No.” He shakes his head. “You felt wronged, deprived.”

I glare up at him, his expression serious, his eyes sparkling in that self-assured way only he has. “I don't like you right now,” I say, my voice quiet.

"But you still want me,” he drawls.

I try to push him away, but before I know it my hands stop pushing at his chest and slide upwards as he lowers his head and kisses me. His lips are gentle, his kiss sweet, leisurely. My mouth opens to his tongue, and I lose myself to his seduction and I don’t like myself for it.

“What did Tristan want?” Ethan asks, pulling away and staring me straight in the eye.

“He wanted me,” I answer.

Ethan's expression darkens again, his eyes stormy. “And what did you say?” he asks, and I can tell the control to his voice is forced.

“You know what I said,” I shrug. “I told him I was with you.”

“That you’re mine?” I know I shouldn't indulge this possessiveness, but belonging to Ethan is oddly addictive. I want to be his, I like being his.

“Yes,” I whisper.

He glances down at his watch and curses. “Sweetheart, I've got to go.” He kisses me hard on the mouth, a fleeting kiss that leaves me wanting more.

“I still don't like you,” I say, scared he may have broken something.

“I don’t like me either right now,” he replies.

Chapter Twenty-Seven

Annoyed that at three o'clock the estate agent calls to cancel the viewing, I decide to take my frustration out on the pavement through a quick, fast run. It's cold, the air burning into my lungs as my feet pound angrily, determinedly, music blaring through my earbuds. I run 3K, a shorter run than I'm used to, but faster. I feel the burn of exertion in my legs, adrenaline propelling me onwards, the buzz dispersing the anger, replacing it with a heady euphoria. Pumped, I complete the block route and head for a hot shower.

I'm in the process of drying my hair, sitting on my bed in my fluffy dressing gown, when I'm dragged from my thoughts by the doorbell. I glance at my watch to see it is just past four, and curse Will for uncharacteristically being early. I open the door and before I have a chance to react, a hand slaps hard over my mouth and I'm pushed backwards.

"Do not make a sound," the male voice hisses, his breath a noxious haze of stale alcohol. It happens so quickly: one moment I'm opening the door, then the next second I'm pushed forcefully up against the wall. The clicking sound of the door closing jolts me from the state of shock and I look up into his face, a flash of recognition hitting me. I know him. I'm one of those people that very rarely forgets a face, and instantly I know where I have met this man before, and I know that it is him who has been calling me. This crazy-eyed tramp is Roseman.

His brown hair is tousled, laced with a layer of grease, his leather jacket and jeans tattered, his complexion a jaundiced yellow. My nostrils are affronted by the hideous smell of body odour and booze.

"Get off me!" I struggle, pushing his hand off my mouth. "What do you want?" I ask, trying to control the tremble in my tone. I mustn't let this piece of shit know I'm scared, my brain clamours, I must try to assert some control.

Roseman had interviewed for an IT Developer position in the Summer; in July I think, on a particularly hot day. Drew and I had interviewed him and his putrid smell had filled the room, making it difficult to be able to concentrate on the interview itself. Roseman had arrived wearing an old suit, his shirt having a stain just under the collar, instantly a black mark against his name. I have a bit of a thing about people being well groomed and presentable, brown stains and BO don't cut it for me.

On first impressions I'd felt sorry for him, it was obvious he was in a bad way, but then he spoke, and any sympathy quickly evaporated. It was obvious by the way he spoke that he felt call centre work was beneath him. He had openly leered at me, his eyes hungrily settling on my breasts, where they pretty much had remained for the entire interview. I had felt uncomfortable, and I remember saying so to Drew when he had left, as we both sprayed the room manically with air fresheners, that he had weirded me out. What I had seen then was someone who had wandered off the path, someone who needed a bit of help to get back on track; but now he doesn't look like he's just veered off the path, he looks like he's fucking plummeted off a cliff. His eyes are spheres of crazy, his body now pushing hard against mine.

"Barry, isn't it?" I say placatingly, trying to squeeze to the right and out of his grasp.

"You remember my name?" he slurs, intoxication evident in his tone.

I nod and try to smile. Boozy BO Barry. Drew and I had joked about him being the worst interviewee we'd ever had. "I interviewed you," I concentrate on my words, trying to swallow down the nausea and fear, focusing on the pretence of having the situation under control. "You've been calling me, sending me flowers, notes."

"I hate women like you," he spits, my words not seeming to register with him. I flinch, his saliva splattering against my cheek, making me recoil into the wall, as I wipe it away with my sleeve. He registers my disgust and grabs me by the shoulders. "You prissy little bitch! Judging me, thinking you're so much better than me. I needed that fucking job, you whore," and he slaps me hard on my cheek, a stinging sensation that morphs into a burn.

Fight or flight, fight or flight, the words reverberate through my aching skull, fight or flight. I'm caged in by him, so flight isn't a viable option, but as his clammy hand reaches inside my dressing gown, I fight!

"Get off me!" I push hard against his chest, pulling at his arm, detesting the way his clammy, pudgy hand feels against my bare skin. I lift my knee and aim, but he just laughs, a manic sneering laugh that sends a shiver of dread through me. His laugh is deranged, a horribly low chortle; his eyes are wild, and I know that he is either on drugs or having a psychotic episode, neither boding well for me. He uses my foot off the ground to his advantage, tripping me so that I fall awkwardly. We tumble together, rolling, our limbs entwined in a chaotic mess as we struggle to get the upper hand. He manages to bash the side of my head against the corner of the doorframe; it hurts, blood trickling down my cheek, my vision blurring momentarily. He takes advantage of the situation, pushing me down onto my stomach, his body covering mine, pushing me hard into the carpet.

"My wife threw me out because I didn't get your lousy job," he says. "You ruined me, you pretty little tart, and now I'm going to ruin you. I'm going to fuck up your life, just like you fucked up mine. And," he leans into my ear, "God, I'm going to enjoy it." I try to push him off but his sixteen stone bulk seems immovable, the pressure of his weight bearing down on me, making it difficult to even breathe.

"Barry, please!" My voice isn't calm any more, it's desperate, pleading, as his hand roughly pulls up my dressing gown, exposing my bare skin. I've never felt as vulnerable, as scared as I do when I feel his sweaty palm slide over my skin, up the back of my thigh and he continues to tell me how he is going to screw me and make me suffer. For a moment, I'm stuck motionless, my face down on the carpet, inhaling the Shake 'n' Vac, I'm paralysed. My consciousness detaches itself from reality, propelling me back to this morning with Ethan, the sex that had felt wrong, and there's a clarity suddenly: it was consensual, he had been pissed off at me, but it hadn't been wrong, not like this is. Barry is talking about raping me and if I don't try to stop him he is going to succeed. It takes his hand forcefully trying to pull my legs apart for me to snap out of the passive rigidity and I realise I need to fight him, I need to try ...

I try to buck him off and then we begin to fight, a messy bundle of limbs, of being grabbed, of getting free, of being grabbed again. We tussle, it feels like forever, on and on, his words incessant, nasty vile sickening words about me and what he wants to do. At some point I'm aware of a noise and realise it's me and I'm screaming and he's trying to clamp a hand over my mouth. He is everywhere, the smell of him making me lightheaded and nauseous. It feels never-ending and it feels inescapable, I can feel myself getting tired and if anything the fighting seems to be turning him on even more. I scrunch my eyes shut, wanting to block him out, his look of utter hatred for me. He tells me I'm the worst thing to ever happen to him and that he is going to make sure he's the worst thing that ever happens to me.

And then, through the madness, I hear a voice, a glimmer of hope. I see the letterbox flip up.

I stop screaming, the air now punctuated by the sound of my door being kicked again and again. Barry, Roseman, seems oblivious, his mind set on taking me. I concentrate on struggling and listen to the comforting sound of the kick, kick, kick, knowing that help is on the way. Kick, and then there's no more kicking... There's cold air, the smell of bonfires on the breeze, and there's male shouts, and then his weight is lifted off me and I just lie there, my eyes squeezed shut as I am consumed by shock.

Roseman, I remember, had most recently worked on a website for a florist. The roses had been a clue and I'd completely missed it.

Chapter Twenty-Eight

The next few hours blend into a surreal chaos, my mind unable to focus, detaching itself from my body, from reality. I'm cognisant of the events unfolding around me, I participate in conversation, but none of it feels real. It's like I'm a voyeur, peeking in and watching this awful thing happen to someone else. There had been shouts, several male voices, and the weight of Barry had been dragged off me. I'd been surprised to see the Barretts with Will, remember calling out to Olly, who was about to punch Barry in the face, to stop. The sound of heavy breathing punctuated the silence, adrenaline thick in the air. I'd looked over to Barry, stared straight into chillingly vacant eyes, no sense of emotion whatsoever resonant. Feeling sick, I'd slowly sat, stood, straightened my dressing gown and crept away to huddle on the sofa. Will had sat next to me, and I remember the look on his face as I flinched as he had gone to put a comforting arm around me. His expression was open, a concoction of shock, horror, anger, and sadness. It was a look that confirmed that he knew I was hurt, that this horrible episode would leave an imprint on me forever.

One of the twins must have called the police because they arrived and took Barry away. He made no sound as he left, in fact he hadn't made a noise since the door had burst open, and I had this odd thought that he shared this feeling of not really being in the present, just like I felt.

Calmly I'd answered questions, recounting what had happened. A female officer had led the interview, her Irish accent having a gentle lilt, which was reassuring and soothing. She was calm, controlled, patient, and she made it all somehow bearable. Bizarrely, I felt like I could trust her with every sickening detail of what he said, of what I thought he was going to do to me.

I got dressed in a daze and Will came in the police car with me to the station, the Barretts following to give their own statements. Everyone was kind, not rushing me, but it felt like I'd never answered so many questions. At times it felt like I was being cross-examined for something I'd done and I just wanted it all to go away. I told them about the contact he had been making through calls and notes, told them he had specifically gone out of his way to hurt me, had been watching me for over two months. I was checked over, initially not wanting to be when I arrived, answered more questions and then I was allowed to leave.

"What will happen to him?" I asked with concern. "What if he comes back?"

"He won't be able to get to you and we'll update you tomorrow. Your friend's outside," the Irish policewoman had told me, leading me through the door. "Rosie, you've done really well. I know that wasn't easy but coming here straight away gives us the best chance of being able to capture evidence to help us make a prosecution."

Will was on the phone when I entered, my attention immediately captured as I heard him say Ethan's name. He turned to face me as I pushed open the door.

"She's here now. OK, I'll pass her over." Will lowers his mobile and mouths, "It's Ethan," before handing me the phone. Tentatively I raise it to my ear and take in a deep breath.

"Hi." it's the only thing I can think to say.

"Rosie," his voice crackles down the line, the reception poor. "I'll be with you in two minutes. Stay there, I'm coming to get you."

"OK." I return the mobile to Will and head towards the main door, desperate to get some air. It's cold outside, there's a slight breeze with a frosty bite to it. It feels good. I breathe in, long lungfuls, fireworks screeching and banging in the distance.

"We were supposed to meet the others and go to the display," I remember as Will joins me, standing beside me, his hands in his coat pockets.

"The twins let everyone know."

"What did they say?" I turn on him.

"Just that you'd been hurt, no details. Ethan called me, sounded crazy, he made me tell him where we were. He was worried, I think."

"What did you tell him?" I ask, staring down at the ground.

"The same, that you'd been hurt. I told him it was fine, that he didn't need to come, that you could stay with me, but he was intent on knowing where we were. I'm sorry, have I done the wrong thing?"

"No! I want him here."

I'm about to explain everything to Will, when I hear the roar of an engine on the breeze and the Maserati speeds around the corner, the headlights illuminating the darkness. The door flies open and Ethan jumps out, his eyes wild, his demeanour one of utter fury. His expression crumples when he sees me.

"Please don't touch me," I back away as he reaches for me. "I need to get clean. Can you take me to Tranquillity?"

"Sure," Ethan falters, and I know that he has no idea what to say or do. A feeling of dirtiness punctures my shell of numbness, the need to wash myself overwhelming. I take in a deep breath, fighting down the nausea and concentrating on feeling nothing again. The walls of the protective bubble cocoon me once more, giving me the strength to thank Will, to assure him I'll be fine with Ethan, and to head to the car.

"I don't want to talk," I say as Ethan gets in. "Can you just drive?" He nods, reverses, and accelerates, the force flinging me back against the seat. I scrunch my eyes shut, my fists clenched, resting in my lap. I concentrate on breathing, in out, in out, and disconnect from everything else.

Feeling begins to return with a jolt when I step into the lift and catch sight of my reflection in the mirror. The left side of my face is puffy with swelling already, my hair a mess, blood matted in a clump of hair just above my ear. I see myself pale in the reflection and tentatively I put my hand up to touch the bruised skin.

“It's not that bad,” Ethan reassures, as I find myself stepping back against him in shock. “Can I?” he asks.

“Please?” I whisper shakily, turning into him.

He holds me like I'm a porcelain doll that he's terrified of breaking. I know he's being cautious, gentle, and I love him for that, my heart twisting in my chest. Less is more, less is what I need from him right now. His touch is light, but it's there.

When we get to his suite I head straight for the bathroom.

“I need to be on my own,” I say, putting my hand up to stop him from following me in.

He looks hurt, a tortured expression flashing across his face, and I witness the effort it takes for him to replace it with something more neutral. He nods and bends down to kiss the tip of my nose. I smile weakly at his sweetness, comforted by his fleeting touch, but relieved it wasn't too much. I close the door, lock it and undress.

The beginnings of bruises show on my left shoulder and breast, finger marks apparent. There's a red patch to one side of my stomach, which looks like a friction burn, and I recall the sting as he had dragged me across the carpet as we fought. I inhale deeply and step inside the shower cubicle.

The water is hot, a scorching heat bordering on painful. I like it, need it, because for the first time since it has happened I feel something other than empty. I clean myself meticulously, rubbing the fragrant body wash into my sore, bruised skin. As I clean in between my legs an anger begins to bubble deep within me. Again, and again, I lather body wash across my intimate skin, rinsing the bubbles away, his words whirling around my head, the awful things he said he was going to do to me.

I return to the bedroom and dress, having started to leave outfits here and in Ethan's flat in Knightsbridge. We'd both started entwining our lives together, our belongings filtering into each other's personal spaces. It felt natural, so right that we hadn't needed to discuss it. Right now, I'm thankful for this, glad of my things, glad that being here feels right.

It's really late, but I put on a pair of jeans and a soft woollen pink jumper, not wanting to go to bed. I towel dry my hair, brushing out the knots, and stare at myself in the large mirror. The side of my eye is puffy, my cut is an angry line of soreness, but apart from that I look completely normal. I pull up my top and run my fingers down the friction burn that is forming on my stomach, my skin red and painful to touch. I stand and stretch, aware of a tightness in my shoulders, knowing that in the morning I am going to really feel it.

I stand motionless, listening to the sound of faraway bangs and screeches of the fireworks. It's odd, being conscious of your surroundings, what is going on around you, but somehow not feeling part of it. Everything is hazy, sound audible, but as if it is travelling through cotton wool before reaching my eardrums. A muffled noise reaches me, voices, Josh and Ethan. I focus, listening through the door to Josh telling Ethan to call him if he needs anything, then Ethan saying goodbye and closing the door. I'm touched that Josh must have come to check up on us, but relieved Ethan has had the foresight to send him away.

I take in a deep breath and try to prepare myself for what comes next.

Chapter Twenty-Nine

"Hey." Ethan crosses the room as I step out of the bedroom and gathers me against him. He holds me gently, a hand rubbing my back. "You OK? Can I get you anything?"

"This is good," I murmur, sliding my arms around his waist. "It's been a horrible day."

He cups my chin and slowly tilts my face so that he can stare searchingly into my eyes. I wonder what he sees: does he see the hollowness and numbness? His jaw sets into a hard line as he tentatively trails a finger to my cut, before he leans down to place the gentlest of kisses to the sore skin. His expression is a mixture of unbridled rage, combined with a layer of sorrowful pain, the ache clear in his beautiful blue eyes.

"Are you angry?" I ask.

"Yes."

"With me?"

"Hey, no!" he exclaims, his expression softening. "Of course not. How could you think that?"

I shrug. "I should have come back here, like you wanted." He kisses the top of my head reassuringly and leads me to a sofa, where he pulls me down onto his lap. I snuggle against him, soaking him in, his embrace sending warmth through my icy veins.

Ethan is a protector, sometimes bordering on overly possessive, and I've rebelled against him, needing my independence, needing him to recognise this as a quality of mine rather than to try to control it. And he has; sometimes he's fought me on it, but he's also known which battles to step away from. Letting me stay at home over the last few days had been one of those battles – he'd stated his thoughts, but he'd respected my decision in his own way. Had he been right to? Should he have insisted? Would I have listened? Of course he had been right, because there was no way I would have buckled to his will. Although Ethan is bloody-minded, he's not controlling, there's a line I don't think he'd cross. But he had been right and I'd been wrong... I relax into his hold, feeling safe against his muscular body, my head resting against his chest as I listen to his heartbeat, the baboom-baboom sound comforting me. I need him to be that protector now.

"I'm glad I'm with you," I murmur.

"Good." the corner of his mouth twitches into a slight smile. "I'm not going anywhere."

"I was right. I did know him."

"Who was he?" Ethan asks quietly.

"Drew and I interviewed him back in the Summer." I swallow. "We didn't give him the job. In the interview he mentioned that he had worked on designing the website for a local florist. The roses were a clue."

"Fuck!" He exhales and squeezes me tighter.

"Ouch!"

Ethan's hold immediately loosens and concern flickers across his face. "Did he really hurt you?" he asks fearfully.

"We fought..." I trail off.

"Rosie," he shifts me slightly and I catch a glimpse of his uncertainty, "I don't want to rush you, but I do need to know exactly what happened. When you're ready, OK?"

"I know," I nod. "But can we just do this for a bit longer? I'm not ready to go over it again, not with you."

It's the last bit of that sentence that frightens me the most. It had been horrible going over the details with the police, but the thought of having to tell Ethan is gut-wrenchingly awful. I stand and wander into the kitchen, open the fridge and retrieve a bottle of white wine. I pour myself a large glass, noticing Ethan's half glass of whisky on the table. I take a huge glug, the coldness slipping down my throat, jarring the shell, sensation slowly cracking through as the alcohol fizzes through my body. I drink again, a sudden craving to get absolutely wasted taking hold. I want to obliterate everything, to reduce myself to an alcohol-induced fuck-up where nothing will matter.

"That isn't going to help." He takes the bottle from my hand and puts it back in the fridge before putting my empty glass in the sink.

"It might," I object, opening the fridge again and reaching for the bottle.

"Rosie!" His arm circles me from behind as he tries to pull me away from the booze. It's the man behind me that does it, splinters the shell of numbness, emotions crowding in on me all at once.

"Get off me!" I push backwards, my voice panicked. "Don't!"

I run, only just making it in time to the toilet, where I vomit. I lean over the bowl, my body wracked with waves of nausea, my throat stinging as stomach acid lurches up my oesophagus and bile burns its way down my nose. I heave over and over again, my stomach muscles sore from the exertion. Somewhere mid-vomit, I'm aware of Ethan crouching behind me and holding my hair back.

"You done?" he asks quietly as the retching subsides. I nod and he hands me some tissue to dab my mouth and wipe my nose with.

I stumble to my feet and go to rinse my mouth out and brush my teeth. I look ghostlike in the mirror, my skin drained of colour, my eyes large and spooked.

"I need to get clean," I say.

"You've only just showered."

"I can still feel him," I say breathlessly, anxiety taking hold, my throat constricting as I'm whirled back onto my carpet, Roseman's body crushing me. "I need a shower. Can you go?"

"I'm not leaving you," he says uncompromisingly. "We'll shower together."

"I can't..."

"Rosie." His tone is razor-sharp and drags me back to the present, to me and him. "Look at me." His voice softens. "I need you to trust me now, can you do that?"

I bite my lip. Can I? Crunch time: can I trust him? I want to... He frees my lower lip from my teeth and stoops down to kiss me. His lips are warm and tender against mine and I find myself melting against him, my arms clinging around his waist as his kiss soothes me. Kissing, I think, is something Roseman hasn't ruined for me. I find refuge in that kiss, its tenderness simultaneously calming and breaking me.

"You need to trust that I know what you need." He rests his forehead against mine. "Getting drunk will not make this go away and it won't make you feel better. You need to tell me what happened, and you need to trust me enough to let me in."

"I'm scared," I whisper.

"You don't need to be, not any more. Trust me." I stare into imploring eyes, and I know that I can trust him with this. I inhale a deep breath and with my eyes fixed to the tiled floor I recount every detail. He listens, waiting when I'm silent, not rushing me. I feel his restraint in those pauses, his muscles knotting into acute anticipation. His fingers run through my wet hair, working out the tangles slowly and systematically. I sense his hurt as I describe the assault, and illogically it helps, as if the burden is being shared between us now, and that it's not just suffocating me any more. I don't know if that is selfish, but Ethan hurting for me makes me feel slightly better and consolidates the trust I have for him.

When I have finished, he tilts my face up and stares down at me, angry sorrow clouding his gaze. We're silent, locked in our own thoughts, trying to figure out the next move.

"I need to shower," I say finally. "I can still feel him on me."

"I don't want to leave you," he says quietly. "I will if you need me to. But I don't want you to do this on your own."

"I thought he was going to rape me," I whisper.

"I know," his voice is just above a whisper. "I'll go if you want me to, we'll do whatever you want, OK? But I need you to know that I'm here."

He goes to turn on the shower and I watch him nervously, remaining motionless, a blend of embarrassment and humiliation spreading over me. The thought of him seeing me naked, touching me, it's too much, but the thought of him not is killing me. I'm torn and I'm scared.

"I don't know what to do," I say shakily.

"It's ok. There's no rush. If you want me to go, then I'll wait for you next door. We'll do whatever you want."

I don't want him to go, I decide, I never want him to go. "I need to be with you."

"Ok. Get undressed and let's shower together."

I step back, blinking rapidly, my pulse accelerating. I feel dizzy, the steam from the shower making everything foggy.

"I don't want you to see me how I feel!" I say.

"What does that mean?" He seems confused, and I'm confused too.

"Damaged, dirty!" I choke out. "He touched me, his hands were all over me! I was scared I wasn't going to be able to stop him..."

"Rosie." His voice is reassuring, his tone hypnotic, and I don't fight him when he pulls me into his arms. "I would never make you do anything you didn't want to, you know that, and if you really don't want to then we won't as I just said, I can go next door and wait. But we're just going to wash, that's it, OK? I just don't like the thought of you doing this alone. I'm not going to think differently of you."

"You already do." His eyes follow my gaze to his jeans, where uncharacteristically there is no bulge. "See, you don't want me."

He sighs wearily, his expression hardening. "You don't want me to see you naked – do you really think that I'd think you'd want sex? If I'm not aroused right now it's because you're hurting, not because I don't want you, or because I see you differently. I don't!" His eyes blaze as he cups my face, preventing me from looking away. "Right now you don't need me fucking you, but if you did, trust me, I would. What you need right now is to let me see you, so you don't keep worrying about what I'm going to think, because all I'm going to think is that I want to kill the bastard who did this to you. I'm not going to think differently about you, I'm not going to find you less attractive or less desirable. Now trust me."

His outburst is the Ethan I love: uncompromising, confident, his conviction is contagious. He's right, if he doesn't see me now then I'll just be prolonging the inevitable and worrying for longer. Tentatively I start to remove my top and see the exact moment his eyes register the finger-marks on my chest. I cross my arms, trying to hide the beginnings of bruises, and step backwards.

"Hey, don't do that!" he says quietly, pulling my arms to my sides. "Are you sore?"

"A little bit."

We slowly get undressed, Ethan taking his cues from me, and I let him guide me into the large shower cubicle. The hot water feels good, as it had the first time I had showered. For a long time, we just stand together under the jets, saying nothing, just holding hands. He trails a finger across the marks, then down to the angry friction burn on my stomach. There's comfort in his touch, and I find myself relaxing as I let him rub body wash over me.

"Ethan." I grab at his wrist as his hand moves lower. "I'm not ready for that," I say.

He nods, seeming to understand that touching me between my legs is off limits for now.

When we get out of the shower and dry, Ethan produces some arnica cream from the bathroom cabinet, which he carefully rubs into my bruises. There's something so tender in the way he is looking after me that it warrants a slight smile.

"What?" He notices and raises an eyebrow.

"Thank you." I stand on tiptoes and briefly kiss him. "You've been amazing. It feels right being here with you."

"Good." His eyes sparkle. "It feels right you being here."

A warmth floods my body. Even though it has been one of the most horrendous days of my life, this gorgeous man knows how to make me feel better. Today has been really shitty, and he's here, he hasn't bailed on me. He's been my rock, the person to lean on, and I know that has to mean something. I might not know what exactly it means, but it's more, I'm definite about that.

Chapter Thirty

"You are fucking joking!" explodes Ethan, making me jump.

"I know this isn't what you want to hear," the Irish police officer says quietly, "but I need to be honest with you. We haven't yet been able to link him to the phone calls and the letters, but I promise you we are investigating. At the moment he is still being psychologically assessed and it is just going to take time. We need to get his side of the story, see what he says happened. It's just a process and I know it's upsetting."

I nod, acceptance on my face. He'll be diagnosed with some mental illness, I don't know why I hadn't considered this scenario sooner. I'd seen his eyes, the vacancy, of course he'd be deemed to be suffering from a depressive or psychotic episode.

"So what, you do nothing?"

"Rosie, we are taking this seriously."

"I thought he was going to rape me," I say, my voice sounding stronger than I feel. "He came into my home..."

"And we will deal with it, but we need to follow the correct process so we can get you the right outcome."

I stand, seeing no point in discussing the matter further, and they all follow my lead. The police officers head towards the door and I see them out.

"How are you so calm?" Ethan follows me into the kitchen, crowding me against a work surface.

"What do you want me to do?" I glare up at him.

"Be angry, sad, cry, scream, just something!"

"I can't," I reply quietly.

"Yes you can!" he urges.

I sigh and let him draw me into a protective embrace. He's been amazingly calm, gentle, reassuring. I'd been scared to come back to my flat, to be in the place where it happened, but somehow I'd made it across the threshold, comforted and encouraged by his presence, his arm around me, holding me close.

"I'm not ready, Ethan," I mumble into his chest. I feel his muscles tense, then relax as he regains composure.

"OK." He relents, stroking a hand up and down my back.

"Are you sure it's OK to stay with you?" I ask nervously.

"Of course it is. I want you with me." The doorbell makes me flinch, the sound triggering a memory from yesterday. I'd been expecting Will then too, I realise in panic.

"You're safe," Ethan kisses my mouth fleetingly. "It's Will and Chloe. I'll get it. You stay here."

I hear their familiar voices at the door and the next moment Chloe is darting into the kitchen and squeezing me into a hug.

"Are you OK?" she asks, finally letting me go and surveying me.

"I will be. Ethan's been looking after me. Will," I cross to where he is standing awkwardly and wrap my arms around him, mouthing "thank you" in his ear. He does what he does best and hugs me tight.

"Ethan, hey?" he whispers into my ear. I can sense his cheeky grin.

Ethan clears his throat. "Drink, anyone? Rosie, are you going to pack?"

Will releases me and I head to my room, followed by Chloe.

"I can't be here," I explain. "Ethan said I could stay with him."

"You can always stay with me," she offers.

"I know, thank you. I want to be with him," I admit quietly.

"You sure?" I nod. "Did he hurt you badly?" she asks. "Will hasn't been great with the details."

We sit together on my bed, clasping hands, and I tell her everything. Her expressions and reactions mirror Ethan's last night, and I know they both hurt because I've been hurt.

"I was so lucky Will and the Barrett twins showed up when they did," I conclude.

"I don't know what to say."

I shrug. "I know. It could have been worse."

"I guess, but it's still horrible." Chloe chews her lower lip.

"How were the fireworks?" I ask and start packing a suitcase, adding to my belongings that are already resident at Tranquillity. I smile as Chloe recounts the evening.

"Josh is nice," Chloe says.

I spin around and catch a far-off look in her eye. "He is lovely," I wink.

"Don't look at me like that," she shrugs. "He's too nice for me. He's much nicer than his brother. And God, you were so right about Chelsea, she's such a bitch! Self-obsessed witch. She's just vile, the epitome of American spoilt brat. Having said that, Will seemed to like her."

“Oh no!” I shudder. Chelsea, I realise, is the type of beautiful woman that magnetises Will. How could I have thought letting them meet would be a good idea?

“You need to call Charlie,” Chloe interrupts my thoughts. “He was really worried about you.”

“I texted him earlier.”

“Are you sure you couldn't make yourself fancy him?” grumbles Chloe as she holds down the lid on my case while I battle with the zip. “He'd worship you. He wouldn't hide your relationship from anyone.”

“Don't! I want Ethan, you know I do.”

“I know,” she wrinkles her nose.

“He's been great since it happened.”

“I know,” she says again. “Will said he sounded demented with worry when he told him.”

“Is Will cross I didn't tell him?”

She shakes her head. “Surprised, but happy for you. He likes Ethan, a lot. I think he approves.”

“I wish you would,” I sigh.

“He's OK,” relents Chloe. “And I'm glad he's looking after you now.”

We return to the kitchen to find Will and Ethan huddled together looking over something on Ethan's phone.

“Drew will do most of the talking, but I'd appreciate it if you would go along with him.”

“Of course,” Will enthuses.

“I've emailed you the contract. They'll try and fuck us over with the SLAs, go in with the template version, then you can negotiate, but don't promise anything more than this version; this is really what we'd agree to, but they don't need to know that. You never know, you might be able to get us a better deal.”

“Won't they mind you not being there?”

“Probably.” Ethan drops his phone on the table and slaps Will on the shoulder as he gets up. “William, I'm trusting you to charm them.”

“Thanks for coming into school last week.” Chloe accepts a cup of coffee from Ethan. “You made quite an impression.”

“Really?”

"You know you did. Will you come back in the Spring term? Or maybe your brother could come?"

Ethan raises an eyebrow. "You'll have to ask him, won't you?"

"The twins say 'hi'," Will says as I sit next to him.

"I spoke to Jamie before the police came round. I take it Ethan has updated you?"

"It's ridiculous," Will says. "But they will charge him, they can't not. We saw him."

"I hope you're right. Can you let the twins know what is happening?"

I drink my coffee, occasionally adding a comment to their conversation. Chloe and Ethan snipe at each other, but it's harmless, amusing to watch. Will and Ethan have a genuine liking for each other, which pleases me. I will, of course, need to have a private chat with Will about Ethan and me, but I feel certain he'll be happy for us. Their words drift in and out of my consciousness as my mind begins to wander. This flat, my haven, is no more. I'd hated coming back here today, I hate being here now, and I know I'll never sleep here again, that I'll spend as little time here as possible.

The sound of scraping chairs jolts me and I realise that Will and Chloe are preparing to leave.

"Look after her," orders Chloe.

"I will," Ethan promises.

"Come here," beckons Ethan when he returns to the kitchen, having seen my friends out. I snuggle against him. "I've spoken to Drew, explained the situation, I've told him we're taking some time off. He's going to tell Libby what happened, and she is going to think you've gone to stay with your nan for a few days. You're not ready to go back to work on Monday, and I don't want to leave you."

"You can't just drop everything because of me."

"I can do what I want, I'm in charge, remember? Don't try and fight me on this, Rosie, it's non-negotiable. This is important, I need to be with you."

I agree with a nod. I need him to be with me now more than he'll ever know.

Chapter Thirty-One

Zeus sniffs at a tree trunk, his tail wagging slowly, before he saunters to the next tree and starts the manic sniffing once more. Apart from a gallop after a squirrel, Zeus has shown no sign of urgency, happy to lollop his way around the lake with us. Occasionally, he'll return to Ethan's side to nudge his pocket for a treat. He's a gentle giant of a dog, and having him with us is perfect. I love the way Ethan dotes on him, as though he is his own. It brings out the softer side to his character. It adds to his attractiveness.

"What?" Ethan stops and stares down at me.

I blink up at him. "You're cute with Zeus. It makes me like you just a little bit more."

He reaches for my scarf, pulling me closer. "Is that so?" He grins, his eyes gleaming as he bends to kiss me lightly on the mouth. "Good to know you're getting to like me." He releases me with a wink and continues crunching his way through the leaves.

I've been quiet since we left my flat, a feeling of sad finality washing over me as I walked out of the front door. It would never be my safe place any more, just one horrible incident had trashed the years of memories, generally happy ones. It had been time to move on, that's why I'd put it on the market, but the memory of Roseman pushing his way into my home and everything that followed will overshadow everything else that happened there. I scrunch my eyes shut, rooted to the spot, trying to compose myself. I flinch as a hand touches my shoulder, my eyes flicking open as I stumble back and push Ethan hard in the chest.

"Don't!" The word is panicked, and it takes a few seconds for me to remember where I am, what I'm doing, who I'm with. I blink up into concerned blue eyes, and it's enough to finally push me over and to let go. A tear burns its way to the corner of my eye and scorches down my cheek, followed by another and then another. Angrily, I rub at my eyes, trying to fight the tears, but it's useless as the floodgates open. I'm vaguely aware of a strong arm sliding around my waist, guiding me forward to a bench on the lake's edge. Ethan sits and pulls me down onto his lap and holds me as I cry huge wracking sobs into his shoulder. I tremble against him, finding it hard to breathe, a tension headache thundering behind my bloodshot eyes.

"I'm sorry," I splutter.

"You have nothing to be sorry for," he murmurs against my ear. "Nothing."

His voice is laced with sincerity, he's being genuine, which makes me cry harder. I want this man so much, but I can't tell him for fear he might run away, and I can't express my desire physically because I feel traumatised.

"God, Ethan, you don't need this," I choke out.

"Need what?" His fingers grip at my hair and he pulls gently, so I'm forced to look up at him.

"This! Me!" I exclaim.

"I want to be with you." His tone is calm, patient.

"But what if I can't be with you?" I sniff. "You've got needs."

His eyes penetrate mine, and I feel him physically trying to read my mind. Frustration transitions into realisation as he connects the dots. "Are we talking about sex?" he asks with a sigh.

"I know it's important to you," I blush.

"You're overthinking. Stop it."

"God." A sickening feeling takes hold as a thought develops. "You don't want me any more."

"What?"

"You don't desire me."

He slides me off his lap and stands, raking his fingers through his hair. "Are you serious?"

"Last night in the shower." I swallow. "You weren't hard. You're always hard... You've barely touched me."

"Don't you ever doubt that I want you. I told you that last night," he says harshly. We stare at each other for a long moment, before his voice softens. "Do you want me to take you to bed right now to prove it?"

"No!" I recoil in horror, my eyes widening as I try to look away, but Ethan cups my face and forces me to look directly up at him.

"I want you, I desire you, but not like this, because you're not ready." His finger strokes the cut to the side of my head. "You've been hurt, you need to give yourself time."

"I'm scared that I'll never want you to touch me again," I whisper.

A glint flickers in his eyes and a confident smile settles on his lips as he lowers his lips softly to mine. "You just need time," he murmurs. "Kissing's good, right?" Cradling my face, he kisses me, his lips soft, melding against mine. His fingers tangle in my hair as his tongue languidly explores my mouth. Butterflies awaken in the pit of my stomach and my arms wrap around his neck.

We pull apart, both staring at Zeus as he noisily grumbles, the sound of his German Shepherd complaint distracting us. He is sitting a few metres away, his head cocked to one side, and he is staring at us.

"Come on," Ethan's hand finds mine and he pulls me to my feet. "We have a dog to walk." We walk hand-in-hand around the remainder of the lake, Zeus ambling besides us. We're silent, but it's companionable. It's beautiful out here, the solitude is exactly what I need.

The hotel has started to really pick up trade over the last few months, multinational businesses using it for team away-breaks and conferences. Last week a pharmaceutical group had booked the entire hotel, and the grounds had been overrun by mad scientists in wire-rimmed spectacles. The previous month a TV crew were on location, filming down by the lake. Tranquillity offers luxury in a beautiful setting, which seems to attract a niche, wealthy demographic.

Ethan stops as we round the corner that leads to the inclining path up through the trees to the hotel. He turns me to face him, his hands resting lightly on my shoulders, and stares down at me.

"What?" I ask.

"I shouldn't have fucked you over my desk yesterday like I did. I'm sorry. Sex in the office was off-limits for you, but I wanted to push you. The last thing I wanted to do was to make you feel cheap. I was jealous, and I'm not good with this stuff. I just needed to know you're mine, Rosie, only mine."

"I am," I falter. "I want to be..."

"Then don't keep stuff from me. I need you to trust me."

I start to chew the inside of my cheek, mulling over what he has said. I want to tell him that I hadn't intentionally withheld anything, but deep down I know that is a lie. OK, I had intended to tell him Tristan had visited whilst he was at work, but I hadn't planned to share Tristan's declaration of wanting me back.

"It works both ways," I finally say.

Ethan furrows his eyebrows.

"You never mentioned Tristan had called around whilst I was in the shower. I forgot, Ethan, your mum called and then it didn't come back up into conversation and I didn't give it a second thought. But you, you chose not to tell me, and actually you chose to think the worst of me. You made me feel..." I trail off and look away. "When he had me down on the floor, I thought of you," I swallow, "of us in your office, and I thought how stupid I'd been to think that it had felt wrong because it felt nothing like how wrong it felt with him. There was this moment, it felt like he was everywhere, all around me, on top of me, and I thought of you, it made me fight. You made me fight."

He pulls me hard against him and holds me tightly, his nose buried in my windswept hair. I start to cry again, the tears streaming down my cheeks.

"It's going to be OK," he murmurs against my ear.

"I hated him touching me," I choke out. "I just wanted him to stop, I wanted you."

I feel him tense, his hold tightening on me. I reach up and slowly stroke down his cheek and weakly smile up into troubled blue eyes. He's struggling with this too, I realise.

“Let's go back. I don't know about you, but I could do with a few hours’ sleep before this evening.”

“We really don't have to go,” Ethan says.

“I know, but I think we should. It's important.”

“It really isn't. Josh can handle it.”

I laugh. “That's not what you've been saying all week.”

“You just want to go to the restaurant to ogle the tennis team that is staying,” teases Ethan, bringing us back on to playful, safe ground.

I hold my hands up with a grin. “Damn, and there was me thinking I was being discreet.”

Our attention once again is drawn to a grumbling dog, who is sitting a few metres away noisily yawning, his head to one side. I click his lead and he saunters nonchalantly over so that I can attach it to his collar. We head off together up the path, and I can sense Ethan's smile as he follows behind.

Chapter Thirty-Two

"It's fine." Ethan drops a kiss to my temple. "You can hardly see it with your hair like that."

I sigh despondently and turn away from the mirror. Maybe I should have taken Ethan up on the offer to cancel. The cut to the side of my head is scabbing over and although Ethan is right, you can hardly see it now that I have my hair down, brushed so that it frames my face, I know it is there. I'd wanted to wear a new top, but the plunging neckline had exposed the finger marks, now dark purple, so I'd had to choose something else. I look fine in a dark red turtleneck jumper and black jeans, but irrationally I feel dull, unattractive.

We are supposed to be trialling a new menu suggested by yet another new chef. Tranquillity seems to get through chefs ridiculously quickly. Sometimes I think Ethan should quit the corporate world and take a career sidestep into the kitchen. He gets involved in the culinary running of the hotel, too involved some might say, and maybe that's why the volatile chefs leave so often. He's prone to popping into the kitchen to "check on things," which I think leads to the chefs feeling scrutinised and undermined.

Hussain, the latest chef, has lasted nearly two months, and touch wood, he seems to be doing OK. He doesn't seem to mind Ethan popping in, in fact he seems to quite like it, even encourage it. Tonight's tasting session was Hussain's idea, a way for him to prove himself, to make his mark, but also to let Ethan feel like it is a collaborative effort. I'd inwardly smiled at the excitable young chef when I'd heard.

"Rosie?" Ethan tips my head back and stares down into my eyes, his expression concerned.

I inhale his masculine scent, comforted by the blend of dark florals with an unmissable tone of fruitiness. I wrap my arms around his neck, pressing my nose to his skin, reassured by the sensuous male aroma of him. He slips his hands under my jumper, his fingers lightly massaging up my back. The air thickens as our eyes lock. I relax against him, nuzzling against his chest. He kisses the top of my head. Slowly he manoeuvres us over to the bed and sits, pulling me onto his lap.

"I feel better when I'm near you," I murmur. "I know it's silly."

"Is it? I don't know, I quite like it." His eyes gleam. "I'm happy to be near you, touching you... Do you want to do this or not? It's perfectly fine if you have changed your mind."

"I haven't." I wriggle off his lap. "It will be nice to see everyone, and I want a chance to speak to Will about us before work. Thank you for inviting him."

"I like Will, you know that. I've already spoken to him about us."

I wrinkle my nose at the thought of that conversation.

Before joining the others in the small private dining room, set off from the main restaurant, we visit Hussain in the kitchen. It's all go, him shouting out orders, while his team springs to action around him. It's warm, noisy, my nose assaulted by a variety of herbs and a myriad of cooking smells. Hussain scampers over to gabble something excitedly to Ethan, leaning to kiss my cheek, before he bustles away.

"See you later," calls Ethan, his hand resting on my lower back as he ushers me through the restaurant to our private room. We are the last to arrive, and as we enter all eyes fall on me, the chatter stilling. Ethan's arm slides around my waist as he takes in the situation.

"A word, if you don't mind?" my nan barks and gets to her feet and marches towards me. "In private. And you," she indicates Ethan with a curt nod. She's angry, I realise as we follow her back through the restaurant and out into the quiet foyer. Taking in the situation, Ethan leads the way to an empty office and closes the door behind us.

"Anything you need to tell me, Rosie?" Nan turns and glares up at me.

"What have you heard?" I stammer.

"That your stalker assaulted you yesterday in your flat." There's a heavy silence. "I was unaware you had a stalker."

"I wouldn't describe him as that, exactly," I say.

"Rosie didn't want to worry you," Ethan says calmly.

"I thought better of you. She is the only thing I have left, I should have been told." Nan snaps her head round to shoot a scathing look at him, before returning her acrimony on me. "Start talking."

I give her the basics, the minimum amount of information to make this go away. I'm not sure who let my secret slip, but Will and Chloe are the only ones who know the true extent of my assault, and I'm pretty certain they wouldn't have said anything. I do my best to sugar-coat it for her, giving her enough but not everything. Her anger at being kept in the dark fades as I show her my cut, describe a toned-down version of the fight.

"I wish you had told me," she says, the final flicker of anger dissipating, transforming into concern.

"I'm OK," I reach for her hands and give them a reassuring squeeze. "I'm sorry I didn't tell you. I was wrong."

"Yes, you were," she huffs and pulls me into a hug. "Don't ever keep anything like this from me again."

"I won't," I promise, shooting Ethan a sheepish smile over her shoulder.

"Go back to the restaurant," Ethan says to me. "Give us a moment. Trust me," he lowers his voice, "please?" I stare at him, before turning on my heel and slowly leaving the room. Ethan stands at the open door, preventing me from eavesdropping. He's asked me to trust him, and although I have no idea what he wants to say to Nan, I decide to give him this moment. I return to the dining room and smile weakly.

On the left side of the table sit Will, Chloe and Charlie, whilst opposite are Chelsea, Josh, and Zach.

"Pour the girl a drink." Zach smiles across at me, patting the seat beside him.

I smile, bending to kiss his cheek, and take my place. I accept a glass from Charlie and take a tentative sip, my gaze floating to the open door, my stomach knotting whilst I wait for Ethan.

"Thank you for popping by to take Zeus out this afternoon," Zach says.

"That's OK," I turn to him, giving him my full attention. "We love walking him. I take my Nan's dog for walks when I visit her, but she's an old girl and doesn't like to go far these days. Zeus is a lovely dog."

"He is," Zach beams.

"Ethan adores him."

"Ethan adores you." He pats my hand. It's strange, I ponder: right from the beginning, Zach has always insisted on slipping how much Ethan likes me into our conversations. I like to hear it, hope igniting that Zach's words are true, that he is able to verbalise emotion that Ethan obviously can't.

Ethan and Nan return and he pulls out the chair opposite me for her to sit, before he takes position at the head of the table, his hand finding mine.

Lizzie, a pretty waitress, enters with menus. I watch her young slender body make its way around the room. She's nervous as she places a menu in front of Ethan, a slight but perceptible blush creeping across her face.

"What would you recommend?" Ethan asks smoothly.

"Me?" she asks, startled. He nods.

"Give her a break," Josh says. "Lizzie, angel, we're running low on wine, could you bring us another red and white, please?"

"Of course," she stammers.

"Wait," Ethan orders. "Have you eaten anything off this menu?"

She shakes her head. "You're the first group to test it."

"What about the normal menu out there?" He indicates the main restaurant.

"Erm, a couple of things. I had the linguini last week, that was nice. There's not a great choice for vegetarians..." she trails off, embarrassed.

"OK, well maybe we should look at that," he says encouragingly.

"Really?" she beams.

He smiles. "Talk to Hussain and Josh next week."

"OK, I will," she floats out of the room, as if Ethan has made her day.

The evening is pleasant, the food delightful. We all have feedback cards, and Ethan is insistent that we critique the dishes as we go. The wine flows and conversation is easy. I'm not on top form, my appetite small, but I'm content to eat a little and to sit, watch and listen.

My attention is drawn to Will and Chelsea. I recognise that look, his soft brown eyes following her every movement, his focus on her absolute. Her arctic exterior remains, but sometimes I catch a glimmer of something else, that maybe the ice queen is thawing under Will's warmth. Will and Chelsea, I ponder the idea as I pop a piece of lamb into my mouth, the succulent meat melting against my tongue, rosemary and tarragon teasing my taste buds.

The table's attention turns to Chloe as she narrates classroom antics. Her passion and commitment to her students is obvious, even though she is making fun of the teenagers she teaches. Her eyes are bright, her cheeks flushed from the wine, and I know she's enjoying herself.

"You haven't eaten very much," Ethan observes quietly, his hand resting on my thigh. "Is it OK?"

"It's perfect." I cut him a piece and fork it into his mouth with a smile. "I'm not hungry, but the food is wonderful. Hussain's done a fantastic job."

Ethan chews, swallows, and nods. "He has."

I excuse myself and head to the toilet. Will is loitering outside and accosts me on my way back through the bar.

"How are you?" he says, his hand on my elbow as he guides me to an empty booth.

"I'm getting there," I shrug.

"Tell me about you and Ethan then?" His lips quirk into a goofy grin. "How long's it been going on?"

I blush. "Since the first time we met at the Summer party."

"I can't believe you didn't tell me."

"I wanted to, I'm sorry. Ethan's private, he doesn't want everyone knowing at work."

"Is it serious?"

"We haven't really defined what it is," I reply, twirling a strand of hair around my finger.

"I can't believe I didn't guess," he grumbles. "Yesterday in the kitchen, when I was hugging you, I thought he looked a bit pissed off, now I know why."

"He was annoyed with me, not you. Will, you need to keep it a secret from everyone at work. Nobody knows – well, except Drew, he's always known."

"I know," he sighs. "I've had this already."

"What did Ethan say to you?"

"He made his position clear, put it that way."

"What does that mean?"

"It means your secret is safe."

"Will!" I exclaim.

"Rosie?" he asks innocently.

"What did Ethan say to you about us?"

"Something like..."

"If you want to keep your job then keep your mouth shut." An American drawl makes us both jump.

"Yeah, it was something like that," grins Will, not in the least bit fazed.

"Ethan," I admonish.

"You expected nothing less." Ethan dazzles me with a broad smile that reaches his eyes. He looks happy, and my heart skips a beat. Will clears his throat and stands, and I realise that there had been a moment just then, that it wasn't just my wishful mind playing tricks on me. Will had seen it too.

"Discretion is my middle name," Will says with a wink, and returns to the others.

"He's happy for us." Ethan sits and slides an arm across the back of the bench, his fingers stroking the side of my neck. "What's wrong?" he murmurs into my ear.

"You weren't a total shit to Will about us, were you? He's my friend."

He holds his hand up. "I genuinely like Will. He needed to know about us, so I told him, it was as simple as that. He was surprised at first, but he seemed pleased. I asked him to respect our privacy, *asked*," he emphasises the word.

I meet his gaze. "Ethan, sometimes it feels like we're not real, and then sometimes it feels so real it scares the hell out of me."

"I know." He lifts my hand to his mouth, his lips pressing against my knuckles.

"Are we boring you?" calls Chloe as she heads through the bar to the toilets.

"Well, now you mention it," Ethan stands.

“Ah, Mr Serious has a sense of humour after all,” Chloe teases.

“Leave him alone,” I smile. “Come on,” I put my hand in Ethan's, “I want my lemon meringue cheesecake.”

Chapter Thirty-Three

Hussain's new menu, a mixture of classical English, herby Mediterranean and spice-infused Eastern dishes, is received well. He beams with pride as he joins us in the bar, clutching the bundle of complimentary feedback cards.

"I keep my job?" he asks Ethan.

"Of course! That was never in question. You were right, the old menu needed a shake up. A hotel like this is always going to need the classics, but I think branching out and mixing things up could prove very successful."

It's been a lovely evening, but tiredness crashes over me like a tidal wave, pulling me under. I yawn and lean into Ethan as he draws me closer. It's not even half past ten, but I'm wiped out.

"I'm going to go up," I murmur. "Stay, finish your drink."

Ethan reaches for his whisky and tips it back, stands and announces that we're off. I say my goodbyes, hugging Nan tightly and telling her to text me when Charlie drops her home.

"I hope you feel better soon," Chelsea says in a hushed voice, looking down at her hands in her lap. "Sorry I mentioned it to your grandmother, I assumed she knew."

I stare at her for a long moment, unable to figure out whether she is being sincere or not. There's the slightest suggestion of a smirk; I wonder if I'm being paranoid, but then she turns her back on me in such a way that she might as well have just stuck two fingers up at me. She may not have known that my nan had no idea about Roseman, but I'm sure she enjoyed being the one to tell her. I want to drag her by her hair out of her wheelchair and across the bar. Instead, I let Charlie hug me briefly, before Ethan pulls me away and we leave.

"Thanks for tonight," I say, flicking on the lights as we enter the suite. "For inviting Nan, Chloe, Will, and even Charlie. Hussain's great, isn't he?"

"He is; possibly too good." I raise my eyebrows. "People hear about a good chef, competitors come and try to steal them away."

"I don't know, he seems quite loyal."

Ethan laughs. "You're so naive. It's sweet, one of the many things I like about you."

"I am not!" I protest, unable to hide my smile: he likes many things about me.

"Drink?" he asks.

I yawn. "Just some water, please?"

"Sure. Go get in bed, sleepyhead."

I brush my teeth and undress alone. I climb into bed, fighting the tiredness. I want him here with me before I fall asleep, but every second my eyelids feel heavier and I give way to deep sleep.

It's my parents' car, the same road, the same time of day, the same slow-motion viewpoint, the same lorry. Panic rips through me as I see Ethan's face, his expression controlled; the panic soars as I see Roseman in the lorry cab. I scream: "Ethan, no! I love you..." But it's the same collision, the same sound of metal buckling on impact. My lungs ache as I cry out.

"Rosie, open your eyes, it's a dream, it's just a bad dream. Rosie, come on, it's OK. I'm here."

I struggle against him as I flounder in between the state of nightmare and reality. My heart is pounding, my body trembling as I cry out for Ethan over and over. My cheek crashes against his warm chest, strong arms hold me tight, the smell of his skin, his masculine aroma slowly forcing the nightmare to fade. I put my arms around his neck, gasping for air as I cling to him. He rocks me back and forward, assuring me it's just a bad dream over and over, whilst he strokes my back.

"It's OK," he whispers consolingly, as I whimper into the hollow of his neck. "I've got you. Come on, open your eyes, it's just a bad dream."

My eyelids flutter open, as I blink in the dim light from the bedside lamp. My pulse and breathing slowly normalise, replaced with utter embarrassment. I try to detach myself from his hold, but he doesn't let go.

"I'm sorry."

"You never have to be sorry for having a nightmare." He presses his lips to my cheek. "You want to get up, go back to sleep, tell me about it?"

It's still dark, only 5.30 in the morning. I snuggle with him under the duvet, our limbs entwined. I stroke the bristle forming on his jaw, the roughness super-sexy. If it weren't for Friday's incident I know I'd be initiating sex right now, and from the hooded look he's giving me I know he'd be a more than willing participant. I wriggle closer, my breasts pushing into his chest, the warmth of his skin travelling through the thin fabric of my nightie. I need to feel him, to be consumed by him. I'd lost him in the dream, I can't bear to lose him in real life.

"Can I ask you something?" I whisper.

He nods, trailing a finger down my cheek. "Go on."

"What would have happened Friday if nothing had happened to me? Would we still be fighting?"

"I think we'd probably have made up by now."

“How?” He draws back and positions himself up on an elbow to stare down at me. “How would we have made up?” A sexy grin spreads across his lips, his eyes twinkle with mischief. “Are you asking me to talk dirty to you?”

I blush. “No!” I slap at his arm playfully. “Would you have showed up at the fireworks?”

“I would, but late.”

“And then what would have happened?”

“You'd try and ignore me, you'd try to stay mad at me for my earlier indiscretion in my office. But when I stood next to you, too close, my hand would occasionally brush yours when no one was looking.”

“Go on,” I breathe, easily conjuring the picture up in my head.

“I'd catch your eye, and you'd know I was sorry. We'd sneak away and come back here,” he strokes my arm. “We'd end up in bed, and it would be everything that my office wasn't,” he kisses me softly and murmurs. “You make me want to do better.”

I nestle into him and sigh contentedly. We fall back to sleep entwined in each other's arms. It's intimate in a way that transcends just the physical. My sleepy mind continues his make-up story, my nightmare replaced with raunchy passion as my dream vividly depicts how we would have made up.

Chapter Thirty-Four

I'm nervous: nail-bitingly, ridiculously nervous. I've been awake for ages, lying in the dark, listening to his steady breathing, letting my mind wander. Butterflies flutter in my stomach, excitement and anxiety mingling into a jumbled concoction of sensation and emotion. Today is the day I'm going to meet Ethan's parents for a Thanksgiving lunch.

We're in Knightsbridge, having arrived last night, leaving straight from work. We'd skinny-dipped in the pool, laughing and splashing each other. I'm less self-conscious about being naked around him now, and the marks have faded. Over the last few weeks, he's been nothing but a gentleman.

We'd spent a week off work together, spending a few days visiting the Norfolk coast. We'd walked hand-in-hand along the shoreline, eaten chips and ice cream in the November cold. We'd run in the rain, then dried and warmed ourselves snuggling on the sofa in the cottage he'd rented for our mini-break. We'd drunk too much wine, got up late, and spent the time in a blissful, relaxing cocoon.

Returning to work had been hard – I'd hated going back to the secrecy, the freedom of the last week making it seem harder than before. Unsurprisingly, Ethan didn't seem to be bothered at all, and sometimes I had to roll my eyes at what an absolute arse he could be. But every night I'd end up in his arms, and whatever tribulations of the day would be forgotten.

I disentangle myself slowly from Ethan, lifting his arm from my stomach inch by careful inch so as not to wake him. Quietly I move around the apartment, brushing my teeth and tying my hair up in a high ponytail. I scribble him a note and leave it on the pillow.

The pool water is deliciously warm as I sink my shoulders underneath the surface. Rain streaks down the windows, wind thrusting raindrops furiously against the glass. The sky is slowly turning from the darkness of night to a concrete grey. I shiver, glad I am inside. I stretch out on my back, floating peacefully for a while, before turning to my front and beginning a lazy front crawl. I'm just finishing my second length when I spot him coming through the door. I swim to the wall and watch him dive straight in.

"Good morning," he grins as he swims towards me.

"Good morning to you, too," I smile and meet him, my arms wrapping around his neck as he lowers his lips to mine. It's a long, leisurely kiss, our lips soft, whilst our tongues slide against each other teasingly. He tastes of toothpaste, and his lips are warm against mine.

"You should have woken me," he murmurs, beginning to kiss the hollow of my neck, sending shivers everywhere. I run my fingers down his arms, his biceps tensing under my touch. His toned body exudes strength, a powerful spell of masculinity entraps me. I reach his hands, his fingers entwining with mine as he pulls back to stare down at me. I feel his hardness twitch against my stomach, and feel the air thicken, his eyes locked to mine, his jaw set in a hard line as I watch him battle with his own desire.

"I do want you," I whisper.

"I know." His voice is gentle, patient.

On a couple of occasions we'd started to get intimate, but he'd sensed my uncertainty and had backed off. I'd felt awful, apologising, but he hadn't seemed in the least fazed and had just held me tight. I take a step closer, my nipples hardening as they touch his sculpted chest. My breath catches as I feel liquid desire begin to run through my veins.

"Ethan," I look up shyly at him from beneath my long lashes, "I don't want to wait any more."

"Are you sure?" he asks. I nod, pushing my body hard against his, the ache for him intensifying. I want to feel him take me over, inside and out. I'm ready, desperate even, to be his.

He swallows, his hands going to my hips as he lifts me, my legs circling around his waist as he walks us out of the pool, back through the apartment and to his bedroom, where he drops me dripping water onto the bed. He crawls over me, his body warming mine as skin slides against skin. His lips crash down on mine, his tongue diving deep into my mouth. His kisses are passionate, unrestrained, intoxicating. His lips pepper my skin, his tongue exploratory, his teeth grazing against sensitive spots as he gently nips. He positions himself between my legs, looping a leg over his shoulder as his mouth devours me. I writhe against his touch, my breathing coming in short, ragged pants as his tongue licks and circles. He slides a hand underneath my bum, lifting me up, as he homes in on my clitoris. My orgasm comes quickly, swelling violently before I explode around him. His fingers push into me as the climax hits, and my body accepts him. Every nerve-ending thrums with sensation, the best kind of feeling.

"I want to feel you inside me," I gasp into his mouth as his body pushes me into the mattress.

He pushes into me, his cock reclaiming me inch by delicious inch.

"You feel so good," I murmur into his shoulder, relishing this moment.

"Then look at me," his voice is hoarse, his stubble prickling against the side of my neck. I turn my head to meet his intense gaze, concentration on his face. "You look beautiful." I blush, colour scorching its way to my cheeks and down my neck.

The sex is gentle, long gliding strokes that arouse nerve endings I didn't even know existed. It's intimate, hot, sultry. It's an uncomplicated fuck, and it's perfect, our bodies meld together like they belong. My arms and legs cling to him, like I can never get enough. My mind loses focus, the physical overshadowing everything else as he circles his hips and ups the pace. Our bodies sprint for the finish line, my hips meeting his thrusts. It releases my tension, leaving me feeling weak with happiness as we come together.

I close my eyes and nuzzle into him, inhaling the mixture of chlorine and Ethan.

"I've missed that," he murmurs into my ear. "You OK?"

I sigh against his chest. "Better."

He perches up on an elbow and strokes my cheek. "Let's shower, and then I'll make you breakfast."

"Pancakes?"

He grins, his mirth sparkling in his eyes. "Yes, if that's what you would like."

"I love pancakes," I sigh, closing my eyes.

"Hey," he slaps me playfully on the bum. "You are not going back to sleep. We've got things to do today, remember?"

"Do you think your parents will like me?" I ask.

"They'll love you," he replies, kissing the tip of my nose. "Now get up. I want you in the shower."

"Want me?" I try for flirty.

"Want you," he responds seriously.

"Well, why didn't you say so?" I spring out of bed and head for the bathroom, calling over my shoulder, "come on then."

What we had, the physical attachment, it's back, Roseman has not ruined it, even though I was scared he may have. Ethan had been gentle, his focus was completely on me, and I feel safe. And happy, I feel happy.

Chapter Thirty-Five

"Don't look so nervous." Ethan tucks a strand of hair behind my ear. "You'll be fine." We climb up the steps to the exquisite Kensington town house and he pushes the doorbell, a loud "ding-dong" resonating from somewhere deep inside. I hear a tip-tap nearing, the sound of a heavy bolt being moved, and the door is pulled open to reveal a woman who must be Ethan's mother.

She has his face – high cheekbones, brilliant blue eyes – and dark golden hair is piled up on her head, a few well-placed strands escaping. She's wearing a cream silk blouse, and a fitted black skirt that cinches in her tiny waist. She looks like a film star, smoky eyes, red lips. She's probably in her early sixties, but she looks amazing for it.

"Hey Mom," Ethan stoops to kiss her on the cheek. "This is Rosie, who I told you about."

"Hello, I'm Ellen." She extends a hand, which I take. She doesn't hide her scrutiny of me, her eyes flickering over my face, and then she smiles, a warm smile that reminds me of Josh and helps to put me at ease. "I hope you're hungry." We leave our coats in a cloakroom and follow her.

"This is a lovely house," I observe as we make our way through the marble hallway and up a carpeted staircase that twists off to the left. It's all high ceilings and chandeliers, oil paintings hanging ominously, the people and animals depicted in them seeming to look down at us as if they are real.

"It belongs to Ethan's godparents," she says. "They're on vacation in Sydney at the moment, visiting their son. Chase and I love staying here, it's so English, unlike the horrendous apartment that Ethan has."

"Here we go," sighs Ethan, and winks at me.

"Chase," Ellen pushes open the door to a splendid drawing room, its windows looking down onto an immaculate lawn that I imagine hosts many a garden party in the Summer. "Come and meet Rosie."

"Hey Dad." Ethan slaps the older man on the back.

"Good to see you, son." Chase's tone is full of adoration, it warms me to watch them both.

"Nice to meet you, Rosie," he envelops my hand in a strong warm shake. "Let's get you a drink."

"That'll be Josh and Chelsea," beams Ellen as she hurriedly leaves us.

"Do you visit England often?" I ask, sitting on a huge L-shaped sofa.

"A couple of times a year," replies Chase, pouring me a generous gin from a crystal decanter at a small bar in the corner. "I did a bit of work in London before I retired, and Ellen has some friends here as well. We now, of course, have Ethan living here permanently, much to his mother's disapproval."

"Just stay still!" I hear Josh, and then he walks through the door carrying a wriggling Chelsea.

"I don't know why you had to have lunch here," she protests as her brother settles her on the other end of the sofa from me. "So inaccessible. Why couldn't you have booked a restaurant like normal people?"

"Oh, hush now, pumpkin," Chase soothes. "Your mother misses you all, she wanted to cook for her errant children." Chelsea scowls.

"Ethan, Mom wants you in the kitchen," Josh says, sitting next to me.

"She's trying out a new recipe," confides Chase.

"I don't know why you couldn't have just come to Tranquillity," mutters Chelsea.

"Stop whining," Chase admonishes his daughter. "And to think we were missing you."

"Doubt Mom was." She scrunches up her face.

"Mom only misses Ethan," quips Josh.

"Excuse my brattish children," Chase smiles and sits. "So, tell me about yourself, Rosie. How do you know my son?"

"We work together." I stumble over my words.

"You work for Ed Mosen?" I nod.

"What an insufferable goat he is! We absolutely adore Drew, but Ed is something else. You know he made a pass at Ellen once? She saw him off, lecherous old..."

"Ethan's in charge at the moment," I say, wanting to steer the conversation away from Ed's escapades with women.

"Do you work in the call centre?"

"No, I work in recruitment."

"You like it?"

"For now, yes."

It's a pleasant afternoon. The food is wonderful: pumpkin soup, followed by the traditional turkey and all the trimmings. I'm totally stuffed, only managing a sliver of the gorgeous pecan pie and salted caramel ice cream. Ellen is an amazing cook, and I understand where Ethan must get his culinary skills from. Ellen and Chase are devoted to their children, and I'm fascinated to watch their family interaction. It makes me ache for my own parents, wondering how our relationship would have transformed as I flourished in adulthood. We'd always got on well; even when I had rebelled slightly as a teen, we'd still always laughed a lot. I imagined us sitting together, like the Harbers, sharing dinner and tales of what was happening in our lives.

"Have you ever visited America, Rosie?" Ellen asks me.

"Not yet," I shake my head. "But I've always wanted to visit New York for New Year." Ellen is a proud New Yorker and instructs me with a detailed itinerary on what I need to do when I end up visiting.

"You want to see some photos of our apartment in Manhattan?" Chelsea asks when we settle back into the drawing room for coffee.

"Yes please," I smile at her, pleasantly surprised by her offer.

She smiles back and offers me her phone, photos already on the screen. I swipe through pictures of the family home, of goofy poses (usually Josh), and well-constructed snaps (usually Chelsea). I continue to swipe, noticing a beautiful blonde girl in a lot of the shots. There's one of her and Ethan laughing together, and something deep within me awakens, alarm sirens gradually becoming louder. It's the way he is looking at her, and the way her hand is resting possessively on his arm.

And then there it is, the money shot... I stare at it incredulously, blinking just to make sure my eyes aren't playing a cruel trick on me, but they're not.

My entire body freezes, my heart feeling like it is beating its last beat. Everything around me seems to disappear – noise, smell, sight, all fade into a black chasm. Rationality flitters away, as I lose my mind. The picture is of a devastatingly handsome Ethan, his eyes sparkling, a smile lighting up his face. His arm is around the blonde, their hands entwined, the attention drawn to a glimmering diamond on her ring finger.

"That's Melissa," Chelsea says to me. "Ethan's wife."

"She's very pretty," I swallow, drop the phone in Chelsea's lap and shakily stand.

All eyes are on me, apart from Ethan, who I realise isn't even in the room.

"How could you?" hisses Ellen at her daughter, as she takes me by the arm and leads me out of the room. "Come on, let's get you a drink, my dear."

We end up in the huge kitchen, where Ellen sits me at a large table. She goes to a cupboard and takes down two crystal wine glasses, which she fills with white wine from the fridge.

"Is he still married?" I ask nervously.

"He is," Ellen nods, and joins me at the table. "Please, don't smash the glasses," she smiles weakly, "my friend will kill me. They're an anniversary gift. Drink," she orders, taking a generous drink herself. "I wondered if Ethan had mentioned Mel to you."

I shake my head, my mind foggy. "I wouldn't..."

“Have chosen to be the other woman,” Ellen finishes my sentence, her hand reaching for mine as she comfortingly squeezes.

“Surely you're not OK with this?” I ask, appalled.

“All a mother wants for her children is for them to be happy,” she replies. “I haven't seen Ethan happy for a very, very long time. Today, I watched how he is with you, and I saw that you make him happy. That's all I want. He deserves that.”

The door flies open and Ethan bursts in, his expression one of guilty concern. Our eyes lock for a moment, before my gaze drops. Ellen retreats, patting her son reassuringly on the arm before she leaves, gently pulling the door closed behind her.

Chapter Thirty-Six

"I was going to tell you," he says quietly, remaining by the door. He doesn't look himself, he looks worried.

"When?" I snap out. "When were you going to tell me?"

He crosses the kitchen, and I stand to move away.

"Rosie," he captures me in a corner, his hands reaching for my face as he cups my chin, forcing me to meet his gaze. "I'm sorry."

I slap him hard, the noise cutting through the silence, the impact stinging my palm. "I trusted you. I would have never got involved with you if I had known you were married."

"I know." His voice is low, husky. God, I love that voice... "Look, let's go."

"I'm not going anywhere with you. You're a liar! You've got a wife..." A lump rises in my throat as the enormity of what I have just said hits. He's married, and inadvertently I've become the other woman. I feel the colour drain out of my face.

"Listen, it's complicated," he says quietly, his hand on his cheek where I've slapped him. "Please, let me explain?"

"Where is she?" I ask. "There's nothing of hers in your apartment, at Tranquillity. I'd have noticed..."

"She's in New York."

"And when you went back in October, did you see her?"

He nods. "But not like you think."

"Did you have sex with her?" I whisper, the thought revolting me.

"No." His tone is firm, definite, with a tinge of indignation. "I would never cheat on you."

I laugh. "Just cheat with me, though?"

"It's not like that!" He steps away, obviously affected. "I'm married, yes, but we're not exactly together. I broke every rule when I saw you, Rosie. Please, let's get out of here?"

Weakness cripples me as I nod my agreement. This is it, the cliff-edge I've always feared, and pathetically now that I'm here, poised on the edge, I want to cling to him and never let go. I want to hold on in exactly the same way I had wanted to cling to Tristan when he had shattered my world. What is it with me? I'm not a weak person, but letting go is something I really fight against.

I don't move away when his hand settles on the small of my back as he guides me out of the kitchen.

“We're going!” Ethan bellows up the stairs.

Chase and Ellen descend the staircase, their expressions sombre.

“It was lovely to meet you.” Chase clasps my hand and draws me close. “I hope we'll see you on many more family occasions.”

“I doubt it.” The words fall off my tongue venomously and I regret them instantly, his expression awkwardly apologetic. “Thank you for inviting me.”

“Let him explain,” Ellen whispers into my ear as she envelops me in a tight hug. “You've made him happy, don't give up on him.”

“Just get me in my chair!” screeches Chelsea at Josh as they join us. “Ethan, I'm sorry.”

“Are you?” Ethan turns from where he had been loitering at the door.

She shrugs. “Of course.”

"You know what I think?” He stalks towards his younger sister, his jaw set, his demeanour menacing. “I think you wanted Rosie to find out. You've always been a bitch to her.”

“Ethan,” warns Chase.

“She deserved to know.” Chelsea raises her chin. “Melissa deserves...”

“Chelsea,” Ellen interjects harshly, “that's enough.”

“Take her back to New York with you next week,” Ethan says coldly.

I fumble with the door, leaving them to their family dispute. I don't belong there, I'm not a part of their lives. I stride away down the wide street.

“Rosie, wait up!” Josh calls after me. I turn at the corner of the street and wait for him to join me. “Look, I know Ethan should have told you – God, I should have warned you myself – but please, give him a chance. You're good for him.”

“And his wife?” I spit out.

“Isn't,” he replies simply.

I shrug, turn, and continue to walk away, unsure of where I'm going, not really caring. It's raining, a horrible clinging sheet of drizzle that soaks me to the bone.

“The taxi's the other way,” Ethan falls into step with me.

“Well go the other way then,” I snap.

“Not without you.”

I stare up at him challengingly. “And you'll tell me everything if I go back with you?”

"I'll tell you everything you need to know."

We travel in silence, both soaked. When we get back to his apartment I shower, the hot water scorching away the chill. Whilst I dry my hair Ethan showers, and it's only then I realise he hadn't tried to join me, he hasn't even touched me since we left. For some reason that hurts, like he has already given up on me, on us.

I wait for him to join me in the main room, sitting anxiously on the huge leather sofa, my fingers digging into my lower lip as I wait. My mind is whirling, and I feel like the pieces of my life are shattering all over again. He had put me back together, only to splinter me apart once more. My eyes follow his every movement, watching him pour a whisky and knock it back before he pours another and comes to join me.

"You don't wear a wedding ring." I'm the one to break the silence.

"I don't. Melissa and I... It's complicated, but all you need to know is that we're not together. Not like a normal married couple, anyway."

"What does that even mean?"

"It means that you don't have to worry about Melissa."

"Does she know about me?"

"No. We hardly talk."

"But you talked in October?"

"Not exactly. Rosie," he reaches for my hand, "I want you, that's all you need to know. I've wanted you since the very first time I saw you over Will's shoulder."

"I wanted you too," I admit with a blush.

"I want you right now," he says huskily, his thigh brushing purposefully against mine.

I blink up at him, my heart rate accelerating. I know that look, his blue eyes pulling me into their depths, swallowing me up. He lightly touches my hand, pulling it gently away from my mouth as his thumb brushes against my lower lip. His touch both breaks and calms me at the same time. It's so fucked up, such a mess, but I can't look away.

"I can't be the other woman," I say, my voice shaky. "I won't knowingly be that."

"I told you, Melissa and I, we're not together. She knows I have other women, she has other men."

"Then why aren't you divorced?"

"Because it's not the right time. Forget about her, all you need to know is that I want you."

Slowly he lowers his head, his lips soft, warm against mine. I should stop him, I should, I really should, but instead my hands trail up his arms. I tentatively kiss him back, allowing his tongue to tangle with mine. It's a leisurely but utterly mind-blowing kiss, my muscles clenching in anticipation. I close my eyes, my body buzzing with desire. But apparently my mind isn't as weak as my physical self, and the picture of Ethan and his bride flashes behind my closed eyes.

"Stop," I gasp, pushing him away. "This is wrong! I can't do it."

"It is not wrong," he says fiercely.

"I've fallen in love with you," I say.

Wham. He looks like I just told him I killed the family dog. I watch him reach for his whisky and drain it. He looks uncharacteristically ruffled.

"Don't say that," he says hoarsely.

"Why? It's the truth!" I get up, irritated by his reaction. How dare he dismiss me like that? "I've fallen in love with you, Ethan."

"Well, you shouldn't have."

"Why?"

"Because," he stands, towering over me, "love is not something I want to give or to receive."

"Well, thanks for telling me. I guess that's that, then."

I spin on my heel and begin to march towards the bedroom.

"Hey." He intercepts me, his hands resting on my shoulders. "I still want you."

"Seriously?" I rage. "For a supposedly highly intelligent man, you're being really dense right now. Today, I find out you have a wife who you don't want to tell me anything meaningful about. And then, when I tell you I'm in love with you, you just brush it away as if it doesn't matter. It matters! It matters..." A tear escapes and slides down my cheek. "Don't!" I push against his offer of comfort. "I want someone to love me, for us to live in a pretty house with a pretty garden and a dog, because I can't have children. I want that. What I don't want is to be in love with someone who just thinks of me as a fuck."

"I don't! How many times do I have to tell you that? Can't we just carry on like we have been? Rosie, we're good together, this is good. Don't just throw it away on a technicality."

"I want more! I need more! You said you'd tell me everything when we got back, but you haven't. You never do."

"I told you I'd tell you everything you needed to know," he cuts in, "and I have. Melissa and I, we're married but not together. We've been separated for a long time."

"How long?"

“Six years. It's why I moved to England, to get away.”

“Then why not get divorced?”

“Because I don't want to. Melissa needs me, I can't turn my back on her.”

“Do you still love her?” I ask, my stomach lurching. He doesn't answer, just walks away to refill his glass. It's enough, though, and it gives me the conviction to make the break. Separated or not, there's a history to Ethan and Melissa that he isn't willing to share, suggesting there is probably some unfinished business. I'm not prepared to hang around to see how it unfolds. I'm not going to beg, not going to lose every shred of self-respect like I did with Tristan. This was always going to end, it had been inevitable. But now I’m going to be the one to walk away.

Chapter Thirty-Seven

The rain wakes me, the wind crashing violently against the window, a rumble of thunder rolling in the distance. I hear Milly barking and decide to get up to sit with her, knowing she doesn't like storms. It's four thirty in the morning and I'm tired, but I know I won't return to sleep now that I've woken up. Over the last few weeks, me and four in the morning have become firm friends.

I make myself a cup of tea and settle myself on the sofa, a quivering Jack Russell snuggling into me on my lap. I feed her a cheese slice with some Xanax, hoping it will settle her sooner rather than later. I flick through the Sky channels, settling on the news, knowing perfectly well that I won't concentrate on whatever I choose.

The last few weeks have been miserable. I'd moved my belongings out of Knightsbridge and Tranquillity on the day I found out about Melissa. Ethan hadn't tried to stop me, he'd just continued to drink whisky. I'd moved back to Nan's, unable to return to my flat, which as of Friday is now under offer.

Ethan has been in and out of the office, and now I truly understand why you shouldn't sleep with someone you work with. He had been right about that rule, and so wrong to break it. He toys with me, and however much I try not to play his game, I can't help it. I spend most of days aching to see him, wondering if he is in the building, wondering whether he will walk past my desk, speak to me, or just send an email. It hurts seeing him, but in an oddly addictive way, not seeing him seems to hurt more. Most of the time he ignores me, but occasionally I feel his eyes watching my every movement. A couple of times he has been vile, undermining me in meetings, his arrogance making me mad. These exchanges have been followed by heated arguments in his office, sexual chemistry and pent-up frustration clouding the air.

The spark, the magnetic charge that has been there from day one is still burning brightly, and I have to fight against the desire not to fall back into his arms. I crave him, dream of him, he pervades my thoughts constantly; yet a sense of some kind of morality holds me back. The connection with his wife isn't broken, and as he won't expand on anything to do with her, their marriage, I can't be with him.

“It isn't my place to tell you what has gone on in Ethan's past,” Drew had sighed when I had confronted him.

“They're still married, she's not in his past,” I'd corrected fiercely, glaring at him. “You should have warned me, Drew.”

He had the decency to look guilty. “I wanted to, but it really wasn't my place. Ethan's private, I have to respect that. If he wants you to know, he'll tell you. I'm sorry.”

“That's absolute crap!” I storm, my anger directed fully at him. “You let me get myself into a situation that you knew would hurt me. I thought you were my friend..."

“I am,” he'd sat forward and stared up at me imploringly. “I honestly thought it'd just be a fling. I had no idea that it would turn into a relationship.”

“I fell in love with him,” my voice quavers. “You should have stopped me.” I'd walked out of his office, and I haven't spoken to him since. Blaming Drew is a necessary diversion, steering the responsibility away from myself and Ethan.

The memory of yesterday, of Ethan being an absolute bastard in a meeting, infiltrates my thoughts. He'd marched over to Libby in the morning and told her he needed her to minute a meeting with a prospective partner that afternoon. She'd told him she had a dental appointment but offered my services instead. I'd cringed, and Ethan hadn't looked thrilled either.

The meeting was with two directors from an internet marketing company, who wanted to work with us to increase our online profitability. They were young, full of energy and apparent technical know-how. I sat quietly, scribbling away on my pad, watching Ethan out of the corner of my eye.

“Are you writing that down?” he kept asking me. I'd just nodded meekly, but the more he asked, the more it irritated the hell out of me. The two other men looked baffled, too.

“Write it yourself,” I’d scrawled, after the tenth time he had questioned me. I smiled sweetly and pushed the pad towards him, before getting up and excusing myself. I saw a muscle tighten in his jaw as I walked out of the room. I was being totally unprofessional, but I just hadn't cared. Getting my own back on him had seemed more important.

“My office, right fucking now!” he had boomed down the telephone an hour later.

“I'm busy,” I pushed my luck.

“Don't fuck with me!” he bellowed.

“OK, I'm on my way,” I had soothed.

He was absolutely furious with me, balling me out for being totally unprofessional for walking out. He had a point, but I'd argued back, telling him that he shouldn't have kept asking me if I was writing things down, that I knew how to fucking note-take a meeting! We had glared at each other, neither backing down.

“I'm good at my job,” I'd raised my chin. “I don't need you questioning me.”

“You're gorgeous when you're mad,” his voice had softened, and he had moved close, too close.

“And you're a shit,” I had responded weakly, his scent disarming me.

“You're the only person who has ever walked out on me.” He’d touched my cheek, his finger tracing slowly over my skin. “I want you,” he had bent down, his lips unbearably close to mine. “I really want you.”

I'd blinked up at him, my heart racing, my nipples hardening, which his eyes latched onto through my white blouse: treacherous boobs. He knew exactly what buttons to press, and I loathed him for that. “You look tired,” he had drawled, running a finger across my bottom lip. “Spend the night with me.”

“I am tired because I'm juggling hospital visits with work and I'm not sleeping well.” I had pushed him away.

“What hospital visits?” He had looked appalled, worry spreading across his face. “Are you sick?”

“I'm fine,” I'd snapped and tried to leave his office.

“What hospital visits?” He blocked the door.

“My nan had a stroke.”

“I didn't know.” His eyes had melted into the warmest blue that I loved to see. He had tried to reach for me, and it had taken everything to reject his offer of comfort and to leave.

“You don’t get to know anything about me any more,” I’d said coldly, and I’d meant it.

Chapter Thirty-Eight

"Sorry, I can't stay long." I scrape the plastic chair towards Nan's bed and sit down, reaching for her hand. "Why did they move you?"

"Not sure. The nurse said it would be more peaceful to have my own room. I did sleep better this afternoon."

"How was physio?"

"Tedious."

"Have they said when you can come home?"

"Maybe next week. We'll see. Now, enough about me. You look nice, what are you doing this evening?"

I tell her about work's Christmas drinks in the pub. Usually, Ed throws a Christmas bash at Greenacres, but as he is still away from work there is no party this year. Grudgingly, the Board has put their hands in their pockets and arranged team meals out at a nearby restaurant. Tonight's drinks event is an informal gathering arranged by some of the agents and IT boys. I wonder if Ethan will be there, but I doubt it. I'd left the office early and taken Milly for a short walk, then changed before coming to the hospital for a fleeting visit.

Nan looks brighter today, more colour in her cheeks, her speech pretty much back to normal now. There's a slight weakness to the left arm, but even this is improving with physio. She'd been lucky, the stroke had been minor. Initially, the doctors had been concerned that another, more severe one, could be on the way, but Nan's improvements have been encouraging.

"I don't have to go to the drinks," I say. "I can stay."

"Don't be ridiculous!" she scolds, a twinkle in her eye. "You go, enjoy yourself. Maybe make up with that dashing American chap," she puts a hand up to stop my protest. "I'm not sure what he's done, and I don't need to know, but I'm pretty confident he's as smitten with you as you are with him."

"He really isn't."

"We'll see."

The drugs she is on must be scrambling her brains into misguided sentimental mush. She'd liked Ethan a lot, and I hadn't had the heart to tell her about Melissa. I'd just said we'd decided to end things. I think she knew he'd upset me, but as is her nature she hadn't pressed for details, knowing I'll tell her when I'm ready. Patience is a definite quality of my beloved nan.

I stay for ten minutes longer, before she yawns and dispatches me. I drive to work, anxiety twisting in my stomach. The last few weeks, the heartbreak over Ethan, the gut-wrenching panic over Nan, are beginning to take their toll. I'm going to show my face tonight but slip away as soon as possible. I feel tired, in need of my bed and a restful weekend.

I am greeted by a whistle as I get out of the car, and spy Will over the other side of the car park. He strolls over to meet me, sliding an arm casually around my shoulders.

"William." I smile fondly up at him.

"You have very good legs," he comments.

"Why, thank you," I giggle.

"Are you trying to impress anyone specific?"

"Of course not," I deny. But the truth is that I am, of course I am. If Ethan is here tonight I want him to notice me, to see me and realise what he has let go.

I'm wearing a dark red silk blouse with a hip-hugging black skirt. I have cute red heels to match the top, my hair is pinned up, and I look subtly provocative. Sometimes a little really is more, and I feel I've achieved that with my careful wardrobe selection.

"Let's go and get shit-faced," Will says, leading me across the road.

"I'm not going to stay long."

"We'll see." He pushes open the door to the pub and moves aside for me to enter.

It's busy, too busy, crammed full of Mosen's employees. I'm sure there is some health-and-safety regulation being breached right now. I see him straight away, our eyes locking together over the crowd. It's reminiscent of that very first time I caught sight of him over Will's shoulder. The spark ignites, it always does when I see him.

"Shall we go and say hi?" Will asks, nudging me forward.

I shake my head and drop my gaze. "No." I turn right and head to the other end of the bar, where I find the Barretts.

"How are you?" Jamie jumps down off his bar stool and pats it for me to sit on.

"Thanks," I smile as I slide on to it. "I'm good. You?"

We order drinks and chat. The atmosphere is rowdy, everyone getting into the Christmas spirit.

"You'd have thought Ethan might have offered Tranquillity," Will mutters in my ear.

"I know." I turn to face him. "Although he is too uptight to bring this lot back there. They'd trash the place."

"He keeps looking over," murmurs Will.

"Let him," I say and turn to Olly.

The Barretts have been different with me since they hauled Barry off me and saw me in a state of undress. The harmless flirtatious banter, particularly from Olly, has ceased, replaced by some kind of brotherly protectiveness. I'd been worried that the ordeal would make things weird between us, but the twins have been lovely and although things are different, it doesn't feel awkward.

Libby arrives, and we settle ourselves at a table in the corner. We talk about plans for Christmas and New Year. She's off to Edinburgh to spend two weeks with her in-laws, which she does, and enjoys, every year. Will is off to Surrey for a few days to make the dutiful visit to his parents, something he does every year and detests. Will's parents never got over him not completing his medical training and often remind him that the only reason they moved from Mumbai had been for him to have a chance of a really good education, which he had squandered.

The Barretts leave midway through the chat, bored by our mundane conversation. Drew joins us, taking a seat next to Libby and opposite me. He shoots me a nervous smile.

"When is Ed coming back?" Libby asks.

Drew shrugs. "I don't know. I think the break is doing him the world of good. He's really happy with what Ethan is doing, so I don't think he is in any hurry."

"But he will come back?" presses Libby.

"Honestly, you know as much as me. Ethan agreed to a year. What happens after that is anyone's guess." I excuse myself, the conversation making me feel uncomfortable. I squeeze through the crowd, and then stop, my eyes falling on Jade standing with Ethan. She's too close, her hand resting with some familiarity on his arm.

"Thanks for last night," she says.

"You're welcome. Anytime."

She says something else, which I don't hear because Wham's 'Last Christmas' starts to play. I see him laugh, and it's too much. I want to drag Jade off him by her peroxide hair and scratch out her overly made-up eyes. I march to the door and out into the December chill. My heels tap loudly as I storm across the car park.

"Rosie!" He must have seen me leave and chosen to follow, as his voice carries across the car park. "Where are you going? It's early."

"Go away, Ethan," I rage, jealousy fuelling a volatile anger that is crackling through me. "Go back to the pub. You wouldn't want anyone to see us together, would you? Go back to Jade!"

He laughs, a deep, unrestrained laugh. I hate it, hate the fact he finds this funny. Having already drunk too much wine to drive, I stride back into the office, the building still open for another half-hour. I stomp upstairs and head across the deserted floor to my desk, where I slump into my chair and dump my bag on the desk. I power up my PC.

“What are you doing, you crazy jealous woman?” he teases.

I ignore him, my fingers crashing over the keys as I noisily type out my frustration. This makes perfect sense: my brain congratulates itself on its uncharacteristic decisiveness. This is absolutely the right thing to do, the only thing to do. I hit Print and hear the gentle whir of the printer across the room. Ethan hears it too and saunters slowly over to the printer to retrieve the sheet of A4.

“I don't think so.” He rips the paper in half and tosses it in a nearby bin.

“I'll just print another,” I say, undeterred.

“Sweetheart, you can print as many as you want, you are not resigning.”

“Fine, I’ll just email it to Libby.”

He moves swiftly, wheeling my chair back from the desk, and before I know what is happening he has scooped me up into his arms and is marching down the corridor to his office.

“Put me down!” I wriggle in his arms, but his hold just tightens around me. “Ethan, let me go!”

“I can't.” His tone is so serious that it stops me squirming and forces me to look up at him. He doesn't put me down until we're in his office. I watch him switch the light on, pick up his telephone receiver and dial a number. “Hey Tom, it's Ethan. I'm working late, I'll check around up here before I leave. Don't put the alarm on when you lock up. Thanks.” He hangs up and turns to face me. “In twenty minutes, we are going to have this entire building to ourselves.”

There's definite insinuation to his voice, and it sets excitement fluttering in my stomach. No, no, no! He has a wife, my brain screeches at me, and what about Jade?

“I'm not staying,” I say, but remain motionless.

He moves past me and begins closing the blinds.

“Maybe you should ask Jade, or maybe call your wife, see if she wants to come and share a building with you.”

He spins around, his eyes dark, his expression stormy, like I've pushed it too far. There's something in the way he turns, the speed in his movement, and before I can stop myself I'm flinching away from him. For that split-second he really scared me, and he saw it, I hadn't been able to hide it.

“Fuck!” He looks absolutely appalled. “You thought I was going to hit you! Why?”

"Because I've been hit before." The words come out shakily. My heart races, adrenaline coursing through my veins. I stare at him, my eyes wide, and I witness shock and what looks like disgust cross his face.

He clears his throat. "I need a moment." And with that he opens the door and walks out, leaving me alone in his office. Unsteadily, I make it to his chair and sit. My mind catapults back to being eighteen and a naive fresher at university. The memory is as vivid as if the event is playing over for real. It's not something I'd thought about for an exceptionally long time, but it feels like it happened yesterday. Automatically I put my hand up to my left eye, my fingers gently tracing my cheekbone. I squeeze my eyelids tightly shut, trying to bring myself back to the present. I hear the door open a few minutes later, feel him slowly wheel the chair away from the desk. My eyelids flutter open as I feel his hands cradle my face as he crouches down in front of me.

"I would never hit you." His voice vibrates low in his throat. "Never."

I swallow and nod. I believe him. He looks terrible, crushed that he has scared me. The truth is that it had just been a physical reaction, his sudden, furious movement triggering my body to respond. It had been a split-second, that's all, because I know he would never hurt me – not physically, anyway.

"I know," I say, my hand reaching up to his, our fingers entwining. "You just startled me, It's OK."

He stands, pulling me up with him, spinning us around so that he can sit in his big leather office chair and pull me down onto his lap. I lean into him, my cheek nestled on his shoulder, my body relaxing into his hold.

"Was it Tristan?" he eventually asks, and I look up to see he is still brooding.

"No. It was just the once, some guy at uni. We were arguing, we'd both been drinking, and he just spun around like you did and punched me. I left with a badly bruised eye and never saw him again. It was just a reflex, Ethan, it just threw me for a moment. I know you wouldn't."

"Never," he whispers solemnly and kisses the top of my head. "God, I've missed you, missed this."

"What about Jade?" I ask nervously.

"What about her?"

"Did you...?"

"Of course not," he sounds offended and looks wounded, his eyes crinkling in the corners.

"What happened last night?"

"She had a flat tyre, I helped her sort it out, that's all. You are the only one."

"But that's not true, is it?"

"Melissa needs me, but it's not how you think."

"Then tell me how it is!" I implore him, staring up at him from under my lashes.

"I can't."

"Can't or won't?" I ask fiercely.

He considers. "Both."

I sag against him, the fight leaving me. Just for a moment, a little while, I want to be here with him, to feel him, to be his. It goes against everything I stand for, but the jealousy has sparked an odd possessiveness and I don't want to let him go, even though it's the right, the proper thing to do. Ethan clearly senses my resolve fading, because his hand starts to caress my back in gentle little circles. I sigh and shift to meet his gaze, which is one of lust, coupled with something else, something softer, something tender.

"Please don't fight this," he lowers his head, his lips so close to mine.

"But it's wrong," I stammer, feeling myself teetering precariously off the moral high horse.

"Not everything is black and white, sweetheart," he explains, his finger trailing down my cheek, his touch spiralling sensation through my body. "Please, don't walk away from this, not tonight. I want you. You've been driving me fucking insane these past few weeks. Spend tonight with me?"

The tick-tock of the clock suddenly seems deafening as I fight an internal battle of self-imposed morality. Married men are off my to-do list, but here I am considering his proposal. It had been OK before because I had been clueless about Melissa, but now, even though I know, the desire for him that consumes my entire body still burns.

"I want to kiss you," he says against my mouth, his breath brushing across my lips. "I want to feel your skin under my fingertips. I want to be inside you, to feel the way your body responds to mine."

"You're not playing fair!" I protest.

"Tell me you don't want that." He moves his head back slightly.

I shake my head. "I can't."

He senses my reluctance, sees the inner turmoil playing out across my face, and he squeezes me tighter. He begins to take the pins out of my hair, combing through it as it spills in an unruly cascade down my back. He's being so gentle, his expression one of softness and patience, that it melts any resolve I have left. I turn on his lap and wrap my arms around his neck, resting my chin on his shoulder and close my eyes.

"I wish I'd met you years ago," he murmurs into my ear. "You're so beautiful. Perfect. You make me want to be a better man."

Heat scorches through my body, my muscles clenching, an ache thrumming low down, physical need melting away any moral reluctance. His lips trail kisses delicately up my neck, his tongue circling the sensitive spot in the hollow. I squirm in pleasure against him, my mouth welcoming his as our lips unite together in an intoxicating kiss. Our tongues tangle together, absence making us both crazed with desire. The situation might be wrong, but this feels so right. From the very first time I'd seen him, this current has drawn us together, and not for the first time, I let go, giving Ethan the control I know he craves.

His fingers move to my blouse. He stops at the first button and pulls away to stare into my eyes.

"If we do this here, right now, promise me you won't feel cheap. I don't want it to be like last time. I want you to know how much I want you, and only you."

"OK," I breathe, my heart pounding so hard I am sure he can hear it. "Don't stop," I urge, my mouth seeking out his again. He moves us, perching me at the edge of his enormous desk and beginning to unbutton my blouse, pushing the thin material off my shoulders and depositing it on the floor. His hands skim over my shoulders, my collarbone, my skin coming to life under his touch. His thumbs circle my already hard nipples through the fabric of my black lacy bra and I find myself moving closer to him, needing everything all at once. He unhooks my bra, tossing it aside, and massages my breasts, his eyes locking to mine as he witnesses me unravel before him.

In a swift movement he brushes away the contents of his desk, paper and folders crashing to the floor, and then he pushes me back down onto the polished oak. He looms over me, a glint of victory in his eyes as he begins to kiss his way down my body, his mouth sucking in a nipple roughly, eliciting a gasp from me. His teeth graze against my skin, his tongue following to soothe. His hands move to my black pencil skirt, making short work of the side-zip, and he drags it down my legs along with my tights, pushing my shoes off as he goes. His thumbs hook into the waistband of my knickers and he removes them with equal fervour. He sits in his chair, and I feel his eyes drink me in. Vulnerability tempers the arousal momentarily as I take stock of the situation.

His hands are firm as they pull my legs apart, hooking them over his shoulders. I feel his breath against my sensitised skin, anticipation for him uncoils deep within me. He flashes a devastatingly handsome smile before he lowers his head, his tongue sliding slowly up my aching skin, finding my clitoris, and moving lightly against it. He kisses me, his tongue sliding down, dipping inside and then returning with purpose to my throbbing bud, the flicking movement shooting pleasure through my veins. God, I've missed this. His fingers join in, increasing the heady arousal as he presses into me, my body opening to him. Everything is slow, precise, tantalising, it's frustrating and ecstatic all at once. He teases, nips, kisses, licks, sucks, and my body lights up for him. I feel the buzz of the orgasm spread across my lower stomach, feel my muscles tighten everywhere as his finger hits just the right spot inside, his tongue swirling against me. I'm right on the edge, and then he stills, his eyes blazing as he finds mine.

"Tell me you've missed me," he orders, his fingers drawing back and then plunging back hard into me. "Tell me."

"I've missed you," I whisper, so close that it is painful.

"Tell me you want me."

"I want you," I gasp as his tongue returns, circling.

He brings me back to the crest slowly, drawing out the pleasure, so that when he finally releases me over the brink the release is magnified, powerful ripples consuming me as I call out his name.

Through a post-coital, fuzzy haze I watch him get naked, marvelling at the rippling muscles as he shrugs off his shirt. They look even more defined, and I notice his stomach looks like it has shed a few pounds in the weeks we have been apart. He steps out of his boxers, his impressive erection capturing my attention. I move from the desk, pushing him back into his chair and kneel in front of him, taking his cock into my right hand, pumping slowly. My tongue flicks across his head, before my lips part and I suck him deep to the back of my throat.

"God!" he groans, grabbing a fistful of my hair and moving against me. Gentle Ethan is no more, and he powers into my mouth, his thrusts hard and deep. I take it, relishing his lack of restraint, feeling him come undone, and I become aroused all over again because I know it is me that is doing this to him.

"I want to be inside you," he whispers hoarsely, pulling my head back. "Right now."

He pulls me up onto his lap, guiding his cock to my entrance and pulling me hard onto him. He fills me completely, stilling to give me time to get used to him. He grasps my hips, raising me, and then pulls me back down. His hips begin to move, his thrusts determined, every stroke full of conviction. His lips find me and his kiss is hard, his tongue dominating my mouth with skilled precision. I rest my hands on his shoulders, letting him take control, following his lead as our bodies crash together.

"Wrap your arms around my neck," he instructs. "Don't let go, OK?"

I nod and in one fluid movement he is standing, his cock buried deep inside me, and walking us backwards so that my back is pushed up against the door. My legs instinctively curl around his waist, my heels digging into his glutes as he begins to move. He powers into me, driving hard, fast and deep. It's relentless, and I lose my mind to him as a passionate whirlwind engulfs us both.

"Tell me you're still mine," he says, bending to find the spot that drives me crazy just behind the ear.

"I'm still yours," I pant out, my head banging against the door.

He slides a hand up to cushion the movement, his pace slowing as he shifts us back to his desk. He lowers me carefully onto my back, his body hard against mine as he looms over me. His thumb finds my clit once more, and as he begins to pound his way to his own climax he makes damn sure he pulls me over with him. It's intense for both of us, our cries mingling together as one in the silent office. It's bliss and torture all at once, it was desperate, lustful and beyond satisfying.

His skin is hot against mine, his heart thumping against my ribcage. His bulk presses me into the hard wood, his ragged breath sending goosebumps across my skin. He moves slightly and nuzzles against my breasts. I stroke his short hair and commit this moment to memory.

Chapter Thirty-Nine

"Hey." He props himself up on his elbows and scrutinises my face. "You OK?"

"I don't know," I say honestly.

He strokes my cheek. "Not everything is black and white, remember? That was incredible, you are amazing." He slowly withdraws from me and bends down to place a soft kiss to my lips. "Stay with me tonight? Please?"

I sit up, my muscles complaining from their vigorous, and somewhat unexpected, workout. I rub the back of my shoulder absentmindedly while I ponder his proposal. I shiver, the room feeling cold suddenly. Ethan notices and stoops to collect my discarded clothes. I dress, considering whether I should go home alone or whether to extend this pleasure and delay the inevitable. Milly is staying with the neighbour as I had pre-empted being out late tonight, so there's no reason to return to Felixstowe. The thought of Tranquillity is alluring, the thought of Ethan even more so.

"What are you thinking?" Ethan asks, coming to stand in front of me as he finishes doing up the buttons of his shirt.

I meet his gaze. "That I hate the fact that I'm even considering this."

"Don't." He cups my face. "This is good, so good."

"We're not OK," I say, a shiver travelling through my body.

"I know." He draws me close, his hands rubbing up and down my arms. "I should have told you that I'm still married, but the truth is, I wanted you too much to risk it."

"And now I know, and I feel like I'm suffocating, drowning in it."

Ethan's mobile begins to ring, the vibrations rattling noisily on the desk. I step away, indicating he should get it. I go to the window and open the blinds to look out into the darkness. There's something about his voice that makes my body stiffen: his tone betrays concern, and when I turn to look at him he looks pale, ruffled.

"I'll get the next available flight. I'll let you know when I'm back."

"What's wrong?" I ask when he ends the call.

"I'm sorry, I've got to go back to New York. Melissa needs me."

"Melissa?" I say, the word knocking all of the air out of my body as if I have been physically struck. "You're going back to see your wife?"

"I need to go," Ethan says firmly, his expression returning to its characteristically unreadable, totally controlled expression.

"Why?" I ask, a flicker of anger lighting in the pit of my stomach.

"I can't do this," he shrugs dismissively. "I need to book a flight."

"I don't understand! You just wanted me to come back with you and now, what – you just leave me?"

"Melissa needs me!" His voice cracks loudly through the air, his bellow making me jump.

"Then go," I fire back bitterly. "Who am I to get in the way of you and your wife? This isn't good, this is wrong." I point my finger at him. "You said you wouldn't hurt me, but you lied! You could have stopped this, but oh no, you wanted sex and you let me think it could mean something more when it meant absolutely nothing."

"Please?" He takes a step towards me.

"Don't you come near me," I hiss. "You either explain what is going on right now or you let me walk away this time."

We stare at each other, and in that moment I see it clearly: he's not with me, he's very much with his wife. The clarity stabs painfully through my body, but there's something cathartic about it. This is the ending. This is the goodbye.

"You've made your choice." The words drip off my tongue venomously. "I will resign, and unless you want everyone to know you've been fucking me you won't stop me. This may have meant absolutely nothing to you, but it did to me, and I can't go on seeing you, or worse, missing you when you're not here."

"She needs me, Rosie." His eyes implore me to understand. "You don't."

I nod. "No, I just want you. God," I run my fingers through my tousled hair in despair. "I can't believe you are just going to leave me after what we just did. Do I really mean so little to you?"

"Stop it!" he barks. "You will be here when I get back, OK?"

"Fuck you, Ethan," I say. "You don't get to tell me what to do. Book your flight, go to New York and be with your wife. You were never mine to want, to fall in love with..."

"Go." He slumps into his chair, looking beat. "Leave me."

"Don't you dare look at me like that, like I'm the one finishing this!" I rage. "You're leaving me, be clear about that. You're the one ending this."

"Fine," he snaps. "Just go, Rosie. This can't work, I was stupid to think it could. We're done."

I stoop down to retrieve my bag from the floor, my body shaking with a heady concoction of fear, anger, and self-loathing. How could I have given in to him so easily? Disgust vibrates through me. I've become the other woman, something I had never imagined I could do. Ethan Harber had come into my life like a whirlwind, our connection instantly binding me to him. He'd made me trust again. Fuck, he'd let me fall in love again! And now he is tossing me away like it meant nothing.

“Rosie, wait,” he looks up from his computer screen in panic. “How are you getting home?”

I laugh bitterly. “Like it's any of your business.”

“I need to know you'll be safe.”

“You don't get to know anything about me any more,” I spit. “You've made your choice.”

“It's not...”

“Black and white?” I interject sharply. “Yes it is. It really is, Ethan. You don't love me, you don't want me like I want you. There's no blurriness there. I've already begged someone to stay with me when they didn't want me and I won't do that again, not with you.”

“I'm sorry,” he blinks, and I think I glimpse a flash of pain in his eyes. It's too much, and with that I turn my back and stumble out of his office.

Chapter Forty

The sun is strong, far too strong for Christmas day, I think as I crunch my way up the beach. I mean, when did we stop getting the bitterly cold Christmases? When was the hope of snow just a mere fantasy? It's mild, and the weather seems to reflect my utter disregard of tradition. It is warm, bright, when it should be cold and dull; and I'm flat, miserable, when I should be buoyant and happy. This year has been an absolute bitch, I ponder, stooping down to pat Milly. This time last year I was engaged, life was good, or at least I thought it was...

"Come on," Will snakes an arm around my waist and ruffles my hair. "Cheer up. It's Christmas."

I shrug apologetically. "Thanks for coming today."

"Thanks for inviting me." He grins, bending down to pick up a tired Jack Russell. "It's been so nice spending the day with people that actually like each other. Family Christmases at my parents' always descend into some kind of argument. And they don't even have drink to blame it on."

I turn around, distracted by an approaching galloping sound coming towards us on the pebbles. I smile, a genuine smile that reaches the corners of my mouth as I see a huge German Shepherd barrelling towards me.

"Hello, boy," I croon as he nudges at my jeans pocket. "I've missed you." I kiss him on the head before offering him a biscuit and giving one to Will for a wriggling Milly.

"Happy Christmas!" Charlie says, enveloping me in a huge hug. "Your nan said we'd find you down here. I've left her and Zach drinking port together."

"Those two have more fun than we do," I giggle.

The three of us amble companionably along the beach. Zeus runs to the shore, then darts away as the waves rush in at him. I've missed him, and by the way he keeps returning to my side I'd say he's missed me too.

Nan came out of hospital five days ago and I had planned a quiet Christmas, just the two of us. However, she'd surprised me by telling me she'd invited Charlie and Zach for the day. Unbeknownst to me, Zach and she have kindled quite a friendship since dinner at Tranquillity. Will had some kind of bust-up with his father, so I'd invited him too. I didn't mind the cooking, pleased to have people around me.

I haven't heard from Ethan since the night I left his office, but I'm pretty sure he is still in America, and I'm guessing he'll stay there for the festive period. I'd thought he might text today, a silly whim that only led to disappointment. I know we are over, but there is still a part of me clinging to denial.

"Zeus!" I call him, taking the lead from Charlie. "Do you mind?"

He shakes his head and looks puzzled. “Go ahead.”

“Ethan and I used to walk him a fair bit,” I explain. “I miss him.”

“You can still come and walk him,” Charlie responds.

“Maybe.”

“I thought we weren't mentioning the ‘E’ word?” Will asks.

“I know,” I groan.

“Why don't we all set up dating profiles online after dinner?” suggests Will.

“No. Anyway, aren't you on all the sites already, you huge man-whore?”

“I can update mine then.”

“I don't need one,” Charlie says, his beautiful eyes shining.

“Have you met someone?” I explode with excitement.

“Kind of. It's complicated.”

“How complicated?” Will asks with a mischievous smile.

“She's going through a messy divorce, and I also teach her daughter.”

“You've fallen for one of the school mums?” I wrinkle my nose in mock disapproval. “You catch.”

“Hmm,” Will looks contemplative, “divorcees... Maybe I should give that a go...”

I nudge him in the ribs in exasperation and tell Charlie to tell us all about his new lady. I'm relieved and pleased he has found someone; Chloe's constant warnings that I need to be careful not to lead him on have made me slightly wary whenever I am around him. Now, I don't need to worry about possible misinterpreted signals. We walk back to Nan's, listening to Charlie enthuse about Abby, the prettiest mum at the school gates.

I go straight to the kitchen to check on the turkey, calling my greeting as I pass the lounge. I check my phone: nothing. I drop it despondently on the counter.

“Happy Christmas!” Zach fills the doorway, his eyes searching my face knowingly. “I know he's as miserable as you, if that helps?”

“Happy Christmas, Zach. Thanks for coming today, Nan is thrilled. Have you spoken to him?” I ask, unable to hide my interest.

“Last night.” He goes to the fridge and pours me a crisp, cold glass of wine. “You'll work it out,” he says, rubbing my shoulder and handing me the drink.

“Thanks. I don't think there's anything to work out.”

“Nonsense,” he scoffs. “Sometimes, my dear, you need to fight a bit.”

"Ethan's not."

"And maybe you should find out why."

"You know?" I ask.

"I know that he's a fool, that he takes responsibility for things that he shouldn't. And I know that he's fallen in love with you, and that terrifies him."

"In love with me? Ethan?" I stammer. "That's not right, you're wrong."

Zach shakes his head. "I don't think so."

"He's got a wife."

"Correct, but does she make him happy? They are married on paper, that's all. He pays her bills and looks out for her due to some misguided notion of duty."

"What do you mean?"

"That you should ask him."

"I've tried!" I complain.

"Then try again." Zach surprises me with his curtness. "You let him in, and now it's your turn to break down his walls. Rosie," his tone softens, "Ethan and Melissa have been separated for a very long time, yet you're the only one who has become exclusive for him. He needs you to be the one to fight for this. It's not my place to tell you why, that's Ethan's choice. If you want him badly enough then you'll find a way to make him tell you."

We both turn at the sound of snarling and a yelp. Zeus barges into the kitchen and hides behind my legs as an outraged Jack Russell pursues him.

"Enough," I scold, scooping up a snapping Milly. "You play nicely."

Zach's words rumble around my head throughout the afternoon. Is he right? Did I give up on Ethan without a fight? Did I let my moral compass blind me to everything else? Could he be in love with me too, like Zach said? We enjoy a lovely Christmas lunch together, everyone complimenting my cooking. It's a nice Christmas day, with good company. We end up having a very competitive game of Scrabble, which I win, much to the outrage of Charlie and Will, who are playing together.

"It's been a lovely day," I say, putting a glass of water on my nan's bedside table at bedtime.

"You missed Ethan?" she comments, patting the bed.

"I'm trying not to, but it's hard. Zach said that Ethan's in love with me."

She takes my hand in hers, and smiles a knowing smile. "Of course he is. He came to see me in the hospital, you know? Got me moved to the private room and told me not to mention it to you."

"What, Ethan did?"

"He sat with me for a long time. He looked sad, just like you do. He spoke about how wonderful you are, and that he was sorry things had ended the way they had. I think he thinks you can do better. He's in awe of you."

"Is he?" Butterflies start up in my stomach. "He's never said."

"I don't think he knows how."

"Zach said I should fight for him. I don't want it to be the same as Tristan, fighting for someone who doesn't want me."

"Ssh," she soothes. "That man wants you, of that I am totally sure."

"So what do I do?"

"You go and get him."

"He's in New York."

"Then book a ticket."

Fifteen minutes later I'm in bed with the laptop, my mobile cradled on my shoulder as I talk to Chloe.

"Let's do it," she says excitedly. "Book it. The worst thing that can happen is that Ethan will reject you, and I'll have to deal with your tears in Times Square at New Year."

"That sounds horrendous!"

"But we'll be in New York, so that'll make it better. Come on, Rosie. You've got nothing to lose, and everything to gain."

"I don't know," I falter.

"Book it. This year has been rubbish, let's send it out with a bang."

I stare at the webpage for a moment. It's expensive, but I can afford it with the flat sale. Fuck it, I think: Ethan wanted me to be his, and now I need to make sure he knows I want him to be mine, only mine. I hit the 'Proceed to checkout' button, enter my credit card details, and hit 'Buy'. Chloe and I are off to New York on 29 December.

Chapter Forty-One

New York is bitterly cold as Chloe and I brave the elements, arm-in-arm, walking through Central Park holding polystyrene cups of scalding coffee. We'd flown into JFK yesterday evening, checked into our hotel, and gone to a nearby Italian restaurant for pasta and prosecco, before giving in to tiredness and falling into bed. Today we had got up ridiculously early to cram in some sightseeing. We'd visited The Frick, the Statue of Liberty and my favourite, The Empire State Building.

New York is vibrant, the streets crowded with people enjoying the holiday season; the traffic is full-on, the screeches of sirens never far away from puncturing the air; the staff who work in shops and restaurants are so friendly and welcoming. It's like walking through a film set, and I love it here. It's beautiful, formidable with its tall buildings, overpowering, all-consuming and feels like it could swallow me up at any moment. It's like Ethan, I muse, intoxicating, addictive, and where I want to be.

As if reading my mind, Chloe says, "So, you need to let Ethan know you are here, arrange to meet."

"I don't know what to say," I grumble, knowing she is right.

"Happy birthday?" she suggests.

"Sounds good." I dig deep in my coat pocket, pull out my mobile and call Ethan before I have chance to even think.

"Rosie?" His voice sounds gruff.

"I need to see you," I say, cutting the crap and getting straight to the point. "I have your birthday present. Happy birthday, by the way."

"I'm in New York," he replies sharply. "Anyway, what is this? You walked out, remember?"

"You told me to go," I correct.

"Look," he sighs, "I have no inclination to argue over technicalities."

"I'm in New York," I interrupt. "I've flown three thousand miles to see you, so stop being shitty with me."

"You're here?"

"Yes."

"Where are you?" His voice rumbles low down the phone, my body responding in its normal clenching way.

"I'm walking in Central Park with Chloe."

"Fuck," he groans.

"I need to see you, Ethan," I say bluntly. "I have things that need to be said."

"Couldn't it have waited until I returned to England?"

"Obviously not," I snap. I want him to know I mean business, that I'm not here to fuck around.

"I've got plans," he says dismissively.

I mouth his words to Chloe, disappointment scorching my icy cold cheeks. I've come all this way just to be told he is busy! Chloe grabs for my phone, wrestling it out of my hand.

"Ethan, this is what is going to happen," she says calmly. "You're going to pull your head out of your arse and get out of whatever plans you have. You fucked up Rosie's Christmas, don't you dare fuck up her New Year as well. You've got an hour to rearrange things and text her where you can meet. And if you don't, I'll get her hideously drunk and make sure she sees New Year in with someone else. She's hot, and you know how Americans love an English accent. Tick tock." She ends the call. "Trust me," she says as she hands my phone back, "he'll be in touch. Jealousy is a powerful negotiator, and the thought of someone else's hands all over you will incense him. He'll call."

"I hope so," I say glumly, dropping my mobile into my bag.

I haven't thought this through, I decide. I'd let a romantic notion cloud my usual good judgement. I'd been swayed by talk of love, and as with everything that involves Ethan, I'd thrown caution to the wind. Doubt creeps stealthily through my consciousness, uncertainty blanketing my thoughts, my memories. Everything feels wrong suddenly, so wrong it feels like it's going to crush me. I'd just made the gesture of all gestures, and he had tried to fob me off. America is his world, New York his private domain, and I'd crossed the line, knowing how vehement he is about his privacy.

"It'll be OK," Chloe reassures, rubbing my arm.

"I just need a bit of time on my own," I say, unlinking myself from her hold. "Do you mind?"

She looks at me appraisingly. "Sure, whatever you need. I'm going to head back to the hotel. See you later. Just let me know what you're doing."

"OK," I agree, and walk away.

I ditch my coffee and walk for a long time. The park is beautiful; I'd love to see it in Spring, do a morning run here. Time disappears as I lose myself to chaotic thoughts, all sense of clarity draining away. I end up sitting on a bench, watching some kids play football for a bit, a couple of bouncy Border Collies dragging their owner on a fast dash. It's beginning to get dark, the daylight fading quickly as evening draws in. I should think about making a move, but I find I'm unsure of my bearings. I'm just about to retrieve my phone to pull up Google Maps to navigate back to the hotel when I see him turning the corner. Our eyes lock instantly, and I stand awkwardly.

“I've been calling you,” he says, approaching slowly, his eyes flickering down my body before returning to my face.

“Have you?” I say, pulling out my phone and seeing the missed calls and messages. “I must have knocked it onto silent.”

“It's too cold to be out here sitting on a bench,” he scolds, towering over me. I've flown all this way for him, and the first thing he does is tell me off, it is familiarly comforting. He's right, I'm freezing, bone-cold deep-freezing. I shouldn't have sat down, I should have kept walking. I step back. He’s too close and not close enough all at once. I drink him in, he’s so handsome. He even looks gorgeous wrapped up in a thick black coat, jeans, and boots. He's movie-star good-looking, his dark blond hair and sparkling blue eyes the perfect ingredients, mixed with a hard, masculine jawline and broad, well-defined shoulders. At five feet five, he makes me feel doll-like, his body looming over me like the surrounding buildings.

“Hey.” He reaches forward and trails a finger slowly down my cheek. “You look nervous.”

I swallow and blink rapidly, my words blocked in my throat. I came here to fight for him, but I can't even manage a word. I shiver involuntarily and witness a change in him; everything softens, the hard edges receding.

“Ssh,” he soothes, his finger trailing across my bottom lip. “Whatever it is you flew all this way to tell me, it can wait. Just tell me you're OK?”

“It can’t wait!” I splutter.

“It can.” He cups my face in his hands and leans down, his lips warm on mine, chasing away the cold. “You're here,” he whispers.

“I came to tell you that I don't want this to be the end,” I gasp out, before I fall against him, my arms slipping around his waist.

“Rosie,” he pulls me tight against him and squeezes. “Me neither. Come home with me, let me get you warm.”

“Will anyone be there?”

“No. I live alone. I have done for years. Well, until you. Come on, let's go.” I close my eyes, just feeling him. The way his arms feel around me, the solidness of his body pressed to mine. He's always made me feel so safe, right from the very beginning.

“I can't let you go,” I say into his chest. “I tried, but I can't do it. I came here to fight for you, for us.”

He kisses the top of my head and squeezes me even tighter, his fingers combing through my windswept hair.

"I need to get you home. You're freezing." He releases me and shifts out of my hold, putting his arm around my waist and pulling me close again. I reach for his free hand and we walk through the park in silence.

He flags down a taxi and helps me in before joining me on the back seat, our hands clasped together on his lap. Confidence oozes from him, a self-assuredness that captivates me. I'm under his spell, lost completely to him. I came here to fight for us, for him, for me, but my insides have turned to jelly, my brain unable to process meaningful thought. I'm barely cognisant of arriving, of getting into the lift with him and entering his penthouse apartment.

My attention flickers to the view from the glass wall, recognition pricking sharply through the hazy confusion. I walk across the large living space to look out at the Manhattan skyline, my mind catapulted back to the painting on Ethan's bedroom wall in Knightsbridge.

"It's amazing," I breathe as he comes up behind me, slides his arms around my waist and nuzzles against my neck.

"You're amazing," his words vibrate against my skin. "I can't believe you flew all this way. I don't want to fuck this up, but I don't know how to make this right either."

"I know," I shudder.

"I'm going to run you a bath," he says decisively. "You need to get warm."

"Can I look around?" I ask.

"Sure," he smiles, and I feel the cold beginning to thaw.

"Happy birthday." I reach up to kiss him.

His lips meet mine and what was supposed to be a mere peck turns into something else. His lips press against mine, his tongue searching out mine as it pushes into my mouth. His eyes glaze over with desire, his hands cupping my bum as he draws me close, his erection nudging into my stomach through all our layers of clothing.

"Shower," he growls into my mouth, picks me up and carries me through the apartment to his bedroom. He drops me onto his bed, and I let him undress me and watch him strip. The water scorches between us, skin on skin. Our lips collide desperately, our tongues tasting each other, unable to get enough. He manoeuvres us to a wall, lifting me and telling me to wrap my legs around his waist. I comply, my body yearning for his.

"Tell me there hasn't been anyone else?" he orders, his cock pressing hard at my entrance.

"No one else," I gasp. "You?"

"Of course not!"

He drives into me, filling me completely. He stills, his eyes finding mine, before he starts to move. He slides out and slams back hard into me.

"Tell me you're mine," he demands, pulling out again.

"I'm yours," I whisper.

"And you won't leave me again," he says, his tip teasing me.

"Fuck!" I try to sink onto him, needing him inside me, needing him to possess me from the inside out.

"Tell me," he says, holding my hips still. "Tell me you won't walk out again."

"I won't."

He thrusts hard into me and begins to claim me. His strokes are possessive, rough, and my body accepts him, tension building as he takes me hard, fast. His thumb finds my clit, circling, bringing me quickly to the edge. My muscles clench around him as I let him pull me over with him. I bury my face in his shoulder, my mind lost, my body belonging to him.

"Best birthday present ever," he grins.

"Ethan, I don't think I can stand."

"Was it too much? Did I hurt you?"

"Too much and not enough," I sigh.

"I've got you." He strokes my back, moving us back under the shower stream. "And it's never going to be enough."

"I love you," I say.

"I know." He repositions my head slightly so he can stare down at me. "Just give me time, OK? I'm not good at this. But I'll get there."

"I know." I close my eyes contentedly, knowing he will, sensing it deep within my core...

Chapter Forty-Two

"I hear you resigned?" Ethan props himself up on an elbow and stares down at me.

"I told you I was going to," I say groggily, my limbs still feeling boneless.

"Hmm," he considers. "You don't need to."

I stroke his arm, his muscles bunching under the skin. "It's easier this way."

"I'm not going to be there forever. You like your job. You've told me plenty of times."

I smile, my hand trailing up to graze over rough stubble. "I do, but my flat sold, and it just feels like the right time to try something new."

"We'll talk later," he murmurs and begins to pepper my face with kisses. "God, I've missed you, missed this."

He rolls me onto my back, his kisses travelling lower, his lips pressing harder, his tongue explorative, his teeth biting gently. His hands cup my breasts, his thumbs rubbing my nipples into hard peaks. He rolls on top of me, pushing me into the mattress, his body warm against mine, and I arch my back as his mouth hovers over my right breast, his breath hardening the nipple further. He grins up at me, seeing my need, enjoying making me wait. He bends down, his mouth warm, his tongue hard as it flicks, his teeth scraping against my skin. His hand glides over my stomach, his touch light, his hand skimming between my legs, his fingers barely touching me. His groan vibrates through me as his fingers dip inside, my wetness for him coating them. He trails lazy kisses down my stomach, shifting so his shoulders are between my legs, his tongue tasting me in one languid stroke from my opening to my clitoris. His eyes twinkle; he knows what he does to me, and he enjoys it. His tongue circles my opening before plunging inside, a finger trailing up to circle my throbbing clit, the nerves aching for release.

"Ethan," I gasp out as he drags me up off the bed. "It's too much," I wriggle against him, my hands flailing against his muscular shoulders.

"It's not enough," his words rumble against me, travelling to every nerve-ending. He grabs my wrists with one hand, securing them to the bed, and then slides his tongue up, his mouth tasting, his tongue flicking, his fingers sliding deep inside me, rubbing the spot that he knows sends me over. He makes me come hard and long, my body consumed by it, I tremble as he draws my orgasm on and on. Noises slip from my mouth, uncensored, as I spiral uncontrollably. Release crashes over me, the waves of pleasure fizzing everywhere. His lips stay against me, sucking every last drop. My eyes close, my body is weak, my brain unable to function. Sex in the shower had been quick, hard, rushed, and the release had been drawn out quickly, but this... this was tender, slow, and Ethan had literally sucked every inch of desire to the surface and shattered it into a million pieces. A tiredness shrouds me, oblivion cocooning me.

"Hey, beautiful," he kisses my eyelids and scoops me against his warm body. "Open your eyes," he whispers.

"I can't. I don't have the energy." He chuckles. "No one's ever made me feel like you do," I confess.

"Good. You look so beautiful right now, all fucked and sleepy. I could watch you like this all day, knowing that it's because of me."

"I haven't been sleeping very well," I yawn.

"Me neither."

"I'm sorry I ruined your birthday plans."

"You've ruined nothing." He kisses my forehead. "I told you in the shower. Best birthday present ever. I meant it."

"Sex?" I slowly open my eyes.

"You," he says, his voice husky, sexy.

"Don't," I warn, attempting to wriggle away.

"You," he repeats, his arm vicelike, not letting me go.

"You can't say lovely things like that!" I protest.

"Why? It's true. I've never lied to you, have I?"

"Isn't that why we're here, because you have?"

"No. I kept something from you, that's different. I seem to remember you told me that once. I've never told you something that's not true. Sure, I've not told you stuff, and I know that I've hurt you, but I have never said anything I didn't mean."

"I can't think straight."

"Then don't. Just let me hold you. I want you in my bed, I want to wake up with you in the morning. We'll talk tomorrow. I promise. No lies."

"Promise?"

"Promise," he says, and kisses my forehead. "You want to have a nap, then order take out?"

"A nap?" I snort. "Being forty has changed you."

"You're hysterical," he smiles.

"I've got your present," I say, sitting up. "Sex was just the prelude. Get dressed, I want you to see it. And I want to properly look around your apartment, too. A whistle-stop tour to your bedroom does not count."

The apartment is spacious, and unlike Knightsbridge, it has a more homely feel. Family photographs are dotted around the rooms, as are some spectacular paintings hanging from the bright white walls. Ethan seems to have a penchant for cityscapes: New York, Paris, London, Rome, all adorn various walls.

"Do you get interior designers to help you?" I ask, taking in the magnificent kitchen, all the integrated appliances gleaming as if this is a show-kitchen. Cleanliness is one of Ethan's little foibles, he likes everything to be neat, tidy and in its place. The notable exception is when sex is involved: he doesn't mind making a mess then.

"No," he says, opening the double-doored fridge and taking out a bottle of wine.

"You chose all this? You've got such good taste."

"I know." He pulls me close and bends to kiss me sweetly on the mouth. "I still can't get over the fact you've flown all the way here."

"Present." I break out of his hold, catching the gleam in his eye and needing to stop his distraction tactics. I cross the room and sink onto the huge black leather sofa, retrieving a flat A4 package from my bag. He joins me, putting two glasses on the glass coffee table before he comes to sit next to me, crowding me into the corner of the sofa, mischief clearly on his mind.

"Present," I say firmly and hand it to him.

"Thank you," he grins and carefully unwraps the blue paper dotted with silver stars.

"I did it when you were here in October," I babble, hoping he likes it.

"You painted this?" he asks, his eyes wide.

The picture is of Zeus, who is sitting in his characteristic pose with his head to the side, ears pricked. The lake at Tranquillity is the backdrop. It had taken a lot of time and effort, particularly as I haven't painted for years, but I'd been pleased with the results.

"It's incredible." Ethan concentrates on the painting, his expression one of incredulity. "It looks so real, so like him, like it's a photo. I can't believe you did this for me."

"You like it?"

"I love it," he beams, putting it down gently on the table and pulling me onto his lap. "I don't know what to say. Thank you. I still can't get over the fact you're here."

"Did I do the right thing by coming?"

"Yes." He raises my hand to his mouth, kissing my knuckles. "I'm going to make things better, I just need some time, OK?"

I nod, everything suddenly feeling right.

Chapter Forty-Three

I stare down glumly into my coffee, chewing my lower lip, trying to process what Ethan is saying. I never warned him I was coming, I try to rationalise – it's not his fault he has plans today. But irritation bubbles just under the surface all the same.

"Hey." He slides his arms around my waist and nuzzles into the side of my neck. "I'm sorry. This can't wait."

"You said we'd talk," I say tensely.

"We will, but later. I'll meet you in Long Island later for dinner."

"Can't I just stay here in the city? I'll spend time with Chloe doing touristy things, and then when you're ready you can pick me up."

"Chloe's with Josh," Ethan says, his hands starting to massage my shoulders. "Did she not tell you? He's invited her along to the fireworks, so she'll be there this afternoon. God, you're tense, I really need to up my game."

At New Year, the Harbers spend time at their luxury villa on the beach in Long Island. It's a tradition, and as I had already caused Ethan to cancel his birthday dinner with his parents last night, I guess I shouldn't begrudge him family time. He's returning to England with Josh in a couple of days, and I know Chase and Ellen are going to miss their boys. I'm being unfair, I know, but the fact is that I came here to talk, to get the truth, and I hadn't bargained on a full family gathering as part of the process.

"I'll be as quick as I can," he murmurs into my ear, and presses his thumbs hard into a knotted muscle.

My head snaps back. "Bloody hell, Ethan, that hurts."

His fingers continue to knead, the pain fizzling away into something more pleasurable. I give in and lean back on the bar stool, my back pressing up hard against his chest, and close my eyes. His fingers move up my neck, the pressure lessening, his fingers unknotting tension. He's good at this, too good.

My mind refocuses to Ethan telling me Chloe and Josh are together. I'd caught a glimpse of something from her back in November, but Chloe hadn't said anything further, and I hadn't thought about it until now. She had been very encouraging about my trip; she had been the one to suggest she comes with me, and I now wonder if she had her own agenda. Wait until I speak to her!

"Better?" he asks, interrupting my thoughts. I swivel on the stool and wrap my arms around him, snuggling in. He folds me into a tight hug and strokes the hair away from my face before stooping down and kissing me softly on the mouth.

"I've got to go," he murmurs against my lips. "I'm sorry. I'll drop you back at your hotel."

"One more minute," I urge, slipping off the stool and pressing my body up against his. His eyes soften to the clearest of blues and he squeezes me, one of his big hands splaying over my lower back.

"You said we'd talk?" I say anxiously.

"Look at me." He tilts my head back. "I just need to get some things sorted and then I'll be all yours. We'll talk, I promise you." I push down my needy objections and follow him out of his apartment, wearing the clothes I arrived in yesterday.

Wow. I inwardly whistle as he opens the passenger door to a black Corvette for me. He has great taste in cars! What am I thinking? He has great taste in clothes, in interior design, in food... The man just has great taste, full stop.

"What?" He raises an eyebrow and starts up the engine.

"Another nice car," I grin goofily and click in my seatbelt. "Suits you."

He thrums his fingers on the steering wheel for a moment, then pulls out of the car park. I sit back in my seat and marvel at the way he drives with such control and precision. I never tire of watching him drive, finding watching the way he handles the car with such confidence arousing.

"I'll show you New York for real next time," he says as we wait at a light. "Maybe we could come back for a week in Spring?"

I swallow a lump of emotion that suddenly has formed in my throat. Spring. He's thinking ahead, to the future, and I'm still in it. I want to beg him not to go wherever he is going and to stay with me, to talk this through. We've reached our crossroads now, and the time has come to decide where we go from here. I want to make that decision this instant, to fight for us, but Ethan is delaying, and although he makes references about us being together in a few months it's not enough to give me peace of mind. The knowledge of his wife sits heavy on my shoulders, and he still hasn't tried to explain their relationship. I know I make him happy – I see it, I feel it – but she's holding him back, I sense that too.

"We're here," he says five minutes later, pulling in at the kerb. "Rosie?" He says my name like a command and my eyes flicker to his. "I feel like I lost you back there. Talk to me."

"Later." I fumble with the door handle.

"Fuck later," he grabs my wrist. "Now."

"No," I snap. "You're not the only one who needs time. Go and do whatever you need to do."

He sighs and releases my wrist. "Later, then."

I get out of the car and head into the hotel and up to my room, where I collapse onto my bed in a state of utter despondency. I came here to fight for him, but I'm doing a terrible job. I'm messing this all up and I don't know how to make it right.

A knock on my door stirs me from my despair and I open it to find Chloe, looking sheepish.

“Ethan called,” she says, pushing into my room.

“Called you or Josh?” I ask with a wink.

“Josh,” she replies with a smile. “Apparently you left him in a bit of a mood, he wants me to make sure you come to the New Year fireworks at the beach. What's happened?” She plumps herself on my bed.

“It just feels wrong, going to a family gathering without him, especially as nothing has been resolved.”

“What have you been doing all this time?” She wrinkles her nose. “Actually, don't tell me. He's going to join us later, it'll be fine.”

I blush. “What about you and Josh? Ethan said you were together, and that Josh has invited you tonight.”

Chloe puts up her hands. “It's just fun. He's nice.”

“And how long has this ‘fun’ been going on for?”

“Well, we've seen each other a couple of times. I like him, but it's not serious.”

Chloe doesn't do serious – well, not since her long-term boyfriend outed himself as gay at her thirtieth birthday party. She has trust issues, and although she acts all confident, she isn't, not really. Josh is nice, decent, and I approve of them together.

“You should have told me,” I mock-pout.

She shrugs. “Sorry.”

Josh arrives half an hour later to drive us to the coast. It's kind of awkward seeing him, the last time being when I walked out at Thanksgiving. The whole day is going to be awkward, and seeing Chelsea again just unpleasant. I'd feel better if Ethan were beside me, but he isn't going to make it until much later.

“I forgot my phone in my room,” announces Chloe as we leave the hotel. “I'll be two minutes.”

Josh turns to me as we wait outside, his hands in his coat pockets. “He's been miserable without you,” he says. “You're really good for him, you know? Just give him the time to figure it all out, he's not great with this kind of stuff.”

“I'm here, aren't I?” I respond defensively.

I zone out for much of the journey, staring out of the window from the back seat as we leave the skyscrapers behind. The Harbers' holiday retreat is set off a main road, at the end of a winding track through the trees, which opens up to a clearing with a magnificent sea view, the house situated at the top of a hill which slopes down to a private beach.

"Wow." Chloe voices my own thoughts. "It's beautiful. It must be amazing in the summer."

"It is," grins Josh. "We used to spend holidays here when we were kids. It was great."

We gather our belongings and head inside, where we are met by a smiling Chase and Ellen. She embraces me in a quick tight hug, whispering in my ear how lovely it is to see me again. Chase beams, his expression one of utter welcome. Josh is like his father, I muse, laid-back and friendly.

"Hi." There's a whooshing sound and Chelsea appears in her wheelchair. She's wrapped up in a fluffy pink cardigan, looking the epitome of sweet, a plait trailing over a shoulder. "I'll take Rosie out to the cottage."

"Ethan doesn't stay in the house," explains Chase.

"Oh," I falter.

"Great," Ellen simpers. "I'll start making drinks for all of us. You go settle in and freshen up."

I pick up my overnight bag and follow Chelsea down a long hall, through a huge kitchen and out onto a veranda, heaters already on to combat the December chill. She powers down a sloping path, a meticulous lawned area on both sides, and turns a sharp right to reveal a cute little cottage set at the bottom of the garden, poised on a ledge that drops down to the sand.

"Why does Ethan stay down here on his own?" I ask, dropping my bag and leaning on the white railing that lines the drop.

"You know Ethan, he likes his privacy," she replies. "Look." She turns her chair to face me, her face serious. "I think I might owe you an apology."

"Really? Why?"

"I was wrong to make sure you saw the wedding picture of Ethan and Melissa."

"At least you were honest," I concede. "It's more than anyone else has been, more than your brother."

"It wasn't my place." She looks super-uncomfortable, her fingers playing nervously with the key in her hand. She reaches up, battling with the lock. "This door," she complains, wriggling the key in the hole.

"Do you want me to?" I offer as she leans further forward in her chair.

“Fuck,” she screeches as the door gives way and she topples out of her wheelchair into a heap on the floor.

“Shit!” I bend down. “Are you OK? Should I get someone?”

“Fucking Ethan,” she whines, bashing the ground with a fist. “I've told him about this shitty lock.”

“What shall I do?” I flounder.

“Don't just stand there,” she snaps irritably. “Help me back up.”

She reaches back for her chair and begins to bum-shuffle, pulling herself up, and I reach to help. She grits her teeth, the effort obvious on her face. It's the first sign of emotion that I've really seen from her, with the exception of her characteristic bitchiness.

“Don't look at me like that,” she grimaces as she repositions herself.

“Sorry. Are you hurt?”

She shakes her head and recomposes herself. “I've been a complete bitch to you, haven't I?”

I laugh awkwardly. “Pretty much, yes.”

“I know you love him. He deserves to be happy.”

“Don't we all?” I say, picking up my bag and heading inside.

“Come back to the house when you're ready,” she calls as she turns her wheelchair and powers away.

The cottage is small, but really cosy. A comfortable cream sofa lines one wall in the living room and a log burner is opposite, which I imagine makes the room lovely and snug. There's the expected huge TV screen high up on the wall and to the right is a tall oak bookshelf, crammed full of books. Across the other side of the hall is the bedroom, a four-poster bed dominating most of the room, a walk-in wardrobe on the far wall and a bedside table nestled into the other corner. There's a small kitchen, with basic amenities but none of the flashiness of Knightsbridge or Manhattan. It's practical, not luxurious, as is the bathroom with its tub and shower cubicle.

I return to the bedroom and pull out my mobile from my bag, spying a text from Ethan.

“I might be later than expected.”

I hit his number and stretch out onto the soft mattress, trying to quell my irritation.

“Hey,” he answers in a hushed voice.

“When are you going to be here?” I ask.

"Probably about ten," he sighs. "I'm sorry. ...Rosie?" He prompts after an awkward silence.

"It's weird being here without you," I grumble.

"Chloe's there, you like Josh, my parents adore you."

"I came here to see you."

"I know, and I love that you did that for me, but I need to sort things out here and then I'll be with you."

"Whatever."

"I'm trying." Frustration rumbles down the line.

"Are you?" I serve the frustration right back. "Because it feels like you're delaying."

"I'm not arguing with you on the phone," he bristles. "I'll be there as soon as I can."

He ends the call before I have chance to think of a catty reply. The thought of spending the next few hours with his family, however nice they are, is just hellish. I flop back onto the pillows and scrunch my eyes shut, mustering up the energy to return to the main house with a degree of civility. My issue is with Ethan, not with them, even Chelsea seems to be making an effort, and I need to suck it up for just a little longer.

Chapter Forty-Four

Ellen and Chase are wonderful hosts, creating such a relaxed and homely atmosphere. They're always offering drinks or popping into the kitchen to check on food, bossing their children around playfully whilst treating Chloe and I like princesses. Occasionally, I think I catch them looking pityingly at me, but then they smile reassuringly and paranoia creeps in that I'm imagining things that just aren't there. As every hour crawls by, bringing no arrival of Ethan, my anxiety and irritation levels heighten. I feel like a fraud being here.

"He'll be here," Chelsea says in a quiet voice so only I can hear.

I drop my mobile onto the table and shrug. "He was supposed to be here an hour ago. At this rate he won't even be here for midnight."

"He's trying," she says weakly.

I get up and wander inside to top up my champagne. I'm drinking slowly, not wanting to be a drunken mess when Ethan does eventually arrive, if he arrives...

"Sausage roll?" Ellen passes me one from a nearby tray on the worksurface. "Be careful, they might still be a bit hot," she warns as she retrieves a quiche from the oven. All afternoon and evening she has been in and out of the kitchen, cooking up loads of party snacks, which we have been steadily ploughing our way through.

"Mm," I groan in appreciation. "Best sausage rolls ever."

"Aren't they?" A familiar drawl comes from behind me, a hand stealing the remainder from my hand and popping it into his mouth.

"You're here?" I gasp in surprise, turning and being drawn against Ethan's cold body, his arms sliding around my waist. I hear him swallow before he leans down to whisper, "Hey you."

"Hi," I manage, emotion suffocating me. He kisses my forehead and releases me, going to hug Ellen. They talk, I'm not sure what about because my mind has disconnected from everything apart from how devastatingly good-looking he looks in a sapphire-blue jumper and black jeans. I look at him as if seeing him for the very first time, and my breath catches. I don't think I'll ever tire of just watching him.

The others crowd in and everyone says hello, refills drinks and helps themselves to food. I feel myself getting whisked along with them all back out onto the veranda, where Ethan pulls me onto his lap and kisses me softly on the mouth.

"I thought you weren't going to make it in time," I say quietly.

"There was an accident on the freeway, I got stuck. I would have called, but you were pissed off with me already."

Midnight rushes up on us and the New Year is seen in through beautiful fireworks, Chase in his element as he lets them off, his sons nearby to lend him a hand. Bright colours illuminate the sky, shrill whistles, fizzes, and bangs echoing in the darkness, the smell of smoke clinging to the air. There's lots of hugging and new year wishes. Everyone seems happy – even Chelsea gives me a smile. I want this to be my New Year tradition, I realise.

"Come on." Ethan slips an arm around my waist. "I want you all to myself." He raises his voice. "We're heading off."

I lean against the railings outside the cottage whilst Ethan curses and battles with the lock. I hear the door give way and then his hands are on my hips, turning me, his full lips warm against mine. My hands creep up his chest, my arms looping around his neck, my fingers tangling in his windswept hair. Our kisses are long, our tongues savouring each other, our lips revelling in the touch of skin on skin. Right from the beginning, up high in the dark on a big wheel, his kiss has cracked me open, exposing everything for him to take. And he has taken every bit of me, claiming it as his.

"Happy new year, sweetheart," he whispers in my ear.

"I hope so," I whisper back.

He squeezes me tightly. "Come inside, I want to see you. We've got talking to do."

I watch him as he sets about lighting the log burner, the crackling sound filling the room, combining with the smell of wood burning, the flickering light dancing on the wall. It's just me and him, in our own slice of paradise, and it feels like we both belong here. Anticipation and adrenaline combine with fear and desolation. We've known each other for just over four months and right now, in this moment, everything is going to be laid out there. He finally wants to talk, and I'm terrified of what he is about to say.

"You look worried." He catches my eye and comes to sit next to me. "You don't need to be." He leans forward and opens his briefcase, pulling out an A4 folder which he hands to me. "I went to see my lawyer today." He indicates that I should open the folder and my eyes skim quickly across the writing.

"You're filing for divorce?" I say, my eyes flicking to his.

He nods, returning the folder to the briefcase. "It's the right time. To be honest, it's been time for a good few years, but it just hasn't felt right up until now, up until you. You're everything I didn't know I needed."

"Ethan..." A tear escapes out of the corner of my eye as emotion threatens to overwhelm me.

"Hey," he cups my chin in his hand and stares reassuringly at me. "It's OK. You want me to tell you everything?"

"I can't share you," the words come out shakily and I realise that the possessiveness runs both ways. I need him to be mine just as much as he does me. And that's what monogamy is, isn't it? Just two people committed in their bubble.

"You haven't been. I promise." He takes both of my hands in his, his thumbs brushing over my knuckles in that way he has. "Melissa and I met each other at work," he begins. "It wasn't like when I met you, I didn't notice her over someone's shoulder and know I needed to have her."

"You felt it too?" I ask.

"I knew I wanted to fuck you," he grins.

"You are still such a sweet talker!" I giggle, slapping him playfully.

"To be successful you had to put in long hours, socialise with the right people. Melissa and I were thrust together, I guess, both trying to find our feet in a highly competitive industry. We went to the same parties, it just seemed natural that we ended up together. We were both highly motivated professionally, and I guess quite selfish when I look back at it now. We drank a lot, and we both started taking coke."

"You hate drugs," I say, my eyes widening.

"I hate what they can do to people." He closes his eyes for a moment, composing himself. "My mom and dad weren't great fans of hers, they thought she was self-obsessed, but to be honest so was I. We thought we loved each other, I guess we did in our own screwed-up way. Work was always important to me, I needed to be successful, and I was. Mel lost focus, she started to enjoy the socialising part more than the work. I didn't notice at first, but she became erratic at work, screwed up deals. She took a lot more coke than I was aware of and it became a problem, so much so that she got fired. Not long after that, she found out she was pregnant."

For a moment I stop breathing, my entire body tensing as my brain struggles with the prospect of Ethan having a child, maybe even children, I know nothing about. He wouldn't have kept that from me – he couldn't have kept that from me – could he?

"I don't have kids," he says as if reading my mind.

"I'm sorry." I stand, needing to get some fresh air, to get my thoughts straight. I catch sadness in his eyes, and I hate to see it. I stagger out and cling to the railings, hating myself for being relieved that he doesn't have children, which means he lost a baby.

"Rosie," he stands close behind me, his hands resting over mine. "I wanted to tell you, that day in the boardroom when you told me about your miscarriages, I wanted to tell you so badly."

"I'm sorry," I whisper. "What happened?"

"Well, we were coming up to our thirtieth birthdays and a baby, although unplanned seemed the right thing. She was happy, which made my life easier, and I wanted to be a dad. We got engaged. Melissa had the first miscarriage at ten weeks."

"First?"

"Yeah, we had four altogether." I turn and wrap my arms around his waist, squeezing him as tightly as I can, my heart squeezing for the pain I know he would have gone through.

"When Melissa found out she was pregnant she changed, like she seemed content, I guess. She stopped the drugs, and it seemed like she had a purpose. After the first miscarriage, I thought it was still the right thing to do to marry her. She was so incredibly sad, and a wedding gave her something to look forward to, and we'd agreed to try again. We got married quickly, much to the disapproval of my parents, and we got pregnant again and again and again... Getting pregnant didn't seem to be our problem, Mel just couldn't carry them for longer than three months. The doctors didn't know why. She suffered from serious episodes of depression, and I think somewhere along the way I started to feel like she was a responsibility that I had to look after.

She also struggled with drug addiction on and off. I always felt responsible for that because I was the one to introduce her to coke on a night out, I remember it like it was yesterday, and I used to torment myself with what she'd have been like if I hadn't. Chelsea, unbeknownst to me, was dabbling with pills and they became really good friends. I thought it was kinda sweet. One night, when I was out of town on business, they went out to a party and Melissa drove our car off her face on coke with my kid sister in the passenger seat, they came off the road. That's how Chelsea ended up in a wheelchair six years ago. And that was the end for my marriage."

"That's horrible."

"It made me realise I'd stopped loving Melissa a long time ago, but I still cared about what happened to her. She's not a bad person, she's just vulnerable. Before the accident I think I wanted to believe that I could fix her. Stupid, I know..."

"What kind of a relationship do you have with her now?" I ask.

"We don't really have one of any kind any more. I get told when she's in psych units, or when she goes to rehab, I'm still her next of kin. It's why I came back before Christmas. She was in a bad way, Chelsea was with her. She's in a new rehab centre at the moment and although it's early days, her doctors are pleased. She knows about you, about me wanting a divorce. I can't keep being there for her, it's not my place, it hasn't been for years. I hadn't anticipated getting involved with anyone, not long-term anyway, so it was fine for her to still depend on me, but you changed that..."

We stand in silence, holding each other as our thoughts settle. His story makes me sad for him, sad that he's been in a marriage that doesn't appear to have been full of love. I want him to know what it feels like to be loved, so completely, so devotedly. I look up at him and know with utter certainty that coming to New York to fight for him was absolutely the right thing to do.

"I love you," I whisper.

"You better. Come on, it's freezing, let's go in."

"Why do you have your own cottage away from your family? I ask, following him into the kitchen.

"I like my privacy, my own space. I always have." He frowns and pulls me against his firm body. "Not with you, though. I don't want space from you." His lips slant across mine, his tongue pressing into my mouth, stroking against mine, his teeth sucking at my lower lip. My muscles clench in that way they have when he touches me. He lessens the kiss and rests his forehead against mine, his face suddenly serious.

"I'm not going to get this right all of the time," he says.

"I know," I soothe, my fingers trailing the stubble on his jaw.

"I can be an asshole."

I laugh and push at his chest. "You don't need to tell me that."

"Rosie," he grabs my wrists, intent on remaining serious, "I don't want to lose you. I'm not good at this, but I want to do better, because of you." I blink up at him, my breath catching as I glimpse a flicker of vulnerability. He wants this as much as I do...

A strand of sadness uncurls in the pit of my stomach. What kind of a man stays married to a woman he doesn't even love? He's been shackled to her by some misguided duty or obligation and shut himself off from anyone else. Slowly but surely, he's letting me into his private world. My issue was with trust, the thought of laying it all out there for someone again, but his issue is with trusting himself, not me. He married in haste, repented at leisure, and the years of solitude have made him doubt his ability to love, to be loved.

"Take me to bed," I say, an idea forming.

He grins, releases my wrists and scoops me over his shoulder, his hand slapping my bum as he marches into the bedroom.

"Ethan," I gasp, five minutes later when our bodies are tangled in a naked heap on the bed.

"Hmm?" he asks, his tongue circling a nipple.

I move, positioning myself into a kneeling position, pulling him up. "I want you to take me from behind."

"Are you sure?" His voice is gravelly.

"I trust you," I reply simply.

Since my assault, I'd had issues with him touching me from behind, my mind always tripping back to being pushed down onto the carpet, but right now I need Ethan to know, to feel, that I trust him completely. I want him to know I trust him with everything in the hope that it helps him realise he can trust his judgement when it comes to us. This is for him. I feel his body against mine, his hands reaching around to cup my breasts, his lips kissing the hollow of my neck. I concentrate my mind on him, his touch, his breathing.

"You OK?" he whispers. I nod, my hand reaching back to guide his cock to my entrance. I push back, feeling his head enter me. He winds my ponytail around his wrist and pulls my head back, so our eyes meet. Slowly, gently, he pushes in, his eyes glued to mine.

"Breathe," he whispers, lowering his lips for a swift kiss.

We stay still for a long time, his cock buried completely in me. My mind flips back, my body knotting into a tight rigidity, which Ethan notices. He doesn't move, just strokes my back, as he waits for the tension to lessen. I concentrate on him, feeling his touch, getting lost in his eyes, and eventually he begins to move. He glides slowly at first, rocking into me in long deep thrusts, and everything else ceases to exist. My body responds to him, as it always has, hungry, needy, my hips bucking against him as I ache for more. Gentle and slow transforms into hard, pounding thrusts, our bodies slapping together as we come. He crushes me into the mattress and I soak it in, knowing I'll never get enough of this man.

"Happy new year," I murmur into the pillow.

He groans and rolls off me, scooping me into his arms and kissing my forehead. "Happy new year, beautiful."

Chapter Forty-Five

I wake to the sensation of light kisses on my shoulder, a hand cupping my breast, the feeling of his erection against me. The man is insatiable and seems to have the sexual appetite of an eighteen-year-old.

“I know you're awake,” he whispers, nipping my earlobe.

“I am now,” I grumble. "Aren't you ever tired?" I bury my face in the pillows.

“Never of you,” he replies smoothly.

“Erg, get off me,” I scoff, pushing him away.

“Too much?” he chuckles.

I roll over, getting comfortable in the crook of his arm. “Never enough. Good morning.”

The phone on the bedside table starts ringing, and he reaches for the receiver with a sigh. He listens, and says we'll be over in half an hour.

“We're being summoned for breakfast,” he says apologetically. “Do you mind?”

“Of course not. I'm starving, actually.”

When we arrive, everyone is sitting around the large dining room table, tucking in. We take our seats, Ethan serving me a pancake as I pour us coffee. Everyone looks tired, and the packet of Tylenol by the coffee pot suggests hangovers.

“Your father got out the tequila,” Ellen says, washing down two tablets with some water and sliding the packet across to a green-looking Chelsea.

“They never learn,” Chase says heartily, forking bacon into his mouth, apparently not suffering at all. I eat two pancakes smothered in maple syrup and feel completely stuffed, shaking my head as Ethan offers me bacon.

“When are you heading back to the city?” Chase directs his question to his sons.

“Soon,” Ethan replies. “The girls are flying back first thing in the morning, and we're catching the evening flight after them.”

“Shame you can't all fly together,” Ellen says, rubbing two fingers against her temple.

“That's what happens when they don't tell us they are coming,” Josh says.

“We didn't know we were coming,” Chloe says. “We were being spontaneous. Anyway, I'm sure we'll be fed up with you both by tomorrow and be relieved to get away.”

“Probably.” Josh smiles brightly, his attention totally focused on her. It's sweet.

“I'd like to go for a walk on the beach before we leave,” I say quietly to Ethan.

"Sure," he nods, getting up to help clear things away.

"You OK?" he asks ten minutes later, as we descend the steep steps near the cottage that lead down to the sand. "My family can be a little full-on at times."

"They're really nice. Your mum and dad have been so welcoming. I wish you could have met my parents. They'd have liked you." He wraps me up in a tight hug, his lips pressing against the top of my head. I let him hold me, standing still on the beach, and wait for the sudden wave of sadness to recede.

"Tell me about them," he says.

We spend the next half-hour walking, hand in hand, and I tell him about my childhood, what it had been like to grow up as an only child.

"It'll be fifteen years in July, and most of the time it's just something that is there in the background, but there'll be events that make me wish they were still here. You're a close family, it's lovely to watch, but there's a part of me that's envious. I miss them..."

"Of course you do. If my family gets too much for you, if Mom starts to smother you, then let me know."

"No," I shake my head. "It's not that. Your mum's lovely, really kind. She makes me feel like I belong here."

"You do, with me," he leans down to kiss me hard, possessively, on the mouth. I pull away and stare up at him, uncertain how to ask the question that has been niggling in my head since last night.

"Rosie?" he prompts.

I shrug dismissively, not wanting to ruin the moment. "It's nothing."

He places his hands on my shoulders, his eyes rooting me to the spot. "What is it? Come on, let's get it all out there before we go back to England."

"Last night," I say nervously, "you said you wanted to be a dad."

He blinks, trying to remember, and then his expression softens. "I did. When I found out Mel was pregnant it felt right, I wanted our baby, our babies."

"I can't..."

"I know," he soothes.

"I don't think I can try again, Ethan." I take in a deep breath. "If it is something you still want, I don't think..."

"Look at me." His voice has that commanding edge and my eyes meet his impenetrable gaze. "I want you, just you. I know how much that disappointment hurts, I saw it on your face when you told me what you'd been through. If you're asking me to choose between you and the possibility of children with someone else, then I choose you, every time."

"I'm sorry."

"Don't." He pulls me close and holds me, a hand circling my back. "I don't want to try either. I've been single for six years, if I'd wanted kids I'm pretty confident I could have found someone to give me them. I fucked enough women, I wasn't short of offers." I tense, really not wanting to hear that. "I'm sorry," his voice softens. "I just need you to believe me. You. Us. It's what I want."

I believe him and relief makes me smile up at him. I used to think having my own child was all I really ever wanted, but it broke me, the hope, the disappointment, the pain. I thought I'd always feel an emptiness, but right here, right now, I feel like this is it, that Ethan is all I ever wanted. We kiss tenderly, and it feels like he feels the same too.

"What happens when we return home?" I ask when we are back in the cottage, packing up our things.

"What would you like to happen?" He arches an eyebrow at me.

"I want people to know we're together."

"By people, you mean work?"

I nod, unable to meet his gaze, a flurry of anxiety uncurling in the pit of my stomach. Secrecy at work had been non-negotiable, even though I'd tried to enter into discussions on the matter a couple of times.

"OK." He releases my bottom lip from my teeth. "You're adorable when you're nervous."

"OK?" I blink disbelievingly up at him.

"OK," he whispers.

***

The New Year trip to New York was far too short, the majority of the time occupied by men and not visiting the sights. Chloe and I had spent a ridiculous amount of money on a hotel, which we'd only spent the first night actually staying in. But the trip had been perfect, leaving us with the tantalising prospect of a return some time not so far in the future. We'd driven back to the city, and Chloe and Josh had come to Ethan's apartment for dinner on our final night. It had been a relaxed evening, and the four of us together had just felt right.

Before I knew it I was kissing Ethan goodbye in a busy JFK airport, arranging for him to come and collect me from Nan's when he landed. And then Chloe and I were sinking into our aeroplane seats, both wearing a look of contentment and total tiredness.

“So, best New Year ever?” she yawns.

“Completely. I love New York.”

“Next time we need to do more, go shopping, we really didn't do as much as we should have.”

“I know, I’m sorry,” I say apologetically.

“I'm not,” she sighs happily. “It was amazing, and you got Ethan, which was the entire point of our trip.”

“So, he said we can tell people at work about us,” I say.

“Halle-fucking-luja! Has he dropped the L word yet?”

“No. But I feel it, even if he hasn't said it.”

“He will.” She fixes me with a look of utter certainty. “I wouldn't have let you fly all this way if I wasn't sure. He's obviously emotionally challenged, but he'll get there.”

The flight back is a much more sedate affair than the outward journey, most of it being spent sleeping. We arrive to rain at Heathrow, England's New Year greeting to us both, but the sheet of drizzle that clings to us as we leave the terminal doesn't dampen our spirits. Chloe is glowing, the new beginnings of a romance stirring, and I'm warm with the thought that what started out as an uncontrollable, unstoppable physical attraction has turned into more, so much more...

Chapter Forty-Six

Returning to work after the Christmas-New Year holiday is always an odd phenomenon. Everyone looks well-rested, but all seem to wear the same glum expressions and comments like "Didn't it go quickly?" float around the office. It's like a contagion, sucking away the last of the goodwill and replacing it with a depressive state, with the only hope for a cure being to browse bargain holidays online. Nobody in Head Office is even pretending to work, easing in gently being the mandate for the first week back. Departments schedule planning meetings, senior management and directors closet themselves in the boardroom for hours on end, and everyone congratulates themselves on their commitment to setting objectives, budgets, and the bullshit paraphernalia that comes with January.

Ethan and I had come into the office separately, him dropping me on the usual quiet side-street and me walking the rest of the way. He'd been happy enough to arrive together but I want, no, I owe it to Libby to tell her first, before we go public. I think she's going to be pissed off with me, understandably so, and coupled with the fact she has made it quite clear she thinks Ethan is an arse, I'm not sure she is going to be thrilled with my news.

She arrives at her desk at midday, freed from the confines of the boardroom. She looks bright-eyed, and I wonder how best to tackle the matter in hand. Do I just tell her straight out? Do I let her tell me about her time in Scotland?

"Happy New Year," she says. "Sorry I've not caught up with you earlier. Ethan dragged me into a meeting as soon as I got in. He's been uncharacteristically decent this morning, even made me a cup of coffee. I don't know what's got into him."

"More like who he's got into," quips Will as he walks past.

"Go away, William," she chastises, apparently not noticing my scorching cheeks.

"I need to talk to you," I blurt out.

"Are you OK?" she asks, eyeing me across our desks.

"Can we go and get a coffee?"

"Sure," she stands, her hands straightening her skirt. "Meeting Room B is free." We awkwardly make drinks in the kitchen and then head to one of the small private offices across the other side of the floor.

"Is it about your resignation?" she asks, closing the door. "Do you want to retract it?"

I shake my head. "I need to tell you something. I've wanted to tell you for ages, but..."

"It's me," she encourages. "Just say it."

"I've been seeing someone. It's serious."

She smiles. "Well, that's great. I'm pleased for you."

"You know him," I start to twirl a strand of hair around my finger. "He works here."

"Will?" she breathes incredulously, her green eyes glinting at the prospect. "I always thought there was chemistry between you two."

"Libby, it's not Will."

"Then who?"

I take in a deep breath. "Ethan."

She gapes, her usual unshockable demeanour slipping from her face, replaced with incredulity. "Harber?" she croaks. I nod.

"Fuck," she murmurs.

"I wanted to tell you, but it was complicated."

"I'm forever telling you what a prick he is," she says, tucking a strand of hair behind her ear.

"Most of the time he is, at work," I laugh awkwardly. "And I haven't told him anything you've said."

"I knew he fancied you," she says triumphantly. "When you first met him, I told you. I saw the way his eyes undressed you."

My cheeks heat again. "It started that night."

"In August?" She's surprised. "That long and you haven't said anything. I thought we were friends."

"We are," I reply quickly, a stab of remorse hitting me in the stomach. "I wanted to tell you, but he made me promise not to tell anyone at work. I didn't think it would turn into anything. I thought it was going to be a one-night stand, and then I thought it would fizzle out, that he'd lose interest. It's been complicated. I wanted to tell you so badly..."

Libby regains her composure, and I feel the temperature in the room drop a couple of degrees. She may have been briefly pleased that she had been right about Ethan being attracted to me, but she is pissed off that I haven't told her. I'd known she would be; I'd worried about her reaction from the moment I started to hide it from her. Libby has a reputation for being a bit of an ice queen, and now, for the first time since I've known her, her arctic gaze settles on me. Her frostiness has nothing on the cold wind of Central Park in December.

"Why tell me now?" she asks coolly.

"Because at the beginning we weren't sure what this was, we needed to iron out some issues, and now that we have, we don't want to have to hide it."

“Great.” She doesn't sound sincere. “Well as long as it doesn't affect your work. I know you're only here for another two months, but I do expect you to pull your weight.”

"Of course,” I say.

“Wonderful.” She stands. “Is that it?” I nod and watch her walk out of the room and march back to her desk. I take a few calming breaths before following.

Fifteen minutes later, I can't bear the chilly atmosphere any longer and find myself knocking on Ethan's door. He is on the phone when I enter, and looks frustrated.

“I'll have to call you back,” he says as I enter, dropping his mobile on his desk. “I'm busy, what is it, Rosie?” I stop mid-way to his desk, caught off-guard by his sharpness. He hasn't been like this with me since our last awful time in this office. I blink rapidly, feeling stupid for disturbing him.

“Well, if you're busy,” I stumble over my words and take a step back.

“I'm sorry.” He stands and swiftly comes around his desk. “You OK?”

I shake my head, my bottom lip trembling. Tears begin to slide down my cheeks.

“Hey,” he folds me into his arms and pulls me close. “You told her then?”

“She's really pissed off at me,” I sniff. “And the thing is, I don't blame her.”

“She'll get over it,” he says, his hands stroking up and down my back. “She just needs a bit of time.” He walks backwards and perches on the edge of his desk, pulling me between his legs. “Do you want me to talk to her?”

“God, no!” I exclaim, horrified by the prospect.

“Hmm,” he grumbles, and I can hear him trying to hide a smile in his voice. He knows as well as I do that he would only make things worse.

“She went all ice-queen on me and said it had better not affect my work.”

I feel his body tense and stare up to see irritation cross his face.

“We've been fucking for over four months, and to my knowledge it hasn't affected your work.” A muscle twitches in his jaw.

“I know,” I say, finding his outrage contagious.

He grins and kisses me lightly on the mouth. “Don't stand for any crap. Us, it hasn’t affected your work, and it won’t, make sure she knows that. You still want me to come and collect you from your desk this evening?”

I nod and head towards the door. “See you then.”

Having stopped off at the toilets to fix my red, puffy eyes and touch up my make-up, I stride confidently back to my desk and sit down. Libby looks up, and I return her glare.

"Been to see Ethan?" she asks.

I nod. "Do you have a problem with that? Does it count as affecting my work? I understand you being pissed off at me, but don't question my professionalism. I'm good at my job."

She sighs and we both busy ourselves.

Chapter Forty-Seven

"Go away," I grumble, pulling the duvet over my face.

"I've got something to show you."

"I don't want to see your cock," I say.

"You wish." He pushes me onto my back and pulls the duvet off me.

"It's freezing," I whine, rubbing at my eyes.

"Get in the shower then. Come on, we've got somewhere to be."

"You're so annoying," I complain, getting out of bed. "Where are we going, anyway?"

"You'll see," he swipes at my bum. "Hurry up."

A deliciously warm shower, followed by coffee and a bacon sandwich, seems to revive me. Friday night after-work drinks had gone on way longer than anticipated, and sleep deprivation always screws me up the next day. It was worth it, though, I think as I remember Libby and I making up.

Will – lovely, I-don't-like-conflict Will – had sat us both down and pretty-much called Libby out for being a bitch. He'd told her how good Ethan and I were together, how she needed to see him with me and then she'd understand. And then, as if on cue, Ethan had strolled into the pub, come straight to me, and leant down to kiss me lingeringly on the lips. I'd felt the eyes of all of our colleagues on us: we were officially out there now for all to see. Ethan had sat next to me all evening, holding my hand, or just giving little touches, making it obvious something was going on between us.

"You look good together," Libby conceded as I came out of a toilet cubicle and washed my hands at the sink. "Tell me he makes you happy?"

"Really happy," I'd replied, drying my hands.

"Then I'm pleased for you."

We'd hugged it out and celebrated with another bottle of wine.

"What do I need to take with me?" I ask, scraping my hair back into a ponytail.

"Nothing," he replies impatiently.

Ethan is giving off an I-don't-want-to-talk vibe in the car, so I don't bother trying to engage him in conversation. I stare out of the window, seeing sheep in a nearby field, two horses trotting down a country lane, a fallen-down tree in a ditch. His Audi, his car for country jaunts, or so he calls it, is flying, and I have no idea where we are, but it's leafy and feels like we are the only people for miles. We bump up a dirt track with trees on either side, some overhanging branches scraping against the windows. It's dark, eerie, and then we round a sharp corner which leads to a clearing with a house some distance off up a wide driveway.

“Come on,” he says after parking, “Let's go have a look around.”

“What is this place?” I ask, crunching behind him as he strides up the gravel pathway to the front door.

“So.” He turns to face me and reaches for my hands. “I thought about something you said to me in Knightsbridge when you found out about Melissa. It kept going round and round in my head.”

“What?” I ask nervously, not wanting to think back to that day ever again.

“You said you wanted more, the house with the pretty garden. Do you remember?”

I nod in confusion. He reaches in his pocket, pulls out a key and unlocks the large oak door.

“What are you doing?” I protest as he picks me up and carries me inside and through a vast living room to a set of French doors that lead out onto a patio with steps down to a lawned area and a pond.

“I've been told this garden is really pretty in the Spring when the flowers come out,” he says, putting me back on my feet.

“I don’t understand,” I say, my heart racing.

“I’m buying this place. Move in with me.”

“What?” I feel suddenly faint.

He cups my face in his hands, his eyes fixing to mine. “I'm in love with you. I want you to live with me.”

“You what?” I ask shakily.

“I love you,” he says gently, stooping to kiss me softly on the mouth.

“Say it again?” I ask incredulously.

His thumbs stroke down my cheeks as he speaks, his voice a low rumble. “I love you."

“I've wanted you to say that so badly,” I admit, blinking rapidly, trying to take it all in. “You love me?”

“I love you,” he repeats, his arms sliding around my waist as he kisses me once more. “I wanted you from the moment I saw you.”

“You had me from the moment you met me.” I squeeze him so tightly, needing to feel his solid, strong body against mine. “This is the converted barn you wanted to buy. I thought it got taken off the market?”

did, but then the owner changed his mind. I can pull out if you don't like it, but it felt perfect to me for us, for our home," his palms flatten against my bum, our bodies crushed together. "Tell me you'll move in here with me."

I nod. "I love it. I love you."

"I love you more," he says hoarsely, his lips finding mine in a tender kiss that sends a current through my veins, lust and love buzzing through every nerve-ending.

"I've got another surprise for you." He pulls back, his eyes sparkling. "I need to go and pick it up. You have a look around. I'll be ten minutes."

"What is it?"

"You'll see." He kisses the tip of my nose before heading towards the door.

The converted barn has recently been renovated, the wooden flooring and tiled kitchen completely new. The ceilings are high, oak beams running across the centre of the main room. There's no furniture, but the kitchen is fully fitted with integrated appliances and granite worksurfaces. A steep wooden staircase leads upstairs, where there are three good-sized bedrooms, the master bedroom having an ensuite. There's also a family bathroom, with a huge, deep bath that looks divine. I wander around, beginning to imagine our things here, how we would make it our home together. I sit at the top of the stairs, staring down into the main living room, and am swallowed up by happiness. This was the 'more' I had always wanted, and Ethan is the man that truly stole my heart.

"Hi," I answer my phone with a huge smile.

"I've got your surprise." His drawl crackles down the line. "I need you to close your eyes when you hear the door open and promise not to open them until I tell you."

"OK." I scamper down the stairs and into the main room.

"Wait near the patio doors," he instructs. "Don't look for me."

A minute later I hear the key in the lock and the sound of the door swinging open. My heart thuds as I close my eyes, hearing his footsteps nearing on the wooden floor.

"Keep your eyes shut and turn around," he says, standing at the door. "Put your arms out." I feel him approach, smell the familiar scent of citrus and bergamot. His lips brush against mine as I feel him put something warm into my arms. "Hold tight and you can open your eyes."

I stare down at a black-and-tan German Shepherd puppy, who begins to wriggle, oversized paws scrambling, a twitching nose snuffling at my collarbone, a tail frantically wagging.

"You bought me a puppy?" I breathe, tears beginning to overflow.

"I bought us a puppy. Please tell me those are happy tears?"

"The happiest," I sob.

"Is this more?" he asks, his thumbs wiping away my tears.

"Yes. This is so much more!"